# DEVIL'S KISS

Sunset Cove Series #2

ELLA FRANK

Ella Frank, LLC

# Copyright


www.ellafrank.com
Edited by Arran McNicol
Cover Design © By Jay Aheer
Photography by Eric Battershell
Photography by Wander Aguier
Cover Models – Jason Dickinson & Ryan VanDyke

## Also by Ella Frank

***The Exquisite Series***

Exquisite

Entice

Edible

***The Temptation Series***

Try

Take

Trust

Tease

Tate

***Sunset Cove Series***

Finley

Devil's Kiss

***Masters Among Monsters Series***

Alasdair

Isadora

Thanos

***Standalones***

Blind Obsession

Veiled Innocence

***Co-Authored with Brooke Blaine***

Sex Addict

***PresLocke Series***

***Co-Authored with Brooke Blaine***

ACED

LOCKED

WEDLOCKED

# The Call

*Present Day*

DEREK PEARSON PUSHED open the door of Leighton, Finley & Associates, and stepped out on the paved sidewalk. It was the first day of August, and if the sweltering Florida sun was any indication, today was going to be hotter than hell's waiting room.

As he strolled toward the curb, he pulled a pack of Marlboros from the pocket of his shorts and flipped open the top. He needed a fucking cigarette after watching Daniel Finley and his damn professor get all sappy and shit. That was gonna get old real quick if he had to stomach their nauseating displays of *I love yous* longer than the fifteen minutes he'd been in there. But he'd known he had to make an appearance sooner or later; otherwise Danny boy would've shown up asking questions. Questions he wasn't ready to answer.

There'd been a reason he hadn't come around to see Finn when he first moved back from Chicago two months ago, but it wasn't something he was in the mood to talk about yet, even if he was one of the two people on the planet who would understand all the shit he'd been dealing with.

*Yeah…* He just wasn't ready to go there.

With a smoke between his lips, he lit up, then shoved the pack back in his shorts. He was so damn antsy lately, and for that he could thank his brother, Alan.

He walked around to the side of his Jeep and pulled open the door. After climbing inside, he grabbed his cell phone and stared at the dark screen, contemplating his next move.

*Am I really planning to do this?*

*Fuck,* it seemed that he was, even when he knew better.

If he did this, it would be nothing more than a Band-Aid over the real problem. A shot to numb the more painful issues he was dealing with right now. He would be slipping back into a pattern he had pulled himself out of. An addiction he'd broken free from. But he was also aware that if he didn't do it, the alternative would be to spiral out of control, and solitude was no longer helping his fucked-up nerves.

He brought the phone to his ear and waited. The phone rang and rang, and fucking rang, until he was close to hanging up—and then it connected.

"You free?" were the only two words out of his mouth. He waited, not caring to pursue small talk. That wasn't what this was about. All he cared about in that moment was getting what he needed.

When an affirmative came through the phone, he hung up, tossed it on the dashboard, and brought the Jeep to life. As he sped across town, he white-knuckled the steering wheel and didn't allow himself to think about the consequences of what he was about to do.

It took him less than ten minutes to pull into the underground parking garage of the Palisades and take the elevator up to where his drug of choice waited for him. He glanced up into the camera in the corner of his metallic confines and stared boldly into the face of the one who was waiting at the other end of this ride.

*Yeah,* he was about to fall off the fucking wagon big time. Was about to slide back into the one place he promised himself he wouldn't go again. Yet as the elevator came to a halt and the doors opened, there was no denying this was exactly what he wanted.

"I have thirty minutes," were the words that greeted him.

Derek walked off the elevator and over to the naked man waiting for him. He took the haughty chin between his thumb and forefinger and promised in a voice thick with arousal, "I only need ten. Take me to your room, Jordan. Time's a wasting."

# PAST

*"I wish that I could cry*
*Fall upon my knees*
*Find a way to lie*
*Bout a home I'll never see."*

~ Superman
Five for Fighting

# Chapter 1

*Eleven Years Earlier*

LIFE IN THE Pearson household was pretty standard week after week. That was the one sure thing that Derek relied on to survive, day in and day out. He knew his father's routine as well as his own and made it a habit to give the fucker a wide berth whenever he could—*less trouble for all of us in the long run that way.*

Three nights a week, his dad worked the graveyard shift and dragged his sorry ass in just as the sun was rising. So each morning, Derek's goal was to be out of the house and running his way up the long stretch of hard-packed sand by then. That way, when he finally finished his morning exercise his father would either be passed out drunk in his recliner or facedown in his bed.

*Isn't life grand,* he thought, as he came to a stop at the back of their tiny, run-down home that morning, and looked up at the screen door. The bottom of the three stairs that led up to the patio was broken, and one side of it was wedged down into the sand, making it a hazard to anyone who wasn't aware should they try climbing it. But that wasn't really an issue, considering no one in their right mind would bother coming to visit the Pearson household. If anything, they steered clear of it—one of the perks of being the town's pariahs. Well, *he* wasn't so much because he kept his head down and his attitude in check…most days. His father and brother, however, were a different story.

By some miracle of fate, he'd managed to distance himself from the two men who resided in this home over the past nineteen years. Yet he still hadn't worked up the nerve to leave altogether. Not to mention, he had no fucking money. That was something he was determined to change this year. He was going to find a job. One that paid well. And he was going to work as hard as he possibly could to get the hell away from the clusterfuck that was his everyday life.

*That's the plan, anyway.*

Using the bottom of his shirt, he swiped the sweat away from his face and ran a hand through his short hair. *Fuck, best to get this part of the day over with.* It was such a *fantastic* feeling to be scared to set foot into your own home, and that was exactly the way he felt each morning, knowing he may come face to face with the monster who lurked inside.

After stepping over the broken plank, he carefully climbed the other two steps and winced when his foot hit the washed-out wood of the patio deck. The groaning creak was difficult to avoid because no matter where you trod, the timber was going to protest. He froze in place, hoping the door wasn't about to slap open and reveal his hulking father, but when nobody came out he figured he was safe—for now.

He crossed the deck and slowly opened the door and *yep*, there was good ole Dad sprawled back on the recliner with a beer bottle resting in his lap. It wasn't even seven in the morning.

Keeping a wary eye on the sleeping man, Derek cautiously walked around the footrest and was almost home free when his sneaker landed on an empty cigarette carton his dad must've dumped on his way inside.

"Derek?" his dad slurred out in a low, raspy voice, and Derek bit the inside of his cheek in an effort not to speak. Their encounters were always smoother if he kept his mouth shut. He'd learned *that* the hard way.

"Derek," his father said again, but this time turned in the chair to see where he was. "Didn't you hear me, boy? I'm speaking to you."

Reminding himself that the quickest way out of this situation was to reply and then hightail it out of there, Derek ordered himself to turn around and face the man who was barking at him. "Dad."

"Where've you been?"

Like it wasn't obvious from his attire or that he did the same exact thing every morning. Though it was a testament to the fact that, just as he'd always suspected, his father didn't give a shit about him or what he did one way or another.

"Out for a run."

"With that faggot friend of yours?"

The words were jarring, like a slap to the face, and Derek balled his fists at the familiar slur. It was nothing new. He'd been hearing this homophobic bullshit ever since his father had found out he was gay back when he was sixteen. That didn't mean it galled him any less.

God, he wanted to punch the fucker in the face. He had the muscles to do it now, too. The only thing that held him back was the desire to be the total opposite to the piece of shit now kicking down the footrest and getting to his feet.

Like himself, his father was an intimidating wall of a man. Both topping out at six four, they each looked the other in the eye. He was sure that pissed his father off to no end, too, because it made him harder to push around. So did the big fucking muscles he'd worked his ass off to build.

"No," Derek finally answered. "I was running alone."

"Why?" his father said. "Your boyfriend stand you up?"

Derek prayed for patience as he looked out the lone window in the back of their home. "He's not my boyfriend. And Finn doesn't run. You know that."

His dad half staggered, half walked over to him, and when their shoulders collided Derek glared at him and saw an evil twinkle light his eyes.

"Yeah? Well, good thing. His knees are probably shot from all the cock he sucks."

He should've just walked to the kitchen, but Derek felt the tight leash that'd been holding him back finally snap. He reached out, grabbed hold of his father's thick wrist, and halted him. "What did you just say?"

His father's bloodshot eyes narrowed an inch and he gave a menacing grin. "I said, his knees are probably—" But before he could finish, Derek had swung his arm around and sucker-punched the prick right in the jaw. As if on instinct, and without giving it a second thought, his father backhanded him so hard that he went stumbling across the room.

*Jesus, the fucker can hit. He has that skill down to an art form,* Derek thought as he raised a hand to his eye. *That's gonna leave a goddamn bruise.* There were two things his father excelled at in this life: drinking and fighting. It just so happened the fighting was usually with him.

As his dad seethed, he wiped the back of his hand across his mouth and muttered, "Get out of my sight."

The words didn't hurt, not anymore. Derek had grown used to the idea that he disgusted his father. What he would never be able to understand was the stranger glaring at him. It was hard to fathom you could come from such a vile creature filled with so much hatred. Yet at the same time, the physical resemblance was so uncanny it was difficult to refute.

Cradling the side of his face, Derek congratulated himself on getting one in before he'd been clobbered, and then gingerly stepped around his dad. He knew nothing else would follow.

Ever since the age of seventeen, when he'd packed on the height, weight, and muscle and could actually fight back, it never went further from there. But until the day he moved out, Derek would always be on guard and watching his back, because fuck only knew if one night his father would crack and ambush him.

Stomping down the hall, he told himself over and over that no matter what happened this year he *would* get a job, and he would get the *hell* out of this house for good.

---

JORDAN DEVANEY STOOD under the hard-hitting spray of warm water and let the jets from his three showerheads hit every possible muscle on his deliciously aching body.

*Yesss,* last night had been exactly what he needed. He'd decided to indulge himself in a little nighttime delight before his new rule of *no party shenanigans during the work week* kicked into full effect after accepting his new position at the local university.

He laughed to himself as the water slicked down over him, still unable to believe that *he* was going to be in charge of educating future generations. He'd decided that the dean could quite possibly be mad for giving him such a position of authority, but he knew that wasn't the case.

He was brilliant; there were no two ways around it. A certified genius according to his IQ and the bachelor's degree he'd received at the ripe old age of fourteen before going on to complete his PhD by his twenty-first birthday. And on top of those two facts was the recommendation from one of the university's most beloved professors. The woman whose job he would be taking over—Professor Anne Hamilton. God rest her soul.

When he'd been nothing more than a smartass kid getting in too much trouble for his own good, his mother and father had pulled him from school on the recommendation of his teachers, who said that his test scores may require he have "special" schooling. Soon after, they'd hired several tutors to home-school him.

As money wasn't ever an issue in the Devaney household, his parents threw the best minds in the business at him, and when he showed a special interest in history they hired on the brightest, and toughest, teacher in the nation.

Professor Hamilton. The woman who'd recently recommended *him*, of all people, to take her place when she found out she was going to need her energy to fight a new crusade: her ailing health.

He still couldn't believe it. He had more money than he knew what to do with and he'd always assumed he'd travel to far-off and exotic places to take part in exciting archaeological digs, not be stuck in some stuffy room teaching uninterested teens about ruins from a slide show collection. But around six months ago she'd asked him a question he hadn't been able to answer.

*"Are you satisfied with your life, Jordan? You have so much, and everything has always come so easy to you. But is your mind challenged? Or do you want more? Don't you want to make a difference?"*

He'd taken a long look at his life the night after that conversation and the answer had been simple—no, he wasn't challenged. He'd become bored with his privileged lifestyle, and yes, he wanted to make a difference. He still remembered what she'd said to him moments before she'd passed.

*"You were my biggest challenge,* Professor *Jordan Devaney. Now, go and find what makes you work the hardest, and dare yourself to make a difference."*

That had been a couple of weeks ago.

So there he was—*he,* Jordan Devaney, was going to endeavor to be…responsible.

Her final words still lingered as he stood there under the shower getting ready for whatever life was going to "challenge" him with. He tipped his head back and let the water sluice over his face as he thought about the day ahead.

Three classes before noon and one after. If he managed to get through those in one piece, maybe he could track down that gorgeous Professor Hayes he'd met on his campus tour and see if he would be interested in dinner.

*As a friend, of course,* he told himself. Even he wasn't stupid enough to pursue that. Sex in the workplace was just too messy. Not that he'd know, since he'd never taken a job before, but that was what he'd heard.

With a sigh, he turned off the water and snagged one of the fluffy white towels hanging over the pewter hook on the wall. He rubbed it over his hair then toweled off his body before he headed to his walk-in closet to get ready for the day.

The wooden floors were the perfect temperature under his feet as he threw the towel over an armchair and perused the pants hanging in front of him. As he evaluated his choices, he groaned.

*Ugh,* dressing for school was going to be *so* boring. He much preferred dressing for fun. Maybe when he did finally speak to Hayes he could ask if he had any tips for him that didn't include sweaters. Because really, who wore sweaters in Florida? Then a brilliant idea struck him. He didn't have to dress boringly, just… appropriately. So why not have a little fun with his students on his first day? Go for the shock factor. His age would already be a topic of discussion, so why not add a little outlandish attire to go with?

He reached for the brightest pair of pants he owned and smiled as he tossed them over the top of his back-to-back chest of drawers in the center of the closet. He then slipped into a pair of tight black briefs before searching the opposite rack of hangers for a shirt. *Hmm.* He glanced back at the pants. *What color, what color… Oh! Yes, perfect.*

Settling on a vibrant button-down, he finished getting dressed, slipped his feet into some loafers, and went back to the bathroom to brush his teeth and finish styling his hair. It wasn't until he walked back into his bedroom that he spotted the long line of a muscular leg sticking out from under his navy sheets.

*Oh, shit.* Caught up in his head about his first day of being an adult, Jordan had completely forgotten he'd left a man in his bed. One who was still there. *Awkward.*

Not possessing one iota of shame, he walked to the double sliding doors that led to his balcony and tugged open the curtains. As the morning sun pierced through the glass and right into the sleeping man's eyes, Jordan stopped by the edge of the bed and flung back the sheet, revealing one very *naked* man.

"Good morning, sunshine," he singsonged.

As the mountain of muscle started to shift, Jordan took a moment to admire the play of skin over that firm ass and toned back. The man had such a different physique to his own, one that he had really, *really* gotten off on having under him the night before.

Yes, what a shocker—he liked to top.

"Oh, sorry, man. I didn't realize the time."

"Not a problem, big guy. But alas, our night together is over. I have to go and earn a living, and *you* need to exit the building."

Rob…Rod, *or shit, whatever his name is*, sat up and swung his legs over the bed, and when his giant feet hit the floor and he stood, Jordan grabbed his jeans and held them out to him.

The guy was massive. He had him by at least three inches and fifty pounds, but hell if that hadn't made it more exciting when he'd been begging for Jordan to give it to him harder, harder… *Shit. Focus. He's leaving.* "Seriously, hon, you need to get dressed and skedaddle," Jordan said with a waggle of his fingers toward the bedroom door. "Or I'm going to be late."

Rod—*yes, I'm positive it's Rod*—pulled on his jeans and buttoned them as he gave a shy smile that was at odds with his pierced nipples and shaved head. "Can I call you?"

And there was the rub. The problem he'd always had with letting someone wake up beside him: they never just…left.

Jordan opened his mouth to say something along the lines of *probably not*, but he was saved from having to break the poor guy's heart because his phone started an incessant ring throughout his condo.

He held his finger up and dashed into his closet to hunt down the cell.

*Shit, shit, shit…* Where had he left the damn thing? Flinging several shirts over his shoulder to the floor, he hunted under a pair of shorts, and a bathrobe, then spotted his messenger bag slung over the closet handle. *Jackpot.*

Racing to it, he got his fingers around the noisemaker just as his mother's call went to voicemail. *Oh great. Just great. She will* not *let me hear the end of that,* he thought, as he spotted Rod heading toward the private elevator.

Pocketing the phone, Jordan followed and then leaned around him to press the down button. As the door opened, Rod walked backward inside and raised a brow. "Do you ever visit North Carolina at all?"

Pursing his lips a little, Jordan shook his head. "Hmm, not recently."

"No problem. Last night was…unexpected. You're a real firecracker."

Jordan gave a shrug and winked. "Like lightning in a bottle, baby. I'm hard to capture or contain," he said as the door slid shut and his guest went down one more time during their acquaintance.

Jordan dashed back into his bedroom, grabbed his car keys and the bag he'd been rifling through a minute ago, then snagged a banana and headed back to the elevator.

*First day of college, here I come.* It was time to head for class. *Huh*, he thought with a grin. This felt eerily reminiscent of his teenage years. A boy leaving his bed and his mother calling just in time to ruin the moment, or in this case, save him from an awkward one.

He really was lucky to have such wonderful parents, and he

counted his blessings each and every day for that. It had taken him a few years before he'd been comfortable enough to embrace all that he was, but now that he had, he lived by a simple motto.

No excuses.

No apologies.

And not one damn regret.

# Chapter 2

*THE PEOPLE WHO stand out as special in your life are usually put in your path for a reason.*

Camille Finley, Finn's mom, had said that to him last night as Derek sat at her kitchen nook and ate a "good luck on your first day of college" spaghetti dinner with his best friend. He'd been in the process of trying to work out a way to thank her for being the mother he'd never had. But, as usual, when he'd gotten to the emotional "Thank you. I love you" part, he'd choked the fuck up. That had been when she walked around the counter and gave his large shoulders a squeeze, and whispered those words of wisdom in his ear.

He was starting to think the woman was right, too, because if it hadn't been for her, he sure as hell wouldn't be standing on the perfectly manicured lawn of a university with a swollen eye and one hell of a headache, waiting on her late-ass son.

*Yeah,* today was the first day of the rest of his life. His first day of college. And even though he'd worked damn hard to be there, a part of him already wanted out. The part that was embarrassed to know that he'd have to sit through class with his sunglasses on or look like the kind of dick who got into weekend fistfights. *Fucking awesome.*

The shitty part of the situation was that he *wanted* to be there. But now he was stuck with a shiner developing on his face that would no doubt draw attention and questions about himself, and not the good damn kind.

*I mean, really, can the day get any worse?*

The constant heat that blanketed the small town of Sunset Cove was in full effect as all the students who would be attending college for the upcoming year were trying to find their classes. He glanced at his watch again, and when he saw the time he grimaced. Finn was really late. That was just brilliant. Why not add that to the list of shit that was starting to pile up: late on the first day.

He should've known better. During his run he'd noticed the waves were perfect for surfing, and after years of friendship he should've clued in to what his buddy would be doing this morning, no matter how late it made him.

That didn't help him out, though. He didn't want to get off to a bad start with his professors, so he walked up the path that dissected the lawn and headed toward the front entrance of the History building. After climbing the stairs to the double doors, he heard his name being called from behind and spotted Finn jogging across the lawn toward him.

Daniel Finley—Finn to most, and Danny boy to him on occasion—was his best friend. He understood who Derek was and the situation he came from. That didn't mean the two of them hadn't had their fair share of throw-downs, though.

He was too irritated right now to bother acknowledging his friend, who had finally come to a standstill opposite him with a grin so wide it looked like it was about to slide right off his face. "Where the hell have you been?"

"Jesus. Relax, would ya? I got held up. My first class was an hour before yours, remember? And then the rooms got switched, so I totally missed it. By the time I found the damn thing, it was over and I got stuck explaining myself to my law professor. Why are your panties in such a twist?"

Shit, he'd forgotten that. He'd been too busy trying to work out how the hell to hide his mangled face. "Sorry, man. I blanked. But now I'm late. Not exactly how I wanted to start my academic future. With a professor riding my ass."

Finn opened his mouth and a mischievous light entered his eyes. He was probably about to throw out some jab on how he knew Derek liked to be ridden, but then he caught himself and let whatever comment he'd been about to say go. Derek figured the grim expression he must've been sporting had a lot to do with Finn's silence.

Daniel Finley may have had that easygoing surfer vibe happening, but he was one smart guy. Tall, almost as tall as himself, he was broad-shouldered, with a golden tan, and had shoulder-length blond hair that was currently shoved behind his ears. Most underestimated the guy, and were shocked as hell when this beach boy outsmarted them every damn time.

Wanting to steer the conversation to his own liking, Derek said, "You know, out of all the classes I'm dreading, history has to be top of the list. What the fuck do ancient ruins have to do with a business degree? It makes zero sense to even have it on my syllabus."

Finn held open the door for him, and when he loped past, Finn clapped a hand on his shoulder. "We picked this course because it's pretty much the only class we'll see each other in. So stop bitching and get your ass inside, would you?"

"Yeah, yeah. I just don't see the point," Derek grumbled as they entered the large lecture hall and trudged up the stairs to the middle of the room. He was pleased to find that even though they were late, it appeared their professor was also.

Leaving his sunglasses in place, Derek squashed his large frame into one of the small seats to the left of the aisle and then swept a surreptitious glance over the students already seated. Most looked like your average high schooler. Fresh faced eighteen-or nineteen-year-olds, thinking they were adults now that they'd graduated and moved on to pursue a higher education. Most of them also looked as though they could afford to be there and weren't the owner of a purple bruise forming around their eye courtesy of their father—something he was well aware made him very different to this preppy crowd of overachievers and history nerds.

*Fucking hell. What am I doing here?* It wasn't the first time the thought had crossed his mind, which was insane considering he'd only been at school for… *Shit, twenty minutes. But really, what* am *I doing here?*

He wasn't like these kids. They'd been waiting their whole life for this opportunity. Hell, they probably had career plans mapped out when they were in grade school and then worked toward it in high school.

Him? Not so much. He'd been busy working out at the gym at every opportunity he could get to focus his adrenaline and frustration in a specific and controlled way. Not to mention trying to fucking survive his childhood and adolescence. So yeah, he was totally winging it, and was here only courtesy of financial aid and a scholarship he'd submitted and actually been accepted for.

*Miracle of all fucking miracles.*

Finn leaned over and bumped arms with his. "See, you were worried about nothing."

Derek turned to face his friend and slumped a little farther down in his chair. "I guess."

"What do you mean, you guess?"

"I mean, I fucking guess. Jesus."

"Cool it, would you?" Finn said under his breath. "What's up with you this morning? And what's with the sunglasses? Late night out on the town?"

"No. Early appointment with my father's fist—" His words came to an abrupt halt when the door to the lecture hall swung open and crashed back against the wall, followed by an "Oh, shit!" which echoed off the cavernous ceiling.

The new arrival, a young guy carrying a mountain of books almost taller than himself, then stepped into the room and peered around the stack of literature practically weighing him down.

"Check this guy out," he said, trying to get Finn's attention off him. He knew his friend wanted to ask more, but Finn was smart enough to know that now wasn't the time or the place. So, like a good friend, he let it go while Derek continued on about anything other than himself. "I get wanting to impress the professor if you're his TA, but fuck, man, you can make two trips. He isn't even here yet."

"No lie. He looks like he's gonna fall flat on his face." Finn laughed.

They both watched as the guy barely made his way across the front of the room, where he dumped the stack of books on the wooden table beside the podium. When he straightened up, he placed his hands on his narrow hips and blew out a deep breath.

"Whew. Where's a strapping young man to carry your books when you need one?" he announced loud enough to grab hold of anyone's attention he didn't already have. If the volume of his exclamation didn't do it, then his words sure as fuck did. Not to mention his clothes.

The guy was wearing the brightest pair of yellow pants Derek had ever seen, with a violet button-up short-sleeved shirt. It was tucked in at his trim waist and outlined by a thin belt the same color as the shirt. His lean frame took nothing away from his confidence, though, as he surveyed the faces of everyone now solely focused on him. He didn't seem embarrassed, humiliated, or in any way uncomfortable, except for the fact that he'd just lugged half a damn library into a room.

That confidence instantly intrigued Derek, because while he

himself most certainly looked confident on the outside, there was a whole fuck ton of self-doubt just beneath the tattooed top layer. This man who'd captured his and everyone else in the room's attention, on the other hand, appeared to know exactly who he was.

"Good morning, class. As you can see, I'm a little all over the place, but rest assured now that I've finally located my classroom this won't be an ongoing occurrence," he said, his hands moving right along with his words as though part of a choreographed dance. "Well." He laughed. "The all-over-the-place part, that is. I can't guarantee complete punctuality because I'm always late. *What?* It takes time to look this fabulous every day. But I'll work on that too. As long as you all promise to try and be here on time as well."

The guy aimed a dazzling smile up at them, and the class laughed—everyone except for Derek.

*What the hell is this?* he thought as he sat up a little straighter in his seat. *Who the fuck is this guy?* Derek aimed a look toward Finn, who was grinning like a loon at the extra-perky bottle of energy bouncing around the front of the class, and that only confused Derek more.

*Where is the stuffy old professor? Where is the gray-haired, sweater-wearing, doddering old professor?*

That was when the guy at the front of the lecture hall stood in front of the podium and clasped his hands together.

"I suppose you're all wondering who I am. Well, let me clear that up for you in case you're having any doubts. My name is Professor Jordan Devaney. And over the next few months we'll be exploring Pompeii together. Sounds boring, I know. But do I really look like someone who's going to bore you? I don't think so. Right. So, any questions before we get started?"

*Yeah, just one—what the actual fuck?*

---

JORDAN HAD BEEN WAITING for this moment ever since he'd

decided to take the university job. The moment when that slack-jawed look of *what the hell* hit his students' faces. Yes, that was exactly the expression he'd wanted to see, and they weren't disappointing him in the least.

*In all fairness,* he mused, *it could be my clothes.*

He was glad he'd gone with his gut decision to be himself this morning. It was a good reminder to these kids that people didn't necessarily come in specific molds, and he sure as hell didn't fit into any. Especially not the typical uptight professor type.

He shuddered at the notion. There was only one way he ever wanted to be described as being tight, and it certainly wasn't in regard to his personality.

As he let the announcement of *who* he was settle in and register, Jordan began pacing the front of the room and let his eyes trail over the faces staring down at him. That was when he noted their somewhat stunned expressions morphing into grins. That was the other reaction he'd hoped for.

Shock turned to excitement.

He didn't want their first day to suck. *Hell,* he didn't want his to either. The way he looked at it was that he was going to do everything in his power to make his class so damn exciting they'd be gagging for it.

Okay, so maybe not the best analogy to think of in the same sentence as his students. *Strike one against being a responsible adult.*

As he came to a standstill on the left-hand side of the room, he looked up the stadium seating and spotted two guys seated next to one another midway up the aisle. Each of them had a very different air about them.

One was grinning at him like a fool. *Oh, honey, aren't you a heartbreaker,* Jordan thought, as his eyes trailed over him. The guy had a wide, inviting smile that lit up his whole face with a youthful and beautiful quality. He had long blond hair and twinkling eyes that seemed as bright as his grin. The staple beach boy, harmless and carefree, but the guy next to him…he was the complete opposite. Serious and sunglassed, he caught and held Jordan's attention for very different reasons.

With spiky brown hair and muscles on top of muscles, he was exactly the kind of guy Jordan had imagined carrying his books moments earlier. It was a miracle he could fit into the tiny seat he'd squeezed himself into. As it was, he looked terribly uncomfortable, like a pack of sardines squashed into a tin can. He had a snug black V-neck shirt on and, *hello,* swirling down around those thick arms were several intricate tattoos and, *lord help me is that…yes,* black nail polish.

From where he was standing, Jordan couldn't see what his tattoos were of, but he was acutely aware of them. He was also fairly positive that the ink spread under the student's shirt and across the built body it was molded to, which was the worst kind of torture he could've ever been faced with.

There was nothing he was more of a sucker for than tattoos.

*No.* Thaaat's *a lie,* Jordan thought. *I'm a total fool for muscles* and *tattoos. Strike two against being a responsible adult.*

*Damn it.* This was not what he needed on his first day. He wanted sweet, eager students. Not unreadable ones whose entire demeanor screamed, *Total. Badass.*

But as the student continued to watch him, the barrier of the sunglasses and the tight set of his lips had one very immediate reaction rising to the surface.

*No. No, no. There will be no rising of any kind. None.* But there was no denying it—this guy made Jordan's cock hard. *And there you have it—strike three and I'm out before ten minutes has even passed.*

While he stood there willing his dick to ignore its wayward fantasies of taming the bad boy, he took in the mirrored Aviators hiding the guy's eyes and then walked forward, needing to get closer despite himself.

He was ashamed to admit it, but the unnerving way the student was watching him didn't make Jordan want to tuck tail and run. If anything, it represented the one thing he enjoyed most in the world. The one thing that up until this very second had been missing—a challenge.

"You," Jordan said, singling him out by pointing in his direction. When Mr. Muscles seemed to realize he was indicating him, his brow knitted together in a fierce furrow over those glasses.

"How about you remove your sunglasses while inside and tell us what most interests you about history and what you hope to get out of this class."

Jordan watched as an eyebrow rose over the frame in a *how 'bout you go fuck yourself* expression, and it took everything in him not to respond. This guy's demeanor radiated a silent, otherworldly wisdom, as though he'd seen way more in his life than Jordan could ever begin to imagine, and all because of the *don't mess with me* attitude he was exuding.

Jordan also had a feeling that when the guy decided to finally unfold himself from his seat he would be one hell of an intimidating presence. One that under any other circumstance he'd like to climb like a tree.

"Did you need me to repeat myself?" Jordan asked, knowing he needed to establish a firm line between student and teacher right away to keep his own perverse imaginings at bay, and that was when it happened.

As if he'd prodded the guy to the point of him not being able to resist, the student slowly got to his feet and—*good* God—Jordan hadn't been wrong. He was built like a brick shithouse. A real-life He-Man.

"No. I heard you," he said, his voice dripping with disdain but clear enough to be heard around the room. He then reached up and removed his sunglasses, tossing them down on the seat behind him, and Jordan's breath caught in his throat.

*Oh holy Jesus.* There'd been a reason for the sunglasses beyond the attitude. That was blatantly obvious now as he looked up into a face that had one frosty blue eye pinned on him, while the other struggled to open even a fraction of an inch. The guy had clearly been on the receiving end of a very hard-hitting fist. *Shit.*

Before Jordan could get out the words to tell him to take a seat, He-Man crossed his arms over his chest in a move that dared Jordan to make a big deal out of it. Obviously, he hadn't wanted to draw attention to himself earlier, hence the sunglasses, but now that Jordan had inadvertently outed him, he wasn't backing down for anyone. His attitude oozed agitation and his stance was defiant. All in all, he was pissed, and it was because Jordan had read the signals wrong.

*Great. Off to a fantastic start with this one. How was I supposed to know he had a whopping great bruiser on his face? I wasn't. So no harm. No foul. Act cool.*

"Okay. Go ahead."

He-Man swiped his tongue over his surly lip and then slipped his hands into his pockets. "What most interests me about the class?" he repeated.

Jordan nodded and watched He-Man give a careless shrug, as if he didn't give a shit, which he probably didn't.

*And* why *is it that this kind of guy always floats my boat?*

"Not much, really. I don't see what history has to do with the degree I'm actually aiming for, but it was either this or physics, and I figured I was less likely to fall asleep in this one. So there's that."

Jordan's lips pressed together at the sarcastic response just as the guy's friend let out a disbelieving laugh. He slid his eyes to the blond in time to see him whack the huge thigh of the smartass standing beside him, and Jordan could feel his face flushing with annoyance.

*No wonder he has a black eye. He thinks he's hot shit. Karma,* you *are one fickle bitch.*

As if the guy knew he'd pissed him off, the side of He-Man's mouth quirked, and Jordan could feel the heat from his irritation bubbling under the surface.

"As for what I want to get out of it? A passing grade so I

don't have to retake the class seems like a good goal right this second."

"Derek!"

*And now I have a name...*

"Derek, is it?" Jordan asked, and when Derek nodded once, he continued. "I, too, hope you pass this class, though for reasons I'm sure differ from your own. Why don't you take a seat before you land on a shitlist beyond mine, which you have successfully taken the number one spot on within"—he glanced at the clock on the wall then back to his student—"ten minutes of being in my class."

Deciding he needed to move on and have this exchange be over, Jordan turned his back on Derek and let his eyes rove over the other students watching with a mixture of incredulity and mirth on their faces.

For the rest of the class he didn't call on Derek Pearson—yes, he soon learned his last name—but Jordan felt his gaze on him every time he spoke.

It wasn't the scowl from earlier, or the curious interest of a student. No, it was something much more dangerous. Something he'd never been able to resist in the past. It was something that was going to make teaching this class much more difficult than he ever could've anticipated.

That look was bold and daring, it was in your face, and somehow Jordan knew he'd just met his "challenge."

# Chapter 3

WHEN THE HOUR was over and class was let out, Derek shoved his sunglasses back on and got to his feet, more than ready to leave. But Finn was taking his sweet-ass time packing his notebook and pens away, so it allowed him a moment to look at the man now standing behind the podium.

It hadn't escaped his notice that Devaney had been keeping a close eye on him throughout the rest of the class. The guy was trying to be cool about it, but Derek had been watching him with such a tenacious stare of his own, and each time their eyes met, Devaney paused for a second as though he lost his train of thought.

*Oh yeah,* he'd definitely gotten under this guy's skin, and Derek was slightly stunned by how much that discovery pleased him.

The professor was unlike anyone he'd ever met. His exuberant attitude had remained as he went into detail about what they'd be studying this semester, and it seemed as if the guy's excitement grew with every word out of his mouth. It was contagious, and the class had responded with interest.

*He*, on the other hand had responded with the hard-on he was currently trying to calm the hell down.

"You ready to head out?" Finn asked, breaking his concentration. Derek looked back at his friend, who was getting to his feet and slinging his backpack over his shoulder.

"Sure, let's go." He went to step forward, and when Finn didn't move, Derek spotted his somber expression.

*Oh God, here we go…*

"You're going to tell me what happened this morning, right?"

Running a hand through his hair, Derek sighed. "Just the same old shit that always happens, Danny boy. Nothing I can't handle."

"Come on, Derek. This is me you're talking to. He hasn't done that for a long-ass time."

"Yeah, well, guess he got lucky this morning. Didn't he?"

"What the fuck happened?"

Derek ground his teeth together and shot a glance over his shoulder to the front of the room. This time, he saw that Devaney was once again focused on them where they lingered.

"Do you think we could have this little heart-to-heart away from strangers' ears?"

Finn's eyes drifted past him to the inquisitive ones watching them. "Yeah, okay. Let's go."

They headed for the aisle and then down the stairs toward the front door, then Derek heard a soft cough. Finn stopped first and Derek halted behind him, clutching the strap of his bag.

*Aww hell.* He'd hoped Devaney would let him go, considering he was having a hard time looking at the guy. *Hard being the operative fucking word.* But it seemed he wasn't about to get off that easy.

Finn looked over his shoulder with his brow raised in a *want me to stay?* expression, but Derek gave a shake of his head. It was going to be difficult enough to hear whatever his professor wanted to say to him without having Finn sitting in the peanut gallery watching. "I'll meet you outside."

"You sure?"

He nodded and watched Finn push through the door. Derek pivoted around to find his professor now standing in front of the lectern.

"Derek. If you think you can manage to stay awake for five more minutes, I'd like to talk to you."

*Fuck, this is gonna be awkward as hell,* he thought, as he let his bag slide down his arm so he could hold it in front of his idiotic cock. Was it serious right now? Damn thing had a mind of its own. This guy was likely about to hand him his ass on a platter, and here he was getting a goddamn erection.

"I think I can manage."

"I'm so delighted to hear it," Devaney said as he gestured to a seat in the front of the room. "Won't you take a seat?"

Jesus, couldn't they just get this over with and move on?

"Don't see why not."

With way more attitude than he'd usually adopt, Derek walked over to one of the seats and decided there was no way he was going to be able to conceal what was going on between his legs much longer, and instead dropped his bag by his feet and sat down, deciding, *screw it,* he couldn't control who his dick liked. He wasn't the one standing there demanding a private showing. Although…he didn't hate the idea of Devaney giving him a real live strip show.

Derek allowed his eyes to travel up the man's legs and torso before studying the face looking down at him. When he'd first seen Devaney he'd thought he was the TA, and that was for good reason—he was young. If Derek had to guess, maybe mid-twenties? He was fucking hot, too. Not overly tall, he stood at maybe five ten or eleven at best, and he had sharp, angular cheekbones, and a sculpted jaw that came to a haughty point at his arrogant chin.

"You know, Derek. I don't have too much practice doing

this, but I'm always the first to admit when I'm wrong. And I want to apologize to you for earlier."

*Oh…wow.* Unsure of what was expected of him, Derek sat there silently. He really hadn't been expecting that. When it became obvious he had nothing to say, Devaney slid his hands into the pockets of his skintight pants, and that had Derek's eyes drifting to them.

Damn, they were tight. So tight he wondered how the professor had gotten into them that morning. Did he lie on his bed and wiggle his ass into that stiff fabric? Or did he bend at the waist and pull them up—

"Derek? Did you hear me?"

---

*GOD SAVE ME from men like this.* That was all Jordan could think as he waited for a response from the unreadable Derek Pearson. The guy had his shield firmly back in place, and though Jordan knew why the glasses were now there, he wanted to demand that Derek take the blasted things off so he could see where he was looking.

He had a feeling it was directly at him. Or maybe his package, considering how nicely wrapped and in Derek's face it was right that second. But hell, it wasn't his fault the guy was eye level with his cock now that he was seated. It *was* his fault, however, that the thought of unzipping and really giving him something to stare at briefly, *ever so briefly*, flashed through his mind.

Jordan shoved that aside, though, figuring he'd screwed up with this student enough for one day. Instead, he patiently waited for a response to his apology. Well, he tried to wait patiently, but it wasn't exactly his strong suit. "Derek. Focus. Are you okay?"

Derek raised his chin, and though Jordan couldn't see his eyes, he knew that they were now focused on his face.

"Yeah, I'm fine. It's no biggie. I've had worse."

As Derek's answer registered with him, all other thoughts Jordan was having vanished. Those words did not sit well with him at all. They gave the impression that whoever had done the damage to his face was someone Derek knew, not just a random fight, and that was disturbing.

Jordan wanted to ask more. He had an unexplainable need to know who had hurt this man who seemed larger than life… indestructible. He racked his brain trying to come up with an excuse to dig for details, but nothing was coming. He couldn't just demand answers. Derek didn't know him from Adam, or likely trust him. So maybe his best course of action would be to extend an olive branch. He needed to somehow reach Derek Pearson and let him know that he was there. That he would listen—even if he seemed the most unlikely choice of a confidant at that precise moment.

After walking over to where Derek was seated, Jordan took the spot beside him, thinking it might be easier if he didn't have to look at him. Swallowing back his pride, Jordan said, "I really shouldn't have focused in on you this morning, and I'm—"

"Then why did you?"

*Huh…?* Jordan almost said aloud, tripping over his own words. But luckily he caught himself at the last minute. "Excuse me?" he asked instead.

Derek readjusted his posture and turned his large frame in Jordan's direction. That was when he realized what a monumentally bad idea it had been to sit down next to Derek.

Derek's size and pissy attitude was like a bright neon warning sign flashing: *Danger. Danger.* And it was like a rush of blood to his head, and not the one on his shoulders.

"Why *did* you single me out?" Derek asked again.

*Damn. The guy lacks subtlety, that's for sure.*

"I just—" Jordan stopped himself right there and got to his feet so he could get some much-needed power in this exchange.

*How utterly ridiculous,* he scolded himself. *Do not act unsure for one second. You're the adult here. Don't forget that.*

"I thought you were wearing your sunglasses as a sign of disrespect to me."

Without missing a beat, Derek got to his feet also. Jordan didn't dare move away, even as he had to crane his head up to meet where the guy's eyes would be.

"Why would you think that? I don't even know you."

"Well, your attitude was less than…than…" As Derek stood there waiting for him to finish, Jordan's words trailed off and his eyes narrowed. *Hang on one damn minute, how did this turn into my issue?* They were supposed to be talking about Derek, and there was no way on God's green earth he was about to admit any insecurities to this guy. One of his students. He was fucking fabulous and he wasn't about to let *Derek* believe he'd had any effect on him. So instead of finishing his thought, Jordan held up a hand and shook it in a *forget it* kind of way. "How about we agree that we got off on the wrong foot, and move forward from here."

Derek cocked his head to the side and then removed his sunglasses. His eye looked swollen and painful, and Jordan was alarmed by how much he wanted to reach up and gently run his fingers down the side of his face to make sure he was okay. But really, as if this guy needed coddling.

"Okay."

"O*kay*?" Jordan asked, taken off guard by Derek's easy acquiescence.

"Yeah. It is what it is. Whatever. Is there anything else?"

Jordan wanted to offer his ear should Derek need someone to talk to. But at the same time he wasn't one hundred percent convinced it was his good intentions and not his cock doing the offering, and for that reason all he said was, "No. That'll be all."

Derek picked up his bag and as he walked to the door Jordan spun away and shut his eyes, trying to calm himself.

*Oh my God. Oh my God. Oh. My.* God. *Talk about a first-day impression.*

"Oh, and Professor Devaney..." Derek's voice had him slowly pivoting to see him standing at the door—all six foot whatever-he-was of him.

"Yes, Derek?"

"I just want you to know, I respect who you are, very much."

And with that ambiguous comment, Derek Pearson left his classroom.

---

DEREK CAUGHT UP with Finn just outside the History building, where he sat on one of the stairs waiting for him. *Damn it*, he'd been hoping that moment inside would be the last he'd have to talk about his craptastic morning, but it appeared his torture wasn't over just yet.

As soon as Derek stopped beside his friend, Finn was on his feet and looking at him with expectation in his eyes, and Derek knew the quicker he got this over with, the sooner he'd be able to forget it ever happened.

"Okay, Danny boy. Let's have it," he said as they walked down the stairs. He dug in his front pocket for his pack of Marlboros. "Ask what you want, I'll answer. Then we won't talk about this again. Deal?"

"Deal."

They headed along the path across the lawn toward the east building, and he didn't even bother to ask where they were going. He was too busy inside his head trying to work out a way to phrase his next words so Finn wouldn't feel any guilt over them.

He took a cigarette between his lips and lit up, taking a drag to try and calm his frayed nerves. He really didn't want to get into this, but Finn had other ideas.

"When did it happen?"

One thing that could be said about Daniel Finley was his directness. Derek didn't know any other person as blunt as the guy walking beside him, and if Finn wanted something he would, in the end, always get it. That would make him a helluva lawyer one day, even as it made him a giant pain in the ass today.

"This morning."

"Fuck, Derek."

When several passersby turned their way, Derek scrubbed an agitated hand over his chin. "Would you keep your voice down?"

"Sorry, but damn it. How are you even here? Your face must be killing you."

"Yeah, it hurts like a bitch."

"Let me take you to the ER."

"How about no."

"Don't be stupid. You need to get it checked out. Make sure he didn't fracture your cheekbone."

As they stepped under a covered walkway, Derek tugged on Finn's arm and led him to one of the benches in front of a trimmed hedge. "Nothing's broken."

"How do you know? Your eye is barely open."

"I just need some ice."

"Jesus. When are you gonna pack your shit and get the hell out of there?"

This argument wasn't new, but he didn't want to be a burden to the Finley family. They had gone through enough. Mrs. Finley had raised two children on her own, three if Derek counted himself, which he might as well with the amount of time he'd spent there over the years. There was no way he was bringing his father's wrath to their door. Right now, the only reason his father tolerated him was because he was one hell of a deduction at tax time. But he knew it was only a matter of years before that ran out. "When I can afford to."

"I've told you over and over—"

"No, Daniel." His friend shut up then. Finn knew he was serious when he used his full name. It was a rare event, and Derek's tone said he was done talking about it.

"Then tell me why. He hasn't touched you in at least…I don't know…but it's been a while."

"A year. At least a year. Ever since I started spending time at the gym, the fucker got smart. Decided it wasn't a good idea to pick on someone who outweighed him."

Finn sat down on the bench, and Derek followed suit. When they were side by side, a comfortable silence settled between them, and he marveled at the peace he felt with Finn. He'd often wondered why they didn't work on a level beyond friends. But he knew deep down this was why. They were like brothers. It might not have been by blood, but it sure as fuck was through choice. He would do anything for Finn and he knew that feeling was mutual. They had each other's backs, and he knew no matter what happened or where they ended up, they always would.

"Tell me." Finn's voice was soft, but his tone firm.

"He called you a…" Derek was unable to bring himself to say it. A large, comforting hand touched his shoulder, and when Finn squeezed, Derek tried again. "He called you a faggot."

The word lingered between the two of them for a moment, and before he could open his mouth and say anything further, Finn got in first. "And then he hit you?"

"No. I hit him first."

"Derek." Finn sighed and got to his feet. Then he gripped the back of his neck as he paced, and it had Derek shooting off the bench.

"He fucking deserved it. He's a homophobic prick."

Finn whirled around to face him and poked him in the chest. "You know better than to react to him that way. Especially over me. What do I care if he calls me a faggot or a queer? I *am* queer. But you know what I do care about? I care about my best friend getting a fist in his face. *That* I care about. Who knows what would've happened if you'd fallen to the ground unconscious? I've seen you after his boot has hit your ribs. I don't want to see that again, Derek."

"I know," Derek said, and cursed under his breath as Finn clasped the back of his neck and pulled him into a hug. It wasn't awkward, since the two of them were roughly the same height. It actually felt pretty damn good to be touched that way. To be comforted. Then Finn turned his head and whispered in his ear, "Don't ever let him make you doubt yourself. Not ever."

He hugged Finn a little tighter then, because while he'd reacted to the words on his friend's behalf, the both of them knew the pain ran on a much deeper and more personal level.

One that was dark.

One that was damaged beyond repair.

One that made him wonder if he'd ever be able to find peace in his life. And the only thing he knew with exact certainty was that he would never give up trying.

# Chapter 4

*Two Months Later*

JORDAN TIGHTENED THE knot of the purple tie he'd draped around his neck earlier that morning, and gave himself a final once-over in his black BMW Z4's sun visor mirror. His first class of the day started in —*oh…ten minutes, no big deal*—and as usual, he was running late.

It was amazing, really, that for someone as bright and gifted as he apparently was, dressing himself and driving across town to be somewhere at a specific time always seemed to be a monumental effort. One at which he usually failed.

He flipped the visor up and then snatched his leather bag off the passenger seat. If he hightailed it he should be able to—*Ugh, forget it, there's no way I'm going to make it on time,* he thought, and leisurely got out of the car. *Yep. So why bother running and making myself sweat, not to mention mess up my hair?*

It was mid-October, and the air was still heavy and humid enough that walking from his car across the lawn would guarantee an uncomfortable first period of dress slacks stuck to his ass and his shirt plastered to his back. Not something he enjoyed in front of a room full of students.

As far as he was concerned, there were only two good reasons to ever be covered in sweat, and neither of them involved as many clothes as he was currently wearing, *or* the students from his class—*with the exception of maybe…one*, the devil on his shoulder chimed in.

He was halfway across the lawn when he spotted Professor Brantley Hayes climbing out of his car, and stopped for a second to admire him. *Mhmm, so fine*, Jordan thought with a grin as his friend and colleague shut his car door and headed in his direction dressed in— "A *vest*? Are you serious? How in God's name are you wearing a vest today, Hayes? My balls are sweating, and not in the good *it adds to the friction* way."

"Eloquent as always, Jordan. Good morning." Brantley laughed as they met up along the path leading toward their respective buildings.

"Morning," Jordan replied, then brought his venti peppermint mocha to his lips and took a sip. *Thank God for caffeine, really.* How people functioned without it, he would never know.

"Second month of the semester and you're still alive. How are you feeling, Professor Devaney?"

"*Old* when you call me that. I swear, every time a student raises their hand and addresses me that way, I'm one step closer to a receding hairline and wrinkles around my eyes."

Brantley shook his head. "You're ridiculous. You know that, right? You're barely older than they are, and I'll be damned if I tell you you're good looking when it's clear by the smug smirk on your face that you already know it."

"Well, that's just mean-spirited of you. My ego is *very* fragile," Jordan protested. "Plus, a boy can never be told too many times how pretty he is." He batted his lashes and Brantley shoved him in the arm.

Over the last few weeks the two of them had become really good friends. They'd gone out a few times after work to grab a drink, and ever since, they'd hit it off. They even had a regular Sunday brunch date at a tiny little hole-in-the-wall café down by the beach. It was an easy friendship. One he knew they would share for many years to come. Especially since sex wasn't in the mix. That was now one hundred percent off the table. Not only because they worked together but also because Jordan had found out that they shared a positional preference that just wouldn't work for him.

"I'm sure you have someone on speed dial who can feed your *fragile* ego, should you ever need it," Brantley said.

"I have two, if you must know. But neither are as smart *or* sophisticated as yourself. So you can understand how your opinion would carry more weight."

"You're incorrigible," Brantley said, but grinned as he brought his coffee cup to his lips. He took a sip and then said, "Okay. So be serious for a second. I know you're capable."

"'Tis true, but it's so boring."

"I'm sure you'll manage for all of five minutes. I wanted to talk to you about Derek Pearson."

At the sound of that particular student's name, Jordan immediately sobered and came to a halt. He'd been paying a little more attention to Derek than he knew he should. At first he'd attributed it to their first encounter, but with every passing day the quiet, almost introspective nature of the guy, showed a vulnerability that had peaked Jordan's interest. "What about him?"

"I heard something pretty disturbing going around about his father yesterday afternoon. I'm not one to pay much heed to gossip, but in a town the size of this one, it's bound to happen."

Jordan's stomach tightened when Brantley wrapped his fingers around the crook of his arm and pulled him over to the side of the path out of the way of other students.

"I won't keep you long. I just wanted to give you a heads-up. I remember you telling me about that first day and his black eye."

Jordan fingered the lid of his coffee cup and nodded, hating where this conversation was leading.

"Okay. Well, his father got picked up a couple of nights ago for public intoxication. Apparently one of the law secretaries lives down the street from them. He was brought home in a cop car and was acting belligerent. I heard her say that Derek was the one to smooth things over with the police." Brantley paused and then said exactly what Jordan was thinking: "I have a sneaking suspicion his eye was courtesy of his dad. So you might want to keep tabs on him."

*Damn.* Jordan had had a feeling it was something like that, but having it confirmed made it so much worse than just imagining it. When he remained silent, Brantley asked, "Have there been any more incidents since that day?"

Jordan shook his head and, in a voice much more serious than he was apt to using, said, "No. He's very quiet for the most part."

"A bit of a loner, then?"

"Hmm, I'm not sure about loner so much," he said. "More…private, but that's understandable now."

"Yes. I suppose it is."

Jordan nodded. "I mean, except for his surfer friend. You know, the one with the blond hair."

"Ahh yes, Daniel Finley."

Jordan thought he detected something reverent in Brantley's tone, and couldn't help but taunt him a little. "Know him well?"

Brantley's eyes widened, and Jordan couldn't help but laugh at his friend's shock.

"No. Why would you ask that?"

"You just sounded impressed by him. That's all."

"Well, he's a good student. Very bright."

"Very easy on the eyes too," Jordan teased. It worked, too, because Brantley almost choked on his coffee.

"I hadn't noticed."

Jordan placed a hand on Brantley's arm, schooling his

features to those of someone deeply concerned, and asked, "Why? Are you losing your eyesight? You're not *that* old."

"No, smartass. But I'm his professor."

"Which means…what? That you're dead? Or worse"—Jordan lowered his voice to a whisper—"impotent? Because they're the only two reasons you wouldn't notice that Daniel Finley is sun-kissed and *gor*geous. Not to mention he lights up any room he walks into."

"Oh my God. Stop talking. I need to get to class."

"Mhmm, so do I. First class has a certain Daniel—"

"I'm leaving now," Brantley told him as he started walking away.

"Hey? Thanks for telling me about Derek. I'll keep an eye on him." *Like I really need an excuse.*

"No problem. I figured you'd want to know."

"Yeah, I appreciate it. Oh, by the way. You interested in hitting a club this weekend?" He'd asked Brantley a couple of times now, and each time he'd been turned down. The man was sexy and single, but from what Jordan could tell he was also a little more reserved than he was when it came to what he did in his free time.

"I think I'll pass for now."

"Okay. But one day before we're old and gray…?"

"Yes, okay, one day soon."

Jordan saluted him with his coffee cup and then jogged the rest of the way up the path and stairs to the door of his building. He pulled it open and stepped inside where he was blasted by the cool air offering some relief. Tugging at the collar of his shirt, he tried to extricate the material from his torso the best he could as he walked farther down the hall.

As he got closer to his classroom, he spotted Derek with his back up against the wall, with none other than Daniel resting against it with one shoulder angled toward his friend.

Jordan kept an eye on the two of them as he moved closer. Brantley's words ran around in his head as he observed Derek while remaining unnoticed. Ever since that first day, Jordan had made it a point to keep his distance from Derek. He'd known something was off after their original run-in, and having it confirmed merely made him more curious about the student he'd found difficult to push aside.

He would be the first to admit that these two intrigued him more than they should, and he wasn't quite sure why. There was something about them. Something that was niggling in the back of his mind, and as he stood there observing them, Jordan watched Daniel place his hand on Derek's bicep before smoothing it down his arm to squeeze his fingers.

That was when he got it. When the missing piece of the puzzle finally fell into place. These two were extremely comfortable with touching one another. The same way he was with his friend—*and yeah, okay, on-again-off-again fuck buddy*—August.

It wasn't in a friendly clap on the back, *hey, man, it's cool* kind of way. More like an *I'm here for you and always will be* way. They shared an intimate connection. It was obvious if you took a second to really watch them, and this little glimpse at a private moment made it abundantly clear.

*A couple, maybe? Hmm, they might be,* but Jordan would almost place bets they were just friends. *Friends with benefits, then?* he mused, and wasn't quite sure why he cared. But he did.

He hadn't pegged Derek as gay. Daniel either, for that matter, and he was generally very astute when it came to men of the same feathers who liked to flock together. But then he remembered Derek's departing comment from day one as it came slamming back into his brain.

*"I just want you to know, I respect who you are, very much."*

*And shit.* Maybe he wasn't too far off track in thinking Derek batted for the same team he did. And wasn't that a shocker?

Taking in their close stance a final time, Jordan couldn't help but note that Derek had turned his hand over and was gently squeezing Daniel's fingers in return as he aimed a hell of a disarming smile at the laid-back surfer.

*Well, slap my ass and call me Sally.* It was a rare day when *his* actions weren't the most shocking to take place.

He was about to announce himself, but before he could, Derek's blue eyes drifted past his buddy's shoulder and connected with his own.

*Oh shit. Busted.*

The immediate furrow between Derek's brows and the fierce scowl that twisted his lips conveyed quite clearly that he wasn't happy that their private little interlude was being observed.

*Well…tough shit.* Jordan had no reason to feel bad or even guilty. He was allowed to be there in the corridor. Hell, he was supposed to be there. He was the damn professor.

Mustering up his nerve, and he had plenty when provoked, Jordan straightened his shoulders, knowing he didn't even come close to these guys' heights, and sauntered down the hall.

Deciding he would stick it to Derek in the most *I don't care if you're holding hands, kissing, or making out with your friend* way he could manage, Jordan paused when he got in line with them and said cheerily, "Good morning, boys," then pulled open the door with extra flourish and reminded them, "while usually I'd be the one on the sidelines wondering what was about to happen next here, I'm already running late, which means you are too. So don't linger out here long. You don't want all the seats to be taken. And I know how close you like to sit to one another."

Their mouths fell open, and as Derek pushed off the wall as if to correct or confront him, Daniel touched his shoulder in a *leave it alone* gesture.

Jordan flashed them a grin then, and stepped into the classroom, letting the door fall shut behind him.

*There, let him make of* that *whatever he will.*

---

"WHAT THE HELL WAS THAT ABOUT?" Finn asked, laughing as the two of them stared at the door.

"Who knows," Derek said, racking his brain to work out what the hell was going on with Devaney—but nope. He was coming up with nothing.

Ever since their first and only discussion, he'd sat in the back of the guy's classroom, kept his head down and his mouth shut. He'd also managed to get pretty decent grades on his essays, so he had no idea what the guy's deal was.

One thing was for sure: the man knew how to make an entrance. *Christ.*

"I don't know, something about you sure pushes his buttons. Did you see how pissy he was under that posh *Good morning, boys.* He looked like he wanted to claw your face off." Finn laughed again.

"Posh, that's a good word for him," Derek said. "Loud and in your face. And that perfectly styled hair and those clothes? They look like they cost more than my entire fucking wardrobe."

"I know, right. But you have to admit, he looks damn good. Bet he scores big time when he hits the clubs," Finn said, nodding as though he were onto something. "I was looking at the faculty website the other day—"

"Why?"

"I...I just was."

"O*kay*," Derek drawled, feeling as though he were missing something there, but let it go.

"And did you know he's the second youngest professor to ever be appointed a position in the US?"

"Funnily enough, no. I didn't know that."

"I also Googled him because that's pretty crazy, right. He's a genius or some shit. Can you believe that? And his family is super rich. Like, I don't know, Midas rich."

"What about his dick size, was that on there too?" Derek deadpanned. But really, he was kind of curious.

"Fuck you. I just thought it was interesting, that's all."

"Yeah? Huh. Clearly our opinions vary on what's interesting and what's not. Nerd."

"Okay. I don't think he's *that* interesting."

"So then *why* are we still talking about Posh Spice?"

That made Finn just about double over with laughter. "Posh Spice. Fucking love it. Bet that'd *really* piss him off. Anyway, what was I talking about again?" Finn asked, then he pointed at Derek. "That's right. Bianca's tonight. Why don't we go? She asked me the other day if we wanted to come to the bonfire, and I was going to say no. But I think you could do with it. Plus, I want to talk to you about something."

Derek grumbled a little, but in the end agreed. *What the hell.* Maybe it would do him some good to be around kids who were hanging out with the single-minded goal of drinking themselves into a state where they could find someone passable to make out with. Who knows, maybe he'd find some guy who'd make his dick twitch and be able to forget his jacked-up life for two seconds. He could get on board with that.

A couple of nights ago his father had been ticketed for public intoxication and brought home in the back of a squad car. His older brother Alan had been passed out on the couch when the cops arrived. So who had had to deal with all the nosy neighbors standing on their balconies staring at the flashing red and blue lights at 3 a.m.? *Yeah, lucky fucking me.* The only saving grace was that his father had stumbled into his bedroom, passed out, and Derek had been gone by the time he'd awoken the next morning.

Pushing the disgust and pity on the neighbors' faces from his mind, Derek followed Daniel inside their classroom and snuck a quick look toward the front of the room and the "genius" sorting through his mess of papers at his podium.

Devaney had to be the most unorganized person on the planet. Derek thought it was a miracle he managed to teach a university-level class considering the state of his teaching materials, but teach it he did.

Loved by all of his students, the professor was animated and lively with each topic he covered. But no matter how exciting he made his class, the fact remained that he made Derek cautious as hell. He couldn't remember the last time his cock had been this fixated on someone, and he was starting to think the guy was a sorcerer weaving a spell.

Deciding the idea of a party and a hookup was exactly what he needed to maybe forget this weird infatuation, Derek leaned over to Finn and put his lips by his ear to ask, "What time's Bianca's thing tonight?"

Finn turned his head and grinned. "Ten. Are you going to make sure we get home in one piece or do you need to unwind?"

"Nah, I'll walk your drunk ass home. I think the Pearson household has had enough alcohol within its walls for the week—"

"Mr. Pearson?"

As his name registered in Devaney's familiar tone, Derek froze and saw Finn grimace, then he turned to look down at his professor. Devaney was standing with his arms crossed over his chest and an eyebrow raised in an expectant manner. He'd obviously asked a question, seen that Derek wasn't paying attention, and singled him out—again.

*Is he fucking serious?*

"Yeah?"

"Do you have something to add to the conversation?"

He hadn't been told to stand, but since it seemed that he was about to be made an example of, he got to his feet anyway. *'Cause why the hell not.*

"Not really. I was just squaring up my plans for the weekend. You know, something fun, after enduring an hour of this."

He wasn't sure why he was being such a dick. But just as

Finn had suggested that he pushed Devaney's buttons, there was something about his professor that sure as fuck pushed his. He also provoked him into saying stuff that wasn't true. There was no *enduring* happening in this class. It was actually one of the ones he enjoyed. All he knew was the irritated look his teacher was aiming at him made Derek be sure to add a healthy dose of *fuck you* to the end of his statement, just to ruffle the guy's feathers.

He was *so* going to get booted from this class.

Mirroring his professor's stance, Derek widened his feet and crossed his arms in a defiant show of attitude, and the way Devaney's face reddened was a sure tell that he'd raised the guy's blood pressure which was immensely satisfying. Not to mention a total turn-on.

It had Derek's mind travelling directly south, and imagining Devaney naked and flushed from head to toe.

God, he was being a shit.

Certain he was about to be told to get the hell out of the class, Derek was stunned when he caught the corner of Devaney's lips twitch. That tiny indicator that his professor was enjoying their little sparring match had his dick about two seconds away from embarrassing the hell out of him.

"I couldn't agree with you more, Mr. Pearson," Devaney finally said, and for a minute Derek had to remind himself he wasn't talking about his current situation, but the fact he wanted to do something fun after this long week. "So if you don't have anything to contribute to class, please retake your seat, keep quiet, and let me get through the next fifty minutes without your *mouth* interrupting me."

*No way.* There was no way he'd just said that to him and meant it the way Derek was taking it. But the feisty eyes holding his practically sparkled in confirmation, and Derek knew without a doubt that Devaney had just purposely stroked his cock with his words, and in the next breath denied him.

*And I'll be damned if that doesn't make the guy even hotter.*

---

JORDAN COULDN'T BELIEVE what he'd just done. *Okay,* so he could believe it a little bit. He'd just eye-fucked one of his students and, if he were honest, enjoyed every second of it.

The truth was, Derek was just the kind of guy he was drawn to. Someone who was off-limits. Someone who was troubled. He was a bad boy at heart, and knowing his background a little better, Jordan could understand why he was the way he was.

But there was also something fragile about Derek and the way he kept to himself, and it was *that* quality that saved him from being a total punk.

It also made him extremely appealing and was the reason for Jordan's racing pulse.

It was a totally inappropriate reaction, one he knew he would never in a million years pursue. But there was no way to deny the attraction was there, bubbling between the two of them like lava in a volcano waiting to explode.

*Shit. I really need to get laid.*

As he was finishing up, Jordan decided he'd go ahead and give August a call. The guy had left a message earlier in the week that he was in town to catch some prime waves—*his words, not mine*—so Jordan figured he should take advantage of a sure thing.

It'd been way too long since he'd gone dancing, and there was no way he was going to miss out on getting his groove on. The excuse to dress up and flaunt his stuff was too heady a feeling, especially when he wanted to let loose. So he supposed he really hadn't been telling a lie when he told Derek he wanted the day to be over.

Checking the clock on the wall, he saw there were only five minutes until class was done and clapped his hands together before rubbing them with glee. "Okay, guys, that's it for the week. Remember, you have a quiz Monday. Don't be late or I'm locking the door, and for those with plans," he said, and looked directly at Derek, who, he was surprised to find, was watching him with matching focus, "play safe." He broke the potent eye contact and smiled widely. "Have a good weekend, everyone."

As the students vacated the room one after another, he gathered the papers littering his lectern and the small table beside it. He bundled them and was tapping them on the table to straighten the pile when he heard someone approach behind him. With the papers in order, he turned around to see Derek standing beside the podium with his icy blue eyes narrowed, and his mouth drawn in its usual grim expression.

Jordan let his eyes do a quick sweep of the room, and when he realized they were the only two in there, he made sure to keep his attention focused on the face of the student in front of him.

"Can I help you, Derek?"

"Yeah, I think so," Derek said, and then paused before he asked, "Did I do something to piss you off?"

Taken off guard by Derek's language, Jordan squared his shoulders for the verbal sparring match to come. Not that he was worried. He had no delusions that should he want to take this guy, he could, and would, win every time.

"I'm not sure what you mean," he finally replied.

Derek scoffed and took a presumptuous step forward, and Jordan ordered himself to stay put. There was no way he was about to back down just because Derek was several inches taller than himself, and exuded a pent-up energy that was practically making the room vibrate.

It was time the guy had a little discipline in his life. It was obvious now that he rebelled due to whatever was going on with his family, but one thing Jordan would not stand for in his classroom and everyday life was disrespect. No matter who you were or why you thought it was acceptable.

This close, Derek was—*Oh hell, there's no use trying to deny it. The guy is muy caliente.* Dressed in green cargo shorts and his standard black T-shirt that stretched across his broad chest like a second skin, the words printed at the center of it made Jordan want to smile: *Normal people scare me.*

Well, then Derek should feel right at home with him, because no one had ever accused Jordan of being normal. It was time, however, that Derek was taught a lesson about what Jordan was and wasn't willing to let slide.

"If you're referring to my calling on you—"

"I am," Derek said, and Jordan prayed for patience. "Why do you always do that?"

Jordan placed the papers on the podium behind him and then turned back to aim a pointed look up at Derek. "I don't."

"Yes, you do."

He thought about that for a second and made sure that Derek wasn't right, and when he was satisfied he wasn't actually singling him out, Jordan shook his head and pointed a finger up at him. "No, I don't. In fact, I haven't called on you until today, and that was only because you were being rude and talking through my class. If you don't wish to be singled out, Derek, then show some respect."

As his words lingered between them, Jordan's entire demeanor dared Derek to defy him. He couldn't believe how close they were standing. His finger was practically poking that huge chest in front of him, and Jordan could see it rising and falling with every annoyed breath Derek took.

"I already told you," Derek said, his voice so soft and controlled that Jordan was lucky he was so close or he wouldn't have heard him. "I respect you."

Jordan could hear ringing in his ears as his heart thumped out an insistent tattoo.

*One, two, three.* Move. *One, two, three.* Move. *Move. Back. Now.*

Yeah… But he didn't.

Instead, his eyes ran up the square line of Derek's jaw, and Jordan moistened his bottom lip with his tongue. He wanted to bite and suck his way up to Derek's ear and tell him—*Focus, Devaney. Focus.*

"Then show it. When I speak, listen to me. It's really not that hard."

Derek's eyes dropped to his lips, and Jordan knew he was perilously close to crossing a line. One that was highly inappropriate.

"You're wrong," Derek told him. Then he shrugged his bag up his arm. "It's extremely hard every time you speak. And just so we're clear, I'm *not* referring to my attention span."

*Oh no he didn't,* Jordan thought, shocked right down to his leather shoes. He knew exactly what Derek was referring to, and, never one to act coy, he ran his eyes down Derek's body and finally back up to his face. If he'd been anybody else— *But he's not.*

"Listen to me very closely, Derek. While you are in my class, this is not going to *ever* happen."

When Derek's eyes darkened, and the side of his surly mouth tugged into a smirk, Jordan realized exactly what he'd said, and went to correct himself. But it was too late.

"I can live with that. At the rate I'm going, you'll kick me out anyways."

Jordan couldn't help himself then. He chuckled at Derek's insolence and shook his head. "And that's now a goal of yours?"

"To fuck you or to get kicked out? The way I see it, they kinda go hand in hand now, don't they."

While Jordan was aware Derek was going for the shock factor, there was no way he could let that go without some kind of recourse.

"Seeing as you are here on a scholarship, Mr. Pearson, I hardly think it's wise to aim to be thrown out of class for whatever inane reasoning you think you have." Jordan paused after his scholastically inclined speech, but just as it always did, his lack of filter, subtlety, and patience prodded him to add, "And just so we're clear, *no one* fucks me."

As that little tidbit of information escaped Jordan's lips, Derek's eyes blazed with an emotion that went far beyond challenge and headed straight into a territory that was rife with minefields—curiosity.

He then gave a clipped nod of his head, spun on the heels of his flip-flops, and marched toward the door.

*Shit. Why does he always make me act this way?* Jordan thought, but he didn't take his eyes off the intense man as he silently departed the room.

# Chapter 5

THAT AFTERNOON, DEREK booked it home with one thing on his mind—finding out everything he could about Professor Jordan Devaney. He hadn't thought of looking the guy up online before today. But ever since Finn had mentioned it, the idea had taken root and just wouldn't leave him alone.

When he got home, it was a little after five and he was relieved to find the house empty. He dumped his bag on the floor and went to his room to switch on his old, clunky PC. As the computer booted up, Derek paced back and forth in the small confines of his room, going over his earlier encounter with his professor.

The guy was...damn, he was something else, Derek thought as a grin curled his lips. Smart, sexy, and so out of his league that Derek had no clue what the hell he'd been thinking earlier, saying what he had.

But damn if he'd been able to help himself.

There was something about Devaney that made him want to grab a hold of him and, well, fuck his brains out. Maybe it was his superior attitude. Or the fact that even though he was several inches shorter than himself, he had no problem telling him to pull his head in.

For most of his life Derek's father hadn't given two shits about him, and due to his rapid growth spurt in high school, most of his teachers had avoided any conflict with him, so he was rarely disciplined—at all.

That hadn't stopped the professor, though. This was the second time he'd called Derek's ass out, and he was starting to think Devaney enjoyed dishing it out as much as he was enjoying...well, receiving.

Which brought him back to the other thing that had been bugging him. That final comment to him before he'd left today. The one Devaney had made about no one fucking him. It had been playing on repeat since he'd left. It was also hot as hell.

*Fuck,* he thought as he rubbed his palm over the hard-on now straining against the zipper of his cargos.

While Derek had always been the one to top in his past encounters, the thought of being fucked by that Energizer Bunny had him wanting to get on his hands and knees for Devaney while he kept going and going and going...

He groaned at the image in his head as he walked back to take a seat in front of his computer, and Jesus, he was hard. He unbuttoned his shorts and breathed a sigh of relief as he lowered the zipper.

Maybe he should just take care of himself. Get rid of some of the tension that had him wound up like a damn tightrope. The problem was, the only thing he could seem to focus on was Devaney and the idea that he'd be a total hellcat in bed, judging by his uppity personality and quick-to-fire temper.

*Christ, yep, that's what's doing it,* he thought as he slipped his hand inside his pants. Before he thought about all the reasons he shouldn't do what he was about to, Derek opened up his browser and typed the professor's name into Google. He took a deep breath as he hit search and waited to see what, besides his cock, would pop up.

When the results appeared, Derek scanned down the first three stories. The first one read: *Millionaire's son hailed a prodigy.* The second: *Youngest man to graduate with a PhD.* And the third: *Self-made millionaire's son goes wild.*

*You don't say…* Derek's lips pulled into a slow smile as he clicked on the third headline and waited for the page to load. When the story appeared, he noted the date. It was from two years earlier, and it opened talking about Jordan Devaney the twenty-three-year-old son to Nathan Devaney, the man who'd made millions in oil excavation back in the late eighties. It then went on to explain that his only son, and heir to his fortune, was spotted leaving an upscale gay bar in Wyoming with an unknown "friend" in the early hours of Saturday morning. When approached by the paparazzi for comment on why he was seen leaving such an establishment, young Devaney was reported to have said, "If you're asking about my orientation, don't bother. Because you're not going to get a straight answer."

*Fuck yes.* That was the exact attitude Derek admired and had him circling the root of his shaft. He bucked his hips up so his naked flesh was free of its confines, and as he gave it a firm pull and slowly drew his palm up the length, he shut his eyes, imagining it was Devaney.

He drew his lower lip between his teeth as his cock throbbed in his hand, and then he opened his eyes and scrolled past the rest of the words in the article to the image that had been inserted at the bottom of the piece.

It was a night shot, so it was dark except for the streetlights and the neon sign that read *FUBAR*, but there was no mistaking Devaney from the other man in the image with him.

Devaney was the shorter of the two and was wearing ripped jeans that sat low on his waist, and he had a white shirt on that was pretty tame for him. It was unbuttoned, and the photographer must have taken the shot just as a breeze had caught him, because the shirt was being blown away from his body and —*damn*, that had Derek's hand moving faster.

Tanned and toned, Devaney had a compact body that looked entirely fuckable. Around his neck he wore some kind of beaded necklace, and his hair was styled in messy spikes that were sexy as hell.

All in all, he was exactly the kind of guy Derek could imagine under him, over him, and all fucking around him. Then add in the raised middle finger Devaney had given the photographer, and the attitude sealed the deal.

Derek shut his eyes and imagined himself in place of whoever the hell had his arm around Devaney in that photo. He imagined himself going home with him as he pumped his hips faster, and when his toes curled and the pre-cum leaked from the tip of his cock to coat his hand, Derek growled. And when he thought about the disapproving tone his professor had used that afternoon when he'd told him, *No one fucks me*, he came harder than he'd ever come in his life.

Breathing rapidly, Derek languidly stroked himself as he came down from his orgasm. He had no idea how he was going to survive the next few months in Devaney's class. He couldn't seem to concentrate on anything other than the man when he was talking, and after this, today… He wasn't sure he could look at him and not think about how it would feel to get naked with his professor.

He reached for several tissues to clean himself up, then closed out of the browser so he could go and take a shower. Maybe he would talk to Finn about it tonight when they went to Bianca's.

It always helped when he got shit off his chest. Finn would laugh, tell him he was a douchebag, then that would be the end of that. Because liking his professor—that would be the mother of all stupid ideas. Life and school were hard enough without adding a literal meaning to the word *hard*.

*That's what I'll do*, Derek thought, and turned on the water. He just needed to get to Bianca's and talk this out with Finn, the levelheaded one of them both. Then everything would be back to normal.

At least, he hoped so.

---

"I THINK I like my law professor."

The gulp of soda Derek had just taken sprayed out of his mouth as Finn's words hit his ears. He coughed around the fizzy shit that had gone halfway up his nose as he stared at Finn with watering eyes. *There's no fucking way he just said—*

"You know, Professor Hayes?"

*You've gotta be shittin' me,* Derek thought, as he wiped the back of his hand over his mouth. Finn had a lopsided grin on his face that told Derek his friend was close to shit-faced from the girly Jell-O shots he'd been swallowing all night.

Trying to work out what the hell to say to Finn's confession, he shut his eyes for a second and tried to drown out the loud beat of the dance music that was throbbing throughout the house. He was surprised the windows weren't rattling from the vibration. His head sure as shit was.

He couldn't believe what had just come out of Finn's mouth. He glowered at him, irrationally pissed that the one person he wanted to talk him out of the most moronic idea he'd ever had was having the same damn one.

*Motherfucker.* "Are you out of your damn mind?"

As soon as the words spewed out of his mouth, Derek knew they were the wrong ones to say. The smile that had been across Finn's face slipped a notch. "No. I mean it. I think he's really hot."

"Then you're an idiot. As well as drunk."

He watched Finn's shoulders tense, and even though they were roughly the same height and he was trying to be intimidating, the slight sway to Finn's stance lessened the impact.

"Fuck you, man. I'm not drunk."

"Yeah, you are," Derek said, shaking his head. He threw his cup in a large trash can and took a step toward Finn.

"Am not."

"Listen to what you're saying, Danny boy—"

"What? That I like Professor Hayes?"

"Yeah…," he said, and looked around. "You might want to keep that little tidbit to yourself."

Finn scanned their surroundings and then shrugged. "No one's listening."

"If you think that, you're an even bigger dumbass than I originally thought." He knew he was being a dick, but hearing Finn say out loud what he himself had been tossing around in his head made him see what a gigantic mistake it would be.

"You're being an asshole."

"Why? 'Cause the truth hurts?"

"You know what? I wanted to talk to my friend about this. But maybe you can tell him to come find me when he shows up, because you're acting like a judgmental prick."

Before Derek could grab Finn's arm, his friend walked out of the back door to the strip of beach that Bianca's house looked out over. He sighed and rubbed the bridge of his nose.

*Fucking hell*, he *was* being judgmental. That was totally unlike him. Usually he wouldn't give a shit who Finn liked. He would likely be the one encouraging a sex-a-thon with his hot professor. So what the hell was his problem? Oh yeah, he wanted the exact same thing.

Deciding one shot of tequila was allowed considering the circumstances, he snatched up a glass, downed it, and then walked toward the back door. He needed to find Finn and let him know everything was cool. The guy had been stumbling and swaying on his feet, and just because Derek didn't know what to do about his jacked-up reactions to Devaney didn't mean that Finn was in the same situation. He owed it to his buddy to hear him out.

Heading down the stairs to the long stretch of sand, he

looked to his right and then his left, and there was Finn, a fair way up for someone who was three sheets to the wind.

Derek sucked in a breath and decided right then to forget about his whacked-out fantasies. It wasn't like anything would ever come of it. Devaney was rich as a king, smarter than Derek even knew was possible, and probably thought he was a ridiculous kid he had to teach—if he even thought about him at all. So there was no need to hash it all out.

Finn, on the other hand, obviously wanted to talk, and what kind of friend would Derek be if he wasn't there to listen?

As he caught up with his friend, he called out his name. "Yo, Finn! Finn, you drunk asshole. Wait up. I'm not gonna let you walk home by yourself." And when Finn rounded to face him, he added, "Don't go off all half-cocked—ha! Get it? Half-cocked?" trying to get a grin.

There was no immediate smile, but Finn did stop and wait for him, and Derek gave a sigh of relief, knowing that was his sign. Everything between them would be okay.

---

AS THE INCESSANT beat of the techno dance music throbbed throughout the club and vibrated through his body, Jordan shut his eyes and let his head fall back on the shoulder of the man behind him.

*Mhmm,* he'd needed this tonight. Boy had he been wired when he got home today. Not only wired. But horny. He couldn't remember the last time he'd been so fired up. But *man oh man*, he thought—then laughed despite himself, because, yeah baby, sometimes two men were better than one. He'd tried that in the past, but really, all he wanted tonight was someone fun, frivolous, and very fucking capable of getting him off. And August was that man.

Jordan had his hands looped around the back of his friend's neck as he gyrated his hips against the rigid cock aligning his ass, and he felt fantastic. Several minutes earlier he'd peeled his top off and shoved it into the pocket of his skintight jeans. As August ran his hands down his ribs to his waist and then, *yesss, a little lower*, Jordan let himself get lost in the delicious feel of being seduced.

He knew that's exactly what August was doing, too. He'd known August since he was thirteen and on a family vacation in Lake Como, Italy. *Yeah*, if he and his family were rich, he wasn't sure what that made August. But the term *out of this world* sprang to mind.

From that first vacation when they'd met, the two of them had been inseparable every summer, and when they'd turned fifteen and experimented with a few kisses and fumbling hands, they'd quickly discovered that the both of them were extremely compatible when it came to getting naked and having some casual fun.

August's large palm flattened over the zipper of his jeans, and Jordan quickly added his own to increase the pressure so he could grind a little harder against that hand. He heard August's wicked chuckle in his ear but didn't give a fuck. It'd been too long since he'd been with someone who knew all the right buttons to push, so he was going to enjoy this to its full potential.

When August's mouth skimmed across the shell of his ear, Jordan twisted his fingers under the dark shoulder-length hair that curled against his friend's neck and tugged his head down so he could take those laughing lips in a hot, sweaty kiss.

Perspiration ran down Jordan's temple and his body felt fevered as the song switched and an anthem with lyrics about *respect* blasted from the speakers. Jordan halted as the words filtered through his mind, and then shook his head, trying to shake them loose. He tried to lose himself in the rhythm and his partner, but as the lyrics continued on a loop in his head, a very different face was coming to mind. One with a brazen stare and an audacious tongue, and for a second, he lost his fucking footing.

When the heel of his boot came down on August's toes, August cursed in his ear and tight fingers wrapped around one of his wrists. Jordan was spun around and yanked in close to his date, who lowered his head so he could speak directly in his ear. "Want to watch your feet, J? Or mine, for that matter?"

Jordan found August's dark eyes and smiled apologetically. "Sorry, hon. I got distracted for a second there."

"Yeah, I noticed. It's all good. But now my foot's throbbing as hard as my cock. Why don't we take a breather? I could use a drink anyway."

Jordan smiled and slipped his hand into August's then led him off the dance floor. They ordered a couple of drinks and headed over to a more secluded spot where a booth was being vacated. Jordan slid in one side and patted the faux leather beside him, inviting August to sit close by. When his friend followed his suggestion and took a seat so their thighs touched, Jordan gave a flirty wink and brought his apple martini to his lips. He took a sip and let his eyes roam over August's dark hair, stubbled jaw line, and the dark eyeliner he'd used to make his eyes and lashes stand out.

August was an extremely sexy man. A braided leather strap wrapped around his neck had a stone pendant at the base of his throat, and it invited one to look at the strong column of his neck and fantasize about kissing and licking it. He'd done that on many occasions, and had planned to enjoy the hell out of doing it tonight. But somewhere in the last ten minutes, his desire to let his freak flag fly had fizzled out and he was sitting there thinking about Derek Pearson. *What the hell?*

"Hey," August said, and waved a hand in front of his face. When Jordan blinked and refocused on him, his friend frowned and lowered his glass to the table. "You okay?"

"Yeah, I'm just—"

"Distracted. I know. You're giving me a complex here, J."

Jordan laughed at that. "Oh *please*. As if you could ever have a complex. One crook of your little finger and you could have any guy in here."

August gave a wolfish grin and dipped his head in acknowledgment of the truth, and then he leaned in close and took Jordan's drink from him, setting it on the table. "But I'm not here for just *any* guy. You already know that."

When August traced a finger along his lower lip, Jordan reached out to take a hold of his wrist. This was exactly what he'd wanted tonight. A hot night with an even hotter bed partner, but instead of sucking on that finger and biting down on it, Jordan pulled it away.

Sidetracked by the image of teaching a certain student of his a lesson on respect from down on his knees, Jordan sighed dramatically and let his head fall back with his eyes closed as he cursed his flagging libido. *Fuck.*

"All right. What the hell is going on with you? You're a hot mess. Or not so hot, I should say."

Letting out a breath of air, Jordan brought his head back up to face his friend and rolled his eyes. "Thanks a lot."

August gripped his chin and moved in to press a brisk kiss to his lips. "You know what I mean. You look phenomenal as always, but your mind…it isn't in my pants, where I was hoping it would be. So where the fuck is it?"

*Ugh,* August was right. There Jordan was on a Friday night with the surest thing to an epic orgasm sitting next to him, and he was busy thinking about Derek goddamn Pearson.

"J?" August said again, pulling him from his thoughts.

"Yeah." Jordan sighed.

"What's wrong?"

He reached for the martini August had taken away from him and decided if he was going to actually admit he was sitting there thinking about a student to this playboy, he should do it while sucking back some alcohol. When he finished, he saw one of August's dark eyebrows arch and quickly said, "I was just thinking about one of my students."

When a salacious grin split August's lips, Jordan brought a finger up and wagged it at him. "Oh no, it's not like that." Even though it kinda was.

"Like what?" August asked, feigning innocence.

Jordan couldn't help the grin that tugged at his lips. "Whatever filthy thoughts you're thinking over there."

August let out a deep, rumbling laugh. "I'm not thinking those."

"Bullshit."

"What? I'm not." August winked. "But I bet your students are about you."

He laughed at his friend's audacity. "You're so bad. Not only is that frowned upon, that is *not* the issue here."

"Are you sure?"

*No.* "Of course I'm sure. One of my students is…in some trouble, I think. But he's also a total smartass. Hard to talk to. A real handful."

"How would you know he's a handful, if it's not like that?"

Realizing what he'd said and what August was implying, Jordan screwed his nose up and whacked him on the arm. "Shut up. I'm being serious here."

August flashed his killer grin and shrugged. "Okay, but if we're really going to sit here and talk about work, I need another drink," August said, and Jordan wanted to slap himself on the back of the head.

*What is wrong with me?* August didn't care about his work issues. He was there for a good time, not to hear about Jordan's concerns that one of his students had home problems. The same student he couldn't stop imagining getting naked with.

*Shit.* Maybe he'd talk about this on Monday with Brantley. Someone who could sympathize with him and understand where he was coming from. *Minus the whole "I want to sleep with my student" part.*

Mentally shoving aside any thoughts of work, Jordan pushed up onto his knee and moved until he was straddling August's lap, catching him off guard. He placed his hands on August's shoulders and whispered against his lips.

"Forget it. It's nothing. Maybe I just need some help unwinding."

August's hands stroked up his spine, but the frown he'd adopted earlier remained. "That's not what I meant. I was gonna suggest after this we head out and go somewhere a little quieter. There's obviously something on your mind."

*Or someone. How inconvenient.*

Jordan shook his head. "Nope. You're here for one night, right?"

"Mhmm," August agreed, and Jordan rolled his hips forward and brushed his hardening cock over his friend's obvious erection. "Hell, J. Stop it unless you're going to—"

Pleased he'd finally gotten August's mind back on the night's activities, Jordan climbed off his lap.

"Oh, I'm going to," he assured him, and held out a hand. "Now get your hot ass out of that booth. We're going back to my place."

Somewhere Derek Pearson was certainly not allowed.

# Chapter 6

*Three Months Later*

"WHERE DO YOU think you're goin'?"

At the sound of his father's voice, Derek stopped in the kitchen and clutched the strap of his gym bag. He was dressed for his weekly night shift over at the local twenty-four-hour gym. He'd been doing that on the weekdays the past couple of months and had somehow managed to talk Finn into applying for, *and getting*, a "dancer" position down at club Boyz on the weekends. A shitty home life could make a person very motivated, and no one was more determined than him to make as much cash as humanly possible so he could move the fuck out.

Of course, that now meant he had zero social life, but then again, he hadn't really had one to begin with, so that didn't matter much. Finn was practically missing these days since he'd started sleeping with his professor—who knew he had that in him?—and every other hour Derek had available to him, he'd spent it writing papers and studying for his final exams. He had to maintain a certain grade to keep his scholarship.

The last few weeks had turned into endless hours of switching between one job and another, until this week, when he'd had to scale back so he could be at school for the start of his spring semester. He couldn't find it in him to complain, however, because it had kept him out of the house and, for the most part, away from his father—until now.

His sneakers made the cracked linoleum protest underfoot, and as he faced the man who'd addressed him, Derek braced himself for whatever might follow. His father was standing by the ancient television set holding the shit antenna he was trying to get to work in one hand, and a cigarette in the other.

"I'm going to work."

"You work?"

*Ignore him. Ignore him. Ignore him.* "Yeah. I have a job." *Or don't.*

He took a step in the direction of the front door, hoping that would be the end of that—but he should've known better. His father never let anything go. It was one of the reasons the Pearson household was a minefield. One misstep and a bomb exploded right under your feet before you had a chance to fucking blink.

"Where do you work?"

*Like I'm ever going to tell you, you piece of shit.*

Derek swallowed back his initial thought and closed his eyes. *Just let me go,* he prayed, and took another step toward the front door.

"I asked where you've been workin', Derek. Or you lyin' to me? You doing something you shouldn't be?"

If he were smart, he would walk out the door and keep his mouth shut. However, Derek was coming to realize that maybe he wasn't as smart as Mrs. Finley was always telling him he was.

Pivoting around, he dumped his bag on the floor and walked over to where his father was taking a drag of his cigarette.

"And what do you possibly think I'm doing that I shouldn't be? Drinking? Drugs? What a fucking joke. *You* asking *me* that."

His father scoffed. "Don't get smart with me, boy."

"I wouldn't dream of it. You might not understand me," Derek said as he looked his father straight in the eye and wondered why, somewhere in the back of his head, he was hoping his dad would try and take a swing. Maybe because then he would have an excuse to hit him back.

Instead, his father bent to connect the antenna in and then held it out in front of him, trying to get a signal. Derek looked him over, shaking his head as he took in the grubby white wife beater—*how appropriate*—the black cotton shorts with a hole in the left thigh, and the years-old flip-flops. The man was as run-down as the house he lived in.

"If you're workin', you ought to be contributin'."

Derek's words failed him at that, and then he started to laugh—the sound unhinged and a little bit deranged. "You can't be serious."

His father's blue eyes, identical to his own, found his, and the arctic freeze in them explained the iciness that ran through his own veins.

"Course I'm serious. You live here, dontcha? It's my roof that provides shelter for you. If you're working, I expect rent. Monthly. You can bring it to me tonight. Two hundred'll do."

Derek could feel his disbelief morphing into a full-on boiling rage as his father's words hovered between them, and when he brought the cigarette to his lips, Derek took a menacing step toward the man.

There was no way he was going to give this fucker a single penny of his. Not when he was saving every last cent so he could get the hell away from him.

"I'm not giving you a goddamn thing."

Finally a static-filled image appeared on the tube and his father froze in place, craning his head to see his handiwork. "No skin off my back. It's simple. If you don't have the cash, don't bother coming home."

As if his father had just hit him, Derek reeled back. "What?"

"You heard me. If you don't bring the cash, boy, you ain't welcome."

"Alan doesn't do shit and he's here—"

"Alan's worthless," his father snapped.

"Like father, like son," Derek said, hating that that was the damn truth. He'd been working his entire life to be the exact opposite to the loathsome human currently staring at him, but he recognized threads of the man's genes in him, like his temper and need to release his pent-up anger.

"Apple never falls that far from the tree, Derek. You should know that. You're a chip right off the old block yourself—"

"Shut up," Derek barked, shuddering at that thought. "I'm nothing like you."

"Aren't you? You're such a cocky shit, holier than thou in every way. But look at you; you're not so pure. And I ain't just talking about who you fuck," he jeered, leaning in so close that Derek could smell not only the tobacco, but the alcohol lacing his father's breath. "You're *dying* to take a swing at me right now, aren't you, son?" He cackled and moved back. "You're not so different to me."

Horrified that his father was right, Derek snapped. But instead of going for the hit, he snatched the antenna out of the old man's hands and ripped it from the wall. When the television came with it, toppling to the floor, his father roared at him and then crouched down over it.

*What a goddamn joke,* Derek thought. It was telling how concerned the asshole was for something so inanimate when he hadn't once shown an inkling of compassion for those who lived with him.

"I will *never* be you," Derek said, and his father glared up at him.

"Two hundred. And an extra hundred to replace what you just fucked up. Don't come back tonight unless you have it."

Derek's mouth parted, and he was about to argue that his father owed him fucking millions if they were repaying damages for things they'd broken, but he was done. He was done talking to the man struggling to get on his feet. He was done with it all.

When his father was standing tall once more, Derek took the step he needed to bring them nose to nose and said in a voice he didn't even recognize as his own, "Guess you better hope your *worthless* son finds a job soon, because your little queer is about to leave this hellhole and never come back."

When his father's eyes narrowed, Derek took a fistful of the wife beater, and felt a great sense of satisfaction at the flare of concern he finally saw in those eyes. His father was scared of him, and Derek had no idea what it said about him that he liked that.

"Have a nice life, you miserable fucker. I'd rather live on the street than *ever* give you a goddamn cent."

Shoving him away, Derek gave the house a final once-over and didn't let the fact that he had nowhere to go bother him right now. All he knew was that he was getting out of there and he wasn't going to look back.

---

BY THE TIME DEREK got to the gym, he was late for his shift. He wasn't thinking about the fact that he'd just left his home for good. Really. Instead, he focused on what he could control, and that was getting inside, clocking in, and earning money for the shift he was about to work. He would deal with all the other shit later.

He pulled open the door and stepped inside, and as he did he almost tripped over a man who was crouched in the middle of the entryway fishing through his workout bag.

"Fuck," Derek said, and barely had time to react and catch his footing before he fell face first on the floor. Of all the stupid places to stop— "What the hell, man, think you could move to the side?"

As he steadied himself and the man turned around to peer

up at him, Derek found himself staring into the face of none other than Professor Devaney.

*Holy shit.* This was the last thing he'd expected today. He hadn't seen Devaney since his final exam several weeks ago, and he wasn't sure he was mentally prepared to deal with him after the shit afternoon he'd already had with his father.

Over the remainder of his first semester, he and his professor had come to a mutual agreement of avoidance. He'd purposefully ignored his interest in the man, pushed it aside as nothing more than a stupid infatuation, and Devaney, it appeared, had done the same.

It turned out that was the best thing he could've done in the long run, too, because soon after that night at Bianca's, Finn's "professor" had shown up at Boyz and they'd started their "thing"—and never too far away from Hayes was the ubiquitous Jordan Devaney.

Not that Derek had ever made his presence known. Whenever he'd seen them at his weekend job where he danced around in next to nothing, he did his best to fucking hide. Shit was weird enough between them. Adding the fact that Devaney frequented the hottest gay club in the city, which *he* happened to dance at, would just make everything even more awkward.

"Oh, shit. Derek, I'm sorry," Devaney said as he stood and took a step toward Derek, placing a hand on his arm.

The gesture was innocent. Derek knew it was meant to offer apology and comfort and see if he was okay. But with the adrenaline-charged evening he'd already had, that was so *not* how his body was taking it.

*Hell no.*

His dick was definitely not feeling comforted. It wanted release, and it wanted it with the man currently squeezing his forearm.

He looked down at the hand resting on his arm and said, "It's cool. You might want to move to the side next time. That could've been ugly."

"Right?" Devaney said, and gave a carefree laugh that transformed his entire face and had Derek's heart racing and his cock pounding. *Christ, he's sexy.*

"I'm lucky you caught yourself in time. Otherwise I would've ended up flat on my back. *Not* my favorite position, that's for sure," Devaney quipped. As his flippant words lingered between them and Devaney realized what he'd said, he froze. But Derek had had a God-awful night, and he'd be damned if he didn't feel like taking this moment to distract himself from the crap hand that life had already dealt him today.

He cocked his head to the side and studied the man who looked mortified, and then asked, "What *is* your favorite position?"

As if his arm had burned the palm still resting on him, Devaney snatched his hand away and shook his head. "Ah, no. We are definitely *not* having this conversation." He chuckled as he bent down to grab the strap of his gym bag, and Derek found himself smiling for the first time that day at his response.

Devaney was seriously hot when he was flustered.

"Hey, you started it," he said, knowing it would get under the professor's skin further, and he wasn't disappointed. The second he heard him, Devaney's entire body tensed and he slowly straightened and slung the bag over his shoulder. "I didn't *start* anything."

Derek crossed his arms over his chest, effectively blocking the way out, and noticed that Devaney kept his chin tilted and his eyes locked with his, purposely avoiding looking at his body, and that made him bold. He leaned down and told his flustered professor, "Yeah, you did."

That was when he got what he figured was his first *real* look at the professor as he placed his hands on his hips in what had to be the haughtiest of poses, and then pursed his lips in a deliciously dramatic pout that had every single part of Derek, especially his cock, reacting to it.

In class, Devaney had always been lively, but he had a

professional demeanor about him that Derek had always suspected was tempering *this* side of him—and hell, he had to admit he was glad, because this side flipped his fuck switch like nothing else.

"Are you going to *move*?" Devaney demanded, cocking his hip out as his cheeks tinged a delicious shade of pink, which made Derek even hotter, if that were possible. The man was a total spitfire.

Not wanting the moment to be over just yet, Derek smirked. "I don't think so. You almost caused me great bodily harm."

"I seriously doubt that. You're built like a—" Again, as the words fell from his lips, Devaney's eyes widened and he clapped a hand over his mouth. "Shit."

Damn, he made Derek feel good. He had thought the night would be a total horror story after the way it had started, but three minutes in this guy's presence and he felt alive, happy, and really fucking horny. *How is that even possible?*

Derek chuckled, and Devaney's eyes flared in irritation at his amusement before he dropped his hands to his sides, clearly exasperated. "Look, Derek, move it."

Thoroughly enjoying himself now, Derek feigned a frown. "Well, that's not very nice."

"I'm not feeling very nice."

Still riding the high from earlier when he'd told his father to go fuck himself, Derek decided it was time to finally admit how he felt whenever he had a run-in with this particular man. "Neither am I. Actually, nice is the one thing I never feel around you. And I have *many* feelings when you're close by."

One of Devaney's eyebrows arched at the admission, and he took a step to the left to leave without another word. As he brushed by him, though, Derek couldn't help himself from adding in a low voice, "And flat on *my* back is quickly becoming a favorite fantasy of mine. Just in case you were wondering."

---

*SHIT. SHIT. SHIT.*

Jordan slid behind the steering wheel and lowered his head to it.

*What the hell was that?* Oh, he knew, all right.

That was trouble with a capital T.

He knew the look that had flashed in Derek's eyes, the interested tone of his voice, and he also knew his flight response had been the only thing that had saved him from making the biggest mistake of his overly privileged life.

When the fall semester had ended back in December, he'd congratulated himself on surviving it without having to have any more one-on-one contact with Derek Pearson. Then January had rolled around and he'd received his school roster, and was ashamed to admit he breathed a sigh of relief that Derek wasn't on it.

The guy was too much of a distraction for him to be constantly worrying or thinking about. Especially after watching Brantley try, *and fail*, to keep his latest secret…well, a secret from him.

He had to give Brantley props, though—he was damn good at it. Jordan just happened to be a master at picking up subtle signs and cues. But there was no way that a life of sneaking around with a student was for him.

No one would ever accuse him of being the quiet and retiring type, and the thought of staying at home every night or on the weekends just about repulsed him. He wanted the freedom to go out and have a good time. Not be paranoid that someone would find out he was sitting in his car with a hard-on courtesy of his student, like he was right that second.

*Shit.*

Of all the gyms he could've joined for group classes, of course he'd chosen the one Derek was at. He slapped the steering wheel with the heel of his palm and shut his eyes, and all he could see was the knowing gleam that had entered Derek's gaze when he'd finally let loose that devilish smile.

*Jesus*, he really could've done without seeing that. *Or* hearing that Derek liked the idea of bottoming.

*Double shit.*

Drawing in a shaky breath, he reminded himself that he'd be fine. They would continue to avoid one another, just as they had up until now.

*Yes, that's it. Easy. Avoid. Avoid. Avoid.*

Resolved in his decision, he reached into the side pocket of his bag for the phone he'd been trying to fish out at the gym in the first place, but as he felt around, he realized it wasn't there.

*Great. It must've fallen out inside.*

Sighing, he ran a hand through his hair, resigned to heading back into the gym. As he turned to open his door, though, his breath caught in the back of his throat. A large hand with, *ah hell, black nail polish*, was rapping its knuckles on his driver's-side window, and through the rectangle he could see the tight black material of Derek's tank, and yeah, *fuck*, his red gym shorts.

*Don't look. Don't look. Oh, who am I kidding?* Of course he was going to look while no one was there to see him. The shorts nicely molded over an impressive bulge, one that was more visible than Jordan figured it was designed to be, and that meant he was totally screwed. Because just as he'd suspected, their interlude had turned Derek on just as much as it had him.

Jordan ordered himself to get his shit together, and pressed the down button on his window. As the motor whirred and the window lowered, Derek bent at the waist to rest his forearms on the door, and just like that, he was all up in Jordan's space.

Positioned as they were, there was hardly any room between their faces unless he angled his body back, and Jordan knew that would convey loud and clear that he was unable to control himself or worse, nervous—*and fuck that shit.* No one made Jordan Devaney nervous.

"You forgot something," Derek said, and held Jordan's phone out to him. He hadn't dared to remove his hands from the steering wheel in case he did something stupid, like touch the guy. But he knew he had to or risk looking like a total weirdo. *But…look at him—how can I not touch that?*

Angling himself toward Derek, he reached for the phone, but at the last second Derek snatched it back.

"Give me the *phone*, Derek." Jordan knew his tone was pissy, but that was because he was about five seconds away from doing something stupid. When he got no response, he rolled his eyes.

"I like it when you do that."

Jordan arched an eyebrow as if to say, *do what?*

"The eye roll. You never used to do it in class. But it's hot. Lets me know I'm getting to you."

"Oh please, you're giving yourself way too much credit."

Derek held his phone out again and Jordan dropped his eyes to it.

"No, I'm not. Right now, you look as if you're about two seconds away from losing your shit. Why do you have such a problem with me?"

Jordan snatched the phone out of Derek's hands, and this time he let it go. "I don't have a problem with you. Actually, I don't have *anything* with you. Not even a class anymore. And the fact that you like pushing my buttons only shows that you have some serious issues."

"Yeah, you're probably right," Derek said, his voice having lost the flirtatious quality. "You can thank my piece-of-shit father for that."

Jordan faltered, his next words getting stuck somewhere in his throat at the rapid shift in Derek's mood. He wondered if Derek would say more, but when nothing else came out, Jordan looked away to stare down at his phone, checking…what, exactly? That it was in one piece?

"Don't worry," Derek finally said, and his tone had somewhat thawed. "You only missed one call. From someone named…August?"

Jordan's head snapped around, and when their eyes met he saw Derek's lips tug into a crooked grin, erasing the awkward moment from a second ago. "What kind of name is August?"

Not understanding this man in the slightest, Jordan sighed. He knew he needed to end this conversation, yet at the same time found himself wanting to linger and ask questions about the secrets behind those intense eyes watching him.

In the end, he settled on the most basic of questions. One that would open a whole can of worms but must be done if they were to move on in any kind of normal direction. "What do you want, Derek?"

For a second, Jordan thought he caught a flash of longing in Derek's eyes, but it was quickly replaced by a cocky glint and a smirk to match.

"Hard to know the exact answer to that. But right now, I wouldn't say no to fucking you."

*Yeah, okay, the can of worms is now officially open.*

If Derek had been any other person and they'd met under different circumstances, Jordan would be unlocking his car door in a hot second. But Derek wasn't any other person. He'd been his student, and Jordan wouldn't be touching him with a ten-foot pole—or his own pole, for that matter—regardless of how much he wanted to climb all over him and kiss and bite his bulging muscles.

No. There would be no climbing. No touching. And definitely no fucking.

Knowing his best course of action here was indifference, Jordan laughed as if Derek had just told him the best joke ever. *Time to hit his ego.*

"Of course you wouldn't say no to that. I'm gorgeous," he said, giving a flirtatious wink for added sass. "But we've had this conversation, and unfortunately for you, in my bed, I do the fucking and I have no interest in fulfilling your hot-for-teacher fantasies. Now run along, little boy. I'm busy."

He waited for Derek to explode. To accuse him of being the liar he was. But Derek's stare turned contemplative and he nodded a couple of times. He then tapped a hand on the frame of the car and said, "Right. I do remember that conversation. I also remember you saying that *while* you were my professor it wouldn't happen. And Devaney, I checked my schedule twice, and your name ain't on it. So in case you change your mind, I added my number to your phone. Just hit one on your speed dial. Like I said before, I'd happily lie on my back for you any day." Derek then added a hot-as-fuck wink of his own, straightened up, and left Jordan sitting there in the car watching his fine ass as he walked back toward the doors of the gym.

*Oh my* God.

Jordan looked at the phone in his hand like it was a gun and quickly opened the contacts. He scrolled through until he got to number one, and there it was like the fucking scarlet letter—DEREK—*in caps, too, the little shit.* He really needed to add a passcode to his phone.

He was about to hit delete, but at the very last second swiped over the edit button and deleted just the name instead. Jordan's heart was thundering, as if he was doing something he shouldn't, but all he did was replace Derek's name.

Atop that number now read *He-Man.*

He hit save and grinned despite himself. There was no way he would ever call that number. But for some reason, he couldn't find it in himself to delete it.

# Chapter 7

*One Week Later*

DEREK SWUNG HIS arm around hard and fast, and when his fist connected with the red leather of the punching bag, a bead of sweat fell from the end of his hair to land on his nose.

*Fuck this feels good*, he thought as his muscles tensed and he bounced on his toes, sparring with his inanimate opponent. It was early Friday morning before class, and he'd wanted to get out of the dive motel room he was staying in before all the other occupants surfaced.

He was wound up real good, and he could sense it in the way his skin felt tightly stretched across his bones. Damn, he'd needed some kind of outlet, and this place was perfect.

It had always been a safe haven for him, and over the last week it had been his go-to. He'd been spending more and more time there, largely in part because he could work out, use their showers, and then hit school.

*Just another day in paradise, right? Yeah, hardly.*

Just last night at the motel, he'd gone to sleep to the sounds of an argument in the room next door to his. It had ended with a screaming match, a broken bottle, slamming door, and then the familiar sound of a woman crying. Much like the soundtrack from his early childhood. Which was exactly the reason he was down at the gym beating the shit out of the punching bag swaying in front of him.

Life wasn't cooperating. He was supposed to be living a better life free of his father, not dreading every hour he had to go back to a room that smelled of mildew and likely had some kind of bacteria growing on every surface.

*Grrr…* He brought his leg around in a wide kick and his foot connected with the bag. A couple more minutes of this and then he'd have to quit and head to the showers if he wanted to get to the library before class. He'd missed his first statistics class last week when he'd been trying to track down a place to stay, and they'd been given a take-home exam. But after working out his money situation and what he could afford to spend on a place to stay, which wasn't a hell of a lot if he didn't want to use all his savings, he would try and find some quiet time and knock it out.

Over the last couple of nights he'd wondered, *How much can one person possibly take before they fucking lose it?* He wasn't sure, but when he first left his father's, it had spawned some kind of misguided hope inside him—which listening to last night's shit-storm had dashed.

*There's no hope here,* he thought. *Just plain old desperation.*

He landed his final punch with more force than necessary, imagining his father's face pinned to the bag, and as he dropped his arms to his sides, his chest heaved with his exertions.

After his breathing had calmed, he walked over to where his gym bag lay on the ground and grabbed his towel to wipe it over his face. Squeezing his eyes shut, he willed himself to keep it together. Just go and shower, then head to school. He could decide what to do from there. But as all the decisions and responsibilities started to pile up on top of him, he felt more overwhelmed by the second.

He glanced at the phone sitting inside his bag and picked it up. There'd been so many times he'd thought about calling Finn this past week, but at the last minute he'd stopped himself. The guy still thought he slept several houses down from him, and there was no way he was going to tell his buddy that he'd left home. Finn would make it his mission to coddle him by having him stay at his house, and there was no way he was going to be a burden to the Finleys.

*Yeah, not gonna happen.* So instead, he'd kept it to himself.

The other person he'd found himself close to calling was Devaney. When he'd entered his number into the guy's phone last week, he'd also snuck a look at his contact card and stored the number in his own phone under number one. At the time he'd figured it was good to have in case something bad happened. But now the number seemed to mock him every night, just as it was right then.

Staring at his cell, Derek warred with himself for a few seconds, then decided—*fuck it.* Right now, he needed someone to talk to, someone to listen. He didn't want pity; he just needed to get shit off his chest, and he knew there was no way Devaney would coddle him. If anything, he'd get pissed he had his number in the first place.

He swiped the towel over his face again and hit number one on his speed dial.

It rang several times before it connected, and when Devaney's voice came through the line, the words he said took Derek straight out of his bad mood and slid him right into a good one.

---

JORDAN HAD BARELY stepped off his elevator when his phone buzzed in his back pocket. He fished his phone out as he walked over to the kitchen area, and when he saw *He-Man* on the display, he froze and dropped his canvas grocery bags on the tiled floor.

"No he isn't…" he said as he stared at the vibrating device in his hand, then he shoved that thought aside because he didn't want to be thinking about Derek and vibrating things in the same sentence.

Not having any idea what to do, Jordan answered the phone and said the first thing that came to mind: "How did you get my phone number?"

When Derek's chuckle rumbled through the phone, Jordan found himself grinning despite himself.

"Do you always answer the phone in such a bad mood?"

"I am *not* in a bad mood," he said, instantly defensive. Then he realized that he did actually sound pissed off.

"Could've fooled me."

"Well, how nice. Except I wasn't trying to, and you still haven't answered my question. How did you get my phone number, Derek?"

"Last week at the gym."

Jordan was momentarily stunned, and that was when he noticed milk was spilling onto the floor. "Fuck."

He crouched down and rifled through the bags until he found the carton of almond milk, then Derek said, "Look, I'm sorry. I know I shouldn't have—"

"Hang on a second."

"Sure."

Jordan put the phone on the counter and then picked up the bag and placed it in the sink. He quickly cleaned up the milk and then went back to pick up the phone.

Deciding the rest of the groceries could wait, he took a seat on his couch in the living room and brought the phone back to his ear, curious even as he knew he shouldn't be. "All right, I'm back."

"Everything okay?" Derek asked.

Jordan gave an airy laugh before telling him, "Oh yes. There's no use crying over spilled milk, *dahling*."

There was a pause and then, "Huh?"

Letting out a put-upon sigh, Jordan was saddened no one was around to witness the brilliance of his joke. "Oh, nothing. Now, back to this little business of you stealing my phone number. That's quite the offense, you know. I think they label it under the title 'stalking.'"

Derek coughed, then asked, "You think I'm stalking you?"

"Are you?"

"Hell no."

Jordan pursed his lips as he thought about that passionate reply, then asked, "Why? Am I not stalkable?"

Derek sputtered a little, and when he said, "You're kind of crazy, aren't you," Jordan was quick to point out, "Yet you're the one who went through my phone, stole my number, and called. Don't be pointing fingers."

"Fair enough."

"I think so." Jordan paused and waited to see if Derek would say anything else, and just when he thought he would have to flat-out ask what he wanted, Derek said softly, "Thank you for picking up."

Jordan didn't understand what was going on, but Derek having called at all had thrown him so far off course that he needed the guy to spell it out for him. "You're welcome. But I haven't done anything."

"You answered," Derek said, and Jordan instantly sobered when Derek's voice cracked. "That's everything to someone with nothing."

Jordan froze at the sincerity behind those words, and then curled his legs under himself on the couch. By some lucky chance he had Fridays off this semester, and after a quick look at the clock he realized if Derek had class that morning, then he was likely running late. It seemed he really was in need of someone to listen to him.

"Well, I'm here, and I answered. So…do you want to tell me what's wrong?"

Derek's laugh was devoid of humor this time around. "Umm, how long you got?"

Jordan frowned. "It's that bad?"

"It's pretty fucking close to being that bad."

"Okay, well, we could always meet up? Coffee?" he offered, even though his brain was saying *back away*.

"Can't. I've got to go to the library and then class."

"What about after?" Jordan asked, paying no heed to his conscience, which was screaming, *Stop now before this gets out of hand.*

"I need to go back to the library after classes today, too. I missed a statistics paper last week because of…something."

"Well," Jordan said, "I can always meet you at the library. Just tell me what time."

"Umm, how about… *Fuck*," Derek said, and if Jordan didn't know better, he would think that he was nervous. "It'll be tonight, is that okay?"

"That's fine. I'm sure it won't be *too* far past my bedtime." Jordan's tongue-in-cheek comment earned him a genuine chuckle from Derek.

"Right. And what time's that?"

Choosing to ignore the question, Jordan asked instead, "What time should I meet you at the library?"

"How about six?"

"Okay, six it is."

"Sounds good," Derek agreed, and then smoothly switched gears to ask again, "So, what time's your bedtime?"

Jordan laughed. "Is this a distraction technique?"

"Asking you about when you get in bed?"

"Yes."

"Maybe. Will you answer me if I say yes?"

"*No*."

"Well, damn…"

As Derek's voice tapered off and all that remained was silence, the reason for his deflection remained a mystery even as it lay heavy between them.

"Derek?" Jordan finally said, not wanting to lose sight of the reason Derek had sought him out in the first place.

"Yeah?"

"It'll all work out. I don't know what's bothering you, but whatever it is, we'll talk it through and work it out. Okay?"

Jordan wondered if what he was saying was a bunch of bullshit or if he really could help this guy the same way that Professor Hamilton had helped him. He hoped for both their sakes it was the latter.

"Yeah, okay. I've gotta go. I'll see you at six, Devaney."

"I'll see you then."

When the phone disconnected, Jordan lowered it to the coffee table and got to his feet. He headed back to his groceries, and as he went about putting the food away, he couldn't shake the thought that whatever it was Derek needed to talk about would be something he might be unable to fix… and then what?

---

DEREK YAWNED AS he glanced at the clock on the wall of the library. *Fucking A.* It was a little after five thirty, and he had no idea how his eyes were still open.

He was exhausted.

Grabbing his backpack off the floor, he unzipped it and fished out his notepad and textbooks. He needed to at least *start* writing his paper, but all he could think about was getting some much-needed shuteye in a comfortable, safe place.

He closed his eyes for what he thought was a minute then startled awake, sitting up like a jack-in-the-box in his chair. *Shit,* he'd only meant to doze off for a ten-minute power nap, but as he checked his phone for any missed messages, he saw the time and cursed that forty minutes had passed by just as someone nudged his shoulder.

Derek craned his head to the left, and his eyes travelled up a pair of khaki shorts and an aqua shirt to land on Devaney. He was smirking at him in a way that let Derek know he'd caught him sleeping, and the heat of embarrassment crept up his neck.

"Studying hard, I see."

Derek swallowed as Devaney walked around the front of his chair and tapped the open page of his textbook.

"At least you weren't asleep while studying for *my* class."

Derek's eyes tracked his professor as he moved to the aisle opposite him and leaned back against the bookshelf with his arms crossed. He really could pass as one of the students there. Devaney's chestnut hair had grown a little longer than he'd originally worn it, and lately he'd gotten into the habit of styling the front into that faux-hawk Derek had seen on him in the newspaper article he'd…ahh, enjoyed reading. And damn, he looked really hot.

Derek cleared his throat as he closed his textbook and took a look around to see several students close by, hunkered down over their work, just like he was. He then returned his attention to the man across from him whose eyes were directly focused on his.

Unsettled by the intensity of Devaney's scrutiny, Derek ran a hand down the top of his thigh and then tapped his knuckles on his knee. "I didn't know when you'd be here, so I was catching up on—"

"Some sleep?" Devaney supplied, and then walked over to where Derek was seated. He bent down and placed his hands on both arms of the chair, effectively blocking him in where he sat. That wasn't such an easy feat for someone of his size, but again, that never did seem to deter the professor. "I'm not here to bust your ass, Derek, though I'm fairly certain a little discipline in your life wouldn't go astray. You called me here because you wanted to talk. Am I right?"

Derek swallowed. This close up, he noticed that there were

flecks of gold around Jordan's— *Waitttt up. When did I start thinking of him as that? As…Jordan?*

Had it changed because he was so close that Derek could smell the cologne that lingered over his skin, or was it because Jordan was hovering over him in a way that made Derek want to scoot forward in his chair and press his mouth to the one that had just asked him a question?

He wasn't sure, but one thing Derek knew for certain was if he did this, if he left with Jordan and laid all of his secrets out for him, then it would forever change things going forward.

---

ON HIS WAY over to the library, Jordan had gone back and forth on his motives for why he was doing this. But each time he talked himself out of following through, he thought of Professor Hamilton and her words to him: "*Find what makes you work the hardest, and dare yourself to make a difference.*"

And that's what he was doing. His motives were well intended, Jordan knew that, but as he lingered mere inches from the man peering up at him, he knew those same motives, at least some of them, were less than pure.

"Yes," Derek finally said, his voice pitched so low that if Jordan hadn't been as close as he was he might have missed it. "I want to talk." Then he was moving.

Derek shifted forward in the chair, causing Jordan to back up, and as he straightened to his full overwhelming height, Jordan raised his head so he could look up into Derek's face and suggested, "Then let's go."

Side by side they headed for the exit, and when Jordan caught a crooked smile tug at Derek's lips, he raised an eyebrow at him in question.

"You're kinda short. You know that?" Derek said.

Jordan's mouth fell open with indignation, and then he

jutted his chin out, as if it would help add inches to his height. "And *you're* kinda bulky."

"Bulky?" Derek said as he pushed through the doors and then held one open. Jordan sashayed by, and as it shut behind them they stepped out into the cooler night air. "It's called muscular, and I've worked damn hard for it."

"And this"—Jordan gestured down his own body with a sweep of his hand—"is called lean. Not short and *not* little. Don't let looks deceive you. I am quite capable of handling you, even with all that extra bulk you carry around."

When Derek's eyes tracked down over him and Jordan realized what the hell he'd said, he inwardly groaned and headed for the stairs that led to the parking lot.

"Hey, wait up," Derek called out, but Jordan wasn't stopping —*hell no*. He needed to get in his car and use the time between the drive from there to wherever they decided to go to get himself together.

*Professional*, he reminded himself. You *are a professional.*

When he reached his car, he popped the locks and opened the door just as Derek came to a stop beside him. With the door open and between them, Jordan asked, "Where did you want to meet?"

The puzzled look on Derek's face would've usually resulted in some smartass comment from him, but right now, with the night and a weird vibe settling between them, Jordan wanted an answer so he could get in his car and get away from the guy for a minute…or five.

"I thought this *was* where we were meeting."

*Oh for the love of…* "I just assumed we would go and—"

"Grab a coffee?" Derek supplied. "Yeah, I know. But…" Derek's eyes lowered to his feet and he shuffled back and forth. He appeared nervous all of a sudden. But what Jordan couldn't understand was why.

Frowning, Jordan suggested, "We don't have to do this. We can stay here if you like, or go someplace else?"

"No, no, it's fine," Derek quickly said, and when Jordan shook his head and offered, "Really, we can go somewhere else—" Derek sighed.

"No, it's just… Shit," Derek said as his eyes flicked to Jordan's car and the penny finally dropped.

*Ohh, he has no way to get there.* "Derek."

When Derek didn't look at him, Jordan said his name again in a tone that brooked no argument, just capitulation. "Derek. Look at me."

As soon as their eyes met, Jordan's heart tightened. He looked so…lost.

"Do you need a ride?"

"Yeah," Derek finally mumbled.

"Okay. Then get in and we'll track down that coffee, yeah?"

Derek gave a self-derisive laugh. "Why are you being so nice to me?"

"Hey, don't question it. Just roll with it and take it while you can. I'm too selfish for it to last long." He slid in behind the steering wheel as Derek moved to the other side. That was when Jordan popped back out to look across the roof. "Why don't you stash your wardrobe in the trunk?"

Derek scowled at him. "One bag is hardly a wardrobe."

Jordan had to bite the inside of his cheek to keep from grinning. The guy had attitude times ten when it came to someone telling him what to do, which shouldn't be as appealing as it was—but Jordan couldn't help but get a thrill from the way Derek trudged to the back of the car and grumbled, "Bossy."

Jordan sat back in the driver's seat and waited for Derek to climb in beside him, and the entire time he gave himself a stern talking to.

*You are his professor. This is about helping him. Nothing more. Nothing more. Nothing.* More. *Even if he does have one of the sexiest bodies I've seen and ink I'd love to trace with my tongue—*

"Is there anything else?" Derek said as he bent at the waist to look inside the car. "Sure I don't need to take my shoes off before I get in?"

"Your shoes can stay, smartass. But leave your attitude on the curb. There's only enough room in here for one inflated ego, and tonight it's mine."

Derek lowered himself into the passenger seat, and when the door closed behind him Jordan became hyperaware of how big Derek was and just how tight the confines of his Z4 were. *Jesus Christ.*

As if reading his mind, Derek buckled his seatbelt and said, "Tight fit."

And before he could stop his blasted tongue, Jordan quipped, "That's what all the boys say."

Derek's eyes widened with shock, interest, and what appeared to be a healthy dose of lust, and before Jordan could say something to excuse his flippant remark, Derek got there first. "I didn't think that's the way you liked it."

Jordan opened his mouth about to admonish him, but the guy was already shaking his head as if to say, *Don't even try to deny it.* Who the fuck was he kidding? It was too late to take *that* back.

"How I prefer it isn't really relevant, is it?"

"No, but you keep bringing it up, so maybe you *want* it to be relevant."

Appalled, Jordan shook his head. "I do *not* keep bringing it up." Then he scoffed and turned the engine on. "And don't you think highly of yourself?"

"Am I wrong?"

"Yes."

"You're lying. But that's fine. I get it. I just have way too much shit going on in my life right now to try and deny I get a hard-on thinking about you fucking me, sooo…"

Jordan's jaw fell into his lap at that. "You did *not* just say that to me."

"Yeah…I'm pretty sure I did. I mean, I'm just trying to be up front about it with you, otherwise it'll be all awkward and weird. We both know that my friend is fucking yours—worst secret on the planet. And even though you're sexy as hell, that's not why I called. Just in case you thought it was."

*The arrogant little*— "Fuck *you*," Jordan said, about to tell Derek to get the hell out of his car when he saw Derek's lips twitching. Jordan's eyes narrowed as those lips then parted to let free a boisterous laugh.

"You're way too easy," Derek said, the joyful sound filling the car. As his mirth overtook him, Derek wiped a tear from his eye, and Jordan found himself laughing right along with the moron. "Oh man, your face. Fucking priceless. You get so worked up. All red, like steam is gonna come out of your ears."

"I'm so glad you find me amusing, Mr. Pearson," Jordan replied, adopting his best snotty accent, which made Derek laugh all over again.

"Oh yeah. Please, keep calling me Mr. Pearson like you aren't thinking about bending me over and giving me a whooping for being such a—"

"Disrespectful brat?"

"Sure." Derek shrugged and gave him a disarming grin. "A brat, that's me. And there's that word again."

"Respect?"

"Yeah. It's important to you, huh?"

"Hmm..." Jordan squirmed a little in his seat as he put the car into reverse. When Derek's large hand came down over his on the gear stick, Jordan's eyes flicked up to see that Derek had returned to being serious.

"I meant what I said to you that first day. I respect the hell out of who you are. Not only as a teacher, which you rock at, but as a human being. You're a pretty cool guy. If anything, that only increased with the semester I studied under you. Well...not *under* you."

Jordan rolled his eyes, but couldn't help the way his pulse sped up and his chest filled with pride at Derek's admission. It meant a lot to know that he was touching a student's life through his teachings.

He slowly removed his hand and placed it on the steering wheel, ten and two, and when he finally trusted his voice again, he said, "Thank you. That means a lot. Now, if you're quite done…"

"I am."

"Let's go and get that coffee."

# Chapter 8

AFTER THE SHORT drive to the café, Derek took a seat in the far back corner and waited for Professor—*no, Jordan* to grab their coffees.

He took the moment by himself to watch the man at the counter talking animatedly with the barista, who was giving Jordan a sunny smile as he pointed to two pastries and then tapped his chin, as if thinking about what drink to order. *He's my complete opposite*, Derek thought as he continued to observe the guy, and once Jordan was handed their drinks, he tucked two paper bags under his arm and made his way through the practically empty tables to where Derek sat.

When he arrived and lowered down to place the drinks and food on the table, Jordan sighed. "Geez, Derek. Be sure to pick the farthest table next time."

Derek shrugged, taking the grande coffee as Jordan slipped into the seat opposite him. "Sorry. I didn't really want to have this conversation with anyone else listening."

When understanding dawned in Jordan's eyes, he asked, "Is this to do with your father?"

Derek gave a grim nod. "I see you've heard about the infamous Bud Pearson."

"I haven't heard much. But I'm a smart guy. I can put two and two together."

"Yeah, I've read how smart you are. A real brainiac or something."

Jordan winked as he raised his coffee cup to his lips and said, "Or something. I see you've been doing your homework."

Derek studied the man eyeing him from across the table. "Well, I am in school, *professor*."

Jordan scoffed. "Really? You're calling me professor? You just told me in my car you want to—"

"Fuck you? I know. I also told you that I wouldn't because it's too complicated."

"Don't be glib."

"Who's being glib? I'm dead serious. While it would be"—Derek ran his eyes over Jordan as he eyed him with a piqued expression that made his balls tighten—"an experience I'd never forget, I just have too much going on."

Jordan leaned across the table, and Derek's cock throbbed when he narrowed his eyes on him. "Trying to shock me? It won't work. How about you stick to the real reason you called me. Not the fact that you can't stop thinking about how much you want me to teach you a really solid lesson on—"

"My knees?" Derek offered, and watched Jordan's lips curl into a grin.

"I'm not going to bite, Derek."

Derek flashed his teeth in a wicked grin. "Can I?"

"Lord save me from the bad boys," Jordan said as he aimed his eyes to the ceiling.

"Is that what you think I am? A bad boy?"

"Have you seen you?"

Derek looked down at himself: jeans with a couple of holes in the legs, a white T-shirt, and his boots. Pretty standard for him, and boring compared to the guy seated opposite him. "What about me?"

Jordan reached for one of the paper bags on the table and shook his head. "You really don't see it?"

"No?"

"The muscles, the tattoos, the nail polish. That attitude."

"I don't have an attitude."

"Ha!" Jordan's eyes widened, and then he tore open the brown paper bag. "You, my friend, are full of attitude."

Derek frowned as Jordan pulled out a gooey-looking bar of—

"*What* is that?"

The grin that flashed across Jordan's lips was wicked. Then he swiped his finger through the sticky amber and brought it to his mouth to suck it clean before letting out a dramatic moan. "A salted caramel bar. It's delicious."

*No shit*, Derek thought as he watched Jordan repeat the move. But he wasn't thinking about the caramel bar. *No sir.* He couldn't tear his eyes away from the man now reaching for his coffee as if he hadn't just fellated his finger. After Jordan took a sip of his drink, he glanced over at Derek to see why he wasn't talking. He cleared his throat and tried to remember that they weren't here on a date.

"I'll take your word for it. I don't really like caramel."

"Wait," Jordan said, raising a hand, palm up. "You *don't* like caramel?"

Derek sat back, crossed his arms over his chest, and gave a shrug. "No, not really. Sweets in general, actually."

"Oh my *God*. What is wrong with you?"

"Nothing. I just don't like them."

Jordan looked him over. "Is it because of your workouts? You're worried about putting on 0.001 percent of body fat? Because I have to tell you, one measly little bar won't do it. And I'm sure your metabolism is off the charts anyway."

Derek looked at the sticky bar sitting in front of Jordan and screwed his nose up in distaste. "Nah, that's not it. It's too rich or something. Maybe because I didn't really grow up eating sweets? I don't know. It just doesn't appeal to me."

Jordan slumped back in his chair and shook his head as he licked his fingers clean. "I'm horrified. Give me a minute."

"Take all the time you need. I've got nowhere to go."

Although Derek meant his words in an offhand way, the reality of them was so close to the truth that it automatically pulled him from his easygoing mood and propelled him right into a shit one. Something he didn't hide well, apparently.

"Derek?" Jordan sounded wary as he reached across the table to touch Derek's fingers. "I'm sorry. I didn't mean…" He trailed off as their eyes met, and as the warmth of Jordan's touch seeped into him, Derek stared over at the wide brown eyes looking back at him. "What happened with your dad?"

If he was going to do this, he needed some distance. So Derek slid his hand away and picked up his coffee. He took a sip and then flicked a brief look at the man now waiting for him.

"Nothing," he said, and watched Jordan's eyes rove over his face, as if he were trying to work out the underlying meaning to the word.

"What do you mean, nothing?"

"I'm not sure how much you know about my family…" He let his words hang between them, wondering how much of this festering wound he'd have to expose.

"Like I said earlier, I don't know much, but I heard your father is…" Jordan hesitated, and that made Derek scoff.

"A drunk, homophobic prick?" he supplied.

"Well…"

"It's okay. That's putting it mildly. He's a fucking monster. For most my life he conducted our conversations with his fists and had no problem telling his faggot son repeatedly that he disgusted him. Trust me when I say that nothing you call him is worse than what I've already thought."

Jordan looked stunned by his words, but when the surprise

melted away and was replaced by compassion, Derek got up and started pacing to rid himself of the adrenaline and fear that came from talking about the fucker. It was as if thinking about him, or mentioning him, would somehow conjure his father right there with them.

"Derek, it's okay. There's no rush." Jordan paused as if weighing his next words, then asked, "What happened?"

"He didn't hit me for a change, if that's what you're asking."

"Does he usually?"

"Only when he's been drinking."

"And how often's that?"

"Every hour or so."

Derek thought he heard "fuck," but he'd walked a little ways away before rounding back to head for Jordan.

"Okay. So what happened?"

Derek drew in a shaky breath and slid into the seat he'd previously vacated. "He kicked me out."

To Jordan's credit, he didn't look shocked or horrified. This was actually the most serious Derek had ever seen the other man, and it was appreciated.

"Because you're gay?"

"No. I mean, he always let me know how disgusting that was to him, but that wasn't the reason he told me to go."

"Then what was?"

"Money. The asshole wanted me to give him my paychecks. Man has some nerve asking me for anything after what he's done to me. What he did to my mother…and family." His voice cracked, and he swallowed the best he could around the lump caught in his throat.

Fuck, it all sounded so much worse when he said it out loud, and judging by the concerned expression on Jordan's face, he agreed with that assessment one hundred percent.

---

JORDAN SWORE HE could hear every single sound in the coffee shop in stereo at that moment: the grinder of the beans, the steamer for the foam, and the two baristas gossiping behind the counter as the night slowly settled in.

Meanwhile, he was trying to decipher exactly what Derek was telling him.

Had he moved out? Was he living with his friend Daniel? Seemed like a possible solution, but just as Jordan was about to ask, Derek spoke.

"I've been staying at this piece-of-shit motel for the last week." He paused and then scowled, clearly annoyed. "But last night there was an argument that got heated, and fuck…I don't know. It's a shithole. Who the hell knows what goes on there. When you're paying by the night, no one asks any questions."

Jordan tried to keep any judgment off his face, but he'd never been particularly good at subterfuge, and the outrage he was currently feeling knowing that Derek had been sleeping at some seedy motel was difficult to contain. The only thing that kept him from demanding *why* was the sheer frustration that was pouring off Derek in waves. The guy was struggling to keep a hold on his temper, and he looked one word away from detonation.

Jordan thought about his next words carefully as he wondered what it would take to ease Derek right now. To help him relax back to the cocky badass he'd walked into the café with.

"So…where are you planning to stay tonight?"

Derek shrugged and picked his coffee up to take another sip. "Same place, I guess, until I can figure out an apartment or something."

"Derek," Jordan said, then swallowed his immediate impulse to offer up one of his spare rooms. "What about Daniel? I know the two of you are close."

Derek shook his head. "No. I won't do that to his mom. Mrs. Finley, she's been through enough raising two kids on her own.

She doesn't need a third. Not to mention the added worry of my father turning up and causing shit."

"I'm sure she wouldn't see it that way."

"Yeah, but I would," Derek said softly. "I can't do that to her. I love that family like it's my own. I wish it was."

Jordan's heart ached at the longing he heard in Derek's voice, and he had a sudden thought of his own family. He really should give his mother a call. It'd been a few weeks, and he knew she'd love to hear from him.

As he fiddled with the sleeve of his coffee cup, Jordan knew what he was about to do next was unwise. It was likely the dumbest idea he'd had to date, and really, he didn't do dumb. But there was no way he was going to let Derek leave this café to go back to some motel full of God only knew what.

"What if you come and stay with me?"

The words sounded odd, even to his own ears as they fell off his tongue. But Derek's stunned look of *what the fuck* made them feel even more out of place.

"You can't be serious."

"Why can't I?" Jordan shot back, even as the voice in his head was telling him this was a bad idea. But he was already in it now. If he backed out he'd look like he was worried, or worse, thinking this would be some kind of illicit setup where he moved a sexy student into his rich penthouse to fuck—

"Well, for starters," Derek said, breaking Jordan from his completely inappropriate thoughts, "I'm pretty positive you don't like me too much."

"That's not true."

Derek's eyebrows winged up until they practically hit his hairline. Okay, so they'd had a few run-ins as professor and student, but that didn't mean Jordan disliked him. "It's not my job to make you think that I *like* you or that we're friends, Derek. It's my job to teach you."

An unreadable spark lit Derek's blue eyes, then he sat up in his chair as if he found it difficult to sit still.

"Wouldn't you get in trouble?" he asked. "You know, if someone found out?"

*Yes.* "Maybe. But I can't let you sleep in some flea-infested motel. What kind of person would I be if I saw someone in trouble and didn't help them? It's not like it would be permanent. And I'm not your teacher anymore, so there's no conflict of interest with your grades."

Derek chewed on his upper lip and his eyes narrowed. "I'm not some kind of charity case, you know."

"Oh, for God's sake." Jordan blew out an exasperated breath. Patience was never one of his strong suits. "This isn't charity. Trust me, I contribute to plenty of those and know the difference. This isn't pity either. It isn't anything other than me offering you a spare room and bed to sleep in. My place is—" He stopped himself from saying *enormous*. "I have a couple of spare rooms. You can take one until you can apply for, and move into, an apartment. Much better than wasting your money on some place that isn't safe."

"So, you're doing this because you're worried about my safety? I thought you said I was a badass."

"The only person you're going to require safety from in the next few seconds is me if you don't stop acting like such a shit."

Derek finally relaxed and chuckled, the sound breaking the tension for the first time since the conversation had taken a turn toward the serious.

"You keep implying that you could take me on and win. But I gotta say, Devaney, I'm not buying it."

Jordan finished his coffee then placed his cup on the table, silently sizing Derek up. The guy may have him beat in size, but when it came to confidence, Jordan didn't doubt himself for one second.

He got to his feet and took a step forward so he was standing beside the table and Derek, who was smirking up at him.

"First, don't call me Devaney. My name is Jordan, unless you see me in school, where it will always be *Professor* Devaney." His reprimand was meant to come out professional and keep the two of them on the same page after this odd conversation. But Derek's eyes darkened and Jordan's breath caught at the desire swirling in them.

*Oh shit, he likes it when I get on him like this,* and fuck if that didn't keep his mouth from delivering words he knew that he shouldn't.

"Second. If I ever decided to take you on in *any* capacity, you can rest assured by the end of it *you* would be the one to surrender. Not the other way around. Now, if you're interested in the offer, I'll show you my place."

When Derek pushed his chair back and unfolded himself from the chair, the wooden scrape of the legs on the floor was the only sound Jordan could hear over the thumping of his heart.

God, the guy was overwhelming, but Jordan would be damned if he moved back.

"Duly noted, *Jordan*. And yes, I'm interested." Derek's voice was raspy, and Jordan knew exactly where his mind had gone because, damn it, despite his good intentions, his had gone there too. He wasn't sure if he should stress that this was *just* a living arrangement, but then he remembered their previous conversation in the car and figured it was pretty clear on both their sides that they definitely were *not* interested in something as complicated as fucking each other would be.

So with that in mind, Jordan backed up and picked up the paper bag that held Derek's uneaten salted caramel bar.

"Good. Then let's go. On the way over, you can explain to me again why you don't eat sweets, because *that* is just plain wrong."

# Chapter 9

WHEN JORDAN TURNED the car into a driveway that led down under a high-rise building situated on the main strip of Sunset, Derek leaned toward the window and craned his head to look up at the towering structure.

"Christ, how many floors are in this building?"

A chuckle came from the man maneuvering his car through the rows of pillars until he turned into what had to be a designated spot, because it was the only one free in that row.

"Twenty-eight."

"Twenty-*eight*? Get the fuck out of here. That's insane."

"Mhmm," Jordan agreed. "I know. It seems ridiculous. But I swear the view is totally worth it."

Derek got out of the car and moved to the trunk to get his bag, and when he shut it he saw Jordan standing over by the path that led to a lit private entrance. "The view from where? The roof?"

As they walked toward the glass doors, Derek automatically opened it and Jordan glanced at him, the expression in his professor's eyes warm, as though he appreciated the gesture, before it flashed back to neutral.

"Thank you," Jordan murmured as he passed by and moved toward the only elevator, where he pulled a keycard from his pocket and slipped it into the metallic panel. When the door slid open, Jordan held it and gave a crooked grin, returning Derek's chivalrous gesture. "After you."

Derek walked inside the small confines, and when Jordan followed and the door swooshed shut, he was made highly aware of his size. The elevator was narrow, personal in a sense, and the two of them only just fit comfortably together side by side with their arms touching.

He let his eyes move up the panel, expecting to see twenty-eight buttons to choose from, but there was nothing on the walls except the shiny metallic finish of the elevator. High in the right-hand corner was a small screen that seemed a little odd, but before he could get the words out, Jordan said, "It's a TV screen and camera."

Derek's head whipped around so he was facing Jordan, who laughed. "Oh, no need to panic. It's not currently on."

Derek frowned. "Why's it there? And where's the button for your floor?"

Jordan shifted to rest his back against one side of the elevator. "It's there for me to see who is stopping by, and there are no buttons because this elevator *only* goes to my floor."

*Huh?* Derek was confused. What did he mean, the elevator only went to his floor? Jordan wasn't making any sense, but then Derek remembered that the professor was rich. Very fucking rich, apparently.

He opened his mouth, about to ask what floor they were going to, but before any words could come out, the elevator came to a smooth stop and a soft "ding" sounded.

"Here we are," Jordan announced as the door opened and he pushed off the wall to head out into his condo. "Floor twenty-eight."

Derek watched Jordan head out into a huge open space, and as he stepped off the elevator to follow, his jaw almost hit the floor.

*Oh my fucking God.*

The room that spread out in front of him was ridiculous.

As in it looked ridiculously expensive. Derek froze in place, not willing to take a step further in case he happened to break something with his huge feet or duffel bag.

The room was unlike anything he'd ever seen in his life. As far as the eye could see, the cream marble floors that were accented with flecks of brown shone so brightly that they reflected the elaborate chandelier that hung center stage like an art piece. Hell, it probably was. Directly under the light was an U-shaped couch that beautifully complemented the tones of the space. It sat atop a rectangular rug that Derek was positive looked more comfortable than his bed at home.

Jordan tossed his bag on the couch and made his way over to the floor-to-ceiling doors that provided a stunning view of a deck setting fit for a king. There were chaise lounges, a table that was likely designed to be used indoors but had somehow made it to Jordan's balcony, and, yes, a hot tub and pool at the far end of the balcony. The spread beyond the spacious living room was not only impressive, it was out of this world.

Who lived like this?

Jordan unlatched the doors and shoved them open so the night breeze could filter inside, then he headed into the kitchen to open his fridge and pull out a bottle of wine. When he turned back with a bottle in his hand and two glasses, his eyes found Derek exactly where he'd left him, and he grinned.

"You can come in, you know. Just put your bag there until we can work out all the details."

Derek's heart raced at breakneck speed as he looked around the opulent space and shook his head.

This had been a terrible mistake. What was he doing here? This wasn't where he belonged. This was *so* not what he'd expected when Jordan had said he could come and crash at his place.

He'd stupidly imagined a cramped room where he could stash his bag and do his homework. Not some playboy penthouse that screamed sex, money, and success. He felt like a fucking failure.

A loser failure that was going to throw up at any moment.

"I don't think this is such a good idea. I'm just gonna go," he said as he backed up, and as he went to hightail it out of there, he noticed two tall podiums flanking either side of the elevator, with beautiful bronze sculptures on it that were likely worth more than he would ever hope to make in his life.

*Yeah, okay, Derek Pearson does* not *belong in a place like this.*

"Wait," Jordan said from behind him, and Derek could hear each footfall on the cream tiles as he came closer. "What is it? What's wrong?"

Derek shut his eyes and willed his voice to sound normal as he turned to Jordan, who was looking at him with confusion and worry written all over his face.

"Derek," he said softly, and reached a hand out to touch him, but suddenly everything about this situation and the reason why Derek was there bubbled to the surface and had him backing up, as if a simple touch would make him fall apart.

"Derek. Let me help you. I *want* to help you."

Derek swallowed past the massive lump and shook his head as his eyes flew around the room again. "Why, Jordan?" he asked. "You don't know me. Hell, for all you know I might rob you blind in the middle of the night."

Jordan took a cautious step toward him and squeezed his arm. "You're right. You could. Don't go for those statues behind you, though—they weigh a ton, and honestly, the silverware in the dining room is worth more and is lighter."

When Derek's eyes widened, Jordan squeezed again. "I'm just kidding. Relax. I don't make it a habit to bring strangers back to my place, but I'm also a pretty good study on people.

And yes, you're right, I don't know you that well. But I once knew someone like you who was in trouble. Someone who needed a little guidance and help." He gave a rueful grin and then added, "Someone who was a bit of a punk."

That made Derek laugh. "Yeah?"

"Oh yeah." Jordan nodded. "He was a total shit. But someone took him under their wing, and I think he turned out okay."

Derek contemplated the man watching him with a steady and friendly gaze, and thought how ironic it was that it was the same man he'd expected to despise throughout college.

"I still think he's a bit of a shit, just for the record."

Jordan's grin was blinding as he dropped his hand. "You're probably right, but now he thinks he can get away with it on the basis of his good looks and charm."

Derek sighed as he let his eyes drift around the condo again, and he couldn't stop himself from asking, "Just how rich are you?"

Jordan gave a fabulously snotty laugh and flick of his wrist. "Beyond your wildest imagination, *dahling*."

Derek scoffed. "You're a little unbalanced, aren't you?"

"No. I'm very well adjusted. Just spoiled rotten. But at least I admit it."

Derek's lips twitched. He knew that Jordan was purposefully overexaggerating to ease the tension that'd been in the room.

"Think you can put up with that?" Jordan asked, his eyebrow raised in challenge.

Was he kidding? This place was a fucking palace. If anything, Derek felt weird just being here in the first place. Who was he to say if Jordan should act one way or another?

"Yeah…I think I can manage. But only if you're sure."

Jordan took on a serious tone that belied his earlier frivolousness. "I am. Of course, we'll need to set up some ground rules. The first of which will be no smoking in or on the premises of the Palisades, Mr. Marlboro Man. *Capiche*?"

Derek dumped the duffel on the floor and nodded. "Got it."

"Second, no strange men in my house. You want to hook up or fuck someone, you do it at their place, in a club, or hell, at the library."

"Are you serious?"

Jordan nodded. "As a heart attack."

"You're giving me permission to fuck someone in the stacks at school? Good to know, professor. Can you write me a note just in case I get caught with my pants around my ankles?"

Jordan walked backward into his living room and shrugged. "Better at school than a stranger in my place. Like you said, I'm rich—"

"And modest," Derek added, finally moving forward, following Jordan into the living space.

When they got to the couch, Derek could see around the corner, where a narrow room housed an elaborate dining table set for eight. It was stunning in its sleek simplicity of a black tabletop and comfortable-looking white lounge chairs surrounding it.

"No. I never claimed to be modest," Jordan said as he flounced down into the plush couch, kicked his shoes off, and then curled his legs up under him. "I'm rich. My parents are rich, and I don't want some random hookup of yours traipsing through my belongings as he sneaks out in the middle of the night. So sue me."

Derek took a seat at the opposite end of the couch and cocked his head to the side. "Assuming it would always be a random."

"Oh, please. Are you trying to tell me you have a boyfriend tucked up your sleeve? I've seen you shaking your ass half-naked at Boyz, Derek Pearson. And there hasn't been anybody *regular* dancing with you. So don't pretend."

Caught totally off guard by the fact Jordan had been paying such close attention, Derek felt his face heat, and Jordan started laughing hysterically at him.

"I'm sorry, was the fact you dance at a gay club supposed to be a secret? I know you always make a wild dash for cover when I show up, but I've seen you there. White short shorts, tattoos all over. You're pretty hard to miss."

"Um…" He paused, and then Jordan flashed a wide *gotcha* grin at him and Derek glowered. "You're being an ass on purpose, aren't you?"

Jordan gave a playful wink and leaned forward to open the wine. "Payback's a bitch, right? I can be too, but I try to keep that for the people who really deserve it." He handed a glass of Merlot to Derek and then leaned back into his couch again. "I was also trying to get your mind off how bomb-ass my place is. Did it work?"

Derek laughed at Jordan's over-the-top attitude, but nodded. "Yeah, it did."

"See, there's a method to my madness. Not *just* madness."

Derek took a sip of his wine, feeling like a bit of a buffoon with his big hands and the tiny glass. "I don't think you're mad at all," he said, surprising himself with his sincerity. "I actually think you're kind of amazing."

Jordan's playful attitude sobered in an instant, and he gave Derek a serious look. The expression made Derek's heart skip, and he wondered if Jordan felt the pull the same way he did. His question was soon answered when Jordan sat forward and placed his glass on the coffee table. He then turned to face Derek and said with the utmost sincerity, "I have to be clear about one thing here, Derek. I won't get involved with you. Not in any way beyond friends."

Feeling like a fucking idiot for his moment of honesty, Derek shot to his feet and cursed. What was he thinking saying that out loud? *Way to make a guy feel uncomfortable*, he thought, as he headed back to his bag where it lay by the elevator. He pushed the down button, hoping it would open up and swallow him whole, then Jordan's fingers touched his arm and he stepped up beside him.

"Hey, don't go. That's not what I meant."

Derek looked down at Jordan, and with his shoes off and a wine glass in his hand, he looked…well… Oh, fuck it. The guy looked gorgeous.

"I just wanted to be clear that this is merely a platonic arrangement. That I don't expect you to pay in"—Jordan frowned and then shrugged—"other ways."

"You mean like sex? Are you trying to tell me I don't have to let you fuck me to stay?"

"Derek," Jordan grumbled, and whacked his arm.

"Well, are you?"

Jordan gave him a pointed look. "Yes. I guess if you want to be crude about it. I'm just saying that this is merely a landlord and tenant situation, and at college, a student and professor one."

Derek nodded and faced him. "Got it. And in there anywhere, are we friends?"

Jordan gave a long-suffering sigh and drained his wine glass. "Well, I guess. I *will* have to see you every day. Now can you please stop bolting for the door every time things don't go your way?"

"Sure," Derek agreed, and dropped his bag to head back through the living room and toward a long, narrow hallway Jordan was walking down.

"So just to clarify, that means we will be sleeping in separate bedrooms…right?"

Jordan smirked as he looked over his shoulder. "Smartass."

"Hey, I'm just trying to be crystal clear and not misunderstand anything, *landlord*."

"I sleep in there." Jordan pointed to an enormous room with floor-to-ceiling doors that were opened to a closet that someone could, in all likelihood, go missing in.

Derek whistled. "Impressive, emperor, and where do the commoners sleep?"

Jordan laughed, and the sound was free and easy, the best fucking noise Derek had heard all day.

"You, lowly peon, may choose from the six spare rooms available."

"*Six?*"

"Yes, six."

"Okay, how about you just point me in the direction of one and I'll take it."

Jordan's grin was cheeky as he walked ahead of Derek with what he could've sworn was added swing to his hips. "I do like a man who doesn't mind being told what to do."

And yeah, *fuck him*, this friendship business was going to be a goddamn challenge. Likely one of the hardest he'd ever face, if his eager cock had any say in the matter.

# Chapter 10

*One Year Later*

FINALS. IT WAS always the most stressful time of the semester, and as Derek stared at the economics textbook in front of him, he swore his eyes were starting to cross. It was well after two in the morning and he had to be up in, *shit*, four hours.

*Jesus*, if he didn't fall asleep during the actual exam it would be a miracle.

He tossed his pen on the desk he was seated at, then leaned back in the leather chair, stretching his arms above his head as a yawn escaped him. It was Thursday night, and tomorrow's exam was the last one he had—and then he would be done with his sophomore year.

*God, where did the time go?* He spun around in the chair and looked toward the open door leading from his bedroom to the long balcony that flanked this side of the building. Most days he still couldn't believe he lived there, in the penthouse of the Palisades, but he did.

Jordan had invited him to stay that first night, and since then the two of them had settled into a comfortable routine of landlord and tenant. Just as Jordan had suggested they should. On one hand it was totally strange, yet on the other it had turned out close to fucking perfect.

Tonight, the penthouse was quiet. Jordan had told him he was going out to celebrate his final day of teaching, and instructed Derek with a sassy wink not to wait up.

As if he ever would.

Considering what close quarters they kept, they lived very separate lives. And just as they'd agreed from day one, there were no strange men in the house, and the two of them had developed quite the unexpected friendship.

Jordan Devaney out of school was exactly as he had been that first semester *in* school—times about ten. He was opinionated, sarcastic, and rather full of himself. But Derek had to admit, the guy could back it up.

Jordan was smart, rich, and smokin' hot—not that Derek would ever mention that these days. *Fuck no.* There was no way he was crossing that line they'd both drawn in the sand that night, and neither had ever stepped over.

However, Jordan wasn't only all about himself. The other thing Derek had learned in the past year was just how generous he was. Not only had he taken him in that day, the guy had refused to take his money for anything other than rent on his small section of the house. Derek couldn't remember how many times they'd argued over the grocery bill. But in the end, even if he got pissed and called Jordan a bossy asshole and left the money on the counter, Derek would find it later that night on the bedside table in his bedroom. *Stubborn ass.*

Deciding he was done for the night, he got to his feet and stretched his neck from side to side, ready to go to bed, but the sound of the elevator dinging echoed throughout the condo. He yawned again and glanced at the digital readout on his phone.

It read 2:45 a.m. *Late night, huh, professor?*

Ready to give Jordan shit for being an old guy able to stay out past midnight, Derek was halfway down the hall when he heard someone giggle and then someone else say, "Shh…"

As more musical laughter floated through the air, Derek froze, waiting to see if he'd imagined it, until "God, J. That last round of Mind Erasers totally did you in. You're trashed," confirmed that he hadn't.

The footsteps shuffling through the condo's main living room indicated there were at least two people, and when he heard an "ompfh" followed by more laughing, Derek contemplated turning and heading back to his room.

Jordan had never brought anyone home with him before, and while Derek was more than aware the guy stayed out every now and then, it was different to know he might have to lie in his bedroom and listen to some other guy get in bed with the man he had secretly been fantasizing about.

*Just great.*

Dressed only in a pair of lightweight sweats, Derek was about to head back to his room when a light was switched on and Jordan's voice sounded throughout the penthouse.

"August!" Jordan laughed loudly, then whispered, "Turn it off. You'll wake—"

"Me," Derek said, figuring that maybe if he announced his presence to the men in the living room, then they might not do whatever they were back here to do.

Jordan was sitting on the couch with a guy dressed in jeans, a loose mauve linen shirt, and about four or five beaded necklaces standing between his legs. With his shoulder-length brown hair and dark scruff, the guy bore a striking resemblance to Johnny Depp, and Derek wondered if that's what he was aiming for. If so, he'd nailed it.

The sound of Derek's voice had the both of them whipping their heads around in the direction of where he stood. If the situation had been anything other than what it was, Derek might have noticed how lecherous the smile was that stretched across the face of the stranger who was now staring at him. As it was, Derek was far too irritated at the thought of these two going back to Jordan's room to fuck to notice that—much.

"Hmm. Well, hello. Who do we have here, J?" the man asked, giving Derek his full attention as Jordan flopped back into the couch.

The man stepped over the leg Jordan had flung out in front of himself and took the couple of steps he needed to stop directly in front of Derek. He was tall enough, probably around six foot, but like most, that still put him several inches shorter than Derek.

"That's Derek," Jordan slurred, then added, "He-Man."

Derek's eyes cut to Jordan. *He-Man? Okay…that one's new,* he thought, keeping a discreet eye on his "landlord" as a sensual chuckle came from the unidentified man, whose eyes were surveying every inch of Derek's naked torso.

"I can certainly see why you call him that."

"Yes…" Jordan agreed, even though his eyes were shut. "Muscles and, ahh, more muscles. Mhmm." That velvety purr he gave at the end traveled straight down Derek's spine to his balls, and was as good as a caress.

*Jesus, how much did he drink tonight?* Jordan had never come home like this.

"Got it," Johnny wannabe said. "But *who* is he, J? You haven't mentioned a He-Man before now. Especially not a live-in one."

Fed up with the douchebag know-it-all talking as though he wasn't there, Derek crossed his arms and said, "I don't know who you are, but how 'bout you stop talking as if I'm not standing in front of you and able to kick your ass."

"Oh ho." The guy laughed. "Down, boy. You can stop growling. I'm just trying to understand why a giant is sleeping in my best friend's bed. Nothing more, nothing less."

Uncaring of how little he was wearing, Derek stepped forward until he was toe to toe with the man and said, "I'm not sleeping *in* his bed. And who I am is none of your business unless he decides to tell you."

"Boys, boys…" Jordan said as he scooted to the edge of the couch and then pushed up onto his feet. He didn't sway much as he walked their way, but when he stopped beside the both of them and placed a hand on Derek's bicep, it seemed to register with him that Derek was wearing hardly any clothes. Jordan tested the muscles under his palm and then aimed a megawatt smile up at Derek that made his dick instantly hard.

*Motherfucker.*

"Derek, this is August, he's my…my…" Jordan pondered over his choice of words for a second but then became side-tracked when he squeezed Derek's arm again. "Wow. Your arms are huge. I mean, I knew you were big, but damn. And so… so…" He flattened his palm and ran it over the tattoo on Derek's right shoulder before he whispered, "I've always wanted to touch these…"

Before Derek could halt Jordan's wandering hand, he'd trailed a finger over to his chest to trace the script written just below his collarbone.

"They're so sexy," Jordan murmured, more to himself than anyone else, as far as Derek could tell, and then Jordan looked over to his friend, who was watching the exchange with curious eyes. "Aren't these sexy?"

Jordan was so close that the scent of his cologne mixing with his sweat was intoxicating, and it was everything Derek could do not to uncross his arms and grab a hold of the guy. Apparently his reaction was not lost on August.

"No doubt, J. You might want to stop pawing the guy, though. He looks about ready to combust."

Jordan laughed as though that were the most absurd notion on the planet, but when he turned back to face Derek, his laughter ceased.

*Yeah, pretty sure "combustible" is an accurate description of how I'm feeling.*

Realizing that he'd crossed the invisible barrier they'd carefully erected, Jordan cautiously backed away, but it was too late. Derek couldn't tear his eyes from the man who had always been very careful not to flirt, touch, or give any impression he was interested. But the heat in Jordan's cheeks and the alcohol that had loosened his inhibitions were showing Derek what was behind Jordan's carefully manufactured facade.

"I'm August," the guy standing beside Jordan said as he held his hand out in Derek's direction.

Derek tore his eyes from Jordan's then and took a hold of the guy's hand. "Derek."

August shook his hand and then gave a knowing smirk. "Sorry if we woke you. J's had a few too many—"

"*Hello.* J's right here, and quite sober, thank you very much."

August poked his tongue into his cheek as he dropped Derek's hand and nodded. "Sure you are, J."

"I am."

August slipped his hands into his pockets and asked Derek, "Has he ever stroked your tattoos like he wanted to lick them before?"

*Oh, Jesus.* Like he needed that visual. "No."

August turned back to face Jordan then. "Exactly. You, my friend, need water and an aspirin, then bed."

Jordan waved his hand in an *I don't think so* way, and when August made a grab for him, he dodged and giggled and had Derek smiling right along with him. Who knew Devaney was so damn cute when he was plastered?

Jordan spun on his toes and strutted over to the ridiculously expensive sound system, where he took the remote in one hand and aimed it at the entertainment center like he was pointing a Taser at a target—then he pressed a button.

As a familiar beat filled the room, August, who was still

standing beside Derek, sighed. Derek tried to place the song, but as soon as the lyrics started, his mouth fell the fuck open.

"Britney Spears? Is he fucking kidding?"

August looked at him and shrugged. "He's drunk, is what he is."

Derek looked back toward the living room, and sure enough Jordan was swinging his hips and shaking his ass to an anthem about some guy being toxic. It also appeared he knew every single word as he turned to face them and crooked a finger.

"Oh, fuck no," Derek said.

August chuckled and patted his arm as he walked toward the kitchen. "I'm gonna get a bottle of water for me and him. Think you can handle him for a few minutes on your own, He-Man?"

Derek narrowed his eyes on Jordan's friend and nodded. "I think I can manage."

As he walked toward Jordan, Derek heard August warn, "Be careful. He's a handful when he gets like this."

Before Derek could ask what that meant, August was heading for the kitchen and Derek was left in the living room with Jordan, who had his eyes shut and his head tipped back as he waved his hands above his head.

Fuck, the guy was all sex in that moment.

Tight ripped jeans, tight navy blue tank, and lips Derek wanted over every damn inch of him. When he was close enough that he could smell Jordan's cologne again, he saw him open his twinkling brown eyes and aim a teasing smile up at him. Clasping his hands overhead, Jordan gyrated his hips to the wicked beat of the music. As he came closer toward him, Derek shook his head and leaned down to say in his ear, "Britney Spears?"

Jordan turned his head, and when he replied, "Don't you dare make fun of my Brit Brit," Derek felt the warm breath on his cheek and straightened up to go take a seat on the couch. But as he stepped away, Jordan reached for one of his hands and wrapped it around his waist. In an instant their bodies were flush and Jordan waggled his brows at him.

"Come on, He-Man. I know you can dance."

"He-Man?"

"Mhmm," he said as he writhed against him, and Derek had to take a hold of his squirming hips or he'd be really fucking embarrassed in the next few seconds. "Yeah, just like that," Jordan said, and before Derek knew it was happening, Jordan's arms were around his neck and he was grinding against him like the two of them were naked.

Christ, how was he supposed to do this and keep shit as it always was between them? Jordan wasn't playing fair, and the alcohol was unleashing...well, who the fuck knew what it was unleashing. Then Jordan sighed and said, "More," and there was no stopping Derek from slipping his hands from the guy's hips to his ass and yanking him in so they were aligned from head to fucking toe.

---

JORDAN'S HEAD WAS spinning and his cock was pounding in delicious time to the music pulsating through his living room. He felt unbelievable, and so did the thick arms surrounding his waist and the hands molding his ass to pull him in close to a rock-solid body.

*Derek...damn.* The guy was fucking built. And when he'd seen him standing there in nothing but his sweats, Jordan had had an unstoppable need to touch.

So, with a little help from the few too many shots he'd had, Jordan had done just that, and judging from the thick length he could feel pressed against him, he knew that Derek had wanted to touch too.

As the song switched to the sensual beat of Brit wanting to be a slave for whoever, Jordan tipped his face up and looked into

Derek's eyes, and what he saw there almost had his knees buckling.

Intense desire fueled the scorching expression aimed his way. Jordan licked his lips in response, and Derek dipped his knees and dragged his body up in a way that made a strangled groan leave Jordan.

*Shit, that felt…* He did it again, and Jordan's eyes shut. He brought one of his hands around the front of Derek's sweats and trailed his fingers under the elastic. Derek's skin was warm to the touch, and Jordan hummed as he slipped his hand beneath the fabric and between their bodies.

Derek growled and Jordan closed his eyes, reveling in the moment he'd wanted for so long. He was finally—*yes…right there*—touching Derek. He had his hand wrapped around a thick cock that had slicked his palm with the pre-cum leaking from its tip, and when Jordan opened his eyes, he saw Derek's teeth clenched as he rocked into his fist, seeking more friction on his engorged length.

*Again*, he thought, hoping Derek would thrust forward and grind his cock against him, but instead, he lowered his head and the sharp scrape of teeth on Jordan's jaw shot a bolt of desire straight to his dick.

"You need to come with a fucking warning label," Derek said, nipping his ear. Then he raised his head and pulled Jordan's hand away. "You had very specific terms when I moved in, and until I graduate I'm sticking to them. Now, I have a test tomorrow morning and it's gonna be hard as hell to sleep. So do me a favor—don't keep me up by fucking your boyfriend with the cock I just primed, okay? If anything, think about me lying in there getting off on the thought of you fucking *my* brains out with it."

Jordan's breath caught, and Derek raised a brow as if to say, *Problem?* When Jordan didn't say a word, Derek nodded and slowly backed away, keeping their eyes locked. When he got to the hall he smirked, and Jordan couldn't help but reach down and press his hand over his cock as he bit his bottom lip.

"Yeah, just my luck," Derek said. "You probably won't even remember this tomorrow. Night, Devaney."

And before he vanished, Jordan whispered, "Night, He-Man."

# Chapter 11

*Third Year of College*

DEREK STOOD OUTSIDE the law building with a cigarette in one hand and his phone in the other. He'd texted Finn a couple of nights ago and asked if he wanted to meet up for lunch, since he wasn't due at the gym for his shift until later tonight. It'd been a couple of weeks since the two of them had caught up, and as Derek stood there with his back against the bricks and his foot propped on the wall, he wondered when the two of them had started to drift apart.

When they'd first started college they'd been in a couple of classes together, but soon after that first semester, when they'd branched off to do their respective courses, they'd found less and less time to hang out—unless you counted their morning runs.

Finn had started to spend every spare minute he could with his professor, and Derek…well, he'd been dealing with his own shit. Eventually the runs had stopped, and the only time they really saw one another was at Boyz, and then they were working so they rarely had time to sit down and talk.

Derek knew he'd been slack, and honestly, if he really examined the details of their slow disconnect, he would realize it had a lot to do with him not wanting to lie to the guy. Someone he'd been friends with since he was a boy, and who'd likely feel responsible for him should Derek tell him what he'd been going through.

And maybe that was the problem.

Finn had seen Derek at his absolute worst, and when he'd had an excuse to forget about that and distance himself, Derek had allowed it to happen. What a horrible fucking friend he turned out to be.

"Hey, stranger."

He would recognize that voice anywhere, and when he turned to see Finn pushing through the double doors of the building, Derek realized just how much he'd missed the guy.

"Danny boy," he said, and when they met up they hugged one another. When he took a step away, he grinned. "You're looking good, man."

"You too," Finn said as they headed down the stairs. "Except for that damn cigarette."

"Yeah, yeah. That ain't gonna change anytime soon, so best get over it now."

Finn laughed as they walked across the lawn toward the parking lot. "I know, but I have to at least try. You still running?"

"Of course," Derek said, and then bumped shoulders with his buddy and asked, "You? Has the professor gotten you running alongside him yet? Or do you get your workouts in other ways?"

"You're hilarious."

"What? I remember how hard it was to get your lazy ass out there. The only reason you ever did say yes was to run into Hayes."

"True," Finn said. "But there's something totally different about running with him than there was with you."

"Oh yeah, and what's that?"

Finn waggled his eyebrows mischievously. "I have incentive to get home."

"Oh God, spare me the details, would ya? I mean, what are you two now, married and shacked up?"

Finn took a deep breath and then let it out. "I wish."

"No shit?"

Finn shrugged. "Hey, when you know you know, right?"

"I guess."

When they reached the parking lot, Derek spotted Finn's mother's car and headed toward it.

"Yeah. He's a little harder to convince, though." Finn popped the locks, and when they both climbed in Derek looked over at his friend.

"Why do you say that?"

Finn reversed, and as they pulled out onto the main road, Derek asked, "What's going on, Danny boy?"

"Ugh. It's just something stupid, I'm sure."

"What do you mean?"

Finn opened the center console and fished out a crumpled brochure and passed it to Derek. He read over the print, and the fact that it was a law school wasn't anything shocking. He'd known that was what Finn wanted to do. But what caught his attention and held it was— "This is in Chicago."

"I know."

The sober tone of Finn's voice made Derek shift in his seat to face him, and as he took in Finn's stubbled jaw, he frowned. He wasn't sure why the thought of Finn moving across the country was so fucking terrifying, considering they hadn't been real close this past year or so, but it was.

"You're not *going*, are you?"

Finn took his eyes off the road to look at Derek, and the side of his mouth quirked up. "Hell no. I told him to forget it."

"So Hayes brought this up with you?"

"Yeah," Finn said, and looked back at where he was going.

"Told me it was the best opportunity. A smart choice and all that. Blah blah."

"Yeah. Fuck that. Your family's here."

"I know. See, you get it."

Derek turned back to look out the windshield of the car and had a sudden dislike for Finn's professor. Why the hell would he tell Finn to leave? Or even suggest it. His life was here.

Crumpling the pamphlet in his hand, Derek glared out the window and wondered if Devaney knew what Hayes was up to. He'd have to ask him when he got home.

Finn pulled the car into the local burger shop and parked, and once they were inside with their meals, they sat down in a booth at the back of the restaurant.

"So what about you?" Finn asked. "It feels like forever since we hung out."

Derek squeezed a liberal amount of ketchup on his tray and dunked a couple of fries in it before shoveling them in his mouth. As he chewed around them, he considered what he should tell Finn.

He knew Devaney would have an absolute shit fit if anyone found out he was staying at his place, even Brantley Hayes. And really, he didn't want to go into details. So he just nodded and reached for his soda. "Good, good. Nothing unusual happening over here."

Finn picked up his burger and took a bite, then around his mouthful he said, "A wealth of information."

"Always," Derek agreed, and popped another fry in his mouth.

Finn put his burger down and sat back, then he asked, "Do you think I'm stupid?"

Derek's stomach dropped at the question, but he schooled his features to appear unaffected. "Nope. I'd never call you stupid. At least not to your face. Why do you ask?"

After reaching for one of his own fries, Finn chomped down

into it and then shocked the shit out of Derek by leaning across the table and asking, "Who are you fucking?"

Derek almost choked on the bite he'd taken of his burger, and reached for his drink to wash it down. "What?"

"You're seeing someone."

"Nah." He shook his head. "I'm not seeing anyone, Danny boy. Sorry to disappoint you, but you're the only one sitting at this table that's sucked on anything other than a straw in a long time."

Finn eyed him with suspicion. "You sure?"

"That I ain't fucking anyone? Yeah." Derek laughed. "I'm pretty sure."

"Hmm. It's just that I haven't heard shit from you in months, and the last time I saw you we barely spoke. I know my excuse is Brantley, so who is yours?"

*Jordan Devaney. But not the way you think*, he wanted to say. But how did you tell your friend that you'd been lying to him for so long? Instead he shrugged. "No one, man. Just work and school. This year's been kicking my ass."

"Shit, me too," Finn said, letting go of the inquisition, *thank God.*

"Yeah. Gotta say, I can't wait to be done with school."

"I've still got three years to go after this. Consider yourself lucky."

"Yeah. You poor bastard."

Derek laughed and finished off his burger. When he was done and scrunching up the paper, Finn asked, "What are your plans after graduation?"

"You know, I really just want to *get* to graduation first. But when I do, I've been thinking about opening up my own gym."

"Really? That's a fantastic idea."

"Yeah? You think?"

Finn nodded and then piled his trash onto the tray. "Of course. It's the perfect job for you. Where are you thinking about opening it?"

Derek grinned at Finn's enthusiasm. "Slow down over there, would you. I've gotta finish school first and work out how the hell a bank would ever give me a loan."

"True. But cool idea."

"Yeah, I think so. I'd love to do it down on the beach. You know, like Muscle Beach?"

"Oh, that would be totally hot."

"Right? All those hot, oiled bodies. Hmm, this is sounding better and better. I'm a fucking mastermind."

They laughed as they finished off their drinks, and then Finn looked at his watch. "Sorry, I need to bolt. I still have to hit the library to finish up this damn paper that's due tomorrow before I head to Brantley's. But this…it was really great. We need to do it again. Soon."

"Yeah, we do," Derek said as Finn slid out of the booth.

He followed suit and picked up the tray, tossing the trash out. When they got back in the car, Finn asked where to, and Derek pointed him in the direction of the gym. Once there, Finn dropped him off around the back, and just as he was about to drive away Derek looked through the window at his friend.

"Don't be a stranger, okay?"

"I won't. See you soon, Derek."

"See you soon, Danny boy."

As he watched Finn drive out of the parking lot he reminded himself that this was what happened as you got older. Things changed and you got busy. Friendships shifted and sometimes even ended, but that didn't make it hurt any less. At least Finn was still in the same town. Maybe when things were easier, when school was over, they would come back together.

He glanced at the time on his phone. Five o'clock. He was right on time.

He turned, ready to head around to the front doors of the gym, but he didn't get very far—the next thing he remembered was waking up on the concrete where he was curled into a ball.

Exactly where his father left him.

---

JORDAN SAT OUT on his balcony with his feet propped up on the table in front of him and a glass of sweet tea in hand. It'd just turned five thirty on a glorious Wednesday afternoon and he'd decided to spend the evening relaxing while grading a few final papers he had left for the next day.

He was halfway through his stack when the phone he'd placed on the table started to buzz. When he saw Derek's number flashing across his screen, he frowned. He thought Derek had work tonight.

After placing the paper on the table, he picked up his phone, and hit answer. "Shouldn't you be at work, young man?"

He grinned, waiting for some smartass reply, but when all that greeted him was silence, Jordan sat forward in his chair, his stomach dropping.

"Derek?"

Again, nobody said anything, but this time Jordan heard a shuffling sound and then an anguished groan of pain.

"Derek?" Jordan demanded, and shot to his feet.

*Fuck. Oh* fuck.

He wasn't sure how he knew, but somewhere in the pit of his stomach he knew something was terribly wrong.

"Derek, talk to me." He raced inside to his kitchen counter and desperately searched for the keys he knew he'd left there. He checked under pamphlets and magazines, and when he found them, he asked, "Where are you?"

He ran to the elevator, punched the down button, and as the door slid shut he cursed the slow glide of it. He pressed the phone so hard against his ear he was surprised he didn't break the thing, as he waited for anything from the man at the other end.

He prayed the phone wouldn't cut them off during the descent, then right before the elevator hit the ground floor he heard words that made the air get stuck somewhere in the back of his throat. "Gym. Back of the gym. My father..."

Jordan's hand shook as he pulled open the car door and slid inside. "Derek?"

When he got no answer, he turned the car on and the cell connected with the Bluetooth. He could hear Derek's harsh breathing through his stereo, and the sound was haunting.

"Derek?"

There was a dreadful gurgling sound, an expulsion of air, then, "Yeah?"

Steeling his initial reaction to freak out, Jordan turned onto the main road and sped down the street like a racecar driver. "You keep talking to me, got it? Don't you dare hang up. I'm maybe five...six minutes from you."

More coughing, and Jordan wondered for a second if he should call an ambulance. "Derek? Do you need an—"

"No." The word was brutal and harsh, then in the silence of his car Jordan heard Derek's raspy, broken whisper. "Just you."

He tightened his fingers around the steering wheel and nodded. "You got me. Three minutes."

Jordan zoomed past the strip of convenience stores, and when he got to the turnoff he needed he barely slowed. He entered the lot, and his eyes scanned the area as he drove down the side of the gym to the back—and that was where he spotted him.

Derek was slumped against the brick wall beside the dumpster, and the sight just about broke Jordan's heart. After putting the car in park, he jumped out and ran to Derek's side, where Jordan went to his knees and raised his hands, which were now shaking like a motherfucker.

*Jesus Christ.* Derek's face was hard to look at. The skin on his cheekbone was split open, blood was oozing from it, and the left eye reminded Jordan of that first day in class. It was swollen and angry, and the actual eye wasn't even visible. Just the lid, which was triple the size of the right. The left side of his lip was bloodied and split also, and Jordan didn't know what to do first.

"Derek… I think I need to—"

"No," Derek grunted, and then leaned to the side to spit out the blood that had pooled in his mouth. "No hospitals."

Jordan touched a tentative hand to Derek's arm. "Something might be broken."

"It's not," Derek argued, and then let out a labored breath. "He knows better."

"Your father?"

Derek nodded. His arm was wound tightly around his waist, and his long legs were pulled into his body as he leaned his shoulder against the bricks.

"Still, we should get you checked—"

"No. You do that and I have to give an address. *Your* address."

"Derek, I don't—"

With a monumental effort, Derek pushed off the wall and reached for his shirt with a bloodstained hand. As Derek's fingers curled into his shirt, Jordan kept his eyes on the damaged face staring up at him.

"No."

Finally giving in to an urge he'd had since they'd met, Jordan stroked his fingers down the unaffected side of Derek's face and heard him whisper, "Thank you."

"You don't have to thank me, Derek. You called and I—"

"Answered."

Understanding dawned, and Jordan leaned forward and promised something then that would forever change their lives. "Always."

Derek took in a shuddering breath and Jordan looked around them. "Do you think you can get to your feet? Or do I need to go and get help from inside? I'm not sure if you realize this, but you kind of outweigh me."

When Derek's lips parted on a warped angle to smile, he winced and Jordan apologized. "Shh. Don't talk *or* laugh."

"Bossy."

"Mhmm, and you are in no position to argue. Think you can get to your feet?"

Derek nodded and Jordan maneuvered himself so he was on his right side. It was clear from looking at Derek that when he'd taken the initial hit, and likely fallen, it had been on his right side, because while it still seemed tender, his left had taken the full brunt of the attack.

Once Jordan got Derek to the car, he ran around to the driver's side and buckled in. When he raised his head, he noticed Derek's right eye falling shut, and instructed, "Do *not* fall asleep."

"But I'm so tired."

"No falling asleep, or I'm taking your ass to the hospital."

"'Kay, professor," Derek managed, and Jordan put his foot on the gas and headed straight for home.

---

DEREK DIDN'T REMEMBER much of the drive back to Jordan's or the ride up the elevator. But when he was led down the hall and into a room that was not his own, he paused on the threshold and looked toward Jordan, who was over at the balcony opening the doors to let in some air.

When Jordan glanced back at him, concern marred his expression. As he came back to Derek's side, he reached out a steadying arm and asked, "Are you okay? You need to get off your feet."

Derek swallowed at the kindness in those brown eyes, and braced himself against the emotions welling up inside of him.

Of course Jordan was concerned. Who wouldn't be when faced with someone who'd just had the shit beaten out of him? That was all this was. But as Jordan placed a hand gently on his chest, Derek couldn't stop the way his heart ached.

"This isn't my room."

"No," Jordan whispered, and took Derek's right hand, drawing him farther into the room. He stopped them at the base of the wide bed in the center. "But since I'm not letting you out of my sight for the next"—he looked to the clock on the wall—"oh, twenty-four hours, you are going to be in here, where I can harass you incessantly about whatever comes to mind."

Derek's lips pulled into a tight line and the split on his lip cracked open. *"Ow, fuck."*

"Okay, this is the one time you have permission not to laugh at my jokes."

Derek grimaced.

"So come on, we're going to clean you up. Then rest." Jordan let go of his arm and asked, "You okay on your own for a second?"

Derek gave a nod and Jordan disappeared into the connecting bathroom to flick on a light. When he came back, he took Derek's hand again. "All right. Let's go."

Derek followed him into the bright bathroom, and when his eyes narrowed and he groaned a little, Jordan apologized and moved to the light switch to turn it down.

"You have a dimmer in the bathroom?"

Jordan looked over his shoulder and shrugged. "Mood lighting."

"Only you," Derek mumbled.

"Oh, hush." Jordan chuckled when he came back toward him. "Actually, no. Feel free to speak as much smack talk as you like. You get a pass tonight, and it will keep you awake. Now sit."

Jordan pointed to a chair he must've moved into the bathroom, and Derek gingerly took it.

"Okay, let's get this face cleaned up first."

He watched Jordan move around the bathroom as he gathered a washcloth and cotton balls. Then he disappeared and came back with a first-aid kit and—

"What's that?"

Jordan looked at the little leather kit in his hand and grinned. "A manicure set. I usually use it for a weekly mani-pedi, but tonight I need the tweezers. You have some gravel in the cut above your eye."

Once he placed that on the basin and filled it with warm water, he held up a finger and then vanished. As Derek looked around the opulent bathroom, he saw Jordan's whirlpool tub and decadent shower and pushed aside any images he had of the guy in there. He remembered when he'd moved in and Jordan had told him that he could use either one. *Yeah,* that'd never happened, but fuck, he'd had no problem fantasizing about Jordan in it.

"Okay, mister. I think you should swallow this," Jordan said, handing him a shot glass full of clear liquid. "Tequila, hopefully, can numb some of the pain but not put you to sleep."

Derek brought the glass to the non-swollen side of his mouth and tipped his head back. As the fiery liquid burned a blazing path down to his gut, he handed the glass to Jordan.

"I know, but you needed something. This *is* going to hurt."

For the next half-hour, Jordan washed, cleaned, and meticulously removed gravel from the wound above Derek's eye, and when he was finished, he gently patted his face dry and took a step back.

"How much do you like this shirt?"

Derek looked down at the black tee he was wearing that had some band's slogan on the front, then shrugged. "It's okay."

Jordan picked up a pair of scissors. "So it's replaceable?"

Gathering what was about to happen, Derek nodded. "Yeah."

"Good. Because I don't see you raising your arms anytime soon," Jordan said, and then reached for the hem of Derek's shirt and cut a straight line up the center to his neck. As the material parted, Jordan tossed the scissors on the counter and gently pushed the fabric aside.

When it was falling off Derek's shoulders and arms, Jordan sucked in a breath, and Derek glanced down his body to see what he was looking at. Sure enough, there was a huge red welt that covered half of his ribs and would most certainly leave a bruise tomorrow. It was already starting to turn a bluish purple.

Jordan brought a hand up to cover the gasp that escaped his mouth, and then he raised his eyes to meet Derek's. "Why did he do this?"

*I have no fucking idea.* "Wish I could tell you why he ever did it. If I had to guess, he was drunk, somehow found out where I was working, and came to pay his boy a visit. Last thing I remember was the first hit. He knocked me out cold. The rest must've happened after."

"Oh, Derek," Jordan whispered, his breath leaving him on a shuddering exhale.

"Hey, this is nothing new."

"It is to me. And whether it's new or not doesn't matter. You need to report him."

Derek's hand whipped out to grip Jordan's wrist. "No fucking way. If I do that, I have to file where I'm living, and somehow he'll find out. I will not bring him to your doorstep. Do you hear me? Even calling you, coming back here, was stupid. He might've followed."

Jordan knelt down until he was between Derek's spread legs and looked up at him, and in that moment something between them shifted. The landlord and tenant. The professor and student. They vanished. And all that remained was one man who needed the other to survive.

"Listen to me, Derek Pearson. I don't care. I wasn't about to leave you there. You called me. You needed me. I answered."

Derek released his hold on Jordan's wrist and brought a trembling hand up to touch his fingers to his chin. He needed to know in that moment that Jordan was real. That he wasn't hallucinating and lying out in the middle of the parking lot bleeding to death. But when Jordan got up on his knees to bring them closer, Derek's breath caught and he worried his lower lip with his tongue.

"Careful," Jordan whispered, and gently touched his fingers to the swollen flesh before leaning forward to press the softest kiss Derek could've imagined to the corner of his mouth. "You don't want this to start bleeding again."

When Jordan was about to pull away, Derek tugged him back in close, and miracle of all miracles, Jordan came. Their breaths mingled as the connection between them blazed, and then Jordan's fingers were trailing down the uninjured side of his jaw.

"Derek…" he said, and then angled his head to the side and gently kissed Derek's lower lip.

Derek sat frozen in place at that first intimate connection, as the sweet glide of Jordan's mouth brushed over the top of his. He couldn't believe that Jordan Devaney was finally kissing him. There'd been so many times he'd fantasized about this, but never had he imagined it would happen like this.

"Are you okay?" Jordan whispered against his mouth.

Derek didn't want to move, but managed a slight nod before he leaned forward again, as if in a dream, to steal another kiss. Jordan slid his fingers to the back of his head to stroke through his hair, and this time when their lips parted, Jordan placed several kisses down his neck and nuzzled in there, where Derek heard him whisper, "What am I going to do with you?"

And all Derek could think was, *Good fucking question.*

---

EARLY THE NEXT MORNING, Derek stared across Jordan's bedroom at the man who'd taken such care with him the night before. He needed to get out of there and away from Jordan before his father tracked him back to his place.

He had no idea how his father had found out where he worked, but all he had to do was ask the right person for an address and he could show up there, and… Derek shuddered at the thought of what that no-good piece of shit would, or could, do to Jordan.

Jordan had class this morning. He'd told Derek he only had one today and then he would be back, and Derek knew that would give him the perfect opportunity to do what needed to be done.

Jordan had gone above and beyond in giving him a room to stay in for as long as he had. He'd been beyond generous, and it was time to return that kindness with his safety.

It was time for him to move on.

# Chapter 12

*One Week Later*

JORDAN SAT ON his couch staring at reruns of some city's "real" housewives as he sipped on a glass of Cab Sav. He wasn't really paying any attention, though, as one of the main women slapped another across the face, and considering what a spectacular blow it was, that was saying something. Usually he would be on the edge of his seat cheering a bitch on. But that wasn't happening right now.

*No.*

He was too busy replaying for the millionth time the voice message he'd received from Derek the other day while he'd been in class. *"Hey, Devaney, by the time you get this I'll be out of your hair and house for good. I think it's the best for everyone. It's nothing personal, you know. I just don't think it's smart to stay with you anymore after…well, after what happened with my father."* Derek paused, and Jordan still wondered what he'd really been thinking when he ended the call, because his lame *"It's been cool"* wasn't it. Of that, Jordan was positive.

That message had been followed by one that was short and

to the point: *"Oh, and Devaney, don't try and change my mind either, okay? I know you'll want to. But it's time for me to move on. I'll see you around."*

Then the message ended.

*Impossible man*, Jordan thought, as he tossed his phone down on the couch.

He had no idea where Derek had gone, but when Jordan had gotten home that afternoon, he sure as hell hadn't been there. The empty spare room had made it seem as if he'd *never* been there, and Jordan hadn't been prepared for how much that hurt.

For the rest of the week that followed, he'd been obsessed with tracking Derek down. He'd waited in the gym's parking lot like a total stalker, and even waited outside of Brantley's class to see if Daniel met up with him—but nothing. It was as if Derek had disappeared off the face of the planet, perhaps so he could heal, and finally Jordan had caved and called him, only to be greeted with his voicemail. That'd been on Wednesday, and now here he was on Friday night still worrying over the thoughtless jerk.

He wasn't really a jerk, though. Jordan knew why Derek had done what he had. He thought he was protecting him. But would it have killed him to let Jordan know where he was? That he was safe and okay?

Sighing, Jordan stood, headed out to the balcony, and looked out at the lights lining the path along the beach. He missed him. *That* he hadn't expected.

It wasn't as if they'd spent hours hanging out or anything like that, but it had been nice to come home to someone each night. He wasn't sure if it was Derek in particular or just the comfort of another human being in his life, but clearly Derek was determined to do this his way, and who was Jordan to stop him? They both had very different lives, and it was time Jordan got on with his.

He needed to get out, needed to go and meet some new people.

Yes, that was what he'd do. If Derek wanted to be left alone, then Jordan would follow his wishes. After all, the guy knew where he was should he ever need him.

---

DEREK CLIMBED THE flights of stairs to the top balcony that ran across the front of four apartment doors and prayed this was not going to be a dead end. He must've gone to six—*no, seven*—"interviews" with potential roommates this week, and each one, for some reason or other, hadn't been the right fit.

He'd figured this was the best route for him, since rooming with Jordan had turned out pretty well considering, so he really needed this to pan out. It was the last one on his first-choice list, and the idea of a weekend at Motel Hell wasn't something he was looking forward to.

He walked down to the final door and checked the paper in his hand and the number in front of him. *Yep, this is it,* he thought, as he gripped the straps of his backpack and shut his eyes, sending up a quick prayer. After taking in a deep breath, he exhaled and raised a hand to knock, but before his knuckles connected with the wood, the door swung open.

Derek startled and took a step back. "Shit. You gave me a heart attack."

He heard a chuckle come from the guy in front of him and saw a man wearing a wetsuit and holding a surfboard under his arm. Actually, he was half wearing a wetsuit, because it was unzipped and hanging on the guy's hips.

When the surfer stepped out the front door and leaned his board up against the wall, Derek stood there like an idiot until he turned and aimed a smile at him. That was when Derek got his first good look at his face and was struck by the sheer perfection of it.

The guy had brown hair, cut short on the sides, and up top the strands were longer, with light highlights, probably from his time in the sun. His eyes were the color of green sea glass, and with the sun setting and casting a golden glow over everything it touched, it gave the guy an almost ethereal look.

*Hell, is it possible that surfer guy's my guardian angel?* Derek thought with uncharacteristic optimism. God only knew he could do with one at this point.

No matter who he was, though, he was fucking gorgeous. Beautiful, in fact.

When Derek realized he'd been staring a little too hard, he averted his gaze and looked over his shoulder to the road that separated the small apartment building from the beach. The guy hadn't said anything yet, and since he hadn't told him to get lost, Derek figured he must be in the right place.

"So," Derek started, searching for something…anything, really. "I'm the guy who called about the spare room."

*Jesus. Pretty sure he knows that,* he chided himself as he shoved his hands into the pockets of his shorts and fiddled with his phone. He was well aware he didn't look his best. The cut above his eye was finally starting to heal, but it had one hell of a nasty color highlighting it, not to mention what was under his sunglasses. He just hoped surfer guy didn't take one look at his face then, let's face it, his tattoos, and say, *Forget it, dude.*

The man said nothing like that, though. Instead, he looked over his shoulder at his surfboard and then back to him. "Yeah, I figured. I was hoping you'd get here soon because I really wanted to hit the waves, and here you are. Perfect timing."

*Oh, thank God.* "Yeah, I would've come earlier, but work was slammed."

"No sweat. Let me show you the place real quick so you can see what you think, and we can go from there."

Derek nodded, and when the guy opened the door and held it for him, Derek stepped forward and said, "I haven't seen you around here before."

The guy's eyes travelled over Derek's face then down to his chest, and as they drifted lower, Derek hoped his body fucking behaved, because wow, that stare was bold.

After what felt like several minutes, instead of the few seconds it had really taken, the surfer's gorgeous eyes came back up to lock with Derek's, and he shrugged. "No, you wouldn't have. I'm new to town. Family moved this way a few months back and I arrived a couple of weeks ago."

"Gotcha. That makes sense."

"Does it?"

Derek nodded. "Yeah. Most everyone knows everyone in Sunset Cove. And as a village native, I would've remembered you."

A twinkle lit the guy's eyes, and he grinned. "You think so, huh?"

Derek felt his pulse skip at the interest in that look and those words. Surfer guy was flirting with him.

"I do," Derek said, and held his hand out. "I'm Derek Pearson."

Surfer guy looked down and then slipped his hand into Derek's large palm. After they greeted one another, Derek figured that would be that, but when the guy didn't immediately release his hand and instead held Derek's stare with a teasing one of his own, Derek felt a grin curve his mouth. He'd had such a shit week, and honestly, this guy's flirtation was a welcome distraction.

"I'm Dylan Prescott. And you are seriously built. God. Do you live at a gym?"

Not expecting that at all, Derek couldn't help the laugh that rumbled free. "Nah. But I work at one."

"Well, shit. You're a great promo for them."

"You think so, *huh*?" Derek joked, throwing Dylan's words back at him. If he thought for one second he would embarrass him, though, Derek had another thing coming. Because daring as you please, Dylan's eyes lit as they tracked him again.

"I do. *Damn…*"

*Oh shit, guy isn't shy, that's for sure.* Derek wanted to say something quick-witted, but he kept getting so stuck on how beautiful Dylan's face was that he found it difficult to string two coherent words together. In the end he settled for the obvious. "I kinda need my hand back."

One side of Dylan's mouth pulled up, and as that grin grew wider to extend into the same smile from earlier, two dimples appeared on either side of his cheeks, and Derek thought it was a miracle his knees didn't buckle.

How was one guy so fucking blessed in the looks department?

"Yeah, okay. I guess I can give it back." Dylan let go of Derek's hand and gestured inside with a tilt of his head. "Come on. I'll show you around."

The tour was quick. The place would've fit into Jordan's living room, but it was clean and didn't smell funky, and when Dylan shoved open the door at the far end of the hall and said that would be Derek's room, he felt the weight he'd been carrying around this week lift from his shoulders.

"So what do you think?"

Derek turned back to see Dylan standing with his arms crossed over his naked chest. "It's perfect."

"Yeah?"

"Yeah. Exactly what I'm looking for."

"Great. Then it's yours."

When Dylan left to walk back down to the small kitchen, Derek frowned and asked, "Do you want references? I can—"

"Nope."

*No? What the…?* Everyone wanted references. Derek didn't really want to go to Jordan for one, but he would, and he could get one from his job, but— "What do you mean, no?"

Dylan leaned up against the sink and shrugged. "You seem chill. That's what I'm looking for."

"I seem *chill*? I have a purple face and you haven't even seen the worst of it."

"Hmm, yeah. That bothered me at first, but not so much now."

Not understanding this guy in the slightest, Derek frowned and took his glasses off.

"*Jesus*, that looks painful."

"Yeah," Derek agreed. "And this is a week later."

"Damn. And the other guy?"

The way Dylan asked, Derek figured this was an important answer, so he was brutal in his honesty. "He doesn't have a fucking scratch on him."

Dylan nodded slowly and pushed away from the sink. When he stopped opposite Derek, he studied him in silent contemplation. "I figured. And just so there's no confusion, I'm gay, in case you didn't get that from the way I was looking at you. That gonna be a problem?"

He'd figured, but having it confirmed made this an even better fit. "Not a problem at all."

"Good," Dylan said, then, as if they weren't discussing such serious shit, he asked, "You surf?"

"Ehh…not really."

"What? What kind of Floridian are you?"

Derek laughed, thinking how well this guy would get along with Finn. "Apparently a bad one? I love the beach, but I'm not coordinated enough to balance on a board."

"Well, *Derek*, if I can pretend to be a surfer and I'm not even from here, you can at least try to fit in."

"Is that right?"

"Yeah. You should be ashamed of yourself."

"I'm deeply ashamed. And where are you originally from, Prescott?"

"Prescott, huh? I can work with that. And the answer to that would be San Francisco," he said, his voice taking on a slightly wistful tone. "I'll get back there one day. Or at least to the West Coast."

"Never been. Hate to say it, but I've never been much farther than an hour out of Sunset Cove."

Dylan walked toward the front door and Derek followed. Once Dylan locked up and they were both standing on the little balcony overlooking the waves, he clutched his surfboard under his arm and headed toward the stairs leading down to the parking area.

Before he got too far, though, he said over his shoulder with a carefree laugh, "Not a bad place to be, all in all. Nice to meet you, Derek. I'll see you tomorrow at ten. Don't come earlier than that or you'll be sorry. I am *not* a morning person."

As Dylan disappeared down the stairs, Derek looked over the balcony and watched him cross the road and jog down onto the beach, and wondered if he really was an angel.

A beautiful figment of his imagination.

Guess he'd find out tomorrow—after ten.

---

"JORDAN? HEY, JORDAN. ARE YOU OKAY?"

Jordan blinked and looked across the table to see Brantley frowning at him. It was Sunday morning, and the two of them had met up for their usual brunch and mimosas.

"Hey, yeah, sorry…I spaced for a minute."

"I could tell. Anything interesting?" Brantley asked as he lifted his glass of OJ and champagne to his lips.

Jordan's mouth pulled into a tight smile as he shook his head and pushed his eggs around his plate with his fork.

"Seriously. What is the matter with you? You look as if somebody stole your puppy."

*Well, kinda…* He'd certainly lost someone he cared about—he just hadn't realized how much until they were gone.

"Nothing. I'm just not feeling myself. That's all."

Brantley lowered his arm, placing his glass back on the table. "Is it August?"

"What?" Jordan asked, raising his eyes.

"Your 'friend' August. You told me he was heading overseas last week. I was wondering if he's the reason you're so—"

Brantley's words were cut off by Jordan's phone buzzing on thc table beside his arm. As his eyes flicked to the screen and he saw *He-Man* light it up, he snatched it off the table.

"Do you mind?" he asked quickly. "I've got to take this."

Brantley shook his head and pulled his own phone out, and Jordan thought it funny that the two of them were now likely talking to their "students."

After getting to his feet, Jordan hit the answer button as he wove his way through the tables and out onto the small deck that overlooked the rolling waves.

"Derek?"

He wasn't sure why his heart was thundering like a million horses were galloping through it, but it was beating so hard that Jordan was positive the people seated out on the deck must've been able to hear it.

"You answered."

Those two words made a smile stretch across Jordan's lips. "I already told you—"

"You'll always answer," Derek finished for him.

"If I'm able, then yes," Jordan confirmed as a comfortable silence fell between them. It lasted all of two seconds, and then he had to know: "Are you okay? How's your eye? Your lip? Where are you?"

Derek's chuckle made Jordan want to strangle him. This past week he'd imagined every possible scenario, from the good, to the bad, to the downright morbid. "Don't you dare laugh at me."

"I'm sorry," Derek said, and then he sobered. "I'm not really laughing at you. I was just imagining your face getting all red and cranky."

"I don't get cranky."

"Yeah, you do, Devaney. It's really cute."

Jordan sputtered a little and was about to protest when Derek spoke up again.

"To answer you. I'm okay. Or, at least, I will be. My face is healing. I had a pretty smart guy patch me up…"

As Derek's words trailed off, Jordan pictured the man who'd sat in his bathroom bruised and bloodied just last week and shut his eyes.

God, until this very moment he hadn't realized just how much he wanted to reach out and—

"Jordan?"

His name brought him out of his thoughts and had his eyes opening, almost as if Derek had appeared in from of him.

"Yes?"

"I'm okay. I promise."

"The motel?"

"No," Derek answered. "A roommate. He's pretty cool, I think."

Jordan wasn't sure he was comfortable with the emotion that shot through him at those words, because if he wasn't careful he'd almost believe it was…jealousy.

"Okay. Well, I appreciate you letting me know."

As the silence stretched between the two of them this time, it felt gaping and vast. Final. And it was clear that this, whatever odd arrangement they'd had, was over.

"Jordan?"

"Yes?"

"I wish things were different."

Jordan squeezed his eyes shut and willed himself to stay quiet. He knew exactly what Derek was referring to.

That unspoken element. That moment in the bathroom.

The kiss that had imprinted itself somewhere on his soul.

"I just want you safe, Derek."

"I know. I want the same for you. That's why I left. I took

your address off the records at work and left no forwarding one. You should be safe now."

Jordan swallowed around the words he wanted to say, something along the lines of *I was always safe; no one could get inside my building*, but instead he said, "Thank you." When it appeared neither of them had anything else to say, he added, "If you ever need me…"

"I know. I'll call. Goodbye, Jordan."

"Bye, Derek."

The phone call ended, and Jordan wondered if he'd ever felt such detachment in his life. The answer was simple. *No.*

Never had he permitted someone to rely on him in such a way. And never had he allowed someone to be the reason for his highs, or, he thought as his gut churned, the reason for this all-time low.

But the question he couldn't seem to answer was: how did one survive such disconnect? Could they?

Or would he merely crave that same connection over and over until eventually it destroyed the beauty of what drew him in the first place?

# Chapter 13

*One Year Later*
*Commencement Ceremony*

DEREK CLUTCHED HIS commencement certificate in hand as he walked across the stage and wondered, not for the first time, how the hell he'd managed to get through four years of school and come out on the other side with a degree.

He made his way down the stairs, following behind the line of students who'd filed through in front of him. Today was a day to celebrate, and not even the absence of his father or brother could put a damper on this moment.

As his eyes scanned the crowd, he spotted a somber-looking Finn, whose expression almost had him tripping over his own feet as he continued up the aisle. When he got closer, Derek saluted him with his certificate and tried not to be overly concerned with the lack of response he got.

When he'd called earlier that week, Finn had seemed excited to be invited to the ceremony, and asked Derek if he wanted to come to his, which was to be held later that afternoon. But as

Derek moved to retake his seat, he couldn't help but worry that something had happened. Usually Finn would be the first to flash a grin and cheer him on, but today…today he looked like a zombie.

As he took his seat, his eyes continued to move over the crowd to the faculty members who sat off to the side, and he chided himself for even looking.

*There's no reason for him to be here,* he reminded himself, even as he continued to search the faces of his professors. *I had him for one semester; he isn't going to be—* But he was. There, standing behind the row of professors and university personnel, was Professor Devaney.

He was dressed more conservatively than Derek ever remembered seeing him, and the fact that he was wearing a light gray suit with a very proper blue tie had Derek grinning. It wasn't that the look didn't suit Jordan, because hell, the guy pulled the polished look off to a fucking T. It was that he looked so…proper, so professional, which were two words Derek would never normally think of when he thought of the man who'd danced around a penthouse to Britney Spears.

Jordan's eyes were locked on the speaker announcing the final names, but Derek wasn't about to look away from the man until finally, as if Jordan sensed his focus, his gaze shifted and found Derek's.

He couldn't help himself, and aimed a wink at Jordan. At first he wondered if Jordan had caught the gesture, but when his eyes widened slightly and he quickly averted his gaze, Derek knew that he had.

Damn, it'd been way too long since he'd seen Jordan, and the man looked fucking great. He'd been secretly hoping that Jordan would turn up today, but he hadn't wanted to get his hopes up just to have them crushed. There was no reason to expect that he would show at a commencement ceremony he wasn't one of the teachers for. But Derek had been curious if Jordan would be there for one simple reason—him.

Derek turned back to face the stage with a big, cheesy grin. And as he sat there, not knowing the reason Jordan had showed, the fact that he was there at all meant the world to him.

---

JORDAN FELT AS though the tie around his neck was going to strangle him, but as he stood behind the row of economics and finance professors, he couldn't find it in himself to care.

He'd been keeping an eye on Derek's progress over the past year. His grades, his classes, and yes—*to add to my full-on stalker status*—the day he would graduate. Jordan had told himself he was doing what any concerned teacher would if they were worried about the safety of their student. But as he stood there willing the heat on his cheeks to subside, he admitted to himself that this was about a hell of a lot more than concern for a student.

He'd come there today with two goals in mind.

To see a student he knew had fought tooth and nail through school finally graduate. And his other reason was much more selfish.

He'd wanted to see Derek. Plain and simple.

Throughout the year, they'd run into each other a couple of times, and it had been cordial and polite, but for the most part Jordan hadn't seen him in any capacity other than teacher and student—just as they were right now.

As the ceremony came to a close and everyone stood to go and greet those they were there to see, Jordan's eyes cut through the crowd to where Derek was getting to his feet.

Straightening his suit jacket, Jordan told himself this was an appropriate setting for them to meet up and talk. Surely it wouldn't look odd for him to approach and congratulate a former student on his accomplishment.

He greeted several of his colleagues and wove his way through the crowd, heading toward the tall man he could see wearing his cap and gown. Just as he was about to say his name, though, Daniel Finley slipped between him and his target, and Jordan came to a stop.

*Shit.* He looked around, trying to see if Brantley was there with his man or if… *Okay,* it appeared Daniel was on his own. *Thank God.* Jordan wasn't sure he was that great of an actor. As it was, he was now turning on his heel to walk away from the two students he'd once found so interesting. He needed distance from them, and not to be under any kind of scrutiny. Lord only knew what Derek would do if that wink he'd thrown his way earlier was any indication.

He'd just catch up with him later.

---

"WELL, HELL. WHO would've thought that Derek Pearson would stick with school long enough to actually graduate?"

Derek turned around, recognizing Finn's voice in a second, and pulled him into a tight hug. "Hey, fuck you, man. I can stick with things."

When Finn pulled back, he looked Derek up and down and asked, "Since when? The only two things you've ever stuck with is running and smoking, which seems kind of counterproductive, but…"

Derek chuckled. "At least it proves that I can stick to something."

"Yeah, but only things you enjoy."

"Well, what's the point of doing something you don't like?" He paused and then flashed a grin. "I use the same motto in my sex life."

Finn laughed, but the smile that crossed his lips didn't quite reach his eyes and had Derek instantly concerned. Something was off. Finn was always the jovial one of the two of them, but this guy in front of him, he was trying to put on a good front, and it wasn't fooling Derek for a second.

"What are your plans for the rest of the day?" Derek asked, then looked over Finn's shoulders to see Jordan's back as he walked away from them and into the crowd of students.

*Fuck.* He'd really wanted to talk to Jordan, but he wasn't sure how to do that without alerting Finn. Then there'd be a million questions on why he needed to speak to Posh Spice, and really, he wasn't sure he wouldn't be able to finally spill all his secrets.

Hell, maybe that was what he needed to do. Go and get shit-faced with Finn and finally tell him everything that had been going on with his life. Maybe then Finn would feel comfortable telling him whatever was bothering him.

"Not much. I have my ceremony then I was going to go home," Finn said, and the tone of his voice sent a feeling of apprehension through Derek.

"Do you want to go and grab a couple of beers and chat after you get done?"

Finn's eyes found his, and the pain inside them had Derek taking a step toward his friend. "What's going on, Danny boy? You're starting to freak me out. Is it your mom? Katrina? Is everyone okay?"

Finn nodded quickly at that, easing Derek's concerns over his family and health.

"Then what is it? I know something's wrong. You could never hide anything worth a shit."

As they headed toward the auditorium doors, Finn shoved his hands into his pockets and nodded. "Yeah. I was coming to…" He paused as they stepped out into the sun-filled summer day, and when they moved under one of the pavilion tents that had been erected, Finn toed the grass underfoot and finally looked Derek in the eye. "I wanted to see you graduate and… and to say goodbye."

That brought Derek to a fucking halt. "Goodbye?" he asked, turning to face Finn, who was grinding his teeth like he wanted to scream.

"Yeah."

Finn went to walk away from him, but Derek reached for his arm, stopping him. "Wait up. Where the fuck are you going that you have to say goodbye? I know we haven't been real close lately, but—"

"I'm going to Chicago." The words were clipped and cold, and Finn's expression offered no explanation.

What the hell was going on? "Am I allowed to ask why?"

Finn shoved his hands into the pockets of his slacks and tilted his head to the side. "You can. I'm not sure I know the answer, though. Look, this is hard enough. Don't make it any harder."

"Then help me to understand, because the Finn I know wouldn't decide to just up and leave his family."

Finn's eyes met his then, and the anger that had been cool and collected suddenly roared to life. "Really? *You're* going to say that to *me?*"

The force behind that question immediately had Derek's spine straightening. "Well, it's true. They're here, aren't they?"

"Yeah, they are. You're also here, Derek. Though God knows what the hell you've been doing these past few months or where you've been."

Derek tried to think of an appropriate response, but since he'd been lying to his friend, he really had nothing to say in his own defense.

"You know what," Finn said. "Just forget it. I didn't come here to fight with you. You have your own life, and it's clearly time I went and got one of my fucking own."

Totally shocked by the turn of events and the angry stranger Finn had morphed into, Derek lowered his voice and asked, "Is the professor going with you?"

Finn's eyes went flat at the mention of his boyfriend, and his jaw ticked.

*Fuck, okay. That's answer enough.* Obviously something had gone down there. Deciding the least he could do was act the supportive friend, Derek tapped his certificate on his hand and asked, "So. Chicago, huh?"

Finn nodded, but he looked like he wanted to vomit.

"When do you think you'll be back?"

His buddy shrugged and then said, "When the program is over, I guess. Two years. That's what he said, anyway."

"Hayes?"

This time Finn nodded. "Yeah. Fucking Hayes."

"You don't have to go, you know."

"Yeah, but now I kinda want to. Honestly, I never want to see his face again."

"But—"

"I don't want to talk about it, okay? I just wanted to say goodbye and see you before I left."

"And when's that?"

"Tomorrow."

"Are you serious?" When Finn nodded, Derek took his cap off and ran a hand through his hair. "Jesus. Well, thanks for stopping by."

"You don't have to be a dick about it."

But he did. Because if he wasn't being a dick he might break down and tell Finn that he didn't want him to go, and, more importantly, that he was sorry he'd let their friendship fall the fuck apart.

He didn't tell Finn any of that, though. Instead, he held his hand out and, when Finn took it, pulled him into a hug that made Derek's heart break a little.

"Well, don't be a stranger, Danny boy."

"Ha. You keep saying that to me. And I won't. There's email and text, you know."

"Yeah…I know."

"Hey? Mom wanted to be here today, but she had to work. She told me to give you this."

Finn held a box out, and when Derek opened it there was a wooden plaque with *The people who stand out as special in your life are usually put in your path for a reason* carved into it. He traced his fingers over them, and when he looked up, Finn shrugged. "She's sappy—what can I say?"

"Nah, you're lucky to have her."

"Yeah, I know. Okay, well, I'm gonna head out. Congratulations, man. I hope you get that gym by the beach you talked about."

Derek laughed and shut the lid on the box. "Me too. Good luck in Chicago."

Finn kicked a stone on the ground and didn't respond. He merely gave a tight smile and then turned and walked away.

As Derek watched him go, he thought of the simple words inside the box and wondered if he and Finn would ever cross paths again.

---

IT WAS LATE afternoon and Jordan was about five minutes away from stripping out of the God-awful suit he'd worn and slipping into some shorts and a tank before pouring himself a glass of Merlot.

He'd finally gotten home after the never-ending commencement ceremony, and had wisely avoided all contact with Derek after that one foiled attempt. It was best that things end this way between them. He'd seen Derek through, from start to finish, and somewhere in there along the way become friendly with the guy, but that was it. It was over now. Derek had moved out, graduated, and would start his life and move forward from there.

*Just like I need to do,* Jordan told himself as he removed his jacket and threw it over his couch. When his cell phone started ringing inside the front pocket, he dug it out and almost dropped it as the word *He-Man* flashed across the screen.

As if he'd conjured Derek out of thin air, the guy was calling him, and Jordan wasn't sure if he should let it go to voicemail or… *Hell, who am I kidding?* "Hello?"

"Hi," Derek replied, and Jordan wondered when his cock had become a slave to the man's voice. Every time he heard it, it stood to rigid attention. "You free right now?"

Jordan's pulse raced at the question, and he wasn't sure why. It was innocent enough, but front and center in his mind was the fact that, as of a couple of hours ago, Derek was no longer a student where he worked. Which meant all of the excuses he'd used over the years to keep his distance no longer applied.

"Yes. I'm free."

"Can you let me up, then?"

Jordan whirled around to face the elevator as if Derek was stepping off it and into his condo as they spoke. "You're here?"

"I'm downstairs, yeah. Is that okay?"

Jordan tightened his fingers around the phone as he walked over to the access panel of the elevator and pressed the open button. He watched on the small monitor as Derek stepped inside and then looked up into the camera mounted on the wall of the elevator. That was when he asked again, "Is that *okay*, Jordan?"

Jordan saw his lips move on the camera and knew that if Derek took the elevator up to his condo then everything between them would change. That, however, wasn't enough to stop him from replying, "Yes. Come to me."

## Chapter 14

WHEN THE ELEVATOR came to a stop at Jordan's floor, Derek was positive his heart skipped a few beats. *Christ*, he wasn't sure he had the balls to ask for what he'd come there for. But as the door slid open and Jordan's handsome face came into view, he was determined to fucking try.

On his way over to Jordan's, he'd been running through Finn's words about leaving, and though he knew it wasn't personal, it sure as hell felt that way. Finn leaving Sunset Cove meant the end of an era of sorts. An end of them, for real. Not just because they were busy and doing their own things, but because Finn was putting miles, states, and a plane ride between them.

Thinking about it made him mad all over again, though he knew he had no right, and when he stepped off the elevator and headed toward Jordan, he watched him cross his arms over his chest in a move that Derek knew all too well. It was a blocking move. A *do not come any closer* move. And it had his steps faltering.

When he saw Jordan standing in the crowd today, he'd wanted to go to him for many reasons. One of those was to tell him he looked fucking hot in a suit. But after talking to Daniel, the need to be with Jordan had become more pressing. More desperate. Derek had felt out of control, unable to fix or stop what was happening in his life, and he'd known the only person who would make his world seem stable again was the man opposite him, with narrowed eyes and crossed arms.

"Okay..." Jordan finally said. "What's with the fierce frown on a day where you should be over the moon?"

Derek wasn't even aware he'd been sporting a scowl until Jordan, as always, called his ass out on it. Then before he realized he was going to, he blurted out, "Did you know?"

Jordan cocked his head to the side and asked, "Did I know *what*, exactly?"

Derek wasn't sure why, but he had a feeling that Jordan had known about Finn leaving. But before he could continue his interrogation, Jordan was speaking again.

"That you would graduate? I never had a doubt. Though your smartass mouth and tendency to cause problems for your professors may have given me reason to worry over the last four years."

Derek let his eyes move down from Jordan's styled hair to his high cheekbones, and with his shirt and tie still in place, plus his gray slacks and wingtips, he looked the epitome of sophistication. And just like that, Derek's first line of questioning left him, and instead he asked, "You worry about me?"

"Oh, only whenever I think about you."

"And how often's that?"

The question lingered between them like a dare. One that had been issued four years ago but never acted on. Then... Jordan took him up on it.

He let his eyes trail down over Derek's own shirt, tie, and slacks, then brought them back to his face and answered, "More often than not."

Unable to stop himself, Derek took a step forward and Jordan walked backward. They continued that way until

Jordan's back hit a wall and Derek's polished shoes were touching his.

"Fuck, I want to kiss you right now," Derek said, as he looked into Jordan's eyes and waited for him to tell him no. But he should've known better when it came to Jordan, who angled his chin up instead. His body language screamed out one thing: *I dare you. But if you want me, you better have the fucking balls to take me on.*

*No problem there*, Derek thought, as he placed a hand on the wall by Jordan's head. As all of the feelings he'd squashed down over the years rushed to the surface, Derek brought a hand up to touch Jordan's chin. But before his fingers made contact, Jordan took hold of his wrist and added, "Be sure."

Derek's dick was positive, but as he looked into the dark eyes staring back at him, he sensed there was more to what Jordan was asking him—and he was right.

"What I mean is," Jordan said, "be sure that one night is enough for you."

That brought Derek up short. "Why only one?"

"Because tomorrow I fly to Italy for the summer."

*You've got to be fucking kidding me.* "What's with everyone leaving all of a sudden?"

Jordan shrugged. "This has been planned for months. But I understand if it changes your mind. If you can't *do* one night."

Derek shook his head, not believing that this was actually happening to him. "So basically you want to fuck me then kick me out."

Jordan's eyes widened at his blunt words, but Derek didn't care. It actually felt good to be able to say what he really thought instead of offering a fake smile and going on his merry way, like he'd had to earlier with Finn.

"No. I just don't want you to think this is something it's not. I'm not in the right place for anything serious. I'm going on vacation and you'll be starting work. So I don't want—"

"A boyfriend. Strings. I get it. You want to be able to fuck whoever you want and not worry about the guy back at home mooning over you. Got it."

"Excuse me. It's not like that."

"It's exactly like that," Derek said. Then he sighed. "But I don't even care anymore. I want you. And I've waited for fucking ever to have you."

Derek thought it interesting that Jordan didn't like hearing his terms stated so bluntly. But that was too bad. Jordan had been the first person to really open his eyes and show him it was best to call a spade a spade. And right now, he wasn't about to sugarcoat shit to make it sweet and romantic just so Jordan would feel better.

"Fair enough," Jordan said. Though he looked like he wanted to claw Derek's face off. "As long as we understand each other up front."

"Oh, I understand," Derek said, while inside he was busy thinking, *Fuck this.* On the same day, he was going to lose both Finn *and* Jordan. Sometimes he wished life would give him a break and spread shit out rather than dump it all on him at once.

Jordan's fingers tightened around his wrist, and Derek knew he had to be able to feel the rapid tattoo of his pulse.

"Okay, then," Jordan said. "Go to my bedroom, take off your clothes, and wait for me by the end of my bed. I can't tell you how long I've wanted to see that."

And before Derek could change his mind, he turned on his heel and made his way down to Jordan's bedroom.

---

JORDAN SHUT HIS eyes and counted to twenty as he stood in his living room and watched Derek leave. He needed to get a handle on himself.

*Breathe, Jordan. Fucking breathe. Because if you pass out on the floor and the first time he has his mouth on yours tonight is due to CPR, you will never forgive yourself.*

After his little pep talk, he removed his shoes and socks, unbuttoned the first couple of buttons on his shirt, and then took off the damn tie he'd been wearing all day. Once he was slightly more comfortable, minus the hard-on between his legs, he made his way down to his bedroom.

When he got to the door, the sight that greeted him just about had his jaw on the floor. Derek naked was fucking impressive.

Jordan let his eyes trail over Derek's side profile as he waited at the foot of his bed. His large feet were planted firm, shoulder width apart, and his built calves were rigid as he stood silently. His thighs bunched just as Jordan's eyes trailed over them, and Jordan bit down on his lower lip to keep the groan he could feel bubbling inside him from slipping free.

From the angle he was standing at, Jordan could see the thick length of Derek's erection as it jutted out from his body, and it took everything in him not to go straight to his side and wrap his hand around him and stroke.

Jordan wondered what Derek was thinking right then. He was curious if he was still upset about their previous conversation or if getting naked had brought more carnal thoughts to mind. Because the sight he was seeing had Jordan's hands quickly moving to the button of his pants, and once he had that free, he was unzipping.

The sound must've caught Derek's ear, because his head finally turned, and instead of the irritation Jordan had seen earlier, his eyes were like the center of the hottest flame—blue and blazing.

Half-dressed, Jordan knew he must look completely disheveled as he walked closer to the man he'd been dying to get his hands, mouth, and cock against for years.

When he was finally by Derek's side, Jordan gave a roguish grin and, without touching him, leaned forward and dragged the tip of his tongue up one of the elaborate tattoos decorating Derek's arm.

Derek grunted and Jordan raised his head and winked at him, catching the ticking of Derek's jaw when he clenched his teeth. Then, with a smirk, Jordan lowered his head to do it again and traced his finger over the curve of Derek's back to his tailbone, causing a rumble to escape him this time.

"I've thought about you naked *way* more often than I should've, but, ahh..." Jordan lost his train of thought as he stepped around behind Derek and drew his finger up his spine. He then smoothed his palm over to his shoulder and pressed his lips to the warm skin at the nape of his neck. "God, Derek, you're built like a god. And I have a thing for muscles and tattoos, and *fuck*," Jordan said as he scraped his teeth along his shoulder. "I think I just have a thing for you."

Jordan knew he needed to shut his mouth before he said anything else incriminating. But before he did, there was one more thing... "Turn around for me. I want to look at what's mine for the night."

*Then* he took a step back.

---

DEREK SHUT HIS eyes for a second and willed his dick not to embarrass him. He'd been waiting for this moment for years, and there was no way he was going to come without experiencing, or at least fucking *seeing*, Jordan naked.

*God, please let him get naked...*

He slowly pivoted until he was facing Jordan, and *Jesus*, the guy looked like he was two seconds away from pouncing. His pants were hanging open, his shirt was half undone, and his lips were swollen, as though he'd been chewing on them while he'd been teasing Derek.

As Derek stood there mesmerized, Jordan pulled his shirt

from his pants, undid the rest of the buttons, and stripped out of it, throwing it to the floor.

*Damn*, Derek wasn't sure he'd survive watching Jordan strip in front of him without some sort of… *Oh, fuck it*, he reached down and clamped a tight fist around the base of his cock and squeezed.

When a chuckle echoed around the room and his eyes found Jordan's, the guy shoved his pants to the floor along with his boxer briefs and said, "I'll take *that* as a compliment."

Derek had no witty comebacks in his brain at that moment. All he had was the honest to God truth, which was, "You're gorgeous."

Totally naked now, Jordan, bold as you please, walked over to him and wrapped his fingers around the top of the ones Derek had encircling the root of his shaft. Jordan then tipped his face up and batted his lashes. "I told you so."

The comment was so Jordan, and so fucking arrogant, that Derek scoffed before Jordan twisted his hand and drew it up the length of his cock, making him groan instead.

Jordan waggled his brows and aimed a blinding smile up at him. The guy was a fucking trip, but when he kissed his way up to Derek's ear and said, "Get on the bed," he had Derek's undivided attention.

Derek sat down on the mattress, but before he could do anything else, Jordan bent and took his face between his hands. His lips were against Derek's before he could even blink and the kiss was totally fucking mind-blowing. Jordan's lips were forceful, his tongue rapacious, and any doubt or misapprehension Derek might have had vanished.

As the initial hunger was somewhat tamed, Jordan grazed his lips over the top of his and whispered, "Scoot back to the middle and let me see what you've been teasing me with since day one, Derek."

Not sure if it was the words or the tender touch in amongst the rawness of that moment, but Derek's heart joined his brain and body right then as he sat staring up at Jordan, and a shudder raced throughout his body.

"You okay?" Jordan asked, when he just sat there.

Derek nodded and a seductive smile split Jordan's lips. That was when Derek realized what a gigantic mistake he'd made in coming there tonight. Because even as he moved to the center of Jordan's bed, Derek knew after he left it, his heart would remain right there, where he was about to hand it over to the man looking down at him.

---

AS DEREK MOVED to the middle of his mattress, Jordan thought his bed had never looked more inviting. He was magnificent lying there waiting on him. His colorful tattoos were bright against the crisp white of the bedsheets, and that stiff cock of his was leaking fluid over his abdomen.

Derek was beyond turned on. He looked ready to explode, and Jordan knew their night would be over very quickly, once the touching began. So he was all about taking his time for a moment to enjoy his view.

He'd been waiting to kiss, stroke, and touch Derek Pearson since the first moment he'd seen him, and now that he was his for the taking, Jordan didn't want to rush.

He wanted to savor. To get inside him and stay there. But that wasn't what this was about. This wasn't about forevers. This was about the now.

One night. So they could finally relieve this sexual tension between them and move on.

Ever so slowly, Derek worked his shaft as he raised both feet to plant them on the mattress, and Jordan rolled a condom on. He lubed up, and then tossed the bottle on the mattress before placing a knee on the bed to climb up onto it.

Derek's breathing increased and he pulled his knees up against his chest, waiting for whatever Jordan was going to give to him. He looked beautiful as he lay there, trusting him in that moment with something Jordan knew he'd never given to another, and for that he had to at least tell him… "Derek?"

Derek blinked up at him. "Yeah."

"I've never wanted anyone as much as I want you right now."

The blush that reddened Derek's cheeks made Jordan's confession well worth it as he stroked a gentle finger down the dark channel of Derek's body. He saw Derek lower a hand back to his cock, and pick up the pace as he methodically stroked himself up and down as Jordan probed his body for entrance.

"Yes, Derek. That's it. Let me in."

Derek's body was like a furnace where Jordan was slowly massaging him, and as his finger slipped inside, he heard a moan escape the man he was working over.

"Oh God, Jordan, more."

Jordan shifted to his knees so he could lean over Derek's body and trace the tattoo across his heart with his tongue as he tunneled his finger in deeper, finding and nailing Derek's prostate.

"*Fuck.*"

The curse was like music to his ears as he did it over and over, all the while licking and sucking every bit of ink he could reach on Derek's body. Finally, Derek let go of his knee to grip the back of Jordan's neck and haul his mouth up to his. As their lips met in a molten kiss, Jordan sucked on Derek's tongue. *God*, if he didn't get inside Derek, the guy was going to make him lose it like a damn teenager.

When their lips parted and Derek's breath ghosted over his, Jordan asked, "Ready?"

And Derek's eyes told him all he needed to know.

He moved back, grabbed the lube, and slicked some over his aching length before he poured a nice amount over Derek's waiting body. Then he shifted in between Derek's raised legs and lined the head of his erection up with the tight pucker he'd dreamed of taking many times over.

When Derek's fingers dug into his own knees, Jordan's eyes found his and Derek gave a brief nod. Permission to enter.

With the utmost of care, Jordan pushed inside the man laying his body down for him, and when he breached the first ring of muscle and he heard a curse ricochet around his bedroom, he looked to Derek for direction. He bared his teeth and begged, "Don't stop. Please don't stop."

"I don't plan to," Jordan said, then he was inside and buried to his balls, and Derek's body was clasping his cock like a fucking vise.

He could hear the blood rushing around his head, and when his eyes met Derek's, Jordan knew he'd grossly miscalculated this moment. This was so much more than acting on something they'd been tiptoeing around for years.

This...*this* was everything, and he wasn't ready for everything right now.

Shoving aside his heart and replacing those emotions with the ones making his cock throb, Jordan put a hand on each of Derek's legs just below his knees, and pushed them back high to Derek's chest, spreading him wide open for him. As he gained a nice, deep slide inside Derek's hot body, Jordan's brain shut down on all things emotional and instead flipped to the physical.

"Yes..." Derek said as Jordan pulled out of him and then tunneled back inside. "Again," he demanded, wanting, and, from all accounts, *needing* more, and Jordan gave it to him.

He took Derek in ways he'd never imagined taking anyone. He was more demanding and unapologetic than he'd ever been before, and the entire time Derek lay under him arching up off the bed, giving to him without any complaints. By the time the both of them were close to passing out, Jordan whispered, "Come for me, Derek. Let me see you explode as I take you."

Derek's eyes found his and his Adam's apple bobbed as he swallowed and nodded. Jordan leaned over him and placed a hand by Derek's head, and when Derek's legs shifted down to wrap around his waist, Jordan moaned.

*Yes*… he thought, as he started to piston in and out of Derek, hitting his prostate on every dig. Finally, as Derek's voice cracked and a hoarse cry ripped from his throat, he came in a fountain of hot fluid all over his hand and abdomen.

Mesmerized by the sight, Jordan pulled out of his tight body, rolled the condom off, and watched his cum drip down over Derek's muscles and tattoos as he wrung an orgasm, which just about blew the top of his head off, from his own body.

What a sight Derek was as he lay flat on his back, and in those few seconds, Jordan knew that Derek was his: body, heart, and, as their eyes met, soul—then the moment was gone.

"You need to move," Derek said, his eyes now looking anywhere but at Jordan.

"Derek—"

"Get off me," Derek grit out, and Jordan could feel Derek shudder.

Jordan moved of off Derek's body, and as he shifted to his side Derek rolled off the bed, swung his legs over the edge, and picked up his clothes. Jordan lay still and silent as Derek walked to the bedroom door, and the last thing Jordan heard him say was, "Enjoy Italy. Baggage free."

# Chapter 15

*Three Years Later*

DEREK TOOK A final look at himself in the mirror and then wandered out into the living room he shared with Dylan Prescott. They'd recently moved up in the world. Well, that was what he liked to think. They'd vacated the little dump they'd lived in throughout college and moved into a three-bedroom with two baths that overlooked the beach further down from where they used to live.

With him now managing the gym where he'd worked for years, and Dylan making a living through his catalogue modeling gigs, the two of them made enough to be able to split the rent on the bigger place and enjoy a little more comfort than what they'd once had, and tonight…tonight his buddy Dylan had once again talked him into doing something monumentally stupid.

"I feel like a fucking idiot," Derek grumbled as he walked around the couch where Dylan was sitting.

"Why? Because you actually had to make an effort—"

When Dylan caught sight of Derek, his words stopped and he got to his feet to look him over.

For the first time in his life, and hopefully the last, Derek was dressed in a tuxedo. The jacket and pants he was wearing had been measured to perfectly fit his body, and while he conceded he looked pretty damn good, he'd left his black nail polish on for a bit of *fuck you* flare.

"Shit, man, you look hot. Very James Bond."

Derek tugged on the lapels of the jacket and shrugged. "Yeah? You think?"

"Umm…yeah." Dylan walked over to him, dressed in an almost identical outfit, except for the additions of the black buttons on his white shirt. When he stopped in front of Derek, he laid a familiar palm over the lapel on his chest and smoothed it up to his shoulder, where he flicked away a piece of lint. "You're going to make us a *lot* of money tonight."

Derek screwed his nose up. "I think if anyone's gonna make money for this damn auction, it's going to be you."

"Have you seen yourself? Derek, you look… Just trust me. There's going to be a very broke man tonight because he's going to have to outbid everyone else that's going to fight for you. Including myself." Dylan gave him a thorough once-over. "Damn, I had no idea you'd clean up this good."

"Gee, thanks."

"No, no. I don't mean it like that. It's just…I only ever see you in gym clothes or your jeans. But this. This takes you to a whole other level."

"Down, boy." Derek chuckled. "Put on a suit and Prescott becomes easy—who knew? Stop looking at me like you want to suck my dick or I just might take you up on the offer."

Dylan laughed at that. "Bullshit. We tried that when you first moved in with me, and that was an epic fucking fail. But if you ever think you could be interested in the one whose hand is actually in your pants instead of the one you constantly daydream about…I'm willing to try again."

"You're hilarious, asshole."

"Hey, I'm just saying. You're the one with the little—or should I say *big*—issue. I mean, the equipment is definitely all there. It's just not wanting to come out and play—with me."

Derek raised an eyebrow at his roommate. The pretty bastard was having way too much fun at his expense. "Done?"

Dylan gave a shit-eating grin. "Yeah, I guess. But even you have to admit, it was an *epic* fail."

Derek laughed at the memory. He was right; there were no two ways about it. When he'd first moved in with Dylan, they'd gotten drunk one night and things had progressed from flirtatious comments to a few kisses and a lot of hands. Then, well, Dylan had slipped his fingers down his shorts and Derek had been all for a hand job from the gorgeous guy. However, his cock hadn't cooperated, and even after Dylan had tried his hardest to pump some life into it, it wasn't having any of it.

Nope. His dick had wanted one person only. Jordan. *God.* It felt like that had always been the case, and always fucking would be. But since he avoided Jordan like the plague, Derek had made it somewhat of a mission to track down men of similar builds and temperament to his feisty former professor. He knew that was fucked up, but hey, what else was new when it came to him?

Which got Derek thinking. When *was* the last time he'd gone out and hooked up? Had it really been months ago? He needed to get out more, and his brain and body needed to stop fixating on something he could never have again.

"Yeah, no offense," Derek finally said. "But one major fail with you is all I think my ego can handle."

"Ha," Dylan barked. "Yeah, right. You have more attitude in your little finger than most men have in their entire body. And just because *you* didn't get it up that night, doesn't mean I didn't enjoy imagining it later in my room by myself. You let me see all those tattoos on your body, and… Yeah, that was all it took."

"Damn, I had no idea you were in there jacking off to me each night, Prescott."

"Yeah, right. Don't flatter yourself. After living with you as long as I have, all my fantasies are long since gone. Trust me."

Derek chuckled and snagged the keys off the kitchen table. "Yeah, yeah. Okay, wise guy, remind me again what happens after some strange man purchases me for the night."

"Well, you collect the check. The money goes to the True Colors Fund, then you go on a date with him."

Derek looked doubtful. "And that's it?"

Dylan nodded as he scooped up his own keys. "That's it. Dinner. A movie. Whatever floats his boat."

"What if wall-banging sex floats his boat?"

Dylan headed to the door with Derek following behind. "Then hope it's someone you'd like to crush against a wall?"

"Gee, you're a lot of help, Prescott. Can I refuse? Do they know we aren't on sale for sex?"

"Aww, are you worried about your virtue?" Dylan quipped as they headed for Derek's Jeep. He'd purchased it a couple of months ago, and as he popped the locks, he flipped his roommate off.

"Hey, if I don't worry about it, no one will. And I just want to know the rules up front."

As Dylan climbed inside the car, he shrugged. "The men are aware of the bidding rules, but I've gotta be honest. If I won you for the night, I'd totally try for the wall-banging sex." Derek glanced over at his passenger, and Dylan winked. "I mean, a movie would not be my first choice. At least not the kind of movies they show at public theaters."

Derek raised an eyebrow. "Good to know the way to your heart, and dick, is through a simple tuxedo."

Dylan shrugged. "What can I say—there's something about a man in a tux."

"Oh, I get it. You're looking pretty sharp yourself. But no touching tonight, Prescott…not unless you pay me." Derek laughed at himself. "God, that sounds so wrong. Okay, let's get going. Apparently I have some rich schmuck waiting to take me on a date."

---

JORDAN WASN'T SURE why he'd let Brantley drag him along to the Gay and Lesbian Community Center tonight. This wasn't the way he usually liked to go about donating toward causes he believed in, and he believed strongly in helping the homeless youth among the LGBTQ community. But really, an auction?

He'd almost laughed when Brantley asked him, because he was the last person Jordan would ever expect to turn up to one of these events. But then Brantley had admitted he wanted to get out more and maybe meet someone new and see if...well, just see "if," and who was Jordan to say no to that?

Ever since Daniel Finley had moved to Chicago, Jordan had been trying to get Brantley back out into the dating world for what felt like forever, and he would just about mortgage a fucking house to buy the guy a date if that was what it took to have him sit down and eat a meal with a man whom he might have something in common with. Or at least have really good sex with.

Lord knows the guy could do with a couple of rounds in a bed with a hot guy to remind him how to use the appendage between his legs.

But it was none of Jordan's business what Brantley did, or who, for that matter. He just hated seeing his friend so isolated when he was such a good catch for some lucky guy.

So there he was, standing at the back of an auditorium full of horny men ranging in age, pretending to be there to support a good cause, when really, it was just an added benefit of ogling all the eye candy about to be paraded on stage and the chance to date someone way out of their league.

*Well, out of* their *league. Let's be real.*

With a glass of Chardonnay in hand, Jordan leaned into Brantley and asked, "So do they have a menu of sorts?"

"A menu?" Brantley asked, his eyes wide.

"Why do you look so shocked? Surely it makes sense that we get to *see* what it is we'll be purchasing. Right? You get a catalogue at an auction house, so I figured with all the prime beef they're about to display, we would get a menu here."

"Jordan," Brantley said.

Jordan frowned and then looked back to the stage, where several men were muscling to get closer to the runway. "What? That's why I'm here, right? I mean you. That's why *you're* here. I'm not bidding. I currently have my hands full, thank you very much."

Brantley smiled, and Jordan felt himself reciprocate. He'd been seeing Dr. Stephan Reid for a couple of months now, and things were going…well.

Stephan worked over at the local hospital, and that was where they'd first met. Jordan had been coming out of a meeting where he'd donated funds to an expansion of the children's wing, and they'd literally run into one another and hit it off. Since then, they'd gone out to dinner several times, and one night they'd even gone to the local symphony, and all in all it was going…well.

The only problem was they hadn't quite made it to the bedroom yet. Stephan was a little older. Actually, he was right around Brantley's age, and whenever they'd come close and Jordan would make a move, the guy's pager would go off or he'd be called into work. As frustrating as that was, though, Jordan was beginning to suspect that maybe he wasn't as into Stephan as he should be, considering the lack of sex *wasn't* bothering him. But Stephan was kind and generous, and they had similar interests when it came to giving back to those less fortunate than themselves, and Jordan figured it was worth giving it a little more time to see if it could develop into something more.

"Oh yes, Stephan. How is he?"

"Busy," Jordan replied. It was the truth. He was always busy, but that worked out for Jordan, too, because honestly, he liked his freedom. He not only worked at the university these days but also sat on the board of several charities he found important, and he was the owner of two of the major apartment towers being built down on the main strip of Sunset, and somewhere in the middle there, he saw Stephan when he was free.

"Maybe one day soon when he's *not* busy, we can all get together and have dinner?"

Brantley had asked him this a couple of times now, and while Jordan wasn't opposed to bringing Stephan around, he wasn't sure how permanent he was and would really rather play it by ear.

"Yeah, maybe. I'll have to ask him."

"Please do. I think it's only fair I get to meet the man who's finally held your interest for longer than a night."

*Oh, there's another one, you know...* Jordan thought, and then immediately wondered why the hell Derek Pearson was in his head. He hadn't heard from Derek in years. After the night of commencement, Jordan had gone off on his family's vacation and when he'd come back, just as they'd decided, that had been that.

Jordan had gone back to work at the start of a new semester, and he hadn't run into Derek since.

It hadn't escaped his notice, though, that in a town the size of Sunset Cove, it was likely that Derek purposely avoided him and all his local haunts, because otherwise they would've run into one another by now.

He was about to give Brantley some lame response to the question about dinner when the lights went down and a spotlight lit up a man on the far left-hand side of the stage.

"Good evening, everyone. Are you all ready to part with some Benjamins for maybe a Peter or Paul?"

When the crowd around them whistled their agreement, Jordan glanced over at Brantley. He caught his friend's eye and flashed him a grin before raising his hand and wolf-whistling right along with the other men. As everyone settled, the auctioneer ran through the rules of the event for the crowd. It was simple.

This was *not* a sex for money auction.

If you were interested in someone, you were to raise your hand in a calm manner.

*Yeah, right.* Jordan wasn't sure the crowd currently jostling one another for a prime position by the stage knew the meaning of the word *calm.*

And finally, if you purchased someone and couldn't write a check to be cashed the following day, the man would then go to the next highest bidder.

*In other words,* Jordan noted, *you're shit out of luck.*

The auctioneer then invited them to enjoy themselves and get their wallets ready, because the first man up for grabs that evening was: "The manager of one of the local gyms of Sunset Cove. I'm sure even those in the back of the crowd will have no problem seeing his towering physique. Let me hear your best version of a wolf whistle, boys, because this guy is all kinds of alpha. Derek Pearson."

As Derek's name boomed through the speakers on each corner of the stage, Jordan's jaw almost hit the floor, and then he caught himself right before Brantley glanced over his shoulder and mouthed, "That's Finn's Derek, right?"

When the spotlight moved from the auctioneer to the center of the stage and the curtain drew back to reveal Derek, Jordan's only thought was, *No, that's my Derek.*

He absently nodded as Derek walked forward to center stage, and Jordan couldn't help the small grin that touched the side of his mouth at the expression on Derek's face. The guy was not happy to be the main attraction in a room full of horny men vying for his attention, or, in actuality, bidding for it.

He was dressed the part, though, that was for sure. Derek looked gorgeous in his classic tux, with his hair cut short on the sides and styled back from his face. His broad shoulders filled out the jacket in a way that made Jordan's palm itch to touch, then his eyes moved down to the hands by Derek's side and Jordan noted the black nail polish and felt his dick twitch.

*Jesus,* Derek looked beyond hot. He was attitude and sex in a suit. One that Jordan desperately wanted to peel him out of.

Hands started to fly up around him and the bids rolled in. The auctioneer was going on about "talents" and "measurements" as Derek strolled up the stage to the left then turned to walk back to the center before heading to the right. The more Derek walked, the more confident he became, and on his second pass of the left-hand side his eyes roved over the crowd and found Jordan's.

To Derek's credit, he didn't falter, he merely slowed his pace and narrowed his eyes a fraction, which anyone in the crowd would think he was doing to look suave and sexy, but Jordan knew better.

Derek was watching him now. Had him in his sights, *and hell,* that look had Jordan edging back into the crowd away from Brantley, who'd been swallowed up by the sea of men. When Jordan was as far back as he could get, he looked at the man standing beside him. He was tall, taller than he was, at least, and that was when he was struck with a brilliant plan.

Jordan placed a hand on the man's arm and leaned up to speak in his ear. With the music so loud and the crowd going nuts, the man had to lean down, and Jordan said, "I will give you a hundred dollars to stand here and bid on that man. One dollar over *every* bid, no matter how high it goes, until you win."

The man's eyes widened and Jordan pulled a hundred from his wallet.

"Deal?"

The man looked back to the stage and raised his hand, issuing the first bid. When Derek's eyes flew to his bidder, and then to Jordan, this time his feet did falter.

*Mhmm…* Derek always had been smart, and Jordan was

positive that he knew exactly which man was going to be taking him home tonight.

---

HOLY SHIT. HE would know that face anywhere.

When Derek had first stepped onto the stage and the lights had shone into his eyes, he'd squinted, trying to see if he knew anyone in the crowd. Then about a minute into the ridiculous song, like a magnetic fucking pull, his eyes had drifted to a man watching him, and there, standing in the rowdy crowd of men, was Jordan Devaney. And *God* he looked amazing.

In tight jeans and an even tighter lightweight black V-neck, Jordan looked sexy. So damn sexy. And the heat that fired his eyes when he'd checked out Derek's tux made it close to impossible for Derek to remain decent.

"Okay, it looks like we have a bit of a bidding war happening. The young redhead down the front here and the gentleman in the back."

Derek's eyes darted to the tall man who Jordan had been standing beside, to see that he was now alone. Jordan was nowhere in sight.

*Where the hell did he go?* Derek had been positive Jordan would try and make a play for him. Lord knows he was arrogant enough to buy ten minutes of his time. But he was gone. And it pissed him off that he was disappointed.

"Do I hear a final bid?"

When the man in the back shouted out a preposterous amount of money that Derek didn't believe he *actually* warranted, the auctioneer hit the gavel to the podium and declared him sold.

*Well, fuck.* He'd hoped when he'd seen Jordan that he'd—*Jesus, stop already.*

"Congratulations, to the gentleman in the back. I have to say, you had a real run for your money tonight. If you head out the exit on your left, you can pay the lady by the stage door and then we'll let you back to meet up with your date."

Derek heard the whoops and whistles as his "date" made his way through the crowd. He did as he'd been instructed before heading on stage and took a bow, which the crowd loved, then pivoted on his heel and walked behind the curtain.

As he stepped backstage, Dylan stood there with a huge smile. He was up next, and Derek wondered if the guy was crazy enough to actually enjoy this kind of thing.

"Two thousand and one dollars." Dylan shook his head and then clapped his arm. "I knew you'd break one K, but two? Hot damn."

"By a dollar. That hardly counts," Derek pointed out.

"Someone just paid two thousand dollars for your time, and Derek, it all counts. Now hurry along—your Richard Gere awaits you through those doors."

"I thought you said I didn't have to fuck the guy."

Dylan frowned and then busted up laughing. "You don't. I was thinking more Lancelot and less *Pretty Woman*."

"Oh."

"Yeah. Anyway, I just heard my name, so…wish me luck out there."

"Oh please, you'll bring in three grand easy with that face."

Dylan pulled the curtain aside. "Hey, it's hard being this pretty."

"Yeah, for the other guys looking at you."

Dylan waved his hand over his head and called out, "Have a good time on your date." Then he disappeared out onto the stage.

Derek made his way to the side exit, and as he stepped out into the hall he came face to face with Jordan, who was lounging back against the wall with his ankles crossed and his hands deep in his pockets.

Derek looked him over, and before Jordan had a chance to speak, he said, "You're not supposed to be back here."

He unbuttoned his tux jacket and headed down the narrow hallway. As he did, he saw Jordan out of the corner of his eye and knew that he was following.

When Derek got to the room where he and Dylan had been told they could freshen up, he pushed inside, hoping to find it full, but instead found it the complete opposite.

As the door opened and shut behind him, he knew Jordan was standing there and decided to hell with this. Why was he nervous? It had been three years since he'd seen the guy.

He hadn't called him. He didn't need him. But when he turned around and saw Jordan with his hands on his hips and an exasperated expression on his face, Derek sure as fuck wanted him.

"What are you doing here?" he demanded, as Jordan took a step forward.

"I've come to collect my date."

"*Your* date?" Derek asked, hearing the incredulity in his own tone as he looked around for the guy who had purchased him.

"Yes. I won you, after all. Now I get to take you on a date. So…do you have any place in particular you'd like to go?"

Derek crossed his arms over his chest. "With you? Nowhere. I'm not going on a date with you."

Jordan pursed his lips in a pout, and it galled Derek that he wanted to kiss it right off his mouth. "After all this time, you're still mad at me."

Fuck yes, he was. Not that he'd ever admit that. "Actually, I don't feel anything about you at all."

"Liar," Jordan said as he walked toward him.

"What do you want, Jordan?"

"Well, since I just paid a little over two thousand dollars for your time, how about we start with that."

Derek sighed. "This is insane, even for you."

Jordan laughed, clearly taking that as a compliment. "Oh, I didn't come here tonight with the knowledge that you were going to be up for sale. That was just a happy coincidence. But now that I'm here, I thought it was my duty to let you know how hot you look in that tux."

The guileless eyes Jordan aimed at him didn't fool Derek for a second. The guy was certifiable. They hadn't seen each other in years, yet the second Jordan flashed the right look his way, Derek felt himself wanting to fall back under his spell. Jordan was his fucking kryptonite.

"You paid that much money to tell me I look good in a suit? You shouldn't have bothered. My roommate told me for free."

Jordan's eyes narrowed and he shrugged. "*Hot* is what I believe I said. And I don't care who told you. They're not me. And we both know you like hearing it from my lips best."

Derek close to growled with frustration because, *fuck*, Jordan was right. Then, for the first time in three years, Jordan reached out and touched him. His fingertip grazed the line of his jaw, and before he could remove it, Derek captured Jordan's wrist and held it in place.

"Why?" he demanded again. "Why are you here?"

"I told you, it was a coincidence."

"One you couldn't let pass by. You just *had* to make sure that I saw you up close, huh? Is it a thrill to know that after all these years you still make my dick hard?"

Jordan shook his head. "No. I mean, it is a thrill. But you're wrong. It was the other way around. I wanted to see *you* up close. It's been so long, Derek. You don't call me anymore. And I never see you."

"So you paid two thousand dollars for the privilege? Jordan, I'm pretty easy to find for free."

"Yes, but you made it clear by staying away that you didn't want to be found."

"Did I?"

"Yes."

"Yeah, whatever…" Derek muttered.

"I just thought it would be nice to catch up. I don't know. We were friends too at one point, weren't we?"

Derek laughed, but the sound lacked any kind of joy. "Is that what you want now?" he asked, his voice lowering several octaves. "To be my friend?"

Jordan grimaced, and Derek wondered if the thought of being "just" friends felt as wrong to Jordan as it did to him.

"Has something changed that I don't know about?" Derek asked. "Because I'm sorry, I don't want to be your friend. And the last conversation we had, you told me that you had no desire to date anyone."

As the words left his mouth, Derek saw Jordan's cheeks flame, and he shifted his feet as though he were uncomfortable. The silence that then fell between them was like a dead weight, and as if a light bulb switched on inside of Derek's head, he shoved off the wall and pointed at Jordan.

"You're seeing someone," he said, and Jordan took a step back. Not surprising, considering any idiot could see Derek's temper had just been flipped the fuck on.

He advanced on Jordan, who retreated, and for the first time in their ever-changing relationship, Jordan looked nervous.

"I'm right, aren't I?"

Jordan tilted his chin up, defiant as always, and finally answered, "Maybe. I mean. Yes. Kind of."

When Jordan's back met the wall, Derek kept coming until he had him pinned against it and was now caging him in with a palm on either side of his head. Even after all this time, and with no real claim on the guy, the thought of someone other than himself with Jordan made Derek close to homicidal.

*It should've been me,* he thought, as he fumed down at Jordan. *But it never fucking is.*

"Did you really just pay that much money to tell me you're dating someone else?" Derek was aware that he sounded beyond pissed, but his tolerance for bullshit and etiquette had just run out.

"No, I just wanted to—"

Derek took Jordan's chin in his hand, effectively stopping his words, then he brushed their lips together and whispered, "Don't lie to me. You have never lied to me. Not even when it fucking hurt."

Jordan brought a hand up and encircled his wrist, and the expression that flashed in his eyes made Derek's breath get lodged in his throat. He looked torn.

"I paid that much money on impulse because I saw you and wanted to touch you. That's the truth. It's as simple as that."

"But you're dating someone else?" Derek asked one last time, and Jordan closed his eyes and nodded.

Derek's body trembled at the impact of that silent but final answer, and as he stood there looking down at the one man he'd always wanted but was forever out of his reach, he pressed a kiss to the corner of Jordan's mouth and said, "One of these days, we will get this right."

When Jordan's eyes opened and he stared up at him, Derek released his wrist and said, "But it's not going to be today."

And with that, Derek exited stage left.

# Chapter 16

*Four Years Later*

DEREK STOOD AT the front doors of Pearson's Total Fitness and couldn't wipe the smile off his face. He'd done it. He'd really gone and done it.

Today was the opening of his very own business. The gym he'd been dreaming about owning since he'd finished college, and today it was finally happening.

The red ribbon had been cut, the doors had parted, and the distinct sound of weight machines clinging and clanging as they were used could be heard. He couldn't believe that after all this time he'd finally achieved what he'd set out to do.

His staff were all smiles as they signed up client after client with their opening-month promotion, and Derek was relieved to be past the building portion of the project and into the running and enjoying aspect of his hard work.

He waved at Kelly, his front desk girl on the weekdays, and wove his way through the machines that lined the back mirror toward his office entrance. His office was an additional room he'd had built onto the back of the facility that faced the main strip of the beach.

After stepping out into the fresh air, he inhaled and tipped his face up into the sun. *Yeah,* this was what he'd been talking about. *Living the dream, baby.*

So he had debt he had to pay off, but at least it was his debt. He didn't mind working to pay back loans for a business he loved and would work his ass off to have succeed, and as he unlocked the door to the enclosed patio office, he smiled at his little corner of the world. He loved it there. It might not be an empire, but it was his. All of it. Well, his and the bank's, for now.

He headed for the windows and opened them up to let in the sea breeze before he walked around the small couch to his desk. Sitting behind it, he booted up his laptop to go through his email and saw one from Daniel Finley.

*Jesus,* it'd been a long time since he'd heard from Danny boy —last Christmas, he thought—but the sight of the name in bold staring back at him made Derek smile. He'd missed his friend. He clicked open the message and saw that it was fairly standard, nothing out of the ordinary. It basically updated him on Finn's life and mentioned that someday soon he'd get home and see everyone, and even though Derek knew Finn meant it, he had a feeling that it would be a cold day in hell before Daniel Finley ever set foot back in Sunset Cove. Unless, of course, the one who sent him away groveled, or asked him home. *Like that will ever happen.*

Derek took a moment and sent off a generic letter of his own explaining that everything was fine, home was pretty much the same, and he was single and living the high life. *Footloose and fancy free, Danny boy. Don't be a stranger...*yada yada yada.

It was sad writing that final line, though, because that was what they'd become—strangers. Derek often wondered if things would've been different if he'd made more of an effort to be open with Finn instead of keeping his problems to himself.

Maybe one day he'd be able to find out. Or maybe he wouldn't, and that would be one more relationship he could kiss the fuck goodbye.

No, he wasn't going to do that today. He wasn't going to think of the things he'd lost in his life. Well, namely the two things he'd lost. He was going to focus on the good, and the good was all that he'd accomplished.

Once he'd finished reading his personal mail, he opened the new website's inbox and scanned down the emails asking about group classes and rates until he came across one from Alan Pearson—his brother.

The subject read: *Derek?* And seeing it there in his inbox made him break out in a sweat. It had been a long time since he'd had to deal with Alan. In fact, he couldn't even remember the last time he'd seen his brother.

What the hell could he possibly want? And that had to be it. He had to *want* something, because never did anyone in the Pearson household reach out just to say hi.

He stared at the name for a good ten minutes and seriously considered hitting delete, but at the last minute clicked it open.

**Derek?**

**If this is Derek Pearson, call me. Dad's sick.**

**Alan**

DEREK MUST HAVE READ that one line several times over before he hit delete and stared at the trash bin icon. *Trash…how fitting.* His hand shook as it hovered over the mouse and he clenched his fist to stop the trembling.

*Fuck.* He hadn't thought about his father for years. What did he care if he was sick? He didn't. If anything, he'd pretty much declared the bastard dead the last time he'd raised a hand to him. But as Derek leaned back in his chair and thought about his brother's words, he wondered how long he could ignore them before they'd start eating away at him. How many nights would he lie in bed wondering what was wrong with the fucker and if he was dead or alive? Too many, and that was the sad truth right there.

*Damn it. Why today?* he thought, and scrubbed a hand over his face. Why, when he was finally going places, was he pulled up short and reminded of exactly where it was he came from?

He got to his feet, snatched up his cell phone, and walked over to the window he'd just been admiring. He hated that in less than ten words the one place that wasn't tainted by that bastard had just been infected. And that was exactly how it felt. The second he thought of him, or even let the asshole in through the cracks, all within reach was poisoned. It was one of the main reasons he'd moved out of Jordan's home all those years ago. To not taint what was good.

*Jordan...*

Derek glanced at his phone and saw his number in his contacts list. He shut his eyes and mind against the impulse to call a man he had no right calling, and instead dialed a number he'd all but erased from his head—his old home number.

He told himself he would wait two rings and then hang up. Unfortunately, the phone connected after one.

"Hello?"

Derek shut his eyes against the beautiful view, and then turned his back on it altogether. "Alan?"

There was a pause, as though his brother was trying to place his voice or who he might be, and then he asked, "Derek?"

"Yeah." He wasn't about to offer up more than that. Alan was lucky he was calling him at all.

"So that new gym, the fancy one, *is* yours..."

Derek's spine stiffened at the tone of Alan's words. He had a sneaking suspicion that his brother wasn't calling just to "inform" him of his father's ailing health, and with the next words that came out of his brother's mouth, Derek knew he was spot on.

"You must be doing pretty fucking good to be openin' up some gym down on the beach. Guess leaving your trash behind helped you out, huh?"

Derek ground his molars together and rubbed his fingers over his forehead. "What do you want, Alan? You didn't just email me to shoot the shit. You said he's sick. So what's wrong with him?"

Alan coughed, and Derek held the phone from his ear as he heard some shuffling and then the muffled sound of a television being turned down or off.

"I found him on the kitchen floor the other mornin'. And when they got him to the hospital they did a bunch of scans on him and it turns out he had pneumonia."

Derek waited for the sadness to hit, for something to trigger inside him that would make him feel for the old man. But nothing came.

"They told me he's got COPD. It's pretty advanced. He needs treatment he can't afford or he's just gonna get worse."

Derek's first instinct was to say, *So what?* But he managed to bite that back and instead ask, "And what do you want me to do about it? I'm not giving him any fucking money."

Alan coughed again, and Derek shook his head. He wouldn't be surprised if his brother was in the same boat, or pretty damn close.

"Insurance, Derek. Medical. He doesn't have any since he was laid off."

Derek fumed. The audacity of the guy. There was no way he was asking him what he thought he was. Was he?

"If you add him to yours, then he can get therapy. Some regular help—" and before Alan could say another word, Derek ended the call, throwing his phone on the couch like it'd just transformed into a grenade.

He couldn't fucking believe what had just come out of Alan's mouth. His entire body was vibrating with rage as he stood trapped in his office, looking for a way out.

*Christ.* He wanted to hit something. *Anything.* He had the urge to destroy and get the adrenaline racing through him out of his system. He looked to the door of his gym and thought about going in and seeing if a bag was free, but that wasn't what he really needed right then.

He paced back and forth, running an agitated hand through his hair, and wondered if he should skip out early and hit up a local bar. Maybe knocking back a bottle of bourbon would help numb the anger thrumming through him. But no, doing that made him just like them. He needed something else entirely.

He needed the one person who knew where he came from and everything he'd gone through.

He *needed* the one person who'd told him years ago that if he called, he would always answer.

And like a moth to a flame, Derek reached for the cell phone, pulled up his contacts, and dialed.

---

THAT EVENING, JORDAN was pouring himself a glass of Merlot as he got ready to relax in his tub after a long day at work. He'd had a jam-packed schedule this semester, and tonight was the first night in months he'd had completely to himself. Not only did he have nowhere to go, but he also had nothing to do.

*Thank God.*

He picked up his glass and walked down the hallway in his robe, determined to forget about everything in his head as soon as his tub was full, the lights were off, and his intergalactic bath bomb was working wonders on his body.

After adjusting the lights to a muted glow, he turned on the faucet and dropped the Lush bomb into the tub, then he slipped out of his robe and dipped his toe inside the fragrant water with a sigh.

*Yes…* This was exactly what he'd wanted.

He sank down into the water and stared out the window to the bright lights below.

God, he was tired.

Over the last couple of months he'd had to scale back on his charity work, letting his mother take the reigns, and he'd hired two new property managers for the apartment towers. Unless something else came along that he was passionate about, that was how it would stay. For right now, he wanted to focus solely on his teaching again. Maybe he would even offer up his services as a tutor this coming semester.

He took a sip of his wine and then shut his eyes as he let the warm water ease his body. It felt amazing. Almost better than—*Oh hell no*. His eyes popped open as the thought he'd been about to let slide into his mind was shoved firmly aside. The day he thought a bath was better than sex, he might as well be buried beneath six feet of dirt. But the truth was, it had been a while. A *long* while since he'd had really fantastic sex, maybe even before Stephan, and that was years ago…how depressing was *that*?

In his defense, though, without a steady someone in your life, it took a lot of effort to get laid. You had to dress up, hit the bars or clubs, and even then you didn't know if it would be fantastic. At best it would likely be average, so it wasn't his fault that everyone lately had been *ehh*.

*Wait…what? Ugh, what the hell is the matter with me?* He remembered a time when he couldn't wait to go out to a bar. *Maybe I'm getting old*, Jordan thought, and then shook his head. No, he wasn't old. He'd been bugging Brantley about going to Boyz just the other week, and, as usual, he'd refused. *So it's not my fault. It's Brantley's.* He was just exhausted, and that needed to change also.

He shut his eyes again, and as his mind drifted off to

nowhere in particular, he heard his cell phone ringing where he'd left it in the other room.

*No*, he told himself. *Do not get out and answer it. You can let the call go to voicemail and call whoever it is back…later.* So he let his eyes become heavy as the insistent ringing ceased and he finally dozed off.

When he awoke a little while later, Jordan shifted and screwed his nose up at the lukewarm water now lapping his body. Geez, how long had he been in there?

He'd only wanted to relax for a little while, and now he looked like a glittery prune thanks to the intergalactic bomb. He laughed at himself as he stepped out onto the mat and saw the glitter covering his body.

*Good God*, he should bathe in that before he went out clubbing next time. Because he had no doubt he'd be sparkling for the next few days. He toweled off and then grabbed his robe to slip back into it before heading through to his bedroom to check the time.

After picking up his phone, he swiped the screen and saw two things that shocked him. First, he'd been in the bath for nearly an hour and a half. Damn, no wonder he looked like an eighty-year-old. And second, the missed call from earlier was from *He-Man*.

*Derek?* Derek had called him? *What the…*

It had been a long time since he'd allowed himself to think about Derek Pearson, and Jordan had figured he'd moved on. Especially after the last time they'd seen each other and things hadn't gone so well. Actually, they'd gone horribly wrong. No surprise there, though. It seemed to be the way between the two of them.

But now here Derek was, calling him like he used to back when he'd been in school, and in trouble, and fuck…he hadn't answered.

Jordan sat his ass down on the bed and quickly hit the number, sending up a quick prayer that Derek was okay and that he would answer. Just when he thought it was hopeless and he would never know what Derek wanted, the call connected and Jordan's breath caught at the words he heard at the other end of the phone.

"You didn't answer."

---

DEREK HADN'T MEANT TO say that, but when he'd called earlier and Jordan hadn't picked up, he'd sat at his desk thinking those words on repeat.

*He didn't answer. Jordan didn't answer…*

That was a first.

But what was more surprising was how much worse that had felt than the years where they hadn't spoken at all. Jordan not answering had made it feel final. It had made Derek wonder if he'd moved on and decided that he wasn't worth answering for anymore.

"No," Jordan said, breaking through his thoughts. "I know I didn't answer. I was—"

"With your boyfriend?" Derek asked, and immediately hated himself for it. There was a long pause, one where a fucking pin dropping on carpet could likely be heard, and then Jordan said softly, "No. I don't have a boyfriend anymore. I was in the bath."

Derek shut his eyes as he lay on the couch in his office and imagined the huge whirlpool tub in Jordan's bathroom.

"Are you okay?"

As Jordan's voice drifted through the phone, Derek sighed. "Yeah. I just…" He paused and laid an arm across his eyes. "I just wanted to hear your voice."

He heard some rustling and thought it best that he not ask where Jordan was, because if he said "bed," Derek knew his brain would remind him of the last time he'd been in that bed, years ago.

"Do you want to talk about it?" Jordan asked, and Derek's mouth split into a tight smile at the fact that even after all this time, Jordan was still where he'd always been. One phone call away, ready to talk him out of whatever mood he was in.

"Not really."

"Okay," Jordan said, remarkably good-natured for someone Derek had yelled at the last time they'd seen one another. "Then why don't you tell me what you're wearing?"

Derek started laughing at that and felt his worries lift from his shoulders, as they always did with Jordan.

"I'm serious," Jordan said, feigning offense.

"I'm sure that you are, Devaney."

"I am. I haven't seen you for so long I've forgotten what you look like."

Derek lowered his arm down to his chest and swallowed, debating his next words. Then he decided *what the fuck*, and said what he really wanted more than anything in the world. "Then maybe you should see me."

The silence between them was rife with tension before Jordan said, "Maybe I should."

Derek sat up on his couch, and tried not to read too much into Jordan's words. Then he asked, "Are you serious?"

"Derek?"

"Yeah?"

"I think today is the day…"

As his words from the auction a few years back hung between them, Derek wondered if it was really going to be that simple. They'd been falling together, crashing into one another, since the first day they'd met. Why should now be any different?

"As in?" he asked, wanting clarification.

"As in…let's take it slow. One day at a time, and see where it goes. If that's something you'd want."

Derek wanted to ask what it was about him that made Jordan want to take it slow when usually he was so damn confident. But not wanting him to change his mind, Derek kept his mouth shut. There was obviously a reason, and sooner or later he would find out what it was. "Okay."

"Okay?"

"Yes. Okay. Now what?"

Blood rushed around his ears as he waited for whatever Jordan would say next, and when he whispered, "Come to me," Derek was hanging up the phone and heading to his Jeep as quick as his feet would carry him.

# Chapter 17

*Six Months Later*

"CAN YOU BELIEVE that Brantley and Daniel are back together?" Jordan asked, as he unbuttoned his shirt and tossed it over the end of his bed. "I'm still trying to catch up with the fact that Daniel is even back in town, and now he's shacking up with Brantley and running the poor guy through the wringer."

"You're such a gossip," Derek said, laughing from where he was sitting on the opposite corner of his mattress unlacing his boots. Jordan stopped in front of him with his hands on his hips and waited for him to look up, and when he did, Derek asked, "What?"

"*What?*" Jordan demanded, stepping between Derek's spread legs. "Don't give me that, mister. You're already in trouble for keeping the fact that Daniel was back a secret from me."

"Hey, you didn't tell me that Brantley had sent him a love note in the first place, so I think we're even. Plus, I didn't *know* he was coming back until the night before he arrived. His sister was talking to a friend down at the store and I overheard her.

Trust me when I say that Danny boy was shocked as hell when I turned up at the airport to get him."

Jordan fingered the collar of Derek's black polo shirt and frowned. "What do you think's going on over there?"

Derek ran his hands up the outsides of Jordan's legs to his waist, and then pulled him closer. "You're nosy. And bossy. And if you need me to tell you what they're doing…"

"Not *that*, smartass," Jordan said, swatting at Derek's roaming hands. "I mean, do you think Daniel's going to stay? *Ugh*, I hate the idea of him trampling all over poor Brantley's heart again."

Derek leaned back and raised an eyebrow at him.

"What?"

"Poor *Brantley's* heart? Have you forgotten that Hayes is the one who sent him away?"

"Well, no. But—"

Derek shook his head and sat up, tugging him down onto his lap. Jordan had to either fall over the top of him or straddle his thighs. So he went with option two, placing a knee on either side of Derek's hips and looping his arms around his neck.

"Nope," Derek said, shaking his head. "There is no *but* in the scenario. Brantley sent him away, Finn went, and now they're just going to have to work it out like big boys."

Jordan grinned as Derek stroked his fingers down his spine. "Oh? And how do big boys work things out?"

"Like I said before. If you need me to tell you…"

Jordan gasped as Derek got to his feet with him wrapped around his body in an amazing display of strength, and then laughed uproariously when they tumbled onto the bed.

As they rolled across the mattress, mouths met and tongues dueled while Derek grappled with his shirt, pulling it over his head and throwing it to the floor.

It was always like this with them. Fast and furious. They were both extremely busy in their day-to-day lives, but when the night rolled around and they came together, it just worked. Just as they'd always known it would—and right now was no different.

It had been six months since they'd fallen back into Jordan's bed, and that was pretty much where they ended up whenever they got together. It wasn't that they'd consciously decided to focus only on the physical aspect of their relationship. It just seemed to be the way things went whenever they were around one another. Neither of them had mentioned labels or changing anything about the present situation, so when Derek lowered his head, locked eyes with him, and said, clearly and without one ounce of subterfuge, "I love you," Jordan froze like a deer in headlights.

---

DEREK STARED DOWN into a face he knew as well as his own, and the panic that flashed into Jordan's wide eyes had him rearing back and shifting to his knees.

The man lying on his back looking up at him had lost all the joy that had been stamped over his face a second ago, and Derek's words, his *I love you*, had brought a look of alarm forward to take its place.

As Derek knelt there waiting for some kind of response, Jordan remained paralyzed, as though he were in a state of shock, and with every silent second that passed, Derek felt more and more like a fucking idiot.

How could he have been so damn stupid? To think that after all this time Jordan would finally be ready to admit what it was between them. That he would finally realize that what they had was something people searched their entire lives for and never found.

*But no*, when he'd finally said it, when he'd finally felt the moment was right and told this man he'd known for close to a decade that he loved him, Jordan, the man with an answer for everything, had turned fucking mute.

Derek climbed off the bed and bent down to pick up his shirt. He then straightened and aimed a glare in Jordan's direction as his embarrassment morphed to anger.

"Nothing to say to that, huh? Really?"

Jordan sat up and opened and shut his mouth as though trying to find words, but when nothing came he clamped his lips together and Derek saw his Adam's apple move as he swallowed.

*Wow.*

He grabbed his boots off the floor as Jordan scrambled to stand, but Derek pinned him to the bed with a look that said *don't fucking bother*, and before Jordan could get dressed and follow, Derek was in the elevator and down to the ground floor.

---

THE FOLLOWING NIGHT, Jordan climbed out of the Uber he'd taken to Boyz and checked his phone a final time before he shoved it into his front pocket. Still nothing from Derek.

*Shit.*

He'd been calling him since the night before, and every time he'd gotten his voicemail he'd left yet another "We need to talk" message. He knew he was starting to sound like a robot, but there was no way he was about to have this conversation with a voicemail inbox, where everything he said could be played back on repeat.

So sue him, he didn't like someone having that much proof over him when he was groveling. And he knew when Derek did finally answer, he would be doing some heavy-duty groveling.

But that would now have to wait until tomorrow. Brantley had called him earlier this morning and wanted to catch up with him for brunch. And after putting on an Academy Award-worthy performance, Jordan had somehow agreed to meet up with him and Daniel tonight at Boyz.

Not exactly what he'd had in mind for the evening. The

problem was, if he'd refused, Brantley would've wanted to know why, and since he still hadn't gotten around to telling him that he was sleeping with Derek, he figured he'd keep that little gem to himself until whatever this night at Boyz was was over.

He took a deep breath and shook his hands by his side. *Just go inside, dance for a few hours, and then leave,* he told himself as he continued down the side of the brick building.

He was all set to plaster a smile on his face and maybe drink a few too many shots when he rounded the corner and right there, directly in front of him, was Derek. And not just Derek standing by himself, which would've been awkward enough, considering the circumstances. But Derek, who was leaning against the wall with some twink draped all over his arm like he was an accessory for the night, and hell, maybe he was.

*Unfuckingbelievable.* Jordan fumed as his eyes took in the scene in front of him. The man who, just last night, had pressed him into a mattress and told him he loved him was decked out like a fucking sex god in boots, black pants, and a green vest, and Jordan could see every tattoo he'd licked, sucked, *and yes,* come all over.

He watched as the brunette, who was draped all over Derek, ran a hand up his arm, and Jordan felt his head come close to exploding.

Grinding his teeth together, he stormed over to where Derek was and situated himself so he was directly in his eye line. When the guy stroking Derek's arm moved slightly to the left and Derek's eyes found Jordan's, he had the good grace to look shocked as he pushed off the wall and straightened.

*Yeah, busted,* Jordan thought as he cut his eyes to the brunette now glaring at him over his shoulder. *Oh, honey, don't even try,* he wanted to tell the guy. *Your hands might be all over him, but he's wishing they were mine.*

Jordan could feel his annoyance heating his cheeks as he said to the oblivious man between them, "Scram."

"Fuck off," the guy told him, and Jordan raised an eyebrow

at Derek, telling him, in no uncertain terms, *You get rid of him or I will.*

Derek sighed and leaned down to place his lips by the guy's ear, but as he spoke into it he kept his eyes glued to Jordan's. His version of a fuck you, no doubt.

Once he finished saying whatever the hell he'd said, the guy giggled, tossed a look in Jordan's direction, and then stepped away from them. When he was out of earshot, Jordan took a step forward and asked the most important question first: "Did your fucking phone break last night?"

"No."

"So you *are* just being a dick and not answering my calls."

Derek gave him an *eat shit* smile and said, "How's that feel, Jordan? When someone doesn't answer you?"

*Stay calm,* he told himself. Brantley and Daniel were no doubt about to arrive, and he wasn't sure how he would ever explain this. "Are you serious right now?" he said. "You want to talk about that here? Now? I'm assuming you're here because Daniel asked you."

"Gold star for the genius of the bunch," Derek said as he crossed his arms and glared. *Jesus,* he was angry. Jordan couldn't remember ever seeing Derek this mad before. This…this was a whole new level of pissed. He was vibrating with rage.

"Look. I can see that I hurt you—"

"Oh you can, can you? How fucking astute of you, Jordan. Look, I don't want to talk to you right now. So how about we agree to stay the hell out of each other's way tonight."

Jordan's mouth parted in shock at the low blow, and he ground his teeth together, willing himself to keep his own temper in check. "Fine."

"Fine."

He ordered himself to turn the hell around and walk away from Derek before he did or said something he'd regret, and as he waited further down the line he caught the twink's eye as he gave an *I won* smirk, and headed back to claim his prize.

If Jordan hadn't been so annoyed at himself he might've wished the guy good luck, because with the mood Derek was in there was no chance in hell of him getting out of it anytime soon. As it was, Jordan was too pissed for even a snarky comment.

As he looked out at the street, he saw Brantley and Daniel climb out of a car, and their ridiculously wide smiles made him want to fucking scream at the situation he was now in for the rest of the night.

Well, no one had ever accused him of holding back.

Jordan marched forward to give Brantley a piece of his mind regarding putting him in the same breathing space as the barbarian behind him, and when he'd finished his spectacularly idiotic tantrum he stamped his foot, spun on his heel, and headed inside to track down a drink and forget about the brunette who was back to adorning Derek Pearson's arm.

---

DEREK SCANNED THE crowd of Boyz as he stepped through the doors after much persuasion from Finn. He'd decided to head inside with him and at least get one drink for old times' sake.

One drink, and then he was out. But after Finn had spotted Brantley on the dance floor and they'd both vanished, of course he'd searched out and found Jordan.

He made his way through the crowd and over to where Jordan was standing by the tall tables off to the side of the bar. He had a drink in his hand and an irritated expression on his face, and when he spotted Derek heading in his direction, he gave him a look that screamed, *Stay away from me.*

"I hope that's your first," he shouted so Jordan would hear him.

"It's my second, and last time I checked, I don't answer to you."

"Maybe that's the problem." Derek plucked the drink out of Jordan's hand and placed it on the table. "I've seen you after one too many of these. You need a fucking keeper. Especially dressed as you are. Could your pants be any fucking tighter, Jordan?"

"Do you mind?" Jordan protested.

"Yeah, I do, actually."

Jordan aimed a fulminating glare at him and looked as though he wanted to kick him in the balls. "You made it quite clear outside that you didn't want to talk to me."

Derek scoffed. "Really? That's what you're going with? Out of all that's been said over the last two days." Derek leaned down so his mouth was by Jordan's ear. "I used to think you were so brave, Professor Devaney. The man who wears what he wants and says whatever he's thinking. But in answer to what *I* said to you last night…in answer to something *so* important, you have nothing to say. You *still* have nothing to say. How disappointing that the man I admired so much turned out to be such a fucking coward."

Jordan turned his head, his expression close to murderous, and Derek asked, "Tell me something—do you want to fuck me or kill me right now?"

If smoke could've come out of Jordan's ears it would've, as he replied, "Neither."

Derek let his eyes shift to Jordan's lips and said, "Liar. When you feel like admitting the truth, maybe I'll return one of your calls."

Jordan brushed past him hard enough that their shoulders connected, and as he stormed out the door, Derek turned and watched him go.

# PRESENT

*"Out of the doubt that fills my mind*
*I somehow find*
*You and I collide."*

~ Collide, Howie Day

# Chapter 18

*IT TOOK HIM less than ten minutes to pull into the underground parking garage of the Palisades and take the elevator up to where his drug of choice waited for him. He glanced up into the camera in the corner of his metallic confines and stared boldly into the face of the one who was waiting at the other end of this ride.*

Yeah, *he was about to fall off the fucking wagon big time. Was about to slide back into the one place he promised himself he wouldn't go again. Yet as the elevator came to a halt and the doors opened, there was no denying this was exactly what he wanted.*

*"I have thirty minutes," were the words that greeted him.*

*Derek walked off the elevator and over to the naked man waiting for him. He took the haughty chin between his thumb and forefinger and promised in a voice thick with arousal, "I only need ten. Take me to your room, Jordan. Time's a wasting."*

AS THEIR WORDS echoed around the open living room, Derek devoured the supple skin of Jordan's back as he turned and walked, unapologetically naked, across his tiled floor toward his bedroom.

*Fuck*, he knew he shouldn't be there, especially since this was the first time he'd seen Jordan since that horrible night at Boyz two months ago. But after speaking to his brother yet again about helping out his piece of shit dad, and then going to welcome Finn back to Sunset Cove only to find him and Brantley all over each other, Derek hadn't been able to stop himself from reaching for the phone and the one person who *ever* made any sense in his life.

So much for staying strong and letting Jordan call him. *What a crock of shit.*

Jordan's penthouse was as familiar to Derek as his own apartment, and with every step he took, his cock throbbed a little harder in anticipation. Following Jordan's lead, he kicked off his flip-flops and stepped over the threshold into a room he'd seen in many different capacities. Today, though, he was there for one particular reason, and the naked man heading toward his bedside table knew it.

Once Jordan had tossed a condom and lube on the mattress, he strolled back around the end of the bed and tilted his head so he was looking directly up at him. Derek's chest rose and fell as he waited for whatever Jordan would do next.

It sucked to know that this man was exactly who he needed, even as his brain was calling him a fucking moron for being back there.

Jordan's knowing eyes took his measure, and just as Derek knew he would, Jordan took control. "Get on your knees," he told him, and Derek went to them with no questions asked.

Still dressed in his shorts and tank top, Derek was aware he was several steps behind the man who was about to drive him insane. But that was why he was there, to lose his damn mind, and no one other than Jordan had ever come close to being able to pull him out of his jacked-up headspace when he was stuck there, just as he was now.

He aimed his eyes up at Jordan, and there was no doubt in his mind as to why he was the only one who was able to offer solace while at the same time unravel him. It was the very reason Derek had walked away—he loved him.

"Well, you sure know how to hold a grudge," Jordan said, as he gently stroked the back of his index finger down the line of Derek's jaw. When he reached his chin, he took it between his thumb and forefinger, holding Derek in place as he asked, "What made you change your mind?"

Derek tried to pull his head back, but Jordan held him still.

"I thought you only had thirty minutes," Derek reminded him.

"And you said you only needed ten. That leaves me twenty to listen to your explanation." Jordan moved then so his lips were by his ear and told him, "Start talking, Derek, or you aren't going to get what you want."

"I'm not going to get *that* anyway," he said, and turned his head so he could nip at Jordan's plump lower lip. As he caught and sucked it into his mouth, he reveled in the way that Jordan's pupils dilated and his breath caught. It was intoxicating to be under Jordan's spell again. But to know that he had the power to make Jordan stumble ramped that high up even more.

He brought a hand up to touch Jordan's face, but the guy was lightning quick, wrapping his fingers around Derek's wrist and holding him off.

"Uh uh…talk first."

"Jordan," he said.

"Derek…" Jordan batted his lashes, and Derek shut his eyes, knowing it was the only way to stop himself from begging.

Most days he was convinced that Jordan was the devil. A beautiful seduction put in his path to offer salvation at the cost of one thing—his soul. It was those days that Derek told himself he should steer clear, and he'd finally managed two full months without craving him in some fucking way.

But it was times like this, when Jordan was touching him,

that made him feel like they were the only ones on the entire planet. That was when he wanted to shut his eyes, lie down, and surrender everything to him.

"Where have you been these past couple of months?" Jordan whispered.

"Why?" Derek asked. "Do you actually care?"

"Of course I care. God."

"Well, how should I know, Jordan? You were pretty clear on the subject the last time I was here."

Jordan dropped his wrist as if it had turned to flame. "That's not fair. You blindsided me and you know it. Now take off your shirt."

Derek wanted to tell him to go fuck himself, but he figured that would be a waste of the delicious erection he was staring at. So instead, he reached for his top and drew it over his head. Once it was free, he tossed it aside and went for the zipper of his shorts.

"Are we ever going to be able to *talk* about this, Derek?"

Derek shoved his shorts down to his knees and took hold of his painfully erect cock. He stroked it as Jordan took a step toward him, and when his eyes fell to what he was doing, Derek answered, "We might. But it's not going to be now, and it certainly won't be because *you* demand it. I'll talk when I feel like talking."

Before Jordan could anticipate the move, Derek lunged for him and grabbed his wrist, tugging him forward. Jordan speared his fingers into his hair for balance, then those same fingers twisted and yanked his head back.

"Getting ahead of yourself, aren't you? I didn't say you could touch me."

Uncaring of Jordan's admonishment, Derek brought his other hand around to grab Jordan's ass, and then he was moving to his feet, because while they would both get off on Jordan fucking him through a mattress, Derek sure as hell planned to make him work for it first.

"I don't remember *asking* for your permission."

He hoisted Jordan up his body and felt the sharp bite of his teeth as Jordan sank them into his jaw. The guy wound his arms and legs around him like a fucking vine, then used his body as an anchor as he rolled his hips against Derek's naked abdomen.

"Tell me where you went," Jordan demanded again, nibbling on his earlobe as Derek walked around to the side of the bed.

"No."

Jordan's mouth opened as if he was about to say something more, but Derek cut him off. "Either let go of me or you're gonna end up on your back, and we both know you hate that position."

"In all fairness," Jordan said, "I hate *fucking* while in that position, if we're going to get technical about it. *You* in that position, however, I enjoy very much."

Derek felt his balls tighten at the reminder of the many times he'd had this man inside him, but he wasn't about to cave, so he went with it. "Fine. Have it your way."

With Jordan wrapped around him, Derek fell to the mattress, his weight holding Jordan beneath him until— "Ouch. *Motherfucker.*"

He pushed up on his hands and glared at Jordan, who bared his teeth, the same ones that had just bitten his nipple, in a full-on hellcat grin. Before he could accuse Jordan of being a dirty fighter, he rolled out from under him and Derek gave up. He didn't have it in him to fight this today. Jordan was too sleek and too damn quick, and hell, he wanted him too bad.

He lowered down to his stomach and grunted at the sublime feeling of the cool sheets against his eager cock. When the mattress shifted, he figured the slick glide of lube would be applied next, but instead, the bed dipped a second time, and then there was nothing.

Derek ground his teeth together, fighting back a shout of

frustration as silence descended on the room. He then rolled to his back to search the space for Jordan.

Like a king watching over all he surveyed, he was seated on the plush chaise lounge, which must've been a recent purchase for the elaborate space, with his hands clasped behind his head, his tanned legs crossed at the ankles, and an erection that was primed and ready to fuck.

But looks could be deceiving. So very, *very*, deceiving. As was the case with them.

"What the hell are you doing?" Derek finally asked, even though it was pretty damn obvious. Jordan now had a firm grip of his dick and was leisurely stroking himself while Derek scowled at him.

"I believe they call it…wait…yes, masturbation. I know you're familiar with the term."

*Damn know-it-all,* Derek thought, as he collapsed back onto the bed. He reached down to his own agitated flesh and pressed his palm to it. He needed some friction there, and fast.

"I've missed you, Derek."

"You mean you've missed fucking me," he snapped back. "Because that's all we used to do."

"No. I missed *you*," Jordan said, then sighed. "Why do you always have to be so pigheaded?"

"Me?" Derek asked as he jackknifed up in the bed. His legs now hung over the sides, and he noticed that Jordan had moved from his casual position to sitting on the edge of the couch. "You're the one who freaks out at the first sign of me *ever* wanting more than some scandalous affair with you."

That had Jordan on his feet in a flash. "That's not true. I was sticking to what we agreed to. To take things one day at a time. You changed the terms. Not me."

"Yeah, how dare I," Derek said, as he walked over to where Jordan stood. "I've been thinking about it a lot lately, and I think you get off on sneaking around."

"Fuck you."

"You know what," Derek said as he turned around and grabbed his shorts off the floor. He pulled them on and then reached for his tank. Once that was over his head, he stormed back to Jordan and shook his head. "I've changed my mind. I don't even want *that* now."

The fiery expression that lit Jordan's eyes told Derek he was about two seconds away from getting a piece of his mind.

"Correct me if I'm wrong, but you're the one who called me, Derek."

How Jordan managed to dress someone down in such a snooty tone while stark naked would always be a mystery to Derek. The guy had no shame about his body. He'd once mentioned wanting to be a nudist, and honestly, Derek could totally see it.

"You're right. I did. My bad."

Turning on his heel, he marched out of Jordan's room and headed toward his only means of escape. The elevator.

*I'm such an idiot,* he thought with disgust. *What was I thinking coming to him?* But he knew the answer to that—he loved him. He would always want to go to him. The only problem was that Jordan didn't return the feeling. Or, more likely, he didn't want to *admit* that he did.

*And he has the nerve to call* me *pigheaded.*

Derek jabbed the button of the elevator and stormed inside, ready to get the fuck out of there. But when he turned and saw Jordan, now wrapped in a robe, standing with his arm holding the door back, he sighed.

*Here we go,* Derek thought. *Round two, anyone?*

---

FULLY CLOTHED, DEREK looked just as he had earlier when he'd arrived. Only this time, instead of arousal heating his eyes, rage had taken its place.

Not having a clue what to say but knowing he needed to say

something fast, Jordan wondered when their relationship had gone from easy and sexy to complicated and hard.

"Let go of the door, Jordan. I'm done," Derek announced, his tone defiant and his stance full of conviction, as if daring Jordan to argue. Usually Jordan would respect that and let him go, but not this time. He'd been waiting for two entire months to hear from Derek after he'd dropped his little bombshell, and he'd be damned if he let him go without finding out where the hell he'd vanished to since then.

"Oh, *you're* done, are you?" he asked, and took a step in Derek's direction. Jordan hit the stop button on the interior panel of the elevator and then continued moving forward. "Well, that's too bad. Because I'm not. You want to hash this out, then we'll hash it out."

He could see Derek's cheek tick and knew he was holding back from saying what he really wanted. Probably something along the lines of *Go fuck yourself.* But there was no way he was going to let Derek leave believing the bullshit he'd just spewed out of his mouth. He'd had time to think over these past couple of months too. "I want to talk to you."

"Tough shit," Derek fired back. "Time's up, Jordan. It's too late."

"Too late? You've been *gone,*" Jordan shouted, finally losing his temper with a punctuating stomp of his foot. He could feel the blood rushing to his face as he glowered up at the obstinate man, *and Jesus,* he was perfection.

Derek's blue eyes were locked with his, and he looked like he wanted to strangle Jordan with his bare hands, but never had anyone fit him so damn well. "You have to understand where I was coming from. One day we were—"

"Fuck buddies?" Derek supplied with an arched brow.

"Yes. And you were fine with that, from what I recall."

"I was," Derek agreed, and took a step forward of his own so that they were toe to toe. "But I changed. Maybe I grew up and you didn't? I don't fucking know. But I want more, Jordan.

And when I told you that, when I *told* you that I loved you. Do you remember what you said to me?"

Jordan winced, and Derek nodded. "Exactly. You didn't say a goddamn thing. You looked at me like I'd told you we should get married and have ten kids. So excuse me if I got a little pissed off and didn't want to see your face."

"Pissed off?" Jordan said. "You went to a club the next night and hooked up with someone right in front of me."

"That wasn't intentional. I didn't know you were invited. Plus, I asked you once we got inside if anything had changed, and again—nothing. So what the fuck does it matter to you if I hooked up with him or not? Jealous?"

Jordan poked a finger in Derek's chest as he narrowed his eyes at him. "If I thought for one second you went home with that guy, I wouldn't have answered my phone today."

Derek shook his head and gave a humorless laugh. "Bullshit. You'll answer my calls as long as I keep dialing, and just like the fucking addict I am, I'll never stop calling you."

*Wow*… It wasn't often that he was rendered speechless, but in that moment he had nothing. Jordan wanted to deny Derek's words, to tell him that he was wrong. But he was right.

Whenever Derek's name and number flashed up on his screen, it was like his next fix was delivered straight to his veins. A high he couldn't shake because Derek needed him. He wanted him. But having it reduced to that? Having it labeled in such a way as if it were a bad thing made it feel cheap and…sleazy.

Jordan brought a hand to his mouth and rubbed his fingers over his lips, trying for patience, and then he raised his eyes to Derek's stormy ones. "So, just so I'm clear and I don't misunderstand the next time I see some random guy all over you. You're breaking up with me?"

"Breaking up with you? That would imply that we were together in the first place. Finn and Brantley, they're together.

They go to bed together, they wake up together. They go on dates in public *together*. We don't. We fuck."

"Not *anymore*, apparently."

"Apparently," Derek agreed in a tone that grated on Jordan's last nerve.

He had just about had it. He could feel the angry heat crawling up his neck, and put his hands on his hips, ready to do battle since that was clearly what Derek wanted.

"Be careful, Derek. You're showing signs of being a total asshole."

"Well, if anyone would know what one of those looked like—"

"My, my, you *are* in a particularly caustic mood today, aren't you?"

Derek shook his head but didn't respond, obviously done with the conversation.

*Damn him for being impossibly sexy*, Jordan thought, and in the back of his mind a voice was saying, *Let him go. If he wants to go, then let him go.*

He took a step back, out of the elevator, and wondered if this was it. If this was how they would truly end after everything they'd been through.

As the heavy metal door began to close, Jordan couldn't let him go without asking, "So, this is how it ends? How *we* end? This is what you want?"

Derek's shoulders stiffened and his eyes blazed. "You are so clueless for a man who is supposed to be so fucking intelligent. You know that?"

Jordan flinched at the vehemence in Derek's tone as he released the door and let him go. Nothing he'd said or done tonight was right, and the flame that burned hot and furious between them was finally threatening to consume them. So maybe it was time to put out the fire before it raged out of control.

# Chapter 19

THE NEXT MORNING, Jordan shoved open his car door and squinted at the sun beaming down at him. His head was killing him, but he couldn't blame anyone for that except himself. Once Derek had left, he'd hit his liquor cabinet and wasn't really proud of the fact he was turning up to class today hungover.

Shoving his sunglasses up his nose, he bent at the waist to check himself out in the side mirror and was mortified by what he saw reflected back at him. *Ugh,* it was worse than he thought. He used the palm of his hand to try and smooth down the right side of his hair that was sticking out at all kinds of odd angles. But after two minutes of unsuccessfully trying to tame it, he huffed out a sigh of defeat and straightened.

*Oh, just quit while you're ahead, Jordan,* he told himself, and ran his fingers through it instead, hoping the unruly strands would fall in some kind of way that made him look fabulous instead of fugly.

With his head down and his brain protesting at actually having to make his legs move, he headed across the east lawn and inside to his first class. When he reached his room, he spotted Brantley standing by his door and frowned.

Happy and in love was so *not* what his digestion called for this morning.

"Okay, that face doesn't look happy," Brantley said as Jordan got closer. "Tell me, do you ever wake up in a good mood?"

As Jordan came to a standstill opposite his friend, he glanced at his watch then back at Brantley. "No. And especially not when I have to be up early enough to be here at eight on a Monday morning. So run along. I'm already late—"

"Something unusual for you."

"*And*," he continued, as if Brantley hadn't spoken, "your overenthusiasm is not appreciated or wanted this morning. Please go and be put together elsewhere."

"Rough night? What if I brought coffee?" Brantley asked, as he flashed a charming smile and held out a venti cup.

Jordan eyed the caffeine bribe and pursed his lips. Something was going on. When Brantley was waiting in front of his classroom this early armed with coffee, something was always going on. But *what*, was the question.

He reached for the cup, and as his fingers came close to slipping around the top of it, Brantley snatched it back and that smile of his turned smug.

"Okay." Jordan sighed, placing a hand on his hip. "What do you want?"

"What makes you think I want something?"

"Well, for one, you're holding my coffee ransom." He paused, and then he asked, "Peppermint mocha?"

"Of course."

"Exactly. That's just cruel. You know I'll do just about anything for one of those. Give it to me, Hayes."

"No. No," Brantley said. "First things first."

"I knew it," Jordan said, pointing. "I knew you wanted something."

"Maybe, but let's face it, you aren't your most congenial in the mornings, so I have to use what I can to my advantage. And this morning I'm kind of glad I came armed."

"Oh for God's sake, spit it out. I'm already going to be walking into a room full of zombies. You think it will do them any good if their teacher turns up the same way?"

"*When* he turns up."

"You're hilarious this morning. Married life must be nice."

Brantley chuckled, but quickly said, "We're not married."

*Might as well be,* Jordan thought, and remembered how happy Brantley had been when he'd returned from chasing down Daniel Finley in Chicago, and said he was moving back to Sunset Cove. The guy hadn't stopped smiling for two months straight, and now they were living together, picking out china patterns, and no doubt planning a wedding on the beachfront.

"Mhmm. Are you sure about that? Living it up on the beach in your little love shack with your boy toy." Jordan whistled. "Some have all the luck."

"Actually, that's what I'm here about."

Jordan really didn't want to stand out there talking about happily-ever-afters when the one person who usually gave him his had told him to fuck off the night before. So stepping around Brantley, he placed a hand on the door handle and said, "Aww, thanks for thinking of me. You and Daniel *are* an enticing offer, but I tried being a third once and it wasn't for me. I like to be the main attraction." He added a wink to keep any questions about his surly mood at bay, and it worked. Brantley laughed.

"As thrilled as I am to know *that* piece of information, I'm here to invite you to a kind of housewarming for Finn on Saturday night."

"A housewarming? He's been here for two months."

"I know. But he's finally settled in, his stuff has arrived, and it feels like the right time to welcome him properly."

Jordan shrugged the leather strap of his bag up his arm. "And..." he prompted when Brantley stood there silently, as if trying to choose his next words carefully.

"Well, I was just going to have a small dinner party and I wanted to invite our two closest friends. I'm hoping that we can all start to—"

"Stop. Right. There," Jordan said, shaking his head, knowing exactly where this was going. While he would love nothing more than to be able to sit down and eat a peaceful meal with Brantley, Daniel, and Derek, considering the only time they'd all been in the same vicinity he and Derek had been in a down-and-dirty war with one another, he doubted the likelihood of such an event ever actually taking place. Hell freezing over seemed more likely.

"Come *on*, Jordan," Brantley pleaded. "This is ridiculous. What happened between you two? Daniel called him about Saturday, but as soon as he mentioned you he said Derek got in a foul mood."

*Ass. Serves him right. He ended things with me, not the other way around.*

If Derek had just been patient and given him some time to adjust to the idea that Jordan loved him, then the two of them could be working this out together instead of— *Woah. Wait a minute. Did I really just admit that I…?*

Jordan looked up at his friend and knew the panic he was feeling must be evident on his face, because Brantley reached out a hand and asked, "Are you okay?"

*No. No, I'm not okay.* "I'm fine," Jordan said, and even to his own ears his voice sounded uncertain.

"Are you sure? No offense, but you look terrible."

*God, what have I done?* Jordan thought, as he remembered all the horrible things he'd said the night before. *Shit.* He needed to call Derek, but he had class. All damn day.

*Great,* as if he'd be able to concentrate on anything now other than tracking the guy down and…and… "Brantley?"

"Yes?"

Jordan knew he was about to sound like a goddamn nutcase, but… "Remember when you raced after Finn and told him how pathetic you were without him? How did you know?"

Brantley's eyes widened in surprise, but he didn't ask questions. He just grinned a smug-ass grin, as if Jordan had just told him something he already knew. "If you're asking me that, then you already know." And he was right.

*Oh my God. Brantley is right.*

He *did* know. And somewhere in the back of his mind, Jordan had always known. From the first time they'd met to the night he'd found Derek broken and bloodied. Yes, they'd never labeled it. Probably because the both of them were too scared to ruin a good thing, but when Derek had finally been brave enough to bring it up with him, Jordan had panicked. There was no other way to describe it. He'd had no clue what to say and royally fucked everything up—just like he had last night.

*Oh God. Oh* God.

He needed to fix this. And he would. Somehow.

Jordan grabbed Brantley's arm and gripped it tightly. "I'll be there Saturday. Text me the details." When Brantley's brow rose and his mouth opened to respond, Jordan plucked the coffee out of his hand and said, "Thanks for this. You're a genius."

Brantley laughed. "I didn't do anything."

"Right, well, don't worry. I hear being a genius these days doesn't mean you're any smarter than all those around you. Set two extra places for Saturday. I'll be there. *With* a date."

---

DEREK GOT HOME a little after eight thirty, tossed his keys on the kitchen counter, and made a beeline for the fridge. He needed a beer. Hell, maybe two at this stage.

His day had been busy and long. They were in the middle of adding a sauna to the showers down at the gym, and today there had been one problem after another. Though, he had to admit, he didn't mind standing in a room full of hot, sweaty men as they worked through the issues with the plumbing. They'd estimated the new piping they had to order would set them back about a week with the deadline. Though it wasn't ideal, it was manageable, and Derek figured in the end the payoff would be worth it.

On the plus side, he hadn't had time to think about a certain someone who had a bad habit of always being in his head, and he also didn't have time to think about the other huge problem in his life.

His fucking father.

He'd conveniently pushed him aside in the hope that the longer he ignored the issue there was a chance that Alan would stop leaving messages on his phone. But when he'd looked on his way home this afternoon, there'd been two new messages from his brother.

He twirled the bottle opener around his finger as he turned, ready to head for the living room, and that was when he spotted a huge bouquet of flowers in the center of the kitchen table.

*Okay…* Did someone die he didn't know about?

"Hey, Prescott?" he called out. He waited to see if his roommate was home, and when he spotted him walking down the hall with his headphones around his neck and a grin on his face, Derek popped the top off his beer and aimed it toward the flowers.

"What's the deal, man? You trying to brighten the place up a bit?"

Dylan flipped him off and then walked into the kitchen to grab some chips out of one of the top cabinets.

"Negative. They were on the doorstep when my taxi dropped me off this afternoon. Came in a fancy vase and everything." He chuckled.

Dylan had been out of town for the past week, which was nothing unusual, since he'd started booking some higher-paying gigs. He always had a steady stream of work and was jetting off somewhere to pose for something, and Derek always joked that one day some rich guy at one of those exotic locations would go crazy for his pretty face and up and marry him. Then he'd never see him again. To which he would get the standard Dylan reply: "I don't want someone only interested in my face. He better also want to do something filthy with my body. Fuck you very much."

*'Cause let's face it,* Derek thought, as Dylan rested back against the counter in only a pair of board shorts, *the guy has an incredible body.* He should know. He was his trainer.

"You're not supposed to be eating those." Derek pointed to the chips.

"Yeah? Well, you aren't supposed to be drinking that."

Derek looked at the bottle and shrugged. "Okay, fair enough. But I *need* this. I had a shit day. What's your excuse? Too stressful sipping your whiskey sours up in business class?"

"Hey, flying can be stressful."

"Yeah, when you fly coach like the rest of us lowly peons. Not all of us live the high life, you know."

"I just do what I'm told."

Derek grinned and took a swig of his beer. "Don't advertise that too loudly; you may end up in a precarious position."

"Not a problem, since I'm not opposed to *any* position." Dylan winked and shoved his hand into the potato chip bag.

Derek narrowed his eyes. "You do know I'm going to use the fact you're stuffing your face to my advantage tomorrow, right?"

"Oh, you mean you're gonna kick my ass harder than usual? As if I didn't already know that."

"As if you don't enjoy it."

"Keep telling yourself that. Generally I only like taking orders when fully naked, but something about you bossing me around while I'm in a weight room full of ripped men makes me all tingly. So I keep coming back for more."

Derek chuckled and looked back to the flowers on the counter. "So where the hell did those come from?"

"I have no clue. But they ain't for me."

Derek whipped his head around to see Dylan's pearly grin flashing at him with blinding perfection. "How do you know?"

"Hmm…well, I was going to go with 'I'm not really the roses type.' But really, it was this."

Dylan held out a small envelope and Derek looked at the printed name across the front: *He-Man.*

*Fucking Jordan. What is he up to now?*

"I'm assuming that's you, *He-Man*. Does it ring any bells?"

*Oh, just one,* Derek thought as his balls tightened and he looked back to the roses again. Jordan had sent him flowers? *What the…?*

"Yeah, it's for me."

"Secret admirer?" Dylan asked, chomping down on another chip.

*Secret something, all right.* "Nah, just a friend thinking he's funny, that's all."

Though he'd been headed toward the couch, Derek decided it would be best if he went to his room to open up the card. As he passed by Dylan, he snatched the bag of chips out of his hands, opened the trash can, and tossed it in. "No more of those if you want to make your weigh-in before the shoot next weekend."

"Hardass."

"I'll take that as a compliment, pretty boy."

Dylan made his way to the couch, while Derek headed to his room. Once he was there, he sat on his bed and leaned up against the wall as he opened the envelope.

When he drew the card out he read the words once, twice, and then a third time to make sure he'd read them correctly.

**Date One**

Tomorrow night - Pearson's Total Fitness - Empty it by eight.
*You're* going to work *me* out.
So get ready, I'm coming for you.

*That bossy shit.* What kind of card was that to send with flowers?

Apparently the kind he appreciated, because Derek's palm had moved to the hard length of his shaft beneath his shorts as he read it over and over again.

Jordan had lost his mind. Making demands that he empty out his place of business so he could…could…*what, exactly?* As far as Derek knew, Jordan wasn't exactly the kind to sit through a weight session. He was more the yoga type. And the bossy top type.

Picking up his cell phone, Derek opened the contacts and called Jordan. It connected in less than one ring, and he didn't want to admit how satisfying that felt.

"Derek?"

"Are you out of your mind?"

"Umm, not last time I checked."

Derek shut his eyes and told himself to keep his cool. There was no reason to get mad, because this game Jordan was playing was just that—a game. One that Derek was not going to participate in anymore.

"Well, you must be if you think I'm going to do what you wrote here."

"Ohh, so you got my flowers? Are they beautiful?"

"I told you, I was done with this. With us," Derek said, choosing to ignore Jordan's question.

"No, you said you were done with what we had. And I accept that. 'Fuck buddies' is off the table." Jordan paused and then added, as though checking off a list, "And off the bed, and off the floor, and hell, anywhere else I've had the pleasure of fucking you, *buddy*. Anyway, you get the picture. But this isn't that. *This* is a date."

Derek looked down at the card in his hand and shook his head. "This isn't a date. This is a demand. Actually, it's several fucking demands."

"Well, of course it is. I'm not really the sweet, *tiptoeing around what I want* kind of guy, am I, Derek? If I want something, I go after it. My parents spoiled me as a child, so there's really no helping my bossy nature. On the plus side, I didn't pay two thousand dollars to get your attention."

Derek growled in frustration, and when Jordan chuckled in his ear, his cock got impossibly harder. "You're insane."

"And you love it," Jordan said, and then added with extra flourish, "you told me so."

"Something you have no shame in using against me, obviously."

"*Obviously*." Jordan paused, and then his voice came back through the phone, the most serious he'd been since picking up the call. "Derek?"

"Yeah?"

"I meant what I wrote. I am coming for you, and I plan to get you back."

Derek closed his eyes and ran a hand through his hair. "Why now? Because I walked away? Because *I* told you *no*?"

"Yes."

The answer was so quick, it caught Derek off guard, but what followed next was what truly made him speechless.

"And because one day of knowing that you might not call me at the end of it was one day too many. I know I missed all the signs, and I know the moment of perfection came and went before I even knew I'd missed it. But this is *not* how we end, Derek Pearson."

He swallowed, imagining Jordan's face looking up at him as he said those words. "Because you didn't decide it?"

"No. Because we haven't even begun. Not in the sense where you get to break up with me and walk out. For that honor, you have to date me first."

Derek laughed at Jordan's audacity. The guy was a fucking head trip. But God help him, he wanted him anyway. "And this is your idea of a date? A night at my gym?"

"Not under normal circumstances, but when have we ever

been normal? See you tomorrow, He-Man. And don't wear too much. I want to look at you while I sweat."

Derek swallowed and slipped his hand into his shorts.

"And stop touching yourself—"

"How did you—"

Jordan laughed then, and the pure joy of the sound had Derek grinning like a fool.

"Because I'm doing the same exact thing. Good night, Derek."

"Night, Jordan."

# Chapter 20

DEREK WAS EXHAUSTED. He'd been at work since six that morning and it was just now coming up on eight in the evening.

He still couldn't believe he'd done what Jordan had asked, but he had. He'd shut down the gym half an hour ago and was halfway through closing out the books when there was a knock on his office door.

The sun had now set, and the only lights that could be seen outside his office windows were the lamps lining the path that ran along the beach. There were couples out for evening strolls, and joggers taking advantage of the sun's absence to get in a few miles without the risk of heat stroke. The calmness the night brought was peaceful and relaxing, and it was a welcome feeling after the hectic day he'd put in.

He knew the knocker had to be Jordan. He'd told him to come around the back and he would see a light on. But before Derek got a chance to tell him to come in, the door opened and Jordan stepped inside, dressed for a night at the gym. Red gym shorts and a black tank suited Jordan's toned body to perfection.

Long, lean, and limber, Jordan had proven many times over

that just because he didn't have the bulk and height that Derek possessed, he could still keep up with him for hours at a time in bed. His chestnut-colored hair was all the fuck over the place, and his eyes held a fire that sparked a kindred flame within Derek.

He looked ramped up, and Derek knew the feeling. He was on edge with his own unfulfilled desire. Not that he was about to let Jordan know that. Instead, he leaned back in his chair and clasped his hands over his stomach.

*Play it cool,* he told himself. *Play. It. Cool.*

"Evening, Devaney."

Jordan ran his eyes over him, and when the corner of his lips tugged into an arrogant smirk, Derek felt his dick come to life. *Fucking traitor.*

"Devaney tonight, am I? You haven't used that for a while. If I remember correctly," Jordan said as he placed his gym bag on the ground and walked toward the desk, "you used to call me that to keep me neatly tucked away in the professor box. Did you not?"

Derek got to his feet and rounded the desk until he was towering over Jordan, but as always, the guy didn't back up or budge. Instead, he faced off with him in a way that never failed to get Derek hot and really fucking bothered.

"I did."

Jordan ran his tongue along his top teeth, then flashed the most provocative grin Derek had seen in his life.

"How's that working for you tonight?"

*Yeah,* it wasn't, and Jordan knew it. He was playing to every single weakness he knew Derek had.

Bossy. Daring. And seductive as hell. He was in full-on sex pistol mode, and Derek knew he would be doing whatever the guy wanted by the end of this conversation.

While he tried to locate his tongue, Derek decided it would be wise to put a little distance between them, and sat back down behind his desk. He rolled his chair under it, but if he thought for one second that would stop the man stalking him—he was sorely mistaken.

Jordan's fingertips trailed the top of the wood as he walked around the edge of the desk and stopped beside it. He then hitched himself up onto it and leaned back to kick his leg in an impressive arc over Derek's head, before sliding directly between his legs.

"Are you running away from me?" he asked.

"No."

Jordan raised an eyebrow. "Are you sure?"

Derek grinned at that shameless man eyeing him like his favorite meal, and shook his head. "No."

"Finally. An honest answer." Jordan ran a finger down his jaw to his chin, and when Derek caught his wrist, halting any further touching, he pouted. "Is that any way to treat your date? By manhandling him?"

"You wish." Derek chuckled, and by the way Jordan's eyes darkened, he knew he was right on the money.

Before this went any further, though, before he willingly capitulated, there was something he needed to say, and it had to be now before he lost the ability to speak at all. "Don't do this to me if you're just here to fuck around."

Jordan sucked his lower lip behind his teeth, and when it jutted back out, shiny and wet, Derek had a sudden urge to taste that mouth on his, consequences be damned.

"Oh, I mean it," Jordan said. "You see, I had kind of an epiphany of sorts."

"Did you?"

"Yes, I did."

"And what was that?"

"I want to wake up with you," Jordan said, as he traced his thumb across Derek's lower lip. Then he gave a lecherous grin and said, "After I've taken you to dinner, brought you back to my place, kissed and licked every bit of ink on your delicious body, and had my wicked way with you, of course."

*Jesus, how am I supposed to say no to that?*

"That was my epiphany."

With Jordan's wrist still restrained, Derek got to his feet with enough force that the office chair rolled away from him. He yanked Jordan forward so his ass was right on the edge of the desk and his head was craned back to look at him.

"So you *really* want to date me?" he asked.

Jordan's eyes dilated and he spread his legs apart. Derek took the invitation and moved in between them, cupping the erection now evident in Jordan's gym shorts.

"Yes," Jordan said. "I really want to date you. Among other things." He dropped his eyes to Derek's lips.

*Fucking tease.*

"I meant in public, Jordan. Because you made me shut this place down tonight, and—"

"Shh..." Jordan whispered, and brought a finger to his lips. "That's what I meant too. I just thought tonight being that it's our first time—"

Derek scoffed.

"—we should make it a private matter. But if you want an audience, that's really up to you. I've always been a little bit daring at heart."

"A little bit?"

"Okay, a lot."

Derek then lowered his head to whisper directly against Jordan's lips, "Good. Then you won't have any objections when I tell you I'm about to suck your dick right here, with the windows open."

When Jordan brought his own hand around to press Derek's harder against his cock, his eyes shut. "Not even one."

*God*, he was everything Derek had always wanted, and there was no way he was going to let him get away tonight.

---

SHIT. *I DIDN'T come here just for this,* Jordan thought, as Derek pushed him back onto his desk and moved his hands to the elastic of his gym shorts.

A triumphant smile curved Derek's lips, and somewhere in the back of Jordan's mind he thought, *Please, like I'm gonna stop him. I've wanted this since he left last night.* Sure, it hadn't been his original goal when he drove over there. He'd actually come armed with a bottle of wine and food and was really *going* to have a date with the guy. But hey, if Derek wanted to go this route first, then Jordan was more than happy to accommodate him.

When he'd walked into Derek's office and seen him sitting behind his desk in his tight white polo shirt that hugged his body like a second skin, Jordan had to find a way to get his hands and mouth on him as soon as possible. But it seemed for now the tables had turned.

Jordan arched his head back on the desk, eyeing the open windows, and heard Derek's chuckle.

"Don't tell me you're nervous. I won't believe it for a fucking second."

He wasn't nervous, just curious how much of their performance might be witnessed by wandering eyes. Jordan then turned his head back in time to see Derek's reaction to what he'd worn specifically for his gym date that evening.

"Oh fuck. Jordan…" Derek said as he touched the cotton that was barely concealing his excited cock. "You dressed for the occasion."

Jordan pumped his hips up off the desk and slipped his fingers inside the elastic of his purple jockstrap. "You know me. I always try and dress accordingly."

Derek swatted his hands away and then slowly drew the underwear down until it was beneath his balls. "Liar. You don't dress for anyone but yourself. It's one of the things I love most about you. But I have to say, this…*this* is all for me. When you pulled this on tonight, all you were thinking about was how hard it would make me."

*Shit,* Derek was going to make him come if he kept talking like that. Then he circled his fingers around the base of him and gave a strong tug of Jordan's flesh, making him groan. "God-damn, Derek. Turn the fucking light off."

Derek smirked, and it made Jordan want to kiss it right off his face.

"But if I do that I can't see what I'm doing."

"If you can't find it in the dark, then we're having problems."

"Always a bossy know-it-all," Derek said, and then before Jordan could respond, Derek crushed his mouth over the top of his.

Jordan's lips parted for him, as always. Never would he think to deny Derek access to any part of him. Over the years their connection had changed and grown, but it always held that undercurrent of give and take that each of them coveted from the other. Jordan bowed up off the desk, greedy for Derek's taste as his tongue sampled him, dipping inside over and over again. Then Derek pulled back and told him, "Wait here."

Jordan tracked Derek across the office to the door, where he double-checked it was locked, and then flipped the light switch, plunging the room into darkness.

*Yes… I can work with this.*

The night breeze was blowing through the windows, and, not one to waste a second when it came to getting what he wanted, Jordan kicked his sneakers off and raised his hips, shoving the rest of his clothes down and ridding himself of his socks as Derek came back around to loom over him.

*God, the guy is built.* It was one of the things Jordan loved most about him. His height, his muscles, and the grace with which he moved. There were no questions about it—Derek was a beautiful man.

Once Jordan's eyes adjusted to the dark, he saw that Derek

had pulled his chair back to the desk and taken a seat, putting himself eye level with every vulnerable part of Jordan.

Bold as ever, Jordan leaned up on his elbows and placed a foot on either side of the chair's armrests and heard Derek mutter, "Goddamn, Jordan."

Jordan chuckled as he lay down so his back was flat on the desk, and then he reached for his cock. Just as he wrapped his fist around himself, the warm, wet slide of Derek's tongue over his balls had a moan escaping his throat. He bucked his hips up for more, but Derek's hands came up to hold him still. "Behave."

Jordan scoffed. *Yeah, like that word is even in my vocabulary.* He thrust up again and felt the sharp nip of teeth on his thigh this time. "*Ow.*"

"I told you to behave," Derek said, and Jordan was about to tell him to watch it, but he'd already lowered his head again and was sucking on the skin of his sac, rendering him pretty much useless.

As Derek gave him a thorough tongue lashing, Jordan feverishly pumped his cock before he was hauled to the edge of the desk, and Derek stood to take his length between his lips to the back of his throat.

Jordan's eyes closed and he clamped his teeth shut as he fucked Derek's mouth like he'd never felt anything as good as those lips wrapped around him.

"Derek…" he said, close to losing it. He reached for the head bent down over him, and as he got his fingers tangled in the short strands, he tugged Derek's face up so he could see him. "I want to feel your body against mine."

Derek wasted no time as he whipped his shirt over his head, and the next thing Jordan heard was the sound of a zipper. Derek was over him a second later, lining their erections up, and suggesting, "Wrap a leg around me."

Jordan did as instructed, and when their bodies came into full naked contact, Derek cursed. Jordan's cock was pounding, and he could feel the throb of Derek's as it slid back and forth against his in a hot-as-fuck slide that was about to make his body detonate.

Jordan squeezed his eyes shut as he wrapped his arms around Derek's neck and rubbed himself over every hard surface he could get against. The fact that it was Derek's cock and abdomen worked out perfectly, because nothing was more of a turn-on to him than the guy who he was about to come all over.

"Demanding. That's what you are," Derek told Jordan as he kissed and sucked his jaw and the two of them thrust against one another. "High maintenance, demanding, and insatiable. All the fucking time. And I *love* that about you. Fuck yes, I do. So get used to it. Now, come for me like you told me you would. Pressed against me, just like this."

*Oh God,* it was all too much. The words, the raspy growl coming from Derek every time they moved against each other, and that body. *Shit...*

Jordan brought a hand to the back of Derek's neck and hauled him down so he could take his mouth in a kiss as hot and filthy as what was taking place farther down. Then he slid his lips to Derek's ear and whispered, "If this is what you do on your first dates, I can't *wait* to go on our second."

He wasn't sure what it said about the two of them that *that* was the catalyst that made them both come. But his words, which were seemingly innocent, had Derek's fingers flexing and the two of them exploding in a hot mess of sticky fluid.

*Christ.* Nothing felt as good as when he was with Derek. Not one fucking thing. Jordan could feel Derek's chest rise and fall against his own where they lay sprawled on the office desk, and he started to laugh.

"Guess you really *do* like the idea of dating me," Derek said.

"I guess so, smartass," Jordan said, and shoved Derek away from him.

"This wasn't really a date, though," Derek said as he moved off him and pulled his shorts back into place.

Jordan sat up to get off the table, but Derek stepped back up between his legs and took his face in his hands to kiss his mouth. "I meant what I said. I want to go out with you. In public."

Jordan nodded. "I know. Believe it or not, I actually came here tonight just to be with you. I even brought food…and wine. You just jumped me before I had a chance to offer it."

"Yes. I can see that you put up a real struggle."

"Hey, I'm just telling you the facts."

Derek let him go and handed him a box of tissues. Once he was all cleaned up and Jordan had finished putting his own clothes back in order, Derek wandered over to the door and switched the lights back on. The both of them squinted, and once their eyes adjusted, Jordan flicked his to the desk.

"I have to say, Mr. Pearson. You may have just changed my mind about two things."

Derek slipped his hands into his pockets and waited.

"I think I have a newfound appreciation for one-on-one spot training *and* being flat on my back. Bravo. It's not every day someone can change my mind."

Derek chuckled and Jordan's heart swelled. It had been too long since they'd actually *enjoyed* each other's company.

"So, I'll, umm…call you?" When Jordan stuttered over his words, Derek's chuckle turned into full-on laughter.

"You have no clue what the hell you're doing, do you?"

"Um, no. Not really."

Derek walked across the office to where Jordan was standing, and when he didn't stop, Jordan backed up until he hit the door.

"That's kind of endearing."

"How lovely," Jordan deadpanned. "One thing I do know is: I never want to catch you at some club with another guy again. Got it?"

"I was never with him," Derek clarified, and brushed their lips together. "When are you going to get it? *You* are the one I call. *You* are the one I want. And it's about time we explored that for real. Don't you think?"

Jordan crossed his arms over his chest, irrationally annoyed about that night at Boyz all over again. "I already said yes, didn't I?"

Derek's lips pulled tight—he was trying to restrain a smirk, no doubt. "You're jealous."

"Am not."

"Yeah, you are."

"Ugh," Jordan huffed, and tried to shove Derek away. "Why would I be jealous? I just came all over you. I believe in some cultures, and definitely in the animal world, that makes you mine."

"And don't forget," Derek said boldly, holding Jordan's gaze, "your cock fits my ass like it was designed for it. So yeah, pretty sure that makes me yours. Just time to make it more…public."

"There's that word again."

"You're right. In a sense, it's all about that other word you love so much. Respect, Jordan. It's time that I had yours."

Jordan took a step forward and cupped Derek's face. It was important that it was understood he was telling the truth when he said, "I do respect you."

My, how the tables had turned on *that* particular conversation.

"Maybe," Derek said, and wrapped his fingers gently around Jordan's wrists, before lowering them to his sides. "But it's time to show me. Starting with date two."

# Chapter 21

THE ECHO OF his cell phone had Jordan shutting off his shower early and reaching for his robe. He wrapped it around himself as he padded through his bedroom to his bedside table and smiled when he saw who the caller was. When he hit answer and brought it to his ear, he said, "Ciao, bella."

His mother's laugh trilled in his ear, and Jordan couldn't help but respond in kind to the pure happiness radiating from her. "Hello to you, my sweet boy. How are you?"

"Sweet boy? I think you might have called the wrong number."

"I know exactly who I called."

"Mhmm. Just making sure you're under no delusions as to who you raised."

"Oh, you mean a genius? Yes, I am aware."

Jordan headed through to the kitchen, where he grabbed the carton of OJ before he got ready to head to work. Once he poured a glass, he propped his hip against the counter and took a sip.

"What can I do for you while you *lounge* in beautiful Italy? How I miss those family vacations."

"You're always welcome to come with us, Jordan, you know that. Or visit the lake whenever you wish."

"I know," he said, having a quick fantasy of whisking Derek away to the family villa. "Hard to do that, though, when one has a job. You remember what those are, right, Mom?"

She laughed, unoffended, as she no doubt sipped a cocktail of some kind while basking in the European sun.

"Actually," his mother drawled, and Jordan covered a yawn. Apparently he needed a few more sessions with Derek if his exertions the night before had worn him out. "We're heading home soon, and I was wondering if you'd mind our stopping by so I could talk to you more about that little project you faxed my way. I'd love to be a part of it if you would have me on board, J. It's a very important issue you're dealing with, and I can see you've really put a lot of thought into it."

Jordan perked up at that. He'd been hoping his mother would look over the proposal he'd sent to her on a charity he was looking to fund. Over the years he'd found great pleasure in investing in projects that called to him.

This time around, though, he wanted to start from scratch. He wanted to be the founder of this particular foundation for very personal reasons, and he'd had a feeling if he dropped a few breadcrumbs for his mother, she would be on board in a hot second. She was the best when it came to procuring money for a worthy cause, and this one was more than worthy. It was essential.

"Of course. Come and stay. You never have to ask. How long are you thinking?"

"Just one night to break up the trip, talk this over with you, and, of course, to see our darling boy."

"You really should stop referring to me in such polite terms. I'll start to believe they're true."

"But you're such a good boy, J. And I miss your cute face.

Oh, speaking of cute, August came and said hello the other day. He was staying at his parents' place for the month."

Of course he was, Jordan thought with a smirk. Although there was nothing *cute* about August, at least not since he was maybe ten. From eleven on, the guy had been a hell-raiser, and offered no apologies for the hearts he left broken all around the globe. As far as Jordan knew, August was currently involved with an Italian ar*tist*. Rich, temperamental, and—according to the last email Jordan had received—"a fucking dynamo in bed."

Once upon a time, that jet-setting lifestyle had been so appealing to Jordan. But now here he was, eleven years into a job he adored. It seemed that his professor, Miss Anne Hamilton, really had understood who he was on a level he hadn't even known existed.

Thinking of her brought to mind his first day teaching at the university and, of course, Derek. It was hard to believe they'd known one another for so long. But when he looked back on his career thus far, Derek Pearson was certainly someone who stood out as having made it worth it.

It was funny that in the beginning he'd thought he focused on the surly student with the bruised eye so he could watch him grow and learn. He was proud of all that Derek had accomplished, that was for damn sure, but it wasn't until recently that Jordan realized there was so much more to it than a teacher's pride in his student.

He loved Derek. He'd loved him from that very first day, and it was only now that he was starting to let the enormity of those feelings encompass him.

"Jordan?"

"Oh, sorry. What was that?"

"I'll let you go. I know you have work today," his mother said.

"Yeah, I do. *Shit*. I'm going to be late. Thanks for calling, Mom. I can't wait to see you guys. Love you. Bye."

"We love you too, J. Kisses!"

He made kissing sounds into the phone as though he were ten instead of early thirties, then shoved aside thoughts of Derek that would likely distract him, and hung up to go and finish getting ready for his class.

---

DEREK HAD JUST PUT his Jeep in park when his cell phone rang and his brother's number flashed up on the screen. He really didn't want to answer, especially not before work. But the alternative was to let it go to voicemail, where once again Alan would leave some long-winded message about how it was his duty as a son to help out the family.

*What utter bullshit.*

That didn't, however, stop the guilt that had begun to fester somewhere in the broken parts of him that he'd buried deep down, where he'd hoped they'd never see the light of day. Taking a deep breath, he picked up the phone and brought it to his ear.

"What do you want, Alan?" he said.

"'Bout time you answered the phone."

"Seriously? I'm about to hang *up* the phone, so you best stop running your mouth."

"Calm your tits, would ya? Jesus."

Derek wrung his fingers around the steering wheel and prayed for patience. "What. Do. You. Want? You've got five minutes, and then I'm hanging up."

"I got him an appointment for Friday."

Alan didn't have to say *who* he was talking about. They both knew, and if his brother wanted the conversation to continue, it was best to leave it unsaid.

"So?" Derek said, not giving a shit one way or another.

"I gotta work Friday. So you'll have to take him."

"Fuck you, Alan. I'm not coming back there."

"Derek—"

"No," he snapped. "The last time we talked, I agreed that he could use my insurance, and that was it. He should be fucking grateful I'm doing that much."

Alan coughed, and the sound was so repulsive that Derek looked at the cigarettes on his dash and decided right then he would never touch one again.

"How's he supposed to get across town?"

"I don't know. And I don't care. Tell him to look up a bus timetable, because I'm not taking that piece of shit anywhere. Got it?"

"Yeah, whatever, dude. Must've been nice to just walk the fuck away like you did."

Derek's hand hurt from how hard he was gripping the phone, and when he could finally find the words to actually speak, he said, "I didn't walk away, Alan. I fucking ran and he still found me. So why don't you tell him *that* as he crawls to the closest bus stop."

He hit end on the call and his hands shook as his stomach clenched, and for a minute he thought he was going to see his breakfast again. When he finally got his breathing under control, he squeezed his eyes shut and cursed the hold that asshole still had over him.

Derek hated that his father still had the power to instill fear in him. To make him feel weak. And out of everything the man had done to him over the years, *that* was the one thing he loathed the most.

Fuck, there was no way he was fit for work today.

When he finally felt able to drive again, he put the Jeep in reverse and headed back the way he'd come. He needed to go somewhere where he could think. Where there was nothing but him and his own thoughts, and he knew the perfect spot.

Somewhere he'd been going for years.

---

DATE TWO. JORDAN had thought of little else all day, and he had the perfect idea. As he pulled into a parking spot at the local grocery store, he debated whether to call Derek now or to make dinner and then surprise him by going and picking him up. Either way, he was going to kidnap the guy, bring him back to his place, and feed him until he was so full he couldn't eat another bite *or* find the energy to leave.

After last night, he hadn't been able to stop thinking about Derek's final words on respect. Derek didn't know it yet, but for the past few months Jordan had been working on something that he hoped would show Derek just how much he admired and, *yes*, respected him.

He'd been waiting for the perfect time for a while now. Originally, he'd wanted to tell him when he began working on the idea, but that was the night Derek had first told him he loved him, and after Jordan had sat there stunned into silence, everything had changed and he hadn't had a chance since.

That had all changed, though, in the last couple of days, and now it was time. He knew that it was. He wanted Derek's opinion on this. Wanted to share it with him, and was excited to see his reaction.

He reached for his phone and hit *He-Man* in his contacts with his palms sweating, the equivalent of a twelve-year-old with a crush.

When the call connected and Derek's less-than-enthused "Hey" came through the line, Jordan's all-day smile slipped a notch.

"Hey?" he joked, settling back into the car seat. "Don't sound too excited. My ego won't stand for it."

"Oh," Derek said, and he sounded so distant that Jordan's smile completely vanished. Maybe this had been a bad idea, him calling. Maybe he should've waited. Maybe—

"Yeah, sorry about that. I'm just… It's been… Well, it's been a really shit day, to be honest."

Jordan thought of how wonderful his had been, and

wondered what had made Derek's so miserable. "I'm sorry. Is there something I can do to help? Are you okay?"

He heard the sound of Derek taking a deep breath, then he let it out and sounded stressed.

"I'm okay," Derek said, then gave a mocking laugh. "I mean, I'm not hurt. It's just, my brother called, and…"

That right there was a shocker. Jordan hadn't been aware that Derek still talked to his family.

"I'm just not in a good place right now. I… *Fuck.*"

Jordan heard the sound of something being thrown, and winced. Whatever had happened, he would place bets it had to do with… "Is it your father?"

The silence that fell between them was a familiar sound, and it was a stark reminder of the painful presence that had first drawn them together.

"Derek?" When he got no response, Jordan pushed aside any plans he'd been making in his head and tried again. "Derek?"

"Yeah."

"What do you need? Tell me."

More silence met his ear as Jordan sat there in the car—waiting. Then he heard, "You."

---

DEREK SAT ON the bottom step that led to his apartment and waited for Jordan to arrive. All day he'd been trying to shove aside memories too painful to relive. But the more he'd tried to push them aside, the more they'd come flooding back. Then Jordan had called, and *Here I am, waiting for him to put me back together again.*

He blinked at the night sky and wondered at what moment, what junction in his life, he'd decided that Jordan Devaney was going to be his lifeline.

When did he decree that that was fair to do to someone? Was it the same day he'd decided it was time to free Finn?

Because somewhere along the way he'd distanced himself from the boy who used to pick up his broken pieces, and handed the job off to the man now pulling up by the curbside in front of him.

Was that how you knew you loved someone? When you could show them everything you were and know they wouldn't leave? He had to believe that was the case. Otherwise the burden he'd laid upon Jordan would all be in vain.

As Derek got to his feet, he saw Jordan push open the door and make his way over, a frown marring his forehead. When he finally reached his side, Derek took his face between his hands and lowered his head to kiss Jordan's mouth.

A firm hand pressed over his heart, then Jordan's lips parted for him and Derek lost himself in his taste. The sweet slide into serenity was swift, and when Derek finally resurfaced and raised his head, he whispered, "Thank you."

Jordan traced the angle of his chin and offered a sad smile. "You need to stop that."

"Stop what?"

"Thanking me. I told you. If you ever need me—"

"I know. You'll answer." Derek rested his forehead against Jordan's and shut his eyes.

"Always."

His heart ached at the sincerity behind that one word, and at the same time it conveyed how much Jordan meant what he was saying.

"Sorry I ruined *date two* for us."

"No need," Jordan said with a wave of his hand. "I can work with this. I mean, unless you plan to take me hiking or something."

"Not exactly hiking," Derek said, as he eyed Jordan's clothes with apprehension.

"What?" Jordan asked, then looked down at his gray lightweight pants and plum-colored button-up shirt.

"Yeah, about that. We might have to swing by your place before we head out. If you're still game, that is."

"I am…" Jordan said, as he looked over Derek's khaki cargo shorts and navy-blue polo. Then he narrowed his eyes on the hiker's backpack sitting on the stoop. "I think. Where exactly are we going?"

"Devil's Bend."

"Devil's *Bend*?" Jordan scrunched up his nose. "We have to hike down there."

"Not very far. It's less than a mile."

"In the *dark*," Jordan said, his eyes wide and his expression so full of horror that Derek forgot about his shitty day and instead focused on how adorable the man in front of him was.

"I go there all the time. I could find it with my eyes shut."

"Which is pretty much the equivalent of going there right now, don't you think?"

Derek bent down to grab the backpack off the ground, and then he took Jordan's chin between his fingers and kissed his lips. "Don't worry, Posh. I'll look after you."

He stepped around the now stuttering man and headed toward his car. He knew the nickname he and Finn had given Jordan drove him nuts. But after Brantley had spilled the beans and told Jordan about it, Derek figured it was fair game to use whenever he wanted to get under Jordan's skin. Which, he admitted, was more often than he should.

"Do *not* call me that, Derek Pearson," Jordan said in a tone filled with so much upper-class *fuck you* that Derek couldn't help chuckling. "You know I don't like it."

"I know," Derek said as he leaned back against the trunk waiting for Jordan to unlock it. "But I've had a crap day and you get all feisty whenever I say it, which makes me hot, and then I forget I was in a bad mood and all is better."

Jordan aimed his keys at the car and hit a button so the trunk would spring open and bump into Derek's ass.

"All is *not* better, because now I'm annoyed at you."

Derek swung his bag into the back and slammed it shut. As each of them walked to their sides of the car, Jordan aimed an exasperated look at Derek and asked, "What's at Devil's Bend?"

When they were seated and their belts were buckled, Derek leaned his head back on the headrest and whispered, "Peace."

And no other convincing was needed.

## Chapter 22

"ARE WE NEARLY there yet?" Jordan asked, and chose to disregard the way Derek ignored him. He was several steps behind with a flashlight clutched in his hand as he trudged over sticks and branches and headed directly down a path straight to… *Huh, how fitting. Hell.*

Under no other circumstance would he ever be hiking through the beach scrub at eight thirty at night. *Hell. No.* This was not his idea of a fun time. It was actually, pretty much, his worst nightmare. Not that he would ever tell Derek that.

When they'd talked on the phone earlier, Derek had said he was going to camp overnight at a place he used to go as a boy, and then—*shit, was that a spider web?*—they'd ended up there.

"How you doing back there?" Derek asked, and he sounded way too pleased with himself to fool Jordan into thinking he was concerned for his well-being.

"I'm fine," Jordan said between his teeth, and heard the faint sound of a snort.

If this were any other time, the flashlight in his hand would seem like a fabulous way to teach Derek a lesson when he lobbed it at the back of his head. As it was, apparently hiking in the dark to the middle of nowhere was Derek's idea of catharsis.

"Really, Jordan, anyone would think you never went camping as a kid."

Jordan stopped at that, and when the obvious lack of his footsteps continued, Derek turned around and came back several paces. "Is something wrong?"

"Do I strike you as a child who ever *once* wanted to go camping?"

Derek looked over his pink vertical-striped shirt, yellow shorts with matching pink belt, and olive suede loafers, which each cost well over the hundred-dollar mark. He then reached out, cupped the back of Jordan's neck, and tugged him forward.

Jordan's breath caught as Derek's hand came up to cradle his cheek, and when he smiled, Jordan wondered when he'd become such a damn sap.

"No. You strike me as the type who flew around in private jets—"

"True."

"To exotic places—"

"Also true."

"And missed out on some of the most beautiful sights that were right under your upturned nose."

Jordan huffed. Derek nipped at his lips and said, "*You* are going to love where I'm taking you. You know why?"

Jordan couldn't remember his own name while Derek was tracing his tongue along his lower lip—let alone how to talk.

"Because down there, you can run around completely naked and no one will see you."

Jordan pulled his head back and brought the flashlight up between them to illuminate their faces. "That's not an accurate statement. *You'll* see me."

Derek winked and said, "I fucking hope so."

"*Ahh.* I see what you're up to," Jordan said, and pondered this new information. "And what about you?"

Derek laughed, and then started walking again. "I'll get naked too. *If* you can manage not to complain any more until we arrive."

Jordan aimed the flashlight on Derek's ass. *Okay, I guess I can keep my mouth shut a little longer if I get to look at that naked.*

"Come *on*, Jordan. The quicker we get there…"

"O*kay*. I'm coming. I'm coming," he called out, and hurried along behind.

---

"WE'RE HERE," DEREK announced as the both of them stepped out into the clearing.

"Wow." Jordan dropped his backpack on the sand and walked forward on the isolated stretch of beach. "Look at this place."

That was exactly how Derek felt every time he came down there.

Devil's Bend was on the opposite side of Sunset Cove at the far end of the peninsula, and generally off the public's radar. Most stayed away because it didn't offer a good place to swim or surf. The waves were too rough and the waters too dangerous due to the rocks that littered the shoreline.

What Devil's Bend did offer was a spectacular view of the night sky. With no other lights to be seen, the stars twinkled above like diamonds shining over all they touched. Out in the distance, you could see the faint lights of tankers heading toward the horizon, but here, in this little alcove, the rest of the world—it disappeared.

When Jordan faced him, the smile he aimed his way was so full of glee that Derek thought it made him look like a little boy. Well, maybe not a *little* boy.

"You like it?"

Jordan kicked his shoes off and waggled his eyebrows before he ran up and jumped into Derek's arms. Derek caught him around the waist as Jordan wrapped his arms and legs around him and whispered, "I *love* it."

Derek captured his mouth in a blistering kiss, and as the tempestuous mating continued and he ran his hands up from Jordan's ass to his back, he moaned.

It was then that Derek realized that calling for Jordan in his moments of despair was more than just a hit to take the edge off. He called this man for the pure joy he exuded, which in turn made Derek believe that anything was possible, most especially his own happiness.

Jordan leaned back in his arms and flashed a warm smile. "This place is like something out of a dream."

"I know. It's pretty awesome, huh? Now, you think you can stand on your own two feet for a minute?"

"Sure you want me to?" Jordan asked as he rocked his hips against him.

Derek slapped his ass playfully. "On your feet, Posh. We still have a little ways to go."

As Derek lowered him, Jordan purposely kept them close and let his entire body drag down over the length of his.

"Ohh, looks like someone's *up* for a little fun later. I vote for the nudity to begin now. I behaved. I didn't complain once after you told me what I would get in return."

Derek chuckled and handed Jordan his bag. "Nice to know that all it takes to get you to do something is a bribe."

"As if this is really news. You lived with me for a year, maybe a little more. You already know that I'm selfish."

Jordan slipped his arms through the straps of the bag and hefted it up his back, and then Derek hooked his fingers into the straps and tugged him in close.

"You're not selfish. You're…" When Jordan aimed his stunning face up at him with a cheeky gleam in his eyes, Derek lost his train of thought.

"Yes? Please continue. I do so love hearing about myself."

"Hmm. You're the kindest, most generous man I've ever met."

Jordan's eyes narrowed and Derek brushed a kiss across his lips and added, "As well as self-absorbed and spoiled rotten."

Jordan poked his tongue out. "Whatever. Say what you will. I still want to see you naked. So how about we get wherever we're going so you can spoil me."

Derek held his hand out, and after Jordan had slipped his inside, he tugged him along behind. "All right. Come on, bossy."

They made their way down the beach, and right about the halfway mark, Derek stopped and looked up to the sandy dune he'd been coming to since he was a boy.

There, in amongst the overgrown weeds, sat a beat-up shack. It was so much a part of the landscape that the pieces of broken wood, from what was once a small stoop, were buried under the sand, and half the roof looked as though it had been blown off in the last storm they'd had.

It might not be perfect, or even close to it, but to him it had always looked like heaven.

---

JORDAN FROWNED AT the remains of what had obviously been a delightful little beach hut, but as it stood right now, it reminded him more of pieces of wood on a demolition pile.

"This is it," Derek announced, and walked toward the dunes.

"This is *what*, exactly?"

Derek didn't answer straight away. He just powered on ahead up the sand to where, Jordan assumed, a front door might have been. Once upon a time. A long, *long* time ago.

"*This* is mine."

Jordan stepped over a piece of rotted wood and followed Derek across broken floorboards to stop in the center of the small space. "What do you mean it's…yours?"

Derek looked over his shoulder and shrugged. "I own it."

Before Jordan could ask more, Derek walked through what appeared to have been another doorway at some point in time.

"But…" Jordan said as he followed. He ducked through and spotted Derek putting his bag down in the corner of the second space that was a little more put together. "But it's broken."

Derek was in the middle of unzipping his bag and paused to look over, and the expression in his eyes was heartbreaking. "That's what makes it so perfect."

Jordan walked closer to the man watching him with such focus, and moved to his side as Derek then looked around the space.

"I used to come down here when I was little…"

As Derek's words trailed off, Jordan placed his own bag down and tested the wood panel of one of the walls. Once he was satisfied it was steady, he leaned back against it and waited.

"The first time, I was twelve. About a week after my mother left."

Derek looked over at him, no doubt to see his reaction, and Jordan offered up a tentative smile. A sign that he was there, ready to listen, when Derek was ready to continue.

"Looking back now, I can't really blame her. God knows I did the same thing the second I could. But back then, I didn't understand how she could leave us with him, you know?"

Jordan had borne witness to the handiwork of Derek's father, and the thought that any adult would willingly leave two young children with such a monster made him shudder.

"Anyway," Derek continued. "The night she left, he went on a real bender. He left Alan and me by ourselves, and I remember lying in bed that night wishing he would get home because I was scared. I was scared he'd left us like she had. Ironic, right? Turns out I should've been wishing the exact opposite. He came home that night drunk."

Derek stopped talking and looked away, clearly uncomfortable with the topic he was discussing but needing to share it all the same.

"I came out of my room when I heard him come in. I wanted to make sure he was okay, because it was late. I found him in the kitchen, looking inside the fridge, probably searching for a beer to round out the night, who knows. But when he heard me he turned around, and I'll never forget the look that came into his eyes, Jordan. It was a look that never left—it was pure evil."

"Derek. You don't have to explain—"

"No," he said. "I want to. I *need* to."

"Okay. Then tell me."

Derek scratched his head then continued. "He slammed the fridge shut, and I remember the sound of the bottles rattling inside. It made me jump, and he laughed. Called me a scared little girl. A pussy," Derek scoffed. "Who calls their twelve-year-old son that?"

*A monster,* Jordan thought. "A very sad and cruel man."

"Yeah," Derek agreed, and unfastened the straps around the rolled-up sleeping bag on top of his pack. "Well, that was the kindest thing he did to me that night. I ran back into my room, understanding on some level that I was in danger, I guess. Maybe it was because of the tone he used when he yelled at me? It was the same one he'd used with my mother right before he would— *Fuck.* He followed me, grabbed my arm, and spun me back around. When he asked me why I was still awake, I couldn't answer. I was terrified. He was a big man, as big as I am, and I thought he was going to snap my arm in half. He hauled me inside my room to my bed, and when we got there he realized my terror had gotten the better of me and that I'd pissed on myself." Derek stopped talking and shook his head as he brought his hands up to cover his eyes. He pressed his fingers so hard against his lids that Jordan was worried he would hurt himself, but he knew better. He knew that Derek was just trying to banish what he was seeing, what he was remembering.

He crossed over to him and reached for Derek's wrists. After drawing them away from his face, Jordan brought the palms of each of his hands to his mouth and placed kisses on them. "What happened next?"

"That was the first night he hit me." Derek gave a painful-looking grimace, which Jordan figured he was hoping to pass off as an *it doesn't matter* smile. "He slapped me, shoved me onto the bed, and told me not to bother coming out until I could face him like a man."

Jordan swallowed back the gasp he wanted to let free as he stared into Derek's ice-cold eyes. They'd glazed over, and he knew that Derek was right back there, experiencing it all over again.

"I didn't come out of my room for a week other than to sneak to the bathroom. And after that only because Finn knocked on my window repeatedly and finally helped me pry it open. That was when we came down here and found this place."

"Oh God. Derek. I'm so sorry…"

"No," Derek said, shaking his head. "I didn't tell you so you would feel sorry for that boy. I told you so you could understand why *this* place. This broken-down piece of nothing…it has a fighting chance to be something better. I want to *make* it something better. I want to give it life."

Jordan took in the remains surrounding them and then offered a gentle smile to the truly outstanding man opposite him, and every single part of him called for Derek.

God he loved him, more than he ever thought possible. Why had it taken him so long to see?

"I know it's not much. But it will be."

"I believe it," Jordan said, and he really did. "I believe in you. I always have."

Derek drew him in and wrapped his arms about his waist, and Jordan pressed his lips against the hollow at the base of his throat. "You're daring yourself to make a difference."

Derek pulled back and gave him a quizzical look.

"It's something my professor used to say to me. *Find what makes you work the hardest, and dare yourself to make a difference.* She was a wise woman."

"She sounds like it."

Jordan kissed Derek's lips. "Want to know a secret?"

"Always."

"You dared me."

Derek frowned, and as silly as it seemed, saying those words out loud for the first time brought a blush to Jordan's cheeks, and he felt self-conscious about his reaction.

"I don't understand."

"That first day. I wasn't so sure teaching was for me. Then you stood up and removed your glasses and dared me to make a difference."

Derek's answering smile made Jordan's heart practically thump out of his chest.

"Huh, that's kind of nice when you put it that way."

"I can be nice."

"You weren't that day," Derek reminded him. "You were kind of a jackass, *Professor* Devaney."

"True. You pushed my buttons. It wasn't until much later that I worked out this pearl of wisdom."

When Derek barked out a quick laugh, Jordan nuzzled into his wide chest and asked, "So, *now* is it time to get naked?"

## Chapter 23

AROUND AN HOUR later, Derek sat on his sleeping bag with a bonfire blazing in front of him on the beach as Jordan rustled through his backpack beside him, searching for God only knew what.

"How much stuff could you possibly have in there? We were only at your place for ten minutes."

Jordan's head popped up and he pointed an accusatory finger at Derek. "Listen here. If you expect me to walk to a destination in which I am going to sleep on the *ground*, you best believe that I'm going to pack provisions to get me through the night."

"Well, unless your bag comes equipped with a magical blow-up king-sized mattress, even your delicate ass is going to be sleeping on my sleeping bag with me."

Jordan's eyes shifted to the sleeping bag he'd rolled out and then came back to Derek. "I have no problems with that. Plus, if I get uncomfortable I'll just lie all over you."

"Why do I have a feeling you'll be on top of me either way?"

"Because you're a smart man and you know that's exactly the way I like it."

When Jordan winked, Derek just shook his head. Then he spotted a packet of Oreo cookies in his hand. Jordan and his sweets. The guy didn't go anywhere without those or— "What is that?"

"This," Jordan said, as he held up a palm-sized pouch and grinned, "is wine in a pouch."

"Of course it is."

"Well, you said we were coming out here for our second date and that you needed to talk and relax, and to me that always includes—"

"Wine and Oreo cookies?"

"Hello, it's a dessert wine. Something sweet and something to relax the bones…"

"I can think of something else that would relax me just as effectively."

"I'm sure you can. You have a *very* perverted mind."

Jordan zipped up his bag then stepped over it to come and sit beside him. He offered Derek an Oreo, and when he pulled a face, Jordan screwed his nose up. "I still think you're a weirdo for not liking the sweet stuff."

"Well, I like you, so…I'm pretty sure we solidified my weird factor somewhere back in my first semester of college."

Jordan pulled the chocolate cookie sandwich apart and made an illicit showing of tonguing the cream-filled center before popping the cookie part into his mouth.

As he chewed, he nodded, agreeing. "You know. First time I saw you, I wanted to run my tongue over every single one of your tattoos that I could see. Among *other* ill-advised things. God, from the get-go I knew you were trouble."

Derek faced him, and Jordan shrugged unapologetically. "What? As if you don't know that by now. It was the first thing I did that night after—"

"The commencement ceremony? I remember. You drove me crazy that night."

"Mhmm," Jordan said. "You held out pretty good, all things considered."

"Pretty good?" Derek said. "I didn't come until you'd tongued every damn inch of me and your cock was inside massaging my prostate. Considering I'd been fantasizing about you riding me for years, I deserve a fucking medal for not shooting my load the second you traced your finger across my ass."

Jordan's mouth hung open after Derek's little speech, and then he reached between his legs and palmed himself. "Fond memory of yours?"

"One of my fucking favorites."

"Actually, speaking of tattoos that I've tongued, you owe me," Jordan said with a grin.

"How do you figure that?"

"You told me I could run around naked once I got down here, and that you would too if I didn't complain about how long it took to get here."

"I hardly think a fifteen-minute walk is too long."

"Of course you don't. You run fifty miles a day," Jordan said as he got to his feet and started to unbuckle his belt.

"I don't run fifty miles."

When the belt was undone and Jordan's hands went to the button of his shirt, he paused. "Okay. Twenty?"

Derek leaned back on an elbow and ran his palm up the erection in his pants, as his body prepared to enjoy the show he knew he was about to be the sole audience for. "Try ten."

Jordan undid each of the buttons on the shirt until he reached the top, and then pulled the fabric off and tossed it over on his bag. "Oh, *only* ten? Piece of cake."

"Exactly," Derek agreed as Jordan's hands moved back down to his pants. "Not a big deal at all. And it's not like you object to *all* exercise. Look at your body."

Jordan unzipped his shorts, shoved them to his feet, and then stepped out of them, kicking them in Derek's direction. "I'd rather *you* look at it."

*Fuck*, he'd get no objections on that. In fact, Derek grabbed the hem of his own shirt and pulled it off, then went for the button of his cargos.

Jordan strutted toward him like he was walking a runway, and when he got by Derek's hip he lowered to his knees and traced his fingers over the colorful patterns marking Derek's bicep.

"I remember that first night like it was yesterday. You took your clothes off and it was like I'd never seen you before, because I was actually allowed to touch you. I was allowed to kiss you. And finally… *God*." Jordan moaned, as he gripped his cock, giving it a full stroke. "I was finally allowed to have you. I know it sounds, I don't know, bad, I suppose. But I'd never wanted it so bad as I wanted it that night with you. I don't know what it was, or what it *still* is, but everything about you calls to me." Jordan tilted his head to the side, as though genuinely curious. "How is that possible?"

Derek's breath hitched when Jordan flattened his free hand on his chest and pushed him down to his back on the sleeping bag.

"I don't know," he finally managed. "But trust me. I ask myself daily. We're such an—"

"Unlikely pair?"

"Yeah."

"I know. But I don't care," Jordan said as he shifted up on his knees and moved to straddle the top of Derek's thighs. He then parted Derek's pants so his shaft was visible. "You're just so sexy," Jordan said, and trailed his fingers along the underside of Derek's cock.

Derek shut his eyes, trying to keep control of his body as Jordan slowly teased him, but he wasn't having any of that.

"Open your eyes. You know how much I like them on me."

Derek's eyes opened, and with the fire dancing behind Jordan and the embers flickering up into the night sky he could've very well been the devil himself sitting astride his lap, evoking such carnal reactions.

Derek could feel his ass clenching at the thought of Jordan flipping him over and tunneling inside him. But he also knew from the slow, steady way Jordan was working him that if that were going to happen, it wouldn't be anytime soon. Maybe not even tonight.

"What are you thinking about?" Jordan asked as he drew his fist up to the head of Derek's dick, twisted his wrist, and then reversed course in a delicious hand job that was making it difficult to think at all.

"I was thinking that… Fuck, Jordan—" he said as Jordan brought his hand to his mouth and licked his palm clean of the pre-cum that was coating it. "I was thinking that you're the goddamn devil."

If he'd thought for a second that Jordan would be insulted by the title, he was mistaken. *Oh no,* if anything, a wicked glint of amusement entered those seductive brown eyes, and Jordan leaned down so their cocks rubbed together.

"So…not so *posh* after all, huh?"

When he sank his teeth into Derek's lip hard enough to sting, Derek lifted his head and brought a hand to the back of his head, holding Jordan in place. He speared his tongue deep between Jordan's lips and kissed the hell out of the guy as Jordan grunted and thrust down on top of him.

Derek rolled them to the side until he had Jordan pinned underneath him, and he reveled in the feeling of having his toned body stretched out along his. It was a rare day when Jordan let him get the better of him, and as he lay there panting for breath, Derek knew he'd never seen anyone so breathtaking in all his life. Or someone with such an incorrigible smirk.

"Is there a problem?"

"Yeah," Derek said. "This is only our second date. And I don't put out on second dates."

Jordan's mouth parted, and he scowled up at him. "You can't be serious."

Derek bit the inside of his cheek as to keep his face neutral, and then he glanced down Jordan's very naked and hard body. When he brought his eyes back to the fiery ones locked on him, he shrugged. "Sorry. I'm just not that kind of boy."

"You're not that…" Jordan started, and then stopped as he wound his legs around Derek's waist and used every ounce of muscle he had to pull him down. It was a valiant effort, and if Derek had wanted to, he could've fought him off. But like that was going to happen.

He lowered himself down until he was hovering over Jordan and said, "I'm serious. We're dating now, and last night—"

"Last night you had your mouth all over my cock."

Jordan was something else when irritated. Derek had thought that from day one, and right now was no different. Naked, spread out beneath him, and pinned to the sleeping bag, Jordan Devaney was still ready to tell him to go and get screwed.

"Maybe I want to try out the other part of your little speech before I let you have my body."

Jordan adopted a bored look that had Derek kissing him again until he panted. "And what part is that?"

Derek shifted off the top of him, and Jordan pinned him with shrewd eyes.

"I want to wake up with you."

"You dirty cheat. Using my words against me."

He tugged Jordan to him, and he only put up a token protest before scooting to his other side so he could fit his ass to Derek's cock.

Derek groaned.

"Serves you right," Jordan huffed. "And you better keep your hands to yourself."

"Oh yeah? Or what?"

"Or when you *do* finally decide to put out, I might hold out on you."

Derek chuckled as he draped a leg over the top of Jordan, and marveled at the way he snuggled back, as if he wanted to be completely surrounded by him.

That right there. *That* made everything Derek had been through in life worth it, because there was nowhere on earth he'd rather be.

## Chapter 24

FRIDAY ARRIVED BEFORE Derek was ready, and as he drove down his childhood street at a slow crawl, nausea roiled through his gut. He couldn't believe he was back there—of his own volition.

As he navigated his vehicle between the ones parked at the curbside, he saw Finn's mother's car and stared longingly at the home he'd once wished was his own. It'd been so great to reconnect with Finn recently, and just like back in the day, Mrs. Finley had welcomed him into her home with a warm smile and a hug.

But he wasn't on this street today for a hug and a pat on the back, *no*. He was there to do something he never would've believed himself capable of years ago. It had taken him weeks to come to terms with the fact that he was *helping* his father, but now that he was there driving down a street that for him ended in hell, he wondered if he'd lost his sanity.

As he pulled to a stop at the curb of his father's home, he took a moment to try to calm his nerves. *God,* what he wouldn't do to be anywhere other than there today.

As the engine idled, he tapped his thumb on the steering wheel and counted back from twenty.

*Just get in and get out. You only have to get through the next few hours and then you can forget about this place.*

And therein lay the problem. Knowing that he had to be in the fucker's presence for even five seconds was what caused the heartburn. Because even though he knew he could leave at any time, it didn't do shit to help with the fact that he felt obligated to do this in the first fucking place.

After grabbing the keys from the ignition, he made himself get the hell out of the car before he drove away. He marched up the cracked pavement of the concrete path and shook his head at the weeds growing in between them. The two banana trees he and his brother had planted when they were boys swayed in the breeze, causing the large leaves to drag against the once yellow shutters of the classic-style "Conch House." The paint was chipping off the wooden boards that made up the old shack, and the swing that used to sit invitingly on the porch now hung off one chain broken.

A true representation of the family who'd once lived there.

He hadn't been back in years, and he'd stopped thinking about the occupants the same day he'd left. That was, until his brother had recently tracked him down.

Wanting to get this over with, he didn't bother to stop and knock, and instead opened the door and stepped inside. The depressing gloom that greeted him went hand in hand with the familiar stench of cigarettes and alcohol, and when the door shut behind him the walls seemed to close in, making it even more difficult to breathe.

He peered through the haze and shadows to the place where he knew he'd find him, and sure as shit, there was his father. His ass was planted in his beat-up vinyl recliner facing the one window he'd bothered to open for air—passed out.

*Fucking hell,* Derek thought, as he walked over the crushed beer cans on the floor. He spotted a pizza box on the counter with the lid askew, lifted it the rest of the way, and cringed. Half the pizza was gone, and the other half was at least a couple days old.

"Hey," he said as he came around in front of the recliner. When his father didn't budge, Derek took a second to look over the man whose legs were sprawled out on the ripped vinyl of the upturned footrest.

The greasy hair sticking out at all angles and the unshaven face aged him considerably. He barely resembled the monster that Derek remembered.

"Hey," he said again, louder this time, punctuating it with a kick to the footrest. He'd be damned if he was going to be polite to this piece of trash.

His father roused, and tried to sit up, but his hand slipped off the armrest and he slumped back down, clutching his head. "Fuck, do you gotta be so loud?"

"Apparently," Derek said, crossing his arms. "Why aren't you ready?"

His father hacked and coughed as he struggled to sit up while at the same time tucking the footrest back under the chair. When the task seemed too much of a monumental effort, Derek raised his leg and, with the sole of his boot, shoved the footrest under the couch with a little more force than necessary.

His father rocked forward on the chair and glared up at him. "Watch it, boy."

Derek told himself not to flinch, but old habits died hard. When the asshole got to his towering height of six foot four, Derek took a step back, but he wasn't quick enough. His father got a hold of the middle of his shirt and yanked him forward. Derek's palm shot out to hold him at bay, and his father narrowed his eyes.

"After all these years, you're still a fucking pussy. Afraid of your old man."

Derek wrapped his fingers around his father's wrist and ripped it from his shirt. "You don't scare me," he spat, as he shoved his father away. "And you know why? I got away from you. You hold no power here, *old* man."

"Don't I? Last time I saw you, you were on your ass crying like a little queer—"

"Shut your mouth," Derek barked, the reminder of that final beating his father had dished out bringing to the surface his barely restrained anger.

"What are you even doin' here?"

"I'm here to take you to the clinic. Alan didn't tell you?" Derek looked around the dump he used to call home, and then back to the fucker in front of him. "Of course he didn't," he said. "This place smells like shit."

"I hadn't noticed."

Disgust radiated through Derek as he kicked an empty Chinese container on the floor. "Really?" he asked, and walked back through the living room, past the kitchen, to the front door. "You hadn't noticed this place looks like a fucking pigsty? You're gonna have roaches crawling through here soon enough," he said with his hand on the doorknob. "What time's Alan get home?"

"What's it matter to you? Boy's got a real job, he does. Not like you who thinks he's a real hotshot. Dontcha, Derek? With your overpriced gym full of fags and pretentious dicks willing to pay out the ass to stare at each other bending over all day."

Derek bit the inside of his cheek so hard that the metallic taste of blood hit his tongue and he told himself to just go. *Just leave him there to rot. It's what he deserves.*

But something inside him, obviously some sick and twisted part, couldn't make himself leave.

"I'll be out in the car. You've got five fucking minutes and then I'm leaving. Whether you're dead on the floor or not."

He didn't bother waiting for an answer. He needed to get away from the guy before he lost what little hold he had on his temper. Who knew what he was capable of when pushed far enough, and with the amount of rage he harbored toward that man, it was a miracle he hadn't beaten him and left him dead already.

*Jesus, how is this my goddamn life again?* He was right back in the same fucked-up scenario he'd been in as a child. But what was the alternative? Knowingly letting the man die? Because he would, and soon, without medical intervention.

Derek looked toward the faded yellow door and cursed the universe yet again for the crappy hand he'd been dealt. Why was he the one burdened with the ability to help this man, when he'd done nothing but try to destroy him?

He'd wanted to say go to hell to both his brother and his father…but when it had come down to it, he hadn't been able to bring himself to say no.

The situation was beyond fucked.

He felt cornered. Like a trapped animal, and he knew by the end of today he would either need boxing gloves and a bag—or Jordan.

---

JORDAN SAT ON his couch with the phone pressed to his ear while he and Brantley discussed whether he should serve a rack of lamb or surf and turf tomorrow night at Finn's get-together.

Jordan gave the question careful consideration and then asked, "Surf and turf with lobster?"

"Of course. What do you think?"

"Sounds delicious. Don't even think about buying drinks, though; I've got those covered. Is there anything Daniel doesn't like?"

Brantley covered the mouthpiece and called out over his shoulder, then said, "No. He's easy."

"I was talking about the wine selection, Professor Hayes. Not his behavior in the bedroom."

Jordan heard a smile in Brantley's tone when he answered, "Who said I was talking about his behavior in the *bed*room?"

"Oh, look at you finally making sex jokes about your younger man."

Brantley laughed. "Speaking of younger men. How is *yours* this evening?"

"He is not mine…"

"Isn't he? So you're trying to tell me you won't be turning up to our place tomorrow night with Derek Pearson. A.k.a. owner of Pearson's Total Fitness, a.k.a. He-Man."

Jordan couldn't help the ridiculous grin on his face as he twirled the stem of his wine glass between his fingers. "I'm not telling you anything."

He could practically hear Brantley's frown through the phone as he said his name.

"*What*?" Jordan asked.

"At least have the decency to tell me if I need to hide the fine china if you are bringing someone other than Derek. I'd hate for World War Three to break out in my dining room. Oh, I'm sorry, World War Four. Three happened a few months back at Boyz."

"You know, I think Daniel Finley is rubbing off on you. You've become quite petulant lately."

There was a shuffling sound and then Daniel's voice came through the phone. "Listen up, Posh, I know you're bringing Derek, because he told me. So let me extend the same advice to you that you once gave me: If you hurt him, I will hunt you down and have your perfect, overpriced balls for breakfast, you got that?"

"Overpriced?" Jordan said. "I'll have you know—" He was cut off by the buzzing of his intercom. Getting to his feet, he walked over to press the button to show him who was by the elevator. Derek looked up at him, and any other words that Daniel was saying were drowned out.

If a picture was worth a thousand words, the one he was staring at portrayed anguish and pain in a single image.

Derek's eyes held his as Jordan punched the button to let

him inside, and even as Derek vanished from the screen, Jordan told Daniel he had to go, and switched to the camera inside the elevator. Just as he had a week ago, Derek stared up at him the entire ascent.

He knew that look. He'd seen it on his man before. It was the look of someone who needed his demons exorcised, and knowing where Derek had been today, Jordan knew exactly which demon it was.

He let go of the VIEW button and stood there waiting for Derek's arrival.

When the elevator finally got to his floor and the door opened, Jordan held his hand out and said, "Come with me."

# Chapter 25

DEREK SLIPPED HIS hand into Jordan's and let him lead. After spending a nauseating amount of time with a human being he'd rather never see again, it was a relief to be back in *this* man's presence.

During the hour he'd spent sitting in his car waiting for his father's "therapy" to be done, he'd told himself, over and over, *never again.* He'd had to listen to his father's sick diatribe the entire way to and from the facility, not to mention his entire life, and never would he subject himself to it again. No matter what.

After Derek had dropped him back at the house, he'd driven around for a good two or maybe three hours, trying to calm himself down. But it was no use. Nothing was touching the energy that was coursing through his veins.

Jordan hadn't said a word since he'd stepped off the elevator, but Derek knew by the way his fingers had interlaced through his that what he needed was evident. Instead of heading straight to Jordan's bedroom, Jordan directed him through to the master en suite and flicked on the lights.

This bathroom had always been one of Derek's favorite fantasies. But it was a place he'd never allowed himself to set foot in after the night he'd sat on a chair and Jordan had cleaned up his bruised and broken face. The same night he'd first decided he needed to put some distance between himself and his beloved professor, for Jordan's safety.

Tonight was a different story altogether.

Derek let his eyes sweep around the lavish space and, as always, he got stuck on the massive claw-foot whirlpool tub that stood alone in front of floor-to-ceiling windows overlooking the ocean. It was debauched, decadent, almost to the point of obscene, to think you were stripping down and anyone could see, but really, no one was out there.

On the opposite wall was a shower that ran the entire length of it. There were jets at every possible angle a person could imagine, and at each end was a handheld showerhead. That shower was designed with one thing in mind, and getting clean was *not* it.

"Strip."

The word was clipped, spoken in a voice that sent a bolt of desire directly to Derek's balls, and he immediately went about doing what he was told.

He kicked off his flip-flops and then reached over his shoulder and gathered a handful of his shirt and pulled it off. When he tossed it on the ground, he heard an appreciative groan from the opposite side of the room, where the tub was, and saw Jordan leaned up against it with eyes glued to what he was doing.

"And the shorts," Jordan said, and then dragged his teeth over his lower lip.

Derek unbuttoned his shorts and shoved them and his briefs from his hips, and once he was completely naked Jordan crooked a finger at him. Derek walked across the tiled floor, conscious of the window-lined wall, and when he arrived opposite Jordan he stopped and looked down at the man, still fully clothed, resting against the tub.

Jordan cocked his head to the side and gazed up from his

perch, and Derek was, as always, fascinated by the enigma before him.

No one who met Jordan would ever imagine the side of him that he was about to unleash on Derek, and that was what made him unique. He was carefree, fun, and effervescent. But as Derek had learned over the course of their on again/off again relationship, when that bedroom door shut and Jordan's clothes came off, his partner better fucking brace himself, because he'd soon learn what a bright mind and an endless amount of energy could conjure up.

As a tense silence filled the air, Jordan got to his feet and raised his head until his lips were a whisper away from Derek's jaw. He breathed out and snapped his teeth shut like he wanted to take a bite of him, and the warmth of his breath and promise of that sound had Derek's fists clenching by his sides.

*Fuck.* He hadn't even touched him yet and Derek's cock was so hard it hurt.

Without a word, Jordan stepped to the side and walked around behind him. Derek could see their reflections in the window, but he didn't need it to know that Jordan was close by. He could feel the whisper of fabric from his clothes brushing against his naked skin, just as he could sense Jordan's body heat.

"There are so many things I want to do to you. I'm trying to decide where to begin."

Derek's skin broke out in gooseflesh at the illicit pledge as five strong fingers smoothed up the back of his neck and into his hair. Jordan twisted his hand and caught hold of the strands in a firm grip as his lips landed on Derek's shoulder blade.

"I can't decide what I want to put in you first."

Derek panted as Jordan scraped his teeth along his skin and continued to tug and pull at his hair in a sensual massage.

"My tongue. My fingers. Or should I just bypass those and go directly to my cock?"

Derek groaned at the image the words produced, and let his eyes fall shut as Jordan kept right on seducing him.

"Mhmm, or maybe I should start with none of those. *Maybe* I'll go and get something to ease you back into the idea of me fucking you all. Night. Long."

"Jesus, Jordan," Derek said, and gave up the fight to not touch himself as he wrapped his fingers around the root of his cock.

Jordan ran his fingers down from Derek's hair to the nape of his neck and dug them into the tense cords of muscle there. It felt amazing as Derek continued to stroke his cock in time with each sharp dig of Jordan's knuckles.

"I'm going to work this tension out of you one muscle at a time, if need be. So you better settle in and slow down that hand of yours, because we've got a long night ahead of us."

Jordan punctuated his vow by sinking his teeth into Derek's shoulder and flicking his tongue over the tattooed sword that decorated the skin just below. Then he trailed his fingers down Derek's spine to the crack of his ass and said, "Wash up and meet me in the bedroom. And Derek?"

He waited until he could find his tongue, and then he managed, "Yeah?"

Jordan found his eyes in the window and said, "The first time you come tonight is going to be my way. So don't even think about getting off in the shower or I'll send you home. Understand?"

Derek slowly nodded, and Jordan's inner minx shone through in the grin he flashed, and the way he swatted his ass.

"Good boy."

---

JORDAN LEFT THE bathroom with an erection he was sure he could use to drill through fucking concrete, but no. He had other plans for the painfully stiff dick he was trying to calm somewhat.

He had to get away from Derek for a few minutes and get

himself under control if he was going to give his guy what he needed.

From the second Derek had stepped off the elevator, the tension radiating off him had been evident. His shoulders had been stiff, his jaw set, and even after stripping down to nothing, his body was held at rigid attention.

*Oh yeah,* Derek needed to be worked over, and good.

Jordan threw what he wanted on the bed and dimmed the lights as he listened for the shower in the next room. He was dying to know what had happened today, but he knew now wasn't the time to ask. There would be time for that later.

He looked around the room trying to decide how he wanted the night to go, and when his eyes fell on the chaise lounge he was reminded of the last time they were there in his bedroom and thought it was time to replace that memory.

With a plan in place, Jordan dragged the chaise so it was horizontal with the end of his bed, and then he stripped out of his clothes and waited. Not too long after, he heard the faucet shut off, and he walked around to situate himself exactly where he intended to start this evening's performance. He stretched out along the long line of the chaise, draped an arm over the back of it, and slowly milked his cock as he waited for Derek to join him.

He purposely kept his head turned away from the bedroom door, letting Derek know he was in control and expected him to get his ass over here and on the bed as soon as he was done, and Derek didn't disappoint. Within minutes, Jordan caught the tanned muscles of Derek's physique out of the corner of his eye as he walked between the end of the bed and chaise.

Seated as he was, lounged back with one leg bent and resting against the back of the chair and the other stretched out before him, Jordan knew his body was displayed to Derek like a fucking gourmet buffet.

He tipped his head up, ignoring Derek's very prominent erection, and when he had his attention he raised an eyebrow and asked, "All clean?" Then he dropped his gaze to the straining cock only inches from his face and added, "I sure hope not. Sit on the bed, Derek."

Derek didn't take his eyes off him as he took several steps back, and when the back of his knees hit the mattress, he lowered down until he was seated.

"Spread your legs," Jordan suggested, but he knew his tone was more of an order, and if Derek's quick compliance was anything to go by, he sure as hell didn't mind taking the instruction. "Now show me how you'd fuck my mouth if it was wrapped around you instead of your hand."

Derek's eyes dropped to Jordan's mouth and he made sure to bite and tongue his lips, making them plump and shiny for the man now sliding his large hand up and down his impressive length.

Jordan couldn't keep his own hand still as he trailed his eyes down Derek's serious face to his flexing forearm and widespread thighs. He was phenomenal to look at as his hand moved faster, and Jordan had to clamp his own fingers tight at the base of his arousal due to the threat of explosion.

"Stop," he growled. And just like that, Derek did.

Swinging his legs off the chaise, Jordan got to his feet and took the two steps he needed to be standing directly in front of Derek's face.

"Look at me," he said, needing to see what was going on in those blue eyes of Derek's. When he tipped his face up and Jordan could see the walls in place, he gripped Derek's chin, knowing that gentle wasn't what his man needed right now. Then he bent at the waist to crush his lips against Derek's in a brutal kiss.

Derek grunted at the fierce onslaught, and Jordan took advantage by shoving his tongue deep as he moved his hand to the back of Derek's hair to hold his head in place. He bit at Derek's lips and dug his fingers into his jaw until he heard Derek curse.

Jordan then tore his mouth free and shoved Derek's shoulder back. "Lie down."

Derek lowered himself to the mattress without a word, and Jordan, in turn, sank to the floor between Derek's spread thighs.

This was perfect. He really *was* a fucking genius.

He grabbed the few items he'd dropped at the end of the bed and placed them on the floor beside him, and then he ran his palms from Derek's knees to his ankles, and at the left one he said, "Lift."

When Derek raised his foot, Jordan helped to place his heel on the frame of the bed and felt his dick weep at the sight that was now spread out before him. Derek was a visually stunning man. Jordan had always been taken away by his presence in general. But stripped bare, and laid out for him to do as he pleased, Jordan marveled at the sheer perfection of what made Derek a man.

He had a heavy sac that was currently scrunched up tight to his body, his cock was thick and long when erect, as it currently was, and his hole was so tight that every time Jordan slid inside him, he swore it was the first time.

*God.* That thought was so damn hot that Jordan had to squeeze his eyes shut for a second to control the urge to say fuck it and tunnel into the place he most wanted to be.

Once he was back under some modicum of control, he grabbed the bottle of lube and poured a good amount into the palm of his hand. He slicked it over his fingers and made sure they were nice and wet before he ghosted them across Derek's balls. Derek used the foot he had anchored on the frame to help propel his lower body up and give Jordan better access down to his perineum.

"Oh fuck," Jordan heard from above, and he couldn't help an answering hum of approval as he gently tested the tight pucker under the tips of his fingers.

"Relax for me," Jordan whispered, and blew a warm breath across Derek's cock and balls.

"Sure, let me get right fucking on that."

*Yes…there he is,* Jordan thought. *My badass.*

"Jordan…" Derek said, and it sounded as though he was gnashing his teeth together.

Jordan didn't reply with words. Instead, he moved so his mouth was between Derek's thighs, and flicked his tongue across his balls while his finger slid inside. He thrilled at the shout that met his ears from the penetration, and he could see the muscle of Derek's thigh tense by his head as he thrust down on his hand. Jordan withdrew his finger and then pushed back in, knowing what was to come was going to be a hell of a lot harder than one of his fingers. Raising his head, he took in the view above and shut his eyes for a second, calming himself as he asked, "You okay?"

Derek's hand was moving up and down his cock like his life depended on it, and when Jordan got no answer he pulled his finger completely free and a growl of frustration left the man on the bed.

"I asked you a question. Answer me."

Derek craned his head up and glowered down at him, but Jordan wasn't fucking around; he wasn't about to move on until Derek told him—

"More."

Exactly that.

---

DEREK LAY BACK on the bed and clamped his teeth together at what he knew was about to come, namely himself.

Several times over he'd had to bite his tongue, causing a sting of pain just to stop himself from going off like a rocket. But he knew if he could wait, if he could hold off until Jordan was done tormenting him, the high would be out of this fucking world.

"Bend your other leg, just like this one."

*Christ,* he thought, as Jordan's instruction met his ears. He could feel Jordan's fingers rubbing over his hole, and as soon as he moved his second heel to the bedframe, he saw Jordan raise his hand to pour —*oh, fuck yeah*—a liberal amount of cool lube over him before two fingers were inside him and he was seeing fucking stars.

His fingers clenched in the covers of Jordan's bedding while his others frantically pumped the cock he was hoping would wait, *God please just fucking wait,* for him to really get what he needed.

When he'd walked out of the bathroom and seen the back of Jordan's short hair where he sat on that damn chaise like a king, Derek had known he was about to be worked out, wrung out, and then laid out. Then Jordan had gone to his knees with a bottle of lube and a flesh-covered plastic cock, that he had no doubt was about to be shoved inside of him, and Derek was surprised he hadn't come right then

But no, he would not let this moment escape him because he couldn't keep control of his orgasm. He would wait. Wait until Jordan was in him and pounding him through his ten-thousand-dollar mattress before he gave in to the rush that was building to epic proportions.

Derek's mind had emptied of everything that had been plaguing him when he'd arrived. With every thrust of Jordan's fingers, and suck of his mouth, he was banishing each and every thought, until finally nothing was in his head or body, except the man working him over.

Derek's breathing was heavy as he stared up at the high ceiling of Jordan's bedroom, and with each exhale his body relaxed even further. Just as his eyes were closing, the wide head of what he knew was the dildo pressed forward against his body, and he clamped his fist around the top of his leaking dick, pinching the skin there to hold back the urge to come.

"Jordan…*Jesus.*"

Sharp teeth nipped at his knee, and when the toy slipped

past that first ring of resistance, Derek arched his head back and lifted his hips up off the bed.

"Derek, you look so damn sexy," he heard Jordan say from somewhere between his legs. "Take it."

Derek let his hips fall back to the mattress as more of the toy was slid inside of him, and when he felt as close to full as he could possibly get, Jordan got to his feet, and the look on his face was one Derek was extremely familiar with. His eyes were narrowed, his face was flushed, and his gorgeous, full lips were pulled taut as he said, "On your stomach, Derek. Now."

Derek rolled to his stomach and scooted up the bed a little, groaning at the feel of the phallus still deep inside him. As soon as his engorged cock hit the cool sheets, he moaned from the fucking pleasure of it. He pushed up so his forearms were propped on the bed and braced his knees wide and low so he could rub his dick back and forth against the fabric.

"God," Jordan said as the bed dipped and Derek felt him moving closer to him. "You know exactly what you want tonight, don't you?"

There was no way Derek could deny it as he lowered his forehead to the bed and masturbated against the sheets. He was going out of his damn mind.

Jordan's palm stroked over his ass, and as his fingers gripped the seven-incher inside him and pulled, and then pushed it back in several fucking times, Derek felt the cool splash of more lube hit the hole Jordan was stretching. This time when Jordan pulled the toy free, it wasn't the head of the dildo that grazed over him; it was Jordan's covered cock, and Derek knew he was teasing them both before they tore into one another.

A firm palm began a torturous glide up along Derek's spine as inch by inch Jordan filled him. When that hand then gripped the back of his neck and Derek was urged down until his cheek was on the bed, Jordan's toned body intimately curled over the top of his and Derek heard himself fucking whimper.

Jordan licked the stubble along his cheek, and when he got to his ear he whispered, "Ready?"

Derek licked his lips and swallowed as he closed his eyes and counted back from ten. When his mind was completely blank, he turned his head, met Jordan's eyes, and said the only word he could.

"Yes."

## Chapter 26

"THEN BRACE YOURSELF."

The command made Derek's cock ache as his fingers curled around the bedsheets and he planted his knees as firmly as possible in the mattress. A raspy rumble emerged from his throat and his cheek rubbed against the smooth sheets, as Jordan's hands moved to either side of his hips.

He closed his eyes as Jordan's fingers dug into his skin, and as he slowly dragged his cock out, Derek heard a groan leave the man behind him.

Derek bit his lower lip to keep from begging Jordan to hurry the fuck up, but he didn't dare in case Jordan took that as an invitation to torture him some more.

"How you doin' down there?" Jordan asked, his voice raspy compared to his usual tone.

Derek brought one of his hands down to grip his cock, and as he stroked himself once, twice, and then a third time, Jordan reached around under him and stilled his hand.

"Oh no you don't," he teased as he slowly rolled his hips forward, sliding his cock deep inside. "Don't rush me. Or I'll make you wait even longer."

*God.* Derek was so gone over this guy. Jordan knew him in ways that Derek didn't even know himself, and as Jordan circled Derek's wrist and yanked on it, Derek let him move his hand back to the bedsheet, where he pinned it in place.

"Fuck, Jordan. Hurry up," he said, finally reaching the point where he was about to come with or without Jordan moving inside him, and he knew which he'd rather have. Jordan's chuckle was illicit, and the hands that gripped Derek's waist were his only warning before Jordan slid inside.

Derek's eyes squeezed shut at the sensation, and when Jordan was so deep that Derek could feel his balls against his body, Derek opened his eyes to look back at the one waiting for him to adjust.

Derek concentrated on the scorching brown eyes holding his, the perspiration he could see gleaming over Jordan's body, and the tense muscles that were poised and ready for action the second he gave the go signal.

Jordan was an incredible sight to see as he waited, his own muscles now tense with his restraint, his body trembling with his pent-up desire, and Derek admired him as he licked his full lips.

This was the only moment in this entire scenario where *he* was calling the shots, and he thought it was only fair to make Jordan wait it out a little. That was until he saw one of Jordan's eyebrows arch.

*Busted.*

Before he could utter a word, Jordan pulled out of him and then he surged forward in one smooth thrust.

"Fuck." Derek's curse was loud, and the answering response from Jordan was to do it again. He shifted back and slid his length free until the tip was barely inside of him and then, *holy shit*, plowed back in.

Derek pushed up on his hands and moved into the man behind him, giving as good as he was getting as they moved together in a savage mating. At one point Jordan moved down to brace a hand on the bed and wrap the other around his neck as he kissed Derek's cheek and took him hard, just as he fucking loved it.

Derek shouted as teeth bit his lobe, and the laugh in his ear was arrogant as fuck as Jordan let him have it. Derek reached back and wrapped a hand around Jordan's neck, holding him in place as he craned his head back and sank his teeth into Jordan's jaw and begged, "Give it to me."

Jordan raised his head and brushed a surprisingly soft kiss across his lips, and when he said, "Always," Derek's heart almost stopped.

Jordan moved away to take hold of his waist, and Derek groaned as the thick shaft inside him lodged impossibly deeper. Jordan rolled his hips and pushed in and out of him with more power than anyone would think he possessed from looking at him. The muscles in Derek's arm flexed as they held him in place, and Derek thought it was telling how well Jordan knew him by the exact way he positioned himself so he could reach beneath him to take a hold of his dick and stroke.

Derek arched his head back and growled, and to his own ears he sounded like a wild fucking animal. He was going out of his mind, drowning in a sea of sexual nirvana. Then Jordan lowered down behind him and bit his shoulder and Derek shouted his name so loud, he made his own fucking ears hurt.

The man destroying every semblance of thought in his head then moved to take up a fixed position on his knees behind him, and Derek took over milking his own cock.

He closed his eyes as Jordan methodically took him, and it was rough and raw but at the same time so intimate it made every shit thing that had happened with his father vanish.

It was exactly what Derek needed as his orgasm slammed into him, and then Jordan's fingers dug into his skin and Derek heard him shout out his name as he came too.

*Goddamn.* When Jordan was buried inside him, the rest of the world disappeared, and as soon as he could string two coherent sentences together, Derek was going to work out a way to tell him that and ask when they could start over again.

---

"BETTER?" JORDAN ASKED as he collapsed to the bed beside Derek's brawny frame.

*Hot damn*, his body and mind felt as though it were levitating somewhere above the mattress the both of them were stretched out on. His limbs were loose and his eyes were having trouble staying open, but the delicious feeling of lethargy was a satisfying one, and so was the way his heart squeezed at the one word that just met his ears.

"Much."

"Yeah?"

"Yeah. I had no idea how much seeing him again would affect me. And you know, even though the asshole is sick, he still had the audacity to threaten me. *Me*. The one person who shouldn't even fucking be there helping. I'm such an idiot."

"No. You're not an idiot. You're a human being. Which is more than I can say for him."

Derek turned his head then to face Jordan, and all of the tension that had been evident when he'd arrived was gone. "Yeah, I know you're right. It's just difficult to wrap your mind around it when it's happening. It's hard not to hate yourself for going and helping in the first fucking place." Derek looked up at the ceiling for a few seconds, sighed, and then looked back. A slow smile stretched across his lips. "But damn, Jordan. That side of you, I swear. I'll never get used to it."

Jordan knew exactly what he was referring to. He was aware that his sexual preferences and appetite often shocked those he was with. But Derek had been the first he'd warned from the get-go, and eagerly met him head-on.

"Are you complaining?"

"Hell no. And you know it."

Jordan pushed up onto his hands and leaned in to kiss Derek's cheek. "That's what I like to hear."

"Of course it is. You're totally arrogant."

Jordan got off the bed and scowled at Derek where he lay with his hands behind his head, his gorgeous body on full display. "Well, that's rude."

"Don't try and deny it. It's one of the reasons you're such a phenomenal fuck."

"Derek!"

Derek chuckled. "How are you embarrassed right now? You know exactly who you are and you don't apologize for it—ever. That's totally hot."

Jordan pursed his lips as he thought that over and then grinned, deciding to take the compliment as he turned on the balls of his feet. "I'll be back. I'm going to shower, and you, my filthy-mouthed friend, know where the other bathroom is. You may go and use that."

"I can't use yours?"

Jordan aimed a look over his shoulder as he continued walking through to the bathroom. "No. I don't shower with people who call me arrogant."

As he stepped inside, he heard Derek shout, "I also said you were a phenomenal—"

Jordan slammed the bathroom door before Derek could finish, but not before he could hide his laughter.

*Punk.*

---

AFTER WASHING UP, Jordan strolled back into his bedroom and eyed Derek where he was stretched out as though he hadn't moved. The damp hair, however, proved otherwise.

"So, can I ask you a question?" Jordan asked, and threw his towel over the chaise. "I was thinking about it in the shower, and it's something I've always wanted to know but never really thought it was my place to ask."

As Jordan came around the side of the bed, Derek rolled to his stomach, and the view of all that taut skin on display was too much to resist. Jordan climbed into bed and scooted in until he was practically glued to Derek's side, and then he flung one of his legs over Derek's to settle it between his thick outstretched thighs. He put a hand under his cheek and waited for Derek to look him in the eye.

"*You,* Jordan Devaney, held back on something you want to know? That's fucking shocking."

"I'll have you know, there's a lot of things about me that I'm sure would shock you."

"Oh, I have no doubt."

Refusing to be distracted, Jordan shifted closer. He'd wanted the answer to this question ever since he'd met Derek, so there was no way he was going to miss out on the opportunity to ask now that he had him there pliant and relaxed.

"So…" he started, and then frowned.

"Are you nervous?"

"No."

"You *are* nervous," Derek teased, immediately raising the hackles on Jordan's back.

"I am *not* nervous, I just—"

"What?"

"Oh, fine," he finally said. "You and Daniel, were you ever…" He left the obvious interpretation of what he meant hanging in the air.

Derek eyed him with great consideration and then raised an eyebrow. "Were we ever…?"

Jordan bristled at being the object of Derek's amusement. He pushed up on his hand and glowered at the man now laughing up at him.

"You *know* what I mean."

"Oh, right. You mean running buddies?" Derek asked, and

flashed a grin that had Jordan shoving his shoulder. But before he could retract his hand, Derek took hold of it and tackled him so that Jordan was underneath him. Jordan squirmed halfheartedly, and when it was clear he was going nowhere, he stopped and decided his next best option was to glare Derek to death.

"You're really damn cute when you're pissed off."

"You didn't think I was too cute earlier when I had my—"

"Uh uh," Derek said, and cut him off by pressing a quick kiss to his lips. "You asked me a question."

"And you were a shit about it. So what's new?"

Derek rocked his hips against Jordan, and he spread his thighs, letting the infuriating man settle between his legs.

"Aww, and now you're pouting. See? Cute. Wrap your legs around me. I like how it feels."

"Maybe. If you answer me."

Jordan shuddered as Derek nuzzled into his neck to kiss him, but then gave in and wound his legs over the top of Derek's thighs, stroking his hands down his spine.

"What was the question again?" Derek asked, and when Jordan pinched his ass, he laughed and said, "Okay, okay. Me and Danny boy, huh?" He laughed harder as the words left his mouth, and then he shook his head. "How long have you been wanting to ask me that?"

Jordan gave him a pointed look that said, *Answer the damn question*, which made Derek laugh all over again.

"It's not that funny, Derek."

"It kinda is."

"It is not. That first year, you two were inseparable, and then—"

"And then we had different classes, busy workloads, and for me, a really bad home life. We fell apart, drifted—it happens."

Jordan frowned, still not satisfied with that answer. *Ugh, fine. If I have to spell it out for him.* "So you broke up?"

"No."

"No?" He let out an exasperated breath. "Are you being purposely obtuse?"

"Maybe? If you want to ask me something, then just ask. I'll answer."

"Fine. Were you sleeping with Daniel Finley? As in fucking him? And so help me God, if you give me some ridiculous answer I will murder you and chop your body into a thousand tiny pieces and scatter them all over. And before you doubt me, remember how smart I am. I could totally get away with it."

Derek kissed his lips then whispered, "No. I wasn't fucking Finn."

Jordan opened his mouth, about to demand to know if Daniel was the one doing the—

"And Finn hasn't *ever* fucked me. Happy?"

Jordan wasn't sure why, but this new piece of information made him incredibly happy. He aimed a grin at Derek and nodded, which made Derek laugh all over again.

"What?"

"I was just thinking how ironic this conversation is."

"Why? It's not like it's such a stretch of the imagination. I remember catching you two one day outside my classroom holding hands, and…"

Derek rolled them to their sides and nodded. "Yep, I remember. You got pissed off."

"I did not," Jordan protested.

"Yeah, you did."

"*Any*way, why is it ironic?"

"Because I had a total hard-on for you and Daniel wanted to jump Hayes. I guess you could say we were very happy to be studying *under* our professors."

Jordan laughed and shifted to his back. "Deviants, the both of you."

"Sure, Devaney. Keep blaming me for the fact we're both naked and in your bed right now."

"It's true. I heard all about the way Daniel Finley chased

Brantley during college, but you acted as if you were too busy to be in this bed with me…so, I never really knew if you were interested or just running your mouth to annoy me."

"I was very interested. Which you found out the night you danced around your house to Britney Spears."

Jordan hummed, thinking of that delicious memory. "Yes, I remember. It *was* obvious after that night. You're right."

"Oh yeah. What gave me away? The way I almost came in your hand?"

"Cheeky."

"You were so fucking hot that night. If I hadn't had an exam the next day…"

"Mhmm." Jordan molded his body against Derek's side, and before he knew he was going to, he heard himself ask, "So, why me?"

Derek chuckled. "What do you mean?"

"Oh come on, Derek. We aren't exactly a likely pair."

"Maybe," he said, then turned his head on the pillow. "But from the very beginning we always, I don't know, found each other. More often than not in the middle of arguments or—"

"Sex?"

"Yes," Derek agreed, and reached across to take Jordan's hand. "But it's more than just sex. You ground me. You make me believe in the impossible. You make it all seem obtainable. And you make me want to be better…for you."

Jordan's breath caught when Derek placed a kiss in his palm and then laid it over his heart. The move was so uncharacteristic of Derek, and so intimate for them, that Jordan recognized it for what it was.

This was another perfect moment.

He'd been accused of missing the first one, where Derek had told him he loved him, but Jordan sure as hell wasn't going to miss this. He gently kissed Derek's mouth, about to tell him how much he meant to him when the intercom buzzed and life intruded.

# Chapter 27

DEREK CLOSED HIS eyes as Jordan got off the bed and grabbed a robe from the closet. He heard Jordan huff as he walked over to the intercom panel in the bedroom and then mutter, "Perfect timing."

Pressing down on the button, he said, "*Hello*," sounding extremely put out.

"J?"

The female voice was unfamiliar to Derek, but if the way Jordan's hand flew off the button and he looked at him with huge eyes, she wasn't to Jordan.

"Jordan?"

"Oh my God," he said, and before Derek could ask what the problem was, the intercom started buzzing again. "Oh. My. *God*."

Derek laughed at the usually put together man as he kind of…well, fell the fuck apart. "Jordan? You gonna get that? Who is it?"

Jordan shook his head and then rushed across his room toward the bathroom. When he came out with Derek's shorts and shirt in his hands and tossed them on the bed, Derek frowned.

"Put them on. We don't have long."

Not having a clue what was going on, Derek sat up and reached for his shorts. He'd just pulled them up and was making a grab for his shirt when a woman called throughout the penthouse.

"Oh, J! My sweet boy. Where are you?"

"Jordan? Who the—" Derek didn't get to finish his question because Jordan's bedroom door was flung open, and standing in the massive doorway with a wide-brimmed hat and a set of glasses in hand was a woman who looked as though she'd stepped off an *Italian Vogue* cover.

From her black skyscraper heels, to the snug fit of her cream pencil skirt and fitted black blouse, she appeared elegant and sophisticated. Her mahogany hair was swept off her face and pinned to the top of her head, and around her neck was a cream-colored scarf. She looked as though she was worth a million dollars.

As her dark eyes took in the scene before her—Derek standing by the side of an unmade bed in only his shorts and Jordan wrapped in a robe with his hair every which way—she headed across the room with her arms outstretched to the man who, less than an hour ago, had fucked Derek as though his life depended on it.

"There's my sweet boy. Come give your mother a hug."

---

JORDAN LOOKED PAST his mother's shoulder to where Derek was now pulling his shirt down, and wished that he could see his face.

*What is he thinking?*

"Mother," Jordan finally managed, and pulled out of his

mom's arms. "I didn't realize when you called the other day that you meant you would be stopping in *this* week."

"Well, your father had to come back for some boring business meeting," she said with a flick of her gloved wrist, and then leaned in to press a kiss to his cheek. "And I needed to speak with you. But more importantly, aren't you going to introduce me to the young man standing beside your bed, dear?"

Jordan shook his head and then stepped around her. He loved his mother more than he could put into words, but he knew for some she was more to take than other moms.

He was about to check on Derek when he heard a cough from behind his mother, and she turned so she was standing beside him and they were both staring at a widely smiling Derek.

"Yeah, Jordan. Aren't you going to introduce us?"

*Oh, okay. So* that's *how this is going to go, is it?* Raising an eyebrow at Derek, he accepted the challenge, and gestured from his mother back to the smug man grinning at him.

"Mother, I'd like you to meet Derek."

As she flashed a smile, which Jordan knew was identical to his own, in Derek's direction, he continued.

"He was formerly a student of mine and also lived here at the Palisades for a year or so somewhere in there. Now, don't be all scandalized—back then it was in separate bedrooms, of course." He paused and placed his hand on his mother's arm, and when she looked down at him he thought, *Hell, if ever there's been a time to say it out loud.* "But just recently, he told me in no uncertain terms that he loved me madly and would no longer just let me use him for his body. Luckily for him..." Jordan let his eyes slide to Derek, who was staring at him with his mouth agape until he winked at him, then Derek glared. "I feel exactly the same way."

The room plunged into silence after his monologue, and as he kept his eyes locked with Derek's, his mother was the one to break through the quiet.

"Well, that's quite a story. But I'm positive there's more to it than that. I'm going to go and freshen up and rummage through your wine fridge, J. I'll meet you boys out on the balcony when you're ready." She was about to walk out, but at the last second turned back to Derek and said, "Good for you. He needs someone with a firm hand. And you sure have the muscles for it."

"*Mother.*"

"Okay." She laughed and gave a waggle of her fingers as she turned and headed back toward the door.

When they were alone, Jordan rounded back to Derek and noted the furrowed brow still firmly in place.

"Before you get all mad," Jordan began, and raised his palm. Derek walked forward, backing him up across the room, as was Derek's way. "My mother is under no illusions as to who her son is. So if I'd tried to pretend you were in here looking at my clothing selection, she never would've—" His back hit the wall and he let out a soft "*oomph*" as Derek placed a palm on either side of his head.

"Why would I be mad?"

"Umm…" Jordan floundered for a second. Derek's intense gaze had him unnerved. "You're not?"

Derek lowered his mouth to his and whispered, "Nope."

"Oh," Jordan sighed.

"Mhmm," Derek agreed, and then sucked Jordan's bottom lip into his mouth as he trailed the back of his fingers along his neck and between the lapels of his robe. When his fingers then moved to the knotted belt at Jordan's waist, Derek slipped them behind the loop and tugged him forward from the wall. He pressed a sweet kiss to Jordan's mouth that had him reaching for his arms to keep himself from sliding down to the floor, and then Derek raised his head and *winked* at him.

"You love me."

"Huh?" was Jordan's intelligent answer.

Derek backed away, and as he did, he started doing some stupid little dance with his hands and shoulders that made Jordan snort. Then Derek pointed at him and said, "*You* love *me*."

"And that makes you what…ridiculous?"

Derek nodded as he continued, making his way backward toward the door of the bedroom. "It makes me ridiculously happy. Now put some clothes on. For God's sake, Jordan, anyone would think you spent the last couple of hours having hot sex."

As Derek disappeared, Jordan caught sight of himself in the mirror on the door of his walk-in closet and barely recognized the sap smiling back at him. Derek Pearson had him standing there with hearts in his eyes wanting to twirl around his fucking bedroom, and as he pushed off the wall to get ready for his guy, he couldn't help the chuckle that slipped free.

He'd known from the very beginning that man was going to be trouble, and hell if he hadn't been spot on with that assessment.

---

"SO TELL ME ABOUT JORDAN, the boy."

It was easy to see where Jordan got his love of life from as Gabrielle Devaney tipped her head back and laughed joyously. Derek and Jordan were seated opposite his mother, and they were well into their second bottle of wine as they enjoyed the fire pit and comfy couches out on Jordan's balcony.

Jordan had pulled on some faded jeans with holes all over the place, a gray crew-neck T-shirt, and a navy-blue beanie that was sitting halfway off the back of his head, and he looked fucking hot.

Derek knew that Jordan would've meticulously picked out his look. But as Jordan tucked his feet up under him and leaned into his side, Derek had never appreciated his eye for details more.

"Let me see. Jordan as a boy..." Gabrielle aimed twinkling eyes at her son, and Jordan angled his glass toward her.

"Be nice."

"Why should I be nice? You never are. And Derek here already knows you..."

Jordan took a sip of wine and then looked back over his shoulder at Derek. "Oh, I suppose you're right. No use trying to lie now. Have at it."

His mother grinned at him and then aimed her eyes over at Derek. "He was too smart for his own good. Always getting into trouble—"

"I was not—"

"Always *butting in* with an opinion of his own when people were trying to tell him things. Running with the wrong kinds of boys. You know, the bad ones."

"Imagine that," Derek said, and reached for his wine glass on the table and took a sip.

"Excuse me," Jordan interjected. "I happen to remember another student who tried the badass routine all the time. He tried to get thrown out of my class. *Twice*."

"We're not talking about him, Jordan. So stop trying to distract us and drink your wine."

"You do realize that I'm not five anymore, right?"

"Were you ever five?" his mother asked.

"Good point."

Gabrielle winked at her son, and Derek saw Jordan in every nuance of that expression as she continued.

"I'm sure you know by now how wonderful Jordan is. His father and I couldn't be more proud of him. Bachelor's degree at age fourteen, PhD by twenty-one, and then a university professor to top it all off. Parents couldn't want, or ask, for more of their child. And while the public kept a close eye on him during his *wilder* years, they backed off as he got older. His history professor really helped him to focus his energy and stay on the straight and narrow."

"Well, the narrow, anyway," Jordan added with a laugh.

"One thing, though, that the press will never tell you is what a wonderfully generous person he is. He doesn't even like to advertise it."

"Mom, you don't have to convince him I'm more than just a pretty face. He is aware."

"I know. But you should be proud of these things, dear. Especially this recent charity you've been working on getting up and running for abused and neglected children. The Pearson Project."

As soon as the words left her mouth, Derek stiffened where he sat.

*No…there's no way she just said what I think she did. Did she?*

Derek felt the red-hot burn of embarrassment race up his neck as he stared across at the elegant woman watching him.

Surely he'd misunderstood what she'd just said, because if not, that meant this woman…this sophisticated, worldly woman, who happened to be Jordan's mother, knew all about his appalling past.

*Fuck.* He felt like he was going to vomit. His stomach turned and his palms grew clammy as he looked between mother and son.

How much did she know? What had Jordan told her?

That his father beat him, that he was the town drunk, that he'd mooched off Jordan just so he wouldn't have to live in some fucking dive throughout college?

Jesus, *how fucking mortifying?*

It was bad enough that he was coming into this relationship with Jordan at a disadvantage—the money, the condo, hell… even the brains. *But now this?* What was Jordan thinking spilling all his problems to his mother? To the public?

There was a reason he kept his shit private. He didn't want to be some fucking role model or platform for people to look at and think, *Oh, he's come a long way. No.* He just wanted to be left the fuck alone and forget about the miserable family that spawned him.

Tonight, however, that would not be happening, because without any doing of his own his personal life was now up for fucking discussion.

All other words Gabrielle Devaney was saying faded as *the Pearson Project* continued on a loop in his head—

"Derek?"

He'd completely missed whatever she'd just asked him, and Jordan had sat up and was looking at him with caution in his eyes. He looked like he wanted to speak, to explain away whatever the fuck had just happened here, but Derek was already shifting out of his spot and getting to his feet.

"Derek, wait." That was Jordan. His voice was familiar, but still, the only words Derek focused on were: Abuse. Children. Neglect. *The Pearson Project.*

"I've got to go," he mumbled, and turned like a robot and headed back inside, away from the two watching him.

As he passed by the dining room table, he put his unfinished glass of wine down and continued through the penthouse like a man in a daze. When he was halfway through the living room and making his way toward the elevator, he heard Jordan call out to him again.

"Derek. Derek, wait. I was going to tell you."

He'd been hoping he would escape before Jordan made an excuse to his mother, because the emotion that was now bubbling up inside Derek, past the shock, past the hurt, was embarrassment and anger.

*How dare he do this…*

"Derek."

When the door to the elevator opened, Derek stepped inside, jabbed the button, and then turned to face the man opposite him. Jordan looked as though his entire world was being ripped away from him, but Derek didn't have any words to tell him otherwise.

As it was, he was barely holding on himself, because for the first time since he'd met Jordan, he was the last person Derek wanted to see.

## Chapter 28

JORDAN STOOD AT Brantley's front door the next evening with a cooler full of wine in one hand and his cell phone in the other.

It was Saturday night and he'd been trying to get a hold of Derek without any success ever since he'd left his place. He must've called half a dozen times, left voice messages, and finally texts, and what had he received in return? Radio silence.

This dinner party was the last thing he wanted to do tonight, but he'd figured if he felt compelled to show up and make an appearance then maybe Derek would too. It was wishful thinking, he knew that, but he figured turning up at Derek's place would likely result in a door in his face, so he would try his luck here first, and then go and beat down a door if necessary.

He raised his hand to knock, heard the sound of footsteps behind him, and turned to, *thank you, God*, see Derek, who'd stopped halfway up the deck that wrapped around Brantley's beach house.

Jordan's breath caught at the sight of him. Other than tired eyes, which Jordan knew would match his own, Derek looked perfect. But the closed-off expression on his face told Jordan not to come any closer.

He was wearing black jeans and a tailored army-green shirt with the sleeves rolled up to his elbows, showing off his beautifully tattooed arms. His nails were painted their signature black and he was wearing his favored boots, buckled but not laced. The entire getup was a "back off" signal. It was rife with attitude, and the arms crossed over his chest were a fuck off if ever Jordan had seen one. But he was determined to say something before they were faced with Brantley and Daniel and a dinner that would more than likely be awkward as hell.

Jordan took a step forward just as the door behind him opened and Brantley's voice echoed into the silent night.

"Oh, good. You're both here."

Derek's eyes lifted to where Jordan knew his friend was standing.

"Yeah. We're here," Derek said as he dropped his hands down by his sides and marched forward. As Derek passed by him their shoulders collided, but he kept on going, and Jordan shut his eyes, wanting to scream.

He counted to ten, hoping he had the fortitude to get through this night when all he wanted was five minutes to talk to Derek alone and explain what he'd been thinking when he started up the damn charity.

*Jesus*. This was so *not* how it was supposed to go. He'd wanted to tell Derek about it in private. Invite him to be a part of it. But before he'd had a chance, his mother had unintentionally stepped on a mine. Now, instead of showing Derek how much he admired him and how all that he'd accomplished could be an inspiration to others, he would be explaining what a giant ass he was for not telling him earlier.

When a hand touched his shoulder, he jumped. *Shit, Brantley.* He'd forgotten he was there. He'd called Brantley last night to give him a heads-up that Derek might not show tonight, and by the end of the conversation he'd been drinking wine and spilling his guts about what a colossal mistake he'd made.

"Hey," Brantley said. "You okay?"

Jordan tried for a smile but knew by the concern marring his friend's face that he'd failed spectacularly. "Yes?"

"Want to talk about it?"

"Not if you want me to get through dinner."

Brantley eyed the wine cooler and reached for it. "How many bottles are in here?"

Jordan shrugged. "Not enough to put me out of my misery."

"He's still mad about you not telling him?"

"Mad is an understatement. He won't take my calls, won't text. And, well, you saw him just now."

"Maybe Finn can talk some sense into him. I can understand why he's upset, but what you're doing is a wonderful thing. Surely he can see you weren't doing it to hurt him."

"Yeah, I don't know, Brantley. You didn't see his face when he heard. We'd had such a great evening, and then it all went to shit. So, um, *sorry* in advance for whatever happens in there."

"Hey, I hid all the fine china just in case." Brantley flashed a smile and then looped his arm through Jordan's elbow. "And you brought alcohol. So maybe it will go better than you think."

Yeah, judging from the look on Derek's face a minute ago, Jordan highly doubted it.

---

"HEY, MAN," FINN said as Derek walked through the large archway of the kitchen.

"Hey," he said, crossing over to see what Finn was doing at the sink, and to take his mind off the fact that he wished he was anywhere other than where he was right that second.

*Fuck.* He almost hadn't come tonight, and when he'd walked up to the front door and seen Jordan standing there, his first instinct had been to run. Before he'd had the chance, though,

Jordan turned around, and one look at his miserable expression had Derek frozen in place.

He'd wanted to take Jordan's face between his hands and kiss the hell out of him. But then he remembered *why* he was upset, and the anger at being so blindsided the night before slammed back into him and made him resentful.

After the taxi dropped him home last night, Derek had lain awake in his bed and listened to every single message Jordan had left for him. From the first apology to the very last plea that he pick up the phone and talk to him, but he hadn't been able to bring himself to call him back.

He wasn't stupid. He knew what Jordan had done wasn't meant to hurt him. What he couldn't understand was *why* he hadn't told him. Why wouldn't he have asked him if he was okay with his name being on some national platform for people to know what had happened to him? It made him feel nauseous, but at the same time he knew the importance of what Jordan was trying to do.

"You don't look so hot, man," Finn said, as he peeled jumbo shrimp in a colander.

Derek grunted in response. That was Finn, straight to the fucking point. "Thanks a lot, Danny boy."

"Just keeping it real, man. What's up? You come with Posh tonight?"

When Finn waggled his eyebrows, Derek shook his head.

"But I thought—"

"Yeah, well. We had a fight."

"So I heard. But—"

"What do you mean you heard?" Derek interrupted.

"He was chatting with Brantley last night."

Derek wasn't sure if it was due to the annoyance already festering inside of him, but that little tidbit of information brought the fury he'd managed to keep on a low simmer to a boiling point. "Oh, that's just fucking great."

"Hey," Finn said, and glared at him. "Newsflash. You two

are always fighting. It's like foreplay or some shit. So what's the big deal this time?"

Derek looked at the shrimp, thinking the idea of ripping something's head off wasn't a bad one. "I don't wanna talk about it."

"Well, that's nothing new either, is it?"

He turned his head toward his friend, suddenly finding that every single word coming out of Finn's mouth was rubbing him the wrong way. "What the fuck's that supposed to mean?"

Finn threw the shrimp he was holding back into the sink and turned around. "That you bottle shit up. You've done it for as long as I've known you, and you're *still* doing it."

Derek wanted to tell him to back off and it must have been obvious, too, because Finn called him on it.

"How much do you want to tell me to get fucked right now?"

"About a hundred percent."

"I can tell. But you know what? I'm right. You've always been like that. I'm not saying it's wrong, because it's how you deal with shit, and you've had way more to deal with than others. But maybe it's time to stop bottling things up. Hell, the fact that you couldn't tell me for years that you moved out of your house and moved in with fucking Devaney proves that."

*Okay,* Derek thought as he glared at Finn. *Way to bring up years' worth of resentment, Danny boy.* "If you knew or felt that way, why didn't you say something?"

"Because you were already dealing with enough," Finn shouted. "You didn't *need* me the way you needed him. So I let you go, Derek. It wasn't until I came back that I even realized you gave a shit because you finally told me so."

Finn's words were a punch to the gut, and fuck, that hurt. Where did he get off bringing up all this shit now? Just when Derek needed his goddamn friend, when he'd shown up here even though he hadn't wanted to, Finn was acting like a total dick. And he wasn't finished yet.

"Then we all went out to Boyz," Finn said, on a roll now. "And you told me you loved him but that he didn't feel the same. I wanted to go inside and kick that guy's ass for you." Finn took a step toward him then, brave move, all things considered, and when they were close enough that their shoes touched, he said, "But you know what, Derek? A man who builds a charity in your name for issues that he has watched you *fight* your way through and survive…that's a man who not only loves you but one who admires and respects you—deeply. And you know that. I can see it on your stubborn-ass face. So are you really willing to let him go for doing something because it fucking terrifies you?"

"Are you done?"

"Not quite. I have one more thing to say. There's no excuses here, Derek. He might've gone about this the wrong way. Hell, he probably did. From what I remember, he was never subtle or very good at having a brain around you. But he did this for one reason only. Don't let your fear get in the way of seeing that."

As silence finally descended between them, and Derek was left standing there staring at a man he'd thought was his friend, he shook his head, shell-shocked.

"Wow," he said, his voice low as he tried to control the urge to tell Finn to take his opinions and shove them up his ass. But instead, he reminded himself that he was in Finn's house, as a guest. "It must be nice to be so sanctimonious. Huh, Danny boy? Aren't you the one who got pissed and stayed the fuck away for close to a decade because the man *you* loved did what was best for you?"

"That was totally different, and you know it."

"Do I? Fuck you. I don't need this shit tonight."

Derek turned, ready to leave, only to see Brantley and Jordan standing just inside the kitchen. He had no idea how long they'd been standing there, but judging by Brantley's pissed expression, he'd at least caught the tail end of it, whereas Jordan…he just looked…sad.

"Then maybe it would be best if you left for now," Brantley suggested as he walked into the center of the tense room.

Derek heard Jordan gasp, but before he could say anything, Brantley had taken another step forward, and this time his eyes softened, and Derek hated that worse than the irritation he'd originally seen.

"You are *always* welcome in our home, Derek. But not when you're talking shit about two of the people I love most in this world. Got it?"

Derek swallowed and tried to compose himself. "No sweat, professor. I figured this was a mistake anyway."

He looked over his shoulder to Finn, whose jaw was clenched and his eyes downcast, and then without another word, Derek turned and headed for the door.

---

JORDAN COULDN'T BELIEVE what had just happened and what he'd heard. He watched Brantley walk over to where Daniel stood, offering him a hug, and then…well, then Jordan lost his shit.

"Are you both out of your fucking minds?"

Brantley looked over at him, his eyes wide, and he looked as if he was going to speak, but Jordan didn't want to hear it.

"I can't *believe* you just did that to him."

"Jordan, he was in a foul mood and you heard what he said when we walked in. It was just going to get worse."

"I don't give a shit," he snapped. "You two were hardly hearts and roses when you were working your mess out. How dare you be so judgmental now, especially when there is so much going on with him that you don't even know. Good job, Daniel. Maybe *I* should be the one kicking *your* ass."

"Jordan," Brantley growled.

"Forget it," Jordan said with a shake of his hand as he spun on his heel and made his way out of the kitchen, running toward the front door. He yanked it open and caught sight of Derek walking down the driveway toward the Jeep he'd parked out on the curb.

"Derek," he shouted, and ran after him. By the time he caught up, Derek had the door open and was climbing inside. "Would you wait a goddamn minute?"

"Why?" Derek barked.

"Why?" Jordan repeated, and when Derek looked at him, Jordan gripped the door where the window was wound down and told him, "Maybe because we need to talk?"

"Oh, so *now* you want to talk? What about, Jordan? Charities? Okay," Derek said as he pushed open the door and climbed down before slamming it behind him. He was heaving with pent-up frustration. Yet even with all of the power and fury Derek was radiating, he didn't frighten Jordan in any way.

"Let's talk," Derek said. "I'll go first. Do you remember a conversation you once had with a student of yours where you told him flat-out that he wasn't a charity case?" Jordan opened his mouth to deny it, but Derek got in first. "Do you?"

"Yes."

"Okay. Now, can you possibly understand how it might feel to that same student—hell, let's cut the bullshit—how it feels to *me*, the man who has sat in front of you broken and beaten to a fucking pulp…can you imagine how it felt to *that* man to hear that you…" Derek paused and dragged his bottom teeth over his top lip, then shook his head. "That the one person I believed would *never* do anything to shake the trust I had in him, had gone and done something so personal without asking my permission first."

"Derek—"

"Can you?" he shouted, and Jordan shook his head. He'd never thought of it that way, never even considered that it would be seen as anything other than how he'd meant it—a gesture of love and respect.

"I'm so sorry."

"So am I," Derek said, as he spun away from him and reopened the door. Before he could climb back in, Jordan put his hand over the fingers Derek had on the car and tried again.

"Derek. I wasn't thinking. I never meant to—"

"I know," Derek said, and then glanced over his shoulder. "I know you didn't mean to hurt me. I *know* that, Jordan. But it doesn't change the fact that you did."

Jordan's hand slipped away, and as it fell to his side, he nodded. "I understand."

Just when he thought that would be it, that Derek would get in the car and drive away, he rounded back on him. He grabbed Jordan's shirt and pulled him in to take his mouth in a bruising kiss, and the spark was instantaneous.

They caught alight as quick as gasoline and a match. Tongues tangled, hands fumbled for purchase, and all of the worry and upset Jordan had experienced the night before fueled the passion now blazing back to life between them.

When Derek finally tore his mouth free, he rested his forehead against Jordan's and whispered, "I am *so* fucking hurt right now. But just so we're clear, I'm *not* breaking up with you."

The words from their argument a week earlier registered, and Jordan was amazed at how comforting they were even as his heart splintered in two.

"I'll call you," Derek said, and climbed into the car.

Jordan stepped up onto the curb, and as he watched Derek drive away, the only question that remained was…when?

# Chapter 29

DEREK UNLOCKED THE front door and headed inside, wanting to forget his night from hell. *What a shitstorm,* he thought, as he headed directly to the couch, determined to turn the television on and zone the fuck out.

Not only had he gotten into it with Jordan, who he'd expected things to be tense with, but Finn and Brantley had laid into him. He got it. Brantley was feeling protective. Derek couldn't fault him for that, and at least it proved that the guy had finally manned up and decided that Finn was who he wanted. But Finn had said some stuff tonight that cut deep, and as he'd driven home, Derek couldn't get it out of his head.

Back when he'd been going through all the shit he had with his father and moving out, he'd figured it would be better not to burden Finn, who would feel responsible for him, and in the end had turned to Jordan. *Right?*

Well, that had been what he told himself when he'd been *in* the situation. But looking back on it now and hearing Finn's words playing over in his head about how he'd let him go, Derek realized he wasn't angry because Finn had called him out. He was angry because he was fucking right. He *had* been irresponsible with their friendship.

He'd definitely have to call Finn and patch that up. It had finally felt as though they were getting back on track lately, and he didn't want it to go off course any more than it had tonight.

Closing his eyes, he settled into the couch and let the white noise of whatever show was on fill his head instead of all the other bullshit that was in there. He'd just about dozed off when a hand tapped the back of the couch and had him jerking up in his seat. He turned and saw Dylan with a frown stretched over his face as he strolled around to take a seat on the single recliner they had in the living room.

"When'd you get in?" he asked, as he settled back and Derek took in his outfit.

Dressed in black jeans, a leather belt that had silver buckle holes punctuating it, and *only* a leather jacket, Dylan reminded Derek of James Dean. With his hair styled and tousled up top, his stubble accented his square jaw and perfectly symmetrical features. He really was on another level when it came to looks.

"About a half-hour ago," Derek said.

"Oh, okay. I was showering."

"Figures. Must take you at least an hour to look that good, considering the mess you start with."

Dylan grinned. "You're just jealous 'cause it takes you two."

"Hmm."

Dylan tapped his fingers on the arm of the recliner as he looked him over, and then, blunt as ever, said, "Speaking of a mess. You look pretty beat up right now. What gives?"

Derek flipped him off, but instead of laughing, Dylan sat forward and said, "I'm serious. Last night you came in late, I saw the beer bottles in the trash this morning, and now you're sitting here looking like you ran over someone. What's going on with you? Is it flower guy?"

*Flower guy? Oh shit,* Derek thought as he looked over his shoulder at the roses that still sat in the center of their kitchen table. He'd totally forgotten about those. *Fucking Jordan and his demands.*

"Yeah. Flower guy's part of it."

One side of Dylan's mouth kicked up and his dimple appeared. "So are you finally going to tell me his name?"

Derek narrowed his eyes and sized up his friend. "What do you mean?"

"How long have we lived together?"

"Too fucking long. That reminds me, I forgot to tell you years ago, pack your shit and get out."

That made Dylan laugh. "You need me for the rent and I'm hardly here, so quit complaining. But…what I'm *saying* is, I've roomed with you since the end of college. And I would almost bet my life that the guy who sent you those flowers is the same guy who purchased you a few years back at the auction. He's *also* the same guy you would disappear with for a few nights at a time, am I right? You've never dated seriously—"

"Neither have you."

"Yeah, but I bring guys home. You don't. And he's never sent you flowers before. So…what happened? He fall in love with you?"

Derek nodded. "Yeah. But I did first."

"No shit," Dylan said. "Hang on a minute. Were you serious before? Do I really need to pack my shit and leave?"

Derek wasn't sure why, but that made him laugh his ass off. *Jesus*, here he was after the worst night of his life in a long-ass time, and he was busy crying from laughter. Maybe he was losing his mind.

When he finally settled down, he shook his head and wiped the corner of his eye. "Relax, Prescott. No need to move out just yet. *Jordan*, that's his name, and you're right, it's the same guy since college. We had a fight tonight. Well, it was last night, really, and I'm just… I'm really disappointed with him right now. I'm mad and fucking hurt."

"Shit, man." Dylan put one of his black-booted ankles up

on his other knee and started to tap his leg. "Can I ask what he did? Was it another guy?"

"No," Derek said. "Nothing like that. Actually, he did something pretty amazing, but he missed a few steps along the way. Some really fucking important steps."

Dylan took a deep breath and seemed to be thinking carefully about the next words he wanted to say, and, not for the first time, Derek really wondered about the man sitting opposite him.

He'd known Dylan Prescott for years. But only what he'd been allowed to see. Dylan was an extremely private person when it came to his personal life, yet from all outward appearances he was confident and easygoing. He wasn't egotistical in any way, and Lord knows he could be with a face like his. He just had a way about him that drew people in and that was probably why Derek was sitting there spilling his guts, but Dylan only let people know exactly what he wanted them to.

"I had a difficult upbringing," Dylan finally said, and Derek was stunned that he'd even divulged that much. Feeling that this was something pretty fucking massive for the guy, he said, "So did I."

Dylan nodded. "Yeah, I figured. I'm not sure how similar our stories are. Or even *if* they are, but I bounced around for a while in my teens as a foster kid until I landed with my parents and brother, who moved out here back when we first met."

*Oh wow. Yeah, okay,* he hadn't known that about the guy, and it explained a few things. Including Dylan's nomadic tendencies. He loved travelling from city to city for each modeling job he booked, whereas Derek loved staying exactly where he was.

"They're really good people," Dylan continued. "Some of the best, but my adoptive parents, they made mistakes along the way. Big ones that made me really fucking mad. They made choices for me that I resented, but later I was able to forgive because I understood why they did it."

Dylan scooted to the edge of the recliner and then got to his feet. He aimed his eyes over at the roses on the table and shrugged. "Look, I don't know this Jordan guy. But he's been in your life a long time, and you just told me yourself you both love each other. Whatever he did, or didn't do, I have a feeling he knows it and is regretting it. Maybe instead of sitting here being pissed, you should call him."

Derek nodded. Dylan was right. He knew that, and maybe it had taken someone on the outside to really make him see what was right in front of him. He just needed to call Jordan and talk this out. Clear the air and let him know how he really felt about the entire situation.

"Anyway," Dylan said, recapturing Derek's attention. "I'm heading out for the night. Not sure what time I'll be back. Oh, and don't forget, I have that big shoot in L.A. this Monday, so I'll be flying out Sunday night."

"Oh shit," Derek said, and got to his feet also. "I totally forgot about that. Are you ready?"

"As ready as I can be to stand naked for a bunch of strangers."

"I thought you were going to be in briefs?"

Dylan laughed. "Yeah, and that's about it. Hey, I'm not complaining. This is going to be huge for my career. I'll have men lining up at my door."

Derek gave him a hug before Dylan headed toward the front door.

"I'm pretty sure you could already have that if you wanted to."

Dylan didn't answer as he headed out the front door, but then again, Derek hadn't expected him to.

All right, it was time for shit to get real. First things first, he needed to clear things up with Finn. He fished his phone out of his back pocket and called. When it connected, before he even got the words *I'm sorry* out of his mouth, Finn was right there saying it for him.

"Derek, I was just about to call you, man. I feel like shit about what happened earlier."

He sat down on the couch and shook his head. Then he started to laugh at himself, Finn, and the entire situation. *Jesus*, he felt like a fucking high school girl, and told Finn exactly that.

"Well, you did used to threaten to braid my hair."

"That's because you had braid-worthy hair, Danny boy. Not my fault."

"That's true. I took great pride in my blond locks."

"As you should have." Derek smiled. Then he let it drop, sighed, and ran a hand through his hair. "Listen, I have to say something and I'm only gonna say it fucking once. So listen carefully, okay?"

He heard a door open and close, and had a feeling that Finn had just stepped outside to his and Brantley's balcony.

"I'm sorry."

"Derek, we shouldn't have—"

"Stop it. Let me finish. I'm sorry for tonight. Brantley was right to kick my ass out. But what I'm really sorry about is that I didn't tell you what was going on with me back in school. I don't know why I didn't. Hell, the only thing I can think of is you were like family and I didn't want to burden your mom after all she'd been through, or worse, bring my father to your doorstep. And you were happy with Hayes and busy with your own life, and… anyway. All the excuses I thought made so much sense now sound so fucking lame. I let my best friend go, and I'm sorry."

The quiet sound of Finn breathing and the ocean waves crashing in the background was all he could hear as he sat in his living room waiting for whatever Finn was going to tell him in return, and when he finally spoke, he couldn't have shocked Derek more.

"I was glad."

Derek ran that over in his head. Several times. "What do you mean you were glad? About what?"

"Not the distancing. But the trust I saw you developing with Jordan. I was glad you had someone who you could turn to. Someone who… I don't know how to explain it, but someone who distracted you. He challenged you to get free of the life you were living, because I sure as hell wasn't getting through to you. From day one he pushed your buttons and you pushed his." Finn laughed at that. "You still do. He's exactly what you needed, and I knew he wouldn't come close if I was there, so…I let you go too. Maybe it was just how it was supposed to go, you know?"

Derek nodded, totally speechless as he took in everything Finn had just said, and when his friend said his name, he finally said, "Yeah. I'm still here."

"What are you going to do now? Call Jordan?"

"Yeah, I don't know. But I have a feeling it'll involve shouting, insults, and then wall-banging sex."

Finn chuckled. "Thank fuck I'm not your neighbor."

"Hey, no one's Jordan's neighbor. Aren't you the one who Googled him? Didn't you see his house? It's a goddamn penthouse, dude."

"No shit? So Posh really is the perfect name for him."

Derek laughed at that and thought of his man with a smile. "Oh yeah, it's perfect. Plus he hates it, which makes it even better."

Finn laughed along with him at that.

"Well, if we're good, I better go and work out how to win him back. I'm pretty sure I did the equivalent of kicking a puppy this evening. It's going to take a lot of persuasion for him to even let me in his elevator."

"Elevator?"

"Okay, when this is all worked out again, remind me to invite you the hell over. Brantley can come too, if he promises not to be a dick."

He heard Finn relay his message, and Derek grinned at his

response, "He said if Jordan's wine fridge is full count him in. As long as you promise not to be a dick too."

"Deal," Derek answered. Then he said his goodbyes and hung up, feeling that half of the weight had been lifted from his shoulders. Now he just needed to talk to Jordan, but he wanted to do that in person.

After getting to his feet, he headed toward the table where he'd dropped his keys, and as he walked to the door, his phone started to ring. He flipped it over in his hand, hoping it was Jordan, but instead he saw a number that made his stomach turn.

*Fucking Alan.*

He pulled the front door shut behind him and then swiped the screen as he headed toward the stairs. He was determined to go to Jordan's place no matter what his brother wanted.

"What?" he said, and was shocked when Alan didn't immediately answer. Instead, Derek heard someone asking, "Where do you want us to take him to?"

Derek heard Alan give them the name of their local hospital, and then he came back over the phone. "You there?"

"Yeah, I'm here, Alan."

"Dad was collapsed on the floor when I got home tonight. Unresponsive—"

"But not dead?" Derek asked, feeling a sense of detachment he hadn't expected.

"No, he's not dead. At least not yet."

Derek shut his eyes and wondered if he should be worried he felt nothing in that moment but inconvenienced for being interrupted from going to Jordan's, but then his brother said something that caught his attention.

"When he came to, before they put him in the ambulance, he asked for you."

"Why? What does he want?"

"I don't know. But he asked for you. You know where we're

going if you want to be there. If you don't…whatever. No skin off my back."

As Alan hung up the phone, Derek stared at his for a moment and then thought, fuck it. He threw the phone on the passenger seat of his car and climbed in. Then he started the engine and headed in the one direction that was imprinted on his brain.

Jordan's penthouse.

# Chapter 30

JORDAN SAT IN the dark in his living room staring at the blank television screen that hung on the wall. It'd been over two hours since he'd left Brantley's, and he wondered just how long he'd be able to sit there without food, water, or the need to physically get up. As it was, curling up into a ball and never leaving that spot again seemed like a really great idea.

When he'd arrived home, he'd immediately sent off an email to the project manager of the *Pearson Project* and told her to put on hold all future planned meetings, website implementation, and, well, anything at all, really, and he would get back to her sometime...*this year, maybe?* Jordan thought as he shut his eyes and fell to his side on the couch.

How could he have been so thoughtless? So careless in his single-minded focus that he hadn't thought about the way Derek's name on the marquee might upset him. He'd stupidly thought of it as a way to celebrate him, and all that he'd overcome. He'd never imagined this reaction—

The familiar sound of his phone ringing from the coffee table had him sitting up and grabbing for the device that was vibrating around the glass top. As soon as he saw *He-Man* on the display, he was swiping his finger across the screen to answer it. "Derek?"

"Can you come downstairs?"

Jordan shot to his feet and looked toward the elevator. "You're here?"

"Yes."

"Oh, and you don't want to come up?"

"No. I need you to come down."

Derek sounded odd. He didn't sound angry, but more… distant. Jordan picked up his wallet and keys and slipped into his loafers, all the while holding the phone to his ear. "Are you okay?"

"No."

"Derek, I'm—"

"Jordan, no. Just come down here, okay?"

The elevator door opened, and when Jordan stepped inside, he said, "I'm on my way."

"I'll be waiting."

As the call ended and the elevator started its descent, Jordan had never felt more nervous about anything in his life, including his first day of teaching. Was this to be the day where Derek told him to get out of his life for good? The thought physically hurt, so he shoved it aside, refusing to believe what they had would end this way.

When the elevator came to a stop and the door opened to reveal Derek standing there waiting, Jordan took the steps he needed to reach him, and Derek met him halfway, pulling him into his arms. He had no idea what was going on, but Jordan could feel Derek's entire body shuddering as he wrapped his arms around his waist.

He automatically smoothed his hand up Derek's back, and after what felt like hours instead of minutes, Jordan asked, "What is it? You can tell me anything. Even if I won't like it."

Derek took a step back and looked down, and Jordan knew

that expression. This wasn't about what had happened between them. Something else, even bigger than that, was swimming in Derek's eyes, and with three words he confirmed it.

"It's my father."

---

JORDAN HELD ON to the "oh shit bar" as Derek zipped them through the quiet night streets of Sunset Cove as though he were on a racing track going for first place. As soon as he'd told Jordan what had happened, Jordan hadn't hesitated to go with him to the hospital. Now there he was, fifteen minutes later, buckled into the passenger seat of a Jeep with a man who earlier that night he hadn't been sure he would see again.

Derek hadn't said much of anything since he'd picked him up, but as Jordan sat there and looked at the hands he was wringing around the steering wheel, he wanted to reach out, touch him in some way.

Not sure how he would react, though, Jordan kept his hands in his lap and waited for some kind of direction as to what Derek wanted from him in that moment. It wasn't until they pulled up at a red light and Derek turned to look at him that Jordan saw the silent *thank you* in his eyes. That was when he decided to hell with what may or may not happen, and reached across to the steering wheel to place a hand over the white knuckles there. Derek let go and brought their hands down to the center console, where Jordan entwined their fingers.

*Yes,* he thought as he closed his eyes. While they may not be in the perfect place right then, wherever they were, they were there together.

The light switched to green and Derek looked away and put his foot on the gas, but the rest of the way he kept the connection between them, and when they got to the hospital and had to let go to get out of the car, he didn't waste a second in reconnecting once he rounded the hood to stop by Jordan's side.

As they headed up the walkway to the double doors, Derek pulled him to the side for a moment and touched his fingers to Jordan's cheek. Jordan thought he was going to ask him to wait outside, given the way his father and brother were, but all Derek did was lower his head and brush a whisper-soft kiss across his lips.

There was such emotion in the gentle gesture that Jordan's eyes blurred and he blinked back the tears threatening. Then Derek moved his face to the side of his so their cheeks were touching and whispered, "I love you."

And before Jordan had a chance to respond, Derek had moved away from him, tightened his hold on his fingers, and was walking them toward the double doors.

---

AS DEREK STOOD by the elevator banks with his hand firmly inside Jordan's, he shut his eyes and allowed himself to savor the simple beauty of that moment. Jordan standing beside him in a *public* place with his fingers wrapped around his. In amongst all of the chaos and all of the ugly, Jordan was, as always, there for him. His rock. His everything.

All that he was, and all that he *could* be, he owed to the belief that this man had had in him, the respect that Jordan had shown and taught him from the very beginning, and it was then that Derek really got it. He really understood what Jordan had been telling him since that first day.

He tightened his grip on Jordan's fingers and looked down at him. There were questions in Jordan's eyes, ones Derek knew he would have to answer, but right now, he wanted this moment of simplicity. This moment of standing side by side in a sad hospital hallway, knowing that he would never again stand alone.

As the elevator dinged and they stepped inside, he pulled

Jordan closer to him, and Jordan brought his other hand over to place it on top of their joined ones.

"You okay?" he asked.

Derek nodded. "Yeah."

"If you need anything—"

"You're here," he said, and Jordan fell silent, but his eyes were saying everything Derek was feeling. "That's all I've ever needed."

The elevator hit the floor his brother had texted him, and when they stepped off, Derek spotted Alan standing over by the entrance to the wing his father had been admitted to.

He pulled Jordan to a stop and thought he should give him the choice of what he was about to encounter, because while it was his family and he was used to their bullshit and asshole tendencies, he didn't want to subject Jordan to that unless he knew what he was walking into.

---

"HEY," DEREK SAID as he squeezed Jordan's fingers.

"Hey." He returned the half-smile Derek was aiming his way.

"I wanted to give you the option to wait back here if you want to."

Derek looked over his shoulder to where someone was leaning against the wall watching them. He then turned back to face him, and Jordan asked, "Would you like me to wait here?"

"No," Derek said. "It's just…even though I come from the same household as these two, we are very different men."

"Derek," Jordan said as he touched Derek's arm. "I know that. I know that whatever they do or say is not you or in any way a reflection of you."

"I know, it's just—"

"Derek," he said again, and took a step toward him. "I'm not here to judge you. I'm here to support you. I love you."

As the words hung between them, Jordan noticed Derek's frown tip up into a small smile. He looked…bashful.

"I like how that sounds."

Jordan's heart raced at that as he asked, "Still? Even though—"

Derek put a finger to his lips and nodded. "Even though. Say it again."

"I love you."

When Derek's smile widened, Jordan cupped his cheek and confessed with a grin, "I think I have since you took your sunglasses off and, without a word, dared me to fuck with you."

Derek's eyes roved over his face, and Jordan raised his head to press a kiss to his lips. "I am more than aware of where you come from, Derek Pearson. I know exactly *who* I love. Being confronted with that doesn't scare me, and it won't make me love you any less to see it firsthand. If anything, it makes me love you more to see what you have overcome to be the man you are today. So if you think it would be easier if I waited over here, then I'll wait here. But if you *want* me by your side, if you want my hand in yours, then I will stand there and be in that moment with you. No matter how fucking uncomfortable it might make anyone else."

When Jordan finished talking, Derek took his face between his hands and kissed him so hard that Jordan swore his ears rang. Then Derek recaptured his hand and tugged him along.

When they reached Alan and he took a look at the both of them, Derek pulled Jordan to his side and spoke before his brother had a chance to.

"Say one fucking thing I don't like and you can do this next part all on your own. This is your chance to be a better man than the one in that room lucky that his sons turned up today. So take advantage of this moment. Alan, this is Jordan, my boyfriend."

Alan looked at him, and Jordan noted the bored and somewhat unimpressed look on his face. He was a skinny guy, not much taller than himself, and his coloring was the same as Derek's, as far as his hair and eyes went. But that was where the similarities ended. There was no warmth in those eyes. There actually wasn't much of anything. And Jordan thought it sad that this man had missed out on knowing someone as wonderful as Derek due to his ignorant upbringing.

Alan then shrugged and turned back to Derek. "Yeah, okay. I don't give a shit who you're fucking."

"Well, nice to meet you too," Jordan muttered. "I see candor runs strong through the Pearson household."

Alan frowned, and Jordan wondered if he'd say more, but instead he focused on Derek, obviously deciding he was an easier issue to tackle than the strange guy holding his brother's hand.

"He's been asking for you."

"Why?" Derek said, and to Jordan he sounded as though he couldn't have cared less as to the answer.

"I dunno. Just keeps asking where you are."

Derek shook his head. "Doesn't make any sense, but okay. What room?"

Alan gave them the room number and they headed down the hall. When they reached the door, Derek stopped, and Jordan stepped around in front of him so he could look into his eyes.

"Hey. You don't have to do this if you don't want to."

"No," Derek said with a grim look on his face. "I need to."

"It's going to be okay. Once you're done, come back out here, and I'll be waiting. I promise."

Derek nodded and took a deep breath. As he let go of his hand, Jordan felt as though he were sending a lamb to the slaughter, but at the same time he knew that Derek had to face this if he was ever going to break free from the monster that lay in wait and have a hope of moving on with his life.

---

DEREK STEPPED INTO the hospital room and looked around the stark white walls. On one side was a whiteboard with the nurse's name and the date, but other than that there was nothing. It was a true testament to the fact that this miserable bastard hadn't loved anyone in his life but himself.

As Derek walked farther into the room, he noted how frail his father looked, even in comparison to when he'd seen him just a couple of days ago. He waited for the pain to hit him, the sadness over the fact that his father was the one lying in that hospital bed likely hours away from his lungs giving out.

He stopped at the foot of the bed and shoved his hands into his pockets as he looked down at the figure attached to several IVs and who had a nasal cannula valiantly trying to help him breathe—*yeah, good luck there*—and all he saw was a sad figure of a man who'd terrorized him his entire life.

Thinking that coming here had been a terrible mistake, Derek was about to turn around and leave without bothering to speak, but before he got the opportunity, his father opened his eyes, and Derek immediately found his feet frozen in place.

"I was wonderin' if you'd show."

"You were smart to wonder. It's not like you deserve anyone standing here, especially me."

His father pulled the tubes out of his nose and coughed. "Yet 'ere you are."

Derek walked around the bed, trying to work that out himself. Why had he felt compelled to see him one last time? He had nothing to feel guilty over if he let him rot away all on his own. So why had it seemed imperative that he be there?

As he got closer, his father's eyes followed him.

"I heard you asked for me," Derek said when he was by the side of the bed. "Well, here I am."

His father's eyes tracked over him, and then his dry lips stretched into a smile ripe with malicious intent. "I just wanted to prove to myself that I was right."

Derek narrowed his eyes as his dad started to laugh and then sputter. "And I was. Showin' up to watch your dear old father die. Hoping that maybe he'll reach out a hand and tell you that he loved you all along. Sorry to disappoint, but I just wanted to prove I was right. You're still a fucking pussy."

Derek stared down at the man looking up at him with such hatred, and knew right then *exactly* the reason he was there.

It wasn't to say goodbye. And it wasn't to assuage some misguided sense of guilt he would harbor. No, it was for neither of those two reasons.

"I'm not here hoping you'll tell me that you love me," Derek said. "It would be more traumatizing to know that someone like you *did* love me. I'm here to tell you that you lost. For years you've tried to break me. To hurt me, and you did, physically. But you know what? I wasn't lying when I told you that you no longer have the power. Because when I walk out that door today, I will no longer waste my time thinking about you."

Derek leaned down and braced a hand on the rail of the bed so it looked as though he was hugging his father, but instead he said in his ear, "I'm happy. I'm in love with a wonderful man, and I hope you rot in hell for every evil fucking thing you did to me. Have a nice life, Dad. However long you have left of it. I'm going to go and enjoy mine knowing that what I just told you will eat away at you until you take your final breath."

Then, without sparing his father a final glance, Derek straightened and walked out the door to deliver on his final promise to a dying man.

# Epilogue

*"It's a new dawn*
*It's a new day*
*It's a new life*
*For me*
*And I'm feeling good."*

~ Feeling Good, Michael Bublé

# One Year Later

JORDAN POURED TWO glasses of chilled Chardonnay and was about to put the bottle back in the fridge, but instead re-corked it and tucked it under his arm. Dressed in a fluffy white robe and slippers to match, he scooped up the two wine glasses and headed for the back sliding door.

As he stepped out onto the wooden slats of the deck, a grin split his lips and he used his elbow to flick the switch on the wall panel that illuminated the space. With dancing lights woven around the posts of the trellis and the smooth sound of Michael Bublé crooning in the background, Jordan's eyes found the back of Derek's head and, *oh yeah*, he was feelin' good.

Earlier that morning they had decided they would spend the weekend down at Devil's Bend, and the second he'd been able to get away he was in his car and heading over. It appeared, though, as eager as he had been, that Derek had beaten him there.

Around a month after Derek's father had passed, he'd dived into restoring the little beach hut guns blazing. Jordan could see how beating the shit out of something with a hammer could help a person deal with their confusion over grieving for someone they detested. And out of it all, months later, the little shack that had once sat in shambles had been transformed into one of Jordan's favorite places in the entire world.

Serene, secluded, and sensual. Derek had taken something that had been falling apart and made it a little slice of paradise. He'd also decreed that whenever they set foot inside the intimate space that clothes were to be removed—immediately. Jordan glanced at the robe he'd since changed into with a smirk. *Mhmm…* Derek had given him free rein to be the nudist he truly believed that he was.

As he walked across the small wooden deck, he took in the deep porcelain bathtub that was filled to the brim where it sat outside, overlooking the rolling waves of the ocean. Derek was submerged in the wide oval tub, with his muscular arms resting casually on the edge, and Jordan licked his lips as he came to a stop behind him.

Derek tipped his head back, and as he gazed up, Jordan took in the pleasure warming those blue eyes, and bent at the waist to press his lips to Derek's in a gentle kiss.

"*Dahling*, I'm here."

Derek smiled against his lips. "Darlin', you're wearing too many clothes."

Jordan placed the wine on a small patio table by the tub, along with the glasses, and then unbuckled the tie of the robe and slid it from his shoulders.

As it pooled at his feet, he stepped out of the slippers and moved to the side of the tub. He took in Derek's naked form from head to toe, and every *hard* inch in between, and then dipped his fingers in the water and raised an eyebrow. "And I see you're not wearing anything at all."

"Those were the rules put in place. Were they not?"

Jordan's fingers found Derek's rapidly growing erection, and when he encircled him and found his lips with his own, he said, "They were. But I think you secretly like running around naked as much as I do."

Derek's hands came off the side of the tub to cradle his face, and he pressed a firm kiss to Jordan's lips.

"Around you, I'd be naked twenty-four hours a day if I didn't think I would be arrested for it. Now get in the tub, Posh. I've been waiting for you."

---

DEREK WATCHED JORDAN climb into the water and then settle his perfect ass against him. *Yes*, now his night could begin. He'd been waiting for this moment. Where it was just the two of them and the rest of the world faded away.

Jordan had been heading into town that morning to meet with his mother regarding the Pearson Project. The charity had been up and running for nearly four months now, and they'd already succeeded in meeting the needs of so many unfortunate children who suffered a similar fate to himself, and some even worse.

After the death of his father, Derek had been able to lay to rest with the bastard all of the demons he had created, and thanks to the man currently leaning into his body, Derek had been able to move forward and direct his focus toward people who could benefit from what he had been through.

He would forever be grateful to Jordan for believing in him, and after his initial upset over the way things were handled, the two of them had moved forward on the project and created an important organization that would touch the lives of many. For that, he couldn't thank Jordan enough.

"I never thought you'd get here."

Jordan tilted his head back so their eyes could meet, and he placed a kiss to Derek's chin. "I sent you a text when I left."

"I don't mean that..."

"Oh?" Jordan said, as Derek brought his hand down to interlace their fingers.

"Yeah. *Oh*," he teased, and fingered the sterling silver band he'd slid onto Jordan's ring finger earlier that morning. "I never thought you'd say yes to me. Not like this."

Jordan moved so his back was to Derek's chest once again, and stretched his left arm up in front of him. Under the sparkling string lights that hung down over the tub, the diamonds in the gorgeous silver band shone back at them.

"Oh please, you knew exactly what you were doing, Derek Pearson. I'd never say no to such a gorgeous ring."

When Derek grabbed Jordan around the waist, he gasped as he flipped them, reversing their positions in the tub. Water splashed over the edge, but that didn't stop Derek from bracing his hands on either side of the porcelain and wedging himself between Jordan's legs.

"So it was just the ring, huh?"

Jordan's hands came up to wrap around his neck, and the grin he aimed up at Derek was positively wicked. With his hair wet, and drops of water now clinging to his eyelashes, Jordan was the most beautiful man Derek had ever seen, and he was all his.

"Maybe…" Jordan said.

"Liar."

"Who? Me? I'd never do something like that." Jordan batted his lashes, and Derek rolled his eyes.

"Sure you wouldn't."

Jordan's smile became devilish then as he arched up and wrapped his legs around Derek's lower body. "And yet you want to marry me."

Derek groaned and shut his eyes for a second, but that just made Jordan chuckle even more.

"Clearly I have issues," Derek said as he moved to his knees and Jordan came with him, straddling his lap.

"Clearly," he agreed, as he wound his arms tight around Derek's neck and their bodies pressed together intimately.

"I love you," Derek told him. "For always answering when I

call, and for being the exact person I need at any given time. You found me. *You* made me better."

Jordan's lids lowered as he moved his lips to Derek's ear and whispered, "That's because I love you."

"Always?"

"Always."

*Heaven,* Derek thought, as Jordan brought his lips back to his and kissed him. He was in heaven, being kissed by the devil himself, and, hell, there wasn't one damn thing he would change.

The moment was perfection.

# What to read next

The PresLocke Series
Dylan & Ace's story

ACED
LOCKED
WEDLOCKED

*Note - This is a spin-off of The Sunset Cove Series *and* the L.A. Liaisons Series by Ella Frank & Brooke Blaine

# Special Thanks

I want to thank the powers that be that I made it through the writing, editing, and releasing of Devil's Kiss during mercury retrograde. I also want to apologize to Brooke Blaine for ever making fun of her astrology talk. I mean, if you wanted to prove a point did you have to make it as crazy as this point was made?!?!

In all seriousness, thank you, Brooke, for helping me realize you should *never* hold back for any reason. Balls to the wall. And also, thank you for reading my five thousand beginnings and the 'Boring Files.' ahaha! I couldn't do this without you (best eyes in the business—hands down), and umm…never again! <— You know what I am talking about, woman.

I have to, and by have to, I mean I literally *have* to thank Arran McNicol, my editor. You are a flipping genius, and a speedy one at that. Not only are you a lifesaver, but you turn scripts around so fast you blow my mind. Thank you for being brilliant at your job. It makes it less stressful when I am freaking out over skipping my deadline!

Judy! I am so sorry I always make you work on your vacations. I promise I don't do it on purpose! But thank you for always being willing to put your eyes on my work. I love that we have been working together forever, and this year we will *finally* meet!

This book would not be *this* book without the brilliant cover and for that I have a few people to thank.

Jay Aheer of Simply Defined Art - Every time you send me a cover, you blow my mind. You always take what I ask for and make it original, gorgeous, and flat-out sexy. Exhibit A.) Finley, and Exhibit B.) Devil's Kiss. I love these covers, and you are an absolute pleasure to work with!

The photographers of this project took some amazing pictures that I was able to use as both a cover and as muses for the book. They captured exactly the vibe I was going for.

Eric Battershell - The cover image for this book is probably one of the most striking photos I've ever seen in my life, and everyone who sees it reacts exactly the same way. Jaw on the floor in total awe.

To Wander Aguiar & Andrey - I can't thank you enough for the photo shoot you put together within minutes of me contacting you for images of Jason Dickinson and Ryan VanDyke. It was fate that everything fell into place, and I couldn't be happier with how it all turned out. Your photos are gorgeous. Sexy, strong, and perfect for the message I was wanting to get across with this book. Thank you for working with me. It was an absolute pleasure and I can't wait to do it again.

To the two awesome Facebook groups I am a part of:

The Naughty Umbrella - You are my virtual home and my virtual family! I love you all, and I appreciate you lifting my spirits daily and making me laugh! I love that whenever things get too crazy and intense, I can come into the Brella and within minutes I am smiling. I can't wait to meet many of you in October this year and give you a hug in person. Ohhhh! And thank you to the Floridians for your knowledge on what to call a Coke. ;)

To the M/M Daily Grind - While this is a new group, it has grown so fast and is such a fun group of people! I love the book recommendations and daily chat in the Grind, and I feel extremely lucky to be a part of this group with the wonderful authors in there.

To Between the Sheets Promotions. Natalie I couldn't do this without you! Thank you for putting up with me, and my crazy schedule. I LOVE working with you!

And to the bloggers who continually support me - You are always there, willing to read and give honest feedback on my books. You will never know how much it means to an author to have such support in our wonderful book community. I love the indie world, and while at times it is stressful, finally being able to hand over my baby to the world is always such an amazing feeling!

I hope you all enjoyed Devil's Kiss! Until next time…

Xx Ella

# About the Author

**If you'd like to get to know Ella better, you can find her getting up to all kinds of shenanigans at:**
**The Naughty Umbrella**

Ella Frank is the *USA Today* Bestselling author of the Temptation series, including Try, Take, and Trust and is the co-author of the fan-favorite contemporary romance, Sex Addict. Her Exquisite series has been praised as "scorching hot!" and "enticingly sexy!"

A life-long fan of the romance genre, Ella writes contemporary and erotic fiction and lives with her husband in Portland, OR. You can reach her on the web at www.ellafrank.com and on Facebook at www.facebook.com/ella.frank.author

Some of her favorite authors include Tiffany Reisz, Kresley Cole, Riley Hart, J.R. Ward, Erika Wilde, Gena Showalter, and Carly Philips.

*for more information:*

www.ellafrank.com
admin@ellafrank.com

Printed in Great Britain
by Amazon

35499883R00206